So, THIS IS MAGGIE . . .

"You're afraid of *her*?" Scott whispered to the ghost.

"I ain't afraid of nobody," Cooper snarled, but his gaze shifted away to the tree line.

Shiny, shoulder-length hair bounced with agitation as the delectable Miss Cooper darted between bumpers on impossibly high heels. Her suit flowed with every inch of her body as she charged across the narrow lawn. Worry creased the delicate features of her face. To think Cooper could have sired someone so pretty, so utterly enticing, was beyond comprehension.

"*You*," she said with recognition.

Fame had many benefits. The fact that she already knew who he was would make getting to know her a whole lot easier.

"Nice to meet you," Scott said.

The fire didn't leave her eyes. She didn't even hesitate as she topped the last step and advanced on him. "You owe me five hundred dollars."

A lesser man would have run. Not Scott Templeton. He'd stared death in the face more than once. No way a little slip of a woman like this could back him against the house. . .

By Jenna McKnight

LOVE IN THE FAST LANE
A DATE ON CLOUD NINE
A GREEK GOD AT THE LADIES' CLUB

JENNA McKNIGHT

Love
IN THE FAST LANE

AVON BOOKS
An Imprint of HarperCollinsPublishers

This is a work of fiction. Names, characters, places, and incidents are products of the author's imagination or are used fictitiously and are not to be construed as real. Any resemblance to actual events, locales, organizations, or persons, living or dead, is entirely coincidental.

AVON BOOKS
An Imprint of HarperCollins*Publishers*
10 East 53rd Street
New York, New York 10022–5299

Copyright © 2007 by Ginny Schweiss
ISBN: 978–0–06–084347–2
ISBN–10: 0–06–084347–0
www.avonromance.com

First Avon Books paperback printing: January 2007

Avon Trademark Reg. U.S. Pat. Off. and in Other Countries, Marca Registrada, Hecho en U.S.A.
HarperCollins® is a registered trademark of HarperCollins Publishers.

Printed in the U.S.A.

10 9 8 7 6 5 4 3 2 1

Acknowledgments

Many, many thanks to:

Race car owner and driver Tom Rosemann. If I got anything wrong, it wasn't for lack of his patience and time, the endless supply of research material he provided, or letting me ride in the cars.

Linda Flowers, for sharing her experiences. May you never run out of opportunities to fly around the track!

SK, whose newest ghost is a cat.

 *Chapter 1*

T. S. "Scotty" Templeton was too focused on pushing the Porsche toward two hundred miles per hour to notice exactly when or where he picked up an unexpected passenger. It wasn't your typical race-day casualty, not a bird crammed into the grille or a bug vaporized on the windshield. No, this guy had all appendages intact—two arms, two legs—and was still moving.

"Who the hell—?"

Scott wasn't known for finesse on the best of days, and while racing at night?—forget about it.

The interloper in the passenger seat puffed up with pride and announced, "Larry Cooper, but everyone calls me Speed. Pleased to meetcha."

As if Scott gave a flying fig. It was midnight, with little light bouncing off the moon. If he didn't pay full attention to the road course, it'd chew him up and spit him out.

He hadn't pissed away recent months. He'd quit smoking. He'd given up cookies and hit the gym, and really, for that alone, he *deserved* to win another Rolex. He'd given up drinking; not that he had a problem, except he finally had to admit that booze just tore his stomach all to hell and wasn't worth it. And truth be told, he felt better. Sharper. Quicker. On top of his game.

So why him?

There were a thousand predictable things that could end this race prematurely, and another thousand bumps of the unpredictable variety, but a few things were crucial. He, for one. Besides just loving to race at night for the sheer thrill of it, it gave him a psychological edge over drivers who let the darkness intimidate them. A ten-hour edge, this early in the year. On top of that, the Porsche was running like a striped-ass ape. And the team owner seemed happier than he'd been in years, which meant he'd stay off Scott's back and let him do what he did best—drive.

That was pretty tough, given that he was no longer racing solo. A stowaway was impossible; there wasn't room for a cockroach to hide in the cockpit.

A hitchhiker was out of the question.

The alternative was too far beyond reason even to be considered.

And yet, there sat someone. Sandy hair, mustache, average height and weight, outdated racing suit. Between the tight turns and a plethora of opponents flying along the track, each class running at different speeds, each driver on the alert for accidents and debris, there really wasn't time to take in more than that.

"Uh, you might want to watch the next turn, son."

"Get the fuck outta my car!"

It was second nature to key the radio. Dumb as dirt,

too, because the next thing he heard was the owner's voice crackling over the headset.

"Something wrong, Scotty?"

"Who *is* this guy?"

After a slight pause, the answer came. "There's nobody on you right now, buddy."

As far as the owner could see, that probably was true. It was a perfectly clear night in late January, nice and cool, easy on the engine. The 24 Hours of Daytona was the most difficult road course of all, at times compared to Le Mans. Last year Scott had won the coveted Rolex watch. He intended to start this season with another win, a wider margin. More victories meant more sponsors. More championships meant owning his own team sooner.

But instead of thinking ahead to the next turn, which was coming up in seconds, Scott was obliged to check out a guy who couldn't possibly be there.

"Hey, boss . . ." How to ask this over the two-way without sounding crazy? "The name Larry Cooper mean anything to you?"

"Speed Cooper, sure, stock car great. Back in the seventies. Know why he was a champion, Scotty? Because," the owner roared, "he kept his mind on what he was doing!"

"You gotta watch out up ahead," Cooper warned, and Scott snarled, "I know what I'm doing."

"I sure as hell hope so," the owner shot back.

Scott slowed for a turn. He was covered from head to

fingertip to toe in fireproof gear, and his body strained against the harness. His passenger lounged in the open space beside him, as calm as a statue, and said, "Next corner's a bad one."

"Feel free to step outside."

"Is he on somethin'?" The owner wasn't questioning him now; probably the crew chief. "Goddammit, Scotty—"

Scott tuned out the owner when Cooper said, "I've been waiting for you to come back to the track for weeks."

"You're a hologram, right? Some projected image." Scott was buckled in too tightly to reach up and wrench out the car cam, but at least this time he'd kept his finger off the PTT button.

"Can a projector do this?" Cooper vanished, only to reappear smack-dab in the middle of the hood.

Scott swerved. First out of reflex, then back and forth a few times out of pure orneriness.

"Whoa, watch it there, Scotty," the owner said. "What's up, buddy? Talk to me."

"I'm a little busy right now, boss." Scott tapped the brakes to throw Cooper's ass off the hood, but nothing dislodged him. Nothing even threw him off balance. He just perched there like a friggin' hood ornament.

"Yeah, I can see that. You smoke something a little funny this morning?"

"I don't do funny."

"Great, I always like it when one of my drivers hallucinates. Say, Scotty . . ."

"Yeah, boss?"

"Get your sorry ass in gear before you wreck my car!"

Cooper reappeared in the passenger seat, a self-satisfied smirk on his face. "Say, you're not very good at this."

"You're throwing off my timing. Go away."

From the rattle and thump over the headset, Scott figured the owner had just thrown his across the pit.

"You're a ghost, right? Not an angel."

"An angel?" Cooper sounded stumped for a moment. "Oh no no, nothing like that. I'm not here to take you to heaven." He made *Twilight Zone* noises and laughed at Scott. "I just want you to deliver something."

"Mind if I finish the race first?" At this point, Scott didn't care if it was a ghost or not, but whatever it was was cutting his lead. He'd agree to anything to make it disappear. "If I do, then you'll go away?"

"Upon delivery, you'll never see me again." Cooper crossed his heart.

"I doubt that counts in your condition."

"It's the sentiment."

Scott bit the bullet and sighed, planning how soon after the race he could get his hands on a cigarette. "So what do you want delivered? A secret message from the grave? You annoyed someone until he murdered you, and now you want everyone to know who it was?"

"Son, you got a sinister mind."

"It came with the company." Outside a race, Scott would've glared him right out of the Porsche, but right now he couldn't spare the effort.

"It's an engine."

"Well, at least it's not something stupid."

"No way," Cooper said. "This is a 1971, 426 Hemi."

"That's a bitchin' engine," Scott said with reverence. You didn't have to be a driver or a collector to know one of the great engines of all time. It wasn't a legal racing engine, but any driver's wet dream. He'd bought one three weeks ago and dropped it into the sweetest Charger. "Hey, wait a minute. Not *my* Hemi."

"It's not yours."

"I paid for it!"

"It was mine, and I never sold it. Are you watching this turn?"

"What I'm doing with this turn is none of your business." Scott purposely missed his braking point and moved up on a Ferrari he'd already lapped.

"If you kill yourself, I'll just have to haunt the next guy. And to tell you the truth, I'm getting a little tired of all you piston-headed—"

The Ferrari swerved; Scott had no idea why. If he'd had his full attention where it belonged, he would've remembered he was running on new rubber and adjusted for it. He never would've lost control of the Porsche. Never would've spun out, watching the flash of his headlights go 'round and 'round until he hit the wall.

"Dammit!" Before the car even came to a standstill, Scott had his harness unbuckled. He threw his helmet at *it*, but that had no effect whatsoever, so he pulled the wheel and started to climb out of the Porsche.

Cooper laughed at him. "You can run, but you can't hide."

"Watch me."

Scott wiggled halfway out of the window before he felt something cold on his thigh, right through his racing suit. Icy cold. Freaky. When he twisted to get away from it, he lost his balance and pitched headfirst toward the track. Before his ankle was clear. He didn't hear the bone crack as a Corvette roared by, but he sure as hell felt it.

"Damn."

Cooper appeared beside him, arms akimbo. "Told you to watch the turn. Break anything?"

He was screwed. Back to the crash house.

"Change your mind yet?" Cooper asked.

"Man, you can break every bone in my body, but there's no *friggin'* way you can make me give away my Hemi."

Cooper held his reply until a half-dozen more cars sped by, cutting them a wide berth. Then he hunkered down next to Scott. "You'll be in a cast, what, about eight weeks? I'll be with you every day, Templeton. All day. All night. You'll change your mind."

Scott tried to scoot away on his butt. That's when he figured out his arm was broken, too.

"Oh, seems I was wrong," Cooper said with a smirk. His mustache twitched with suppressed laughter, his voice a ghostly singsong as he added, "You can't run, and you can't hide."

At the end of six long, long weeks, Scott's perpetual roommate had seen to it that he had no love life. Seems women tended to get distracted by an unseen entity doing a war dance on the mattress beside them.

All his friends were suddenly very busy; no one wanted to hear another word about a ghost named Cooper making every day a living hell.

He'd lost all credibility with the team owner, who'd written him off weeks ago and wouldn't put him in a car again if he was down to the dregs of drivers. Even Scott's brother ignored his phone messages after the third week, and Jeremy was about as loyal as they came.

He'd lost weight, no thanks to Cooper making such a nuisance of himself at mealtime.

"What is that? McDonald's?"

"Go away," Scott said with his mouth full of Big Mac. No sense wasting manners on a ghost. He'd hoped when he returned home to Indianapolis to recuperate, Cooper'd stay behind in Florida.

No such luck. He'd known it as soon as he'd pulled out of Daytona—he hated to fly; dangerous damn way to travel, no wheels on the ground. Would've been ten times as bad with a ghost up there, bugging the pilot.

So here he sat in Indianapolis, riding the sofa, same as every day, the foot of his long leg cast resting on the engine block that served as a coffee table. A video of *Le Mans* was on television. Forget that it had a vague plot. Forget that the storyline was slow. He wasn't watching it for that. If he couldn't race, he at least could speed around the track from Steve McQueen's perspective.

Dozens of crumpled hamburger wrappers, french fry containers, and empty soda cups dotted the landscape of

Scott's living room. When he was growing up, his grand-mother's kitchen had been one of his favorite places in the whole world. He'd learned how to cook from her, but two casts and a pair of crutches—one modified to use with a broken wrist—made that downright unenjoy-able. It wasn't that he couldn't get out on his crutches for more than fast food, but what was the point? He took his troubles with him wherever he went.

Cooper closed in from behind and made sniffing nois-es over Scott's shoulder, but that never satisfied him. "Does it smell good? Are the onions hot?"

"Fuck off."

"Come on, you eat that stuff every day and you never tell me nothing. You're driving me nuts."

"Then I was wrong. Things are looking up." Scott grinned, as giddy as if he'd just lapped the second place car for the tenth time.

Cooper grumbled.

Pressing the advantage, Scott set his hamburger down on the wrapper and looked contrite. "Aw, gee, I'm sorry, Coop. I've been a real bear."

The ghost looked suspicious.

"Let me make it up to you."

"You'll deliver it now?" Cooper suggested hopefully.

"What? Oh, the engine. Nah, I'm thinking of doing something special for you tomorrow."

Cooper still looked suspicious, but hopeful, too.

"I was thinking, tomorrow how'd you like a Big Mac of your own?"

It was the first time Cooper threw something at Scott,

who roared with laughter until he fell off the sofa and cracked his arm cast on the edge of the block.

"Hey, look at that." Lying on his back in the narrow gap between the furniture, Scott wiggled the cast and discovered a rough, eighth-inch separation running down his forearm.

"Does it hurt?"

"No," he said with surprise. "Not at all."

"Too bad."

He sat up and played with it until the crack doubled. Still no pain. He wiggled his arm around, flexed his fingers, tried to do the same with his wrist, but that was stiffer than a new truck suspension.

"I need some tools." Scott looked at the ghost expectantly.

"So?"

"So . . . you can move things. Go out to the garage and get something to cut this off."

"Then you'll head for my ma's?" That was where the ghost wanted the engine delivered. Go figure.

"Then I'll think about it."

By the end of the day, Scott had removed his arm cast entirely and cut the leg cast down to below his knee. He hobbled around on it well enough to bag it in a trash bag, seal the top to his thigh with duct tape, and head for the bathroom. His first real, almost-full-body shower in six weeks felt like heaven—until Cooper crammed into the tub with him. It wasn't as if Scott had anything to hide; Cooper'd made a habit of popping into the john just to make him jump.

"How's the water feel?" The ghost sounded jealous enough to start drooling.

"None of your business."

"Don't be a hard ass. Tell me how it feels."

"It feels so good that if you don't get out of here, you're going to see something else that isn't your business."

In a second, the water spray went from hot to frigid, and Scott wrenched his broken leg darting out of the way.

"Ooh, the language," Cooper said when Scott let loose. He laughed and held his ears—a real drama ghost. And he looked too thoughtful for comfort.

Scott's utilities shut off the next day. Now that he could drive again without jutting his right leg onto the passenger side, his truck quit. His cell phone disappeared. The one time he managed to get out with a buddy's help, he discovered his credit cards were demagnetized. Another week of that was all he could take, so Monday morning, with the ghost's permission, Scott drove out to the heated garage he shared with several car buddies and pulled the 426 out of the Charger. It was like ripping out his heart. He dumped the engine into the back of his three-quarter-ton pickup, ready for delivery.

No wonder it had been so cheap.

"Don't feel bad." Cooper stood close to Scott and watched him hang his head over the coveted engine. "I hounded ten other guys who had it before you. You held out pretty long."

"Oh yeah? The guy who sold it to me didn't have a

broken leg." Scott sagged against the side of his black pickup, resigned to his fate. "How'd they manage to get rid of you?"

"Not sure, really. Maybe broken bones sapped your energy. Maybe I'm getting better."

"Mr. Templeton? Scotty?" A boy approached slowly, about twelve, wearing faded jeans and a hopeful smile. "I knew it was you. My dad says you won't mind if I ask for an autograph." He held out a copy of Scott's book, *Going the Distance*. From the tattered looks of it, it had been read many times.

"What's your name?" Scott pulled his pen out of his breast pocket—he always kept one handy—and opened the book to the title page.

"Kenny. Ken," he corrected, as all boys do when they want to appear more grown up.

Scott grinned. He loved autographing anything, anytime. Today, though, he particularly liked someone looking up to him and talking to him without making him the brunt of a joke.

"Hey, nothing wrong with Kenny. I go by Scotty at the track, you know. So, you racing anything yet?"

"Yes sir, I'm doing pretty good. Can you write something to make my friends jealous?"

"Something like, 'Come by anytime and we'll work on the engine some more'?"

"That'd be cool!" After getting his book back, Kenny ran off to show his dad. And maybe his friends.

Scott blew on his pen as if it were too hot to handle, kissed it, and tucked it back into his pocket. Half the fun of racing was driving fast. The other half was being famous.

"You wrote a book?" the ghost said.

Shit; still here.

"The sooner I get rid of the Hemi, the sooner I get rid of you, right?" He was no fool; he'd tried to sell it before his phone had gone AWOL.

"That's what I've been telling you for seven weeks now."

Scott sighed, admitting defeat. "Okay. Where to?"

"You know, I didn't like you at first."

"You're breaking my heart."

"I kinda got used to you now, though." Cooper moved into the passenger side without opening the door. "It's a long way. Somebody's gotta keep an eye on you. I'll tell you as we go."

"Great, a road trip with a ghost."

"I knew you'd like it."

"It's always been my fondest dream." Scott slid behind the wheel, prepared to drive to the ends of the earth to get rid of Speed Cooper, the former champion who'd died on the very track where Scott had acquired him. "If you insist on coming along, open your window."

"You saying I smell?"

"Like a damn pipe."

Coop grinned in memory. "Yes sir, the ladies always liked the aroma of my tobacco. Still hangs around me, huh?"

"I'll have to get my truck fumigated when I get back." Scott pushed the button and lowered the window for him. "Wind won't be a problem, will it? Blow you out on the highway or something?"

"You need to tell anyone you're leaving?" Cooper jabbed. "Friends, maybe?"

"You're not going to talk the whole way, are you?"

"Oh, that's right. I forgot. All your friends don't know you no more."

"Swear to God, if you don't shut up, I'm heading for the nearest priest and getting you exorcised."

"Won't work," Cooper crowed with delight. "I'm not *in* you."

"Hell, according to all the friends I used to have, you're not here, period, so let's just get this over with. Where to?"

"St. Louis."

Home. Connections. Things were looking up already. The pickup roared to life with the first turn of the key. Maybe he'd make it through another day without a smoke. He'd gone through half a pack the day he'd gotten his casts, justifying his slip by thinking maybe he'd been hallucinating from withdrawal, which, unfortunately, turned out not to be the case.

"What're the odds your mother will believe my engine is from the ghost of her dead son?"

"Aw, she won't be any problem," Cooper said. "My wife would be, but she just got married and moved. No, we'll be fine, as long as my first daughter's not there. Now Maggie, she'd be a problem."

* * *

Maggie Cooper risked her peep-toe, crisscross-strapped Manolo Blahniks on the crooked stairs descending into her grandmother's dim, musty, dirt-floored cellar. Come to think of it, she was risking her neck or, at the very least, both ankles. Fortunately, Grammy didn't have to come down here often. Other than the water heater, furnace, and an emergency stash of food, water, and various supplies to weather power outages, the cellar wasn't used for anything.

Grammy followed slowly, using both feet on every tread. Not her normal style, which was darting around at the speed of light, her body keeping pace with her quick mind. Today, however, she was attempting to delay Maggie's departure. Thus the trip into the cellar. Before that, she'd gotten out a rickety cane with no rubber tip, flattened her gray hair, wore a faded blue robe over flannel pajamas, and just generally looked like a sorry old hound dog left out on the porch. It was three o'clock in the afternoon.

"You should hold the railing," Grammy said.

Forget that. Maggie hugged her pearl-colored Armani suit jacket close to keep it from brushing against the damp walls. "I don't know why you wouldn't let me change first."

"There. Look at it."

The only way to avoid hitting her head on the rafters while staring at her grandmother's brand-new water heater was to hunch over. Looked fine to her. "What's wrong with it?"

"It's not strapped to the wall. He should have installed it just like the old one, so it won't fall over." Seventy-year-old Grammy spoke slowly and clearly, as if Maggie were addle-brained.

"It's hooked into a rigid water pipe," Maggie said just as slowly and clearly. "It's not going anywhere."

"Why, an earthquake could rip that right out of there and tumble it over," Grammy grumbled. "Then the gas line would break and start a fire, or worse, an explosion. Do you want us to blow up in an earthquake?"

"Grammy—" Maggie sighed audibly. She gazed into eyes just as green and stubborn as her own and took a deep, calming breath. "There won't be an earthquake."

"We're on the New Madrid fault, you know."

"There won't be an earthquake," she said, trying to soften the frustration in her voice.

"Don't take it out on me just because you got another speeding ticket."

Maggie bit her tongue, counted to five, then calmly said, "It was a warning," for the hundredth time.

Grammy's left-on-the-porch, hound-dog look morphed into that of an arthritic old canine left out all night. In midwinter. "Your mother wouldn't let them get away with this."

Mom, my butt. Grammy always called the shots in this household, which explained why Maggie's widowed mother had finally eloped. Right now, she was on a honeymoon far, far way, with no plans to return.

"Today's Monday," Maggie said, summoning patience.

"I'll be back in a week. If you need help with it before then, tell Ruby."

Grammy scoffed. "She can't even get her makeup on right. Her lipstick is black."

Maggie grinned because, at twenty, her younger sister had a style all her own. "It matches her nails."

"Yeah, the ones dangling from her ears."

"Those are crosses." Maggie checked her watch on the sly, a knockoff, because ninety percent of the time it went walkabout, and she didn't want to worry about never seeing it again. It was getting late. Rush hour started at three-thirty. "Just because she doesn't accessorize your way doesn't mean she can't help."

"But what if—"

"It's only a week," Maggie said gently but firmly. "You'll ace the interviews and then you'll move, I know you will."

If she didn't just go, this could drag on another hour, maybe more. It'd be kinder to get it over with. Maggie tiptoed gingerly back up the stairs, then inspected her shoes for scuffs.

"If you have any questions, I programmed Kevin's number into the kitchen phone. You still push Memory and one to get my cell. His condo is Memory and two. I'll be there in four hours."

"It's a five-hour drive to Chicago," Grammy nagged as she followed her up the stairs at a snail's pace. "You'll get another ticket."

"I have a radar detector, remember?"

"Didn't work this morning."

"It works better outside the city."

Resuming her three-point gait in the kitchen, Grammy shut the basement door. She stared at it wistfully. "Sure would be nice to have a lock on that."

"I know." Maggie smiled to herself and pressed a fond kiss on the older woman's wrinkly cheek. "The odds of someone tunneling into the cellar and coming upstairs in the middle of the night, well, what can I say?"

"It has a door." Leading outside, she meant.

"Solid wood, and you lost the key twenty years ago. It won't kill you to say you're going to miss me, you know."

Grammy sighed heavily, endlessly. "Well . . . I guess I'll just have to get used to it. First your father left. Then your mother. Now you." She didn't mention Ruby's being away at a Goth event in Minneapolis. Or that Maggie's father had died fifteen years ago.

Maggie hugged the older woman soundly, bussed her again, then straightened her back and walked out the door toward her two-year-old red Mustang. She'd planned on changing into casual clothes for the three-hundred-mile drive, but that would have drawn out her grandmother's passive-aggressive role. She could change in a restroom along the way.

With the heat on low to warm her feet, Maggie drove with the windows open and fresh air pouring in. Spring was alive in St. Louis. Redbuds on the bluff along the highway were starting to bloom. The radio was on high. Singing reduced stress, she'd found. So did putting the top down, but that would be silly with hours of highway driving ahead of her. Anyway, those were the nice things about spring in St. Louis. Then there was the skunk in the yard last night. Ticks on the dogs. Chiggers wouldn't be far behind. She looked forward to a high-rise apartment in a concrete city with little patches of green.

She didn't even make it out of the county before her cell phone *ka-ching*ed like an old-fashioned cash register. Grammy, of course. Up went the windows. Off went the radio. With a hands-free connection, Maggie continued to cover miles in the fast lane. Now that she'd made her break, she had everything in perspective again.

"Miss me already?" she asked fondly.

"Maggie, Maggie—" Grammy sounded breathless. "A man just pulled into our front yard."

Surely she meant in front of the yard.

"He's got this really big black truck. He's coming up on the porch!"

"Well, don't open the door. Just ask him what he wants."

"He's dressed in jeans, with one leg tore up the side. He's got on a jean jacket and a cowboy hat."

"Okay, then," Maggie said, her sense of humor still intact. "Thanks for the play-by-play."

"And wait, let's see, what is that? Oh, a boot on his left foot and duct tape on his right."

That seemed a little weird, and Maggie's amusement disintegrated. At least they had three big dogs watching the place.

"I'm telling you all this so you can describe him to the police. You know, in case he kidnaps me. Wait, I'll get the binoculars so I can read his license plate."

"Binoculars, my behind," Maggie muttered. Grammy saw 20/20 with her new glasses.

"S-P-D-D-M-N. That could be demon!"

"It could be Spider-Man, too. Ask him what he wants. Through the door!"

"Okay, hold on."

Maggie toyed with putting Grammy on hold and calling the nearest neighbor to see if there really was a big black truck in the yard, but there was a thick stand of pines blocking the line of sight between their five-acre parcel and the next property.

"It's okay." Grammy laughed, suddenly back to her old self. Probably an old friend she hadn't seen in a while. Someone with a new vehicle she didn't recognize. "Sorry I bothered you for nothing."

"So, who is it?"

"Oh, just the nicest young man, you wouldn't believe. So tall and good-looking. He's here to deliver something your father sent."

"Kind of slow about it, isn't he?"

"What, dear? I couldn't hear you. Scotty was talking."

"He's still there?"

"Hold on."

Maggie drummed her fingers on the steering wheel and wondered what she could promise her grandmother to bribe her into letting her visit Chicago in peace. Today.

"Maggie, you still there? He needs help unloading the truck. It's so late in the day, I told him he could spend the night."

"What?" Maggie shot across four lanes and flew up the next exit ramp.

"Well, none of the rental places will be open late enough. And he's got a cast on his leg."

Visions of Ted Bundy leaped into Maggie's head. "Don't you dare let him in the house! I'm on my way back."

"Don't worry, he's a perfect gentleman." Grammy giggled like a woman a quarter her age. "He took off his hat and wiped his feet on the doormat. I offered him some hot coffee and—"

"Get off the phone. I'm calling 911."

"Oh, don't do that, dear. I'm so looking forward to hearing news about your father."

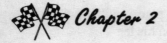 *Chapter 2*

Lucille Cooper, a.k.a. Grammy to anyone she'd known more than five seconds, peered out the sidelight. The instant she spotted the engine in the back of the pickup, her heart leaped with hope.

Maybe this time Lawrence had sent a personal message.

It was an odd lot of people her son had sent her way over the years. A couple from Idaho just passing through Missouri had stopped at a flea market and been harangued by Lawrence into purchasing a set of china and delivering it to her front door; they'd barely said a word, just unloaded boxes and boxes onto her porch and jumped back into their car. A young woman had left two small children peeking out the windows of their minivan while she dropped off a box of faded, cast-iron toys; mostly trains, Model Ts, and banks. A middle-aged gal had delivered a rubber swimming cap, of all the stupid things; she'd talked all afternoon, but not about Lawrence.

They were just a sprinkling of the hundreds who'd crossed her porch. She used to ask about her son. How did he converse with them? What had happened on that racetrack fifteen years ago? What caused the accident that took his life? Was she to blame? Did he come with them?

Nobody answered except to say they'd come alone. Pinned by her plethora of questions, most stammered, stared into space, looked uneasy, and beat a hasty retreat. She'd given up without learning anything, not even what to do with whatever they'd brought.

Collectibles, Lawrence had called them when he was alive. He'd spent his winnings on them and swore they'd make the family rich someday, that they'd put both his girls through college with a lot left over. Mostly they just collected rust and spiderwebs.

This was the first time one of Lawrence's finds had been delivered by such an outstanding specimen of masculinity. Grammy'd always been a sucker for a man in a cowboy hat, which he donned right after raking his fingers through the blackest hair she'd seen this side of midnight.

All three dogs suddenly sat back on their haunches, cocked their heads, and watched. Mighty peculiar for that bunch.

Tall, broad-shouldered, a little rough around the edges, the stranger clunked up the wide porch steps in one cowboy boot. The other foot was duct-taped up to his knee; there might have been a cast hiding under that. Beneath his denim jacket, a cream-colored knit shirt stretched across his chest. If her son weren't already dead, she would've killed him. If he had to send this much eye appeal, why couldn't it be someone her age? Shoot, the same general age bracket would do.

He bypassed the bell and gave the door a good sound thumping.

"Who are you and what do you want?" she asked, her voice wavering purposely. After all, Maggie was still on the other end of the phone.

"Mrs. Cooper? Uh, ma'am, I'm Scott Templeton." He glanced over his shoulder at the truck, shook his head, then spoke to the door again. "I'm here to— I mean, I've got an— Well, ma'am, I'm supposed to deliver an engine to you. It's in my truck. In the back."

Lucille hadn't had any fun teasing anybody in a month of Sundays. Maggie was too focused to be any fun, and as for Ruby, how did you tease someone who lived in the attic and wore black lipstick?

"I don't need an engine," she said, tongue in cheek. "One came with my car."

"Oh no, ma'am, this doesn't go in your car. It's, uh, from . . . someone you used to know." Scott turned his head, held his hand up to his mouth to hide his lips moving, and said, "Shut up, I'm working up to it."

The dogs darted sideways glances at the truck, and the hair stood up on their backs. They slunk off without so much as one bark among them. That could mean only one thing.

Lucille turned the lock and threw open the door. "He's with you? My son is with you?"

Scott whipped off his hat. He held it in one hand and rubbed the back of his neck with the other. For hours, he'd discarded several ways to tell a mother, without scaring her, that her dead son had directed him to deliver an engine to her door. Unless she was a gearhead herself, what the heck was she going to do with his Hemi?

The bright light in the old woman's eyes was at odds with the bathrobe and lifeless gray hair. Her hands trembled, too. His grandmother had been like that near the end. At the very end, he couldn't say; it still ate at him that he hadn't been there when she'd needed him most. That she'd hid her failing health and sent him off to race because his doing what he loved was that important to her.

"He's never come with anyone before," she said.

"You know about him?" Scott asked, dumbfounded.

"Where is he? Right here, on the porch?" Her gaze searched the wide wraparound porch without settling anywhere. "Lawrence, where are you, son?"

"She knows I hate that name," Cooper grumbled.

Scott grinned, pleased to find another way to get Cooper's goat. "Yes, ma'am, *Lawrence* is right here. In fact, *Lawrence* insisted on coming with me to bring you this engine." He considered the icy jab in his shoulder a reward rather than a warning.

Cooper's mother tilted her head back and gazed up at Scott with so much excitement in her eyes, it ate at his resolve to dump the engine and run like hell. He wondered if she made chocolate chip cookies like his grandmother used to, the old-fashioned way. Not with a store-bought mix or a roll of dough from the refrigerator section. Not with a food processor.

"Does he talk to you?" she asked.

"No way to shut him up except do what he wants."

"So . . . you can hear him." Her voice swelled with hope.

"Yes, ma'am."

"You can ask him questions, and he'll answer you?"

"Only if he wants. Most the time, he's just ornery." It felt good to talk to someone about this who, finally, didn't think he was losing it.

She peered around Scott's arm, toward the pickup. "Looks heavy. How're you going to unload it?"

"I've been thinking about that all the way from Indianapolis. The simplest way is to open the tailgate and drive it up a steep hill." Scott grinned when Cooper roared, "It goes in the barn!"

"What? Did he just say something? You look like he just said something."

Scott rubbed his jaw to keep from laughing outright at Cooper's expense. Didn't seem like a good idea. Tempting, though. "Seems *Lawrence* didn't like that idea."

"You call me Lawrence once more, and I'll introduce you to a whole passel of ghosts that'll stay on after I'm done and gone. And won't none of 'em be as nice as me, neither."

"He's talking to you again, isn't he? I can tell by the look on your face. Oh, what's he saying? Please tell me."

"Seems he wants it put in the barn, Mrs. Cooper. So if you're not real particular where it goes, I can just back up real fast and hit the brakes. It should slide right on outta there."

Cooper was fit to be tied. "Didn't the last seven weeks teach you nothing, boy?"

Scott sighed. "Or I can rent a hoist."

"Oh my, this is just so exciting!" Mrs. Cooper grabbed Scott by his sleeve and dragged him into the house, so ebullient that she left the front door standing wide open.

He sniffed the air, convinced he smelled cookies. He could be had for fresh-baked cookies.

"Now you listen. I'm sure it's too late to rent equipment today, so you'll stay right here. And call me Grammy; everybody does."

"Oh no, ma'am, I couldn't," Scott said without an iota of firmness behind it. Truth was, his finances were tied up for the long haul. He'd planned on enjoying the old Hemi for a while, fixing whatever was wrong with it that made it change hands so much, and then taking a nice profit on it. He figured to clear at least thirty times what he'd spent, a nice addition to everything he'd set aside for the team he'd own someday. He didn't have forever; movie stars aside, endurance racing was a young man's sport.

And now he was out one bitchin' engine.

"Nonsense, I wouldn't know you were talking to me if you called me anything else," Grammy prattled on. "You can sleep in Lawrence's old room. It's upstairs. Oh! Can you see him, too?"

"Yes, ma'am."

"Good." She smiled brightly. "Then he can show you where it is while I start supper. You just go on now and make yourself at home. I'll only be a few minutes." She fluffed up her hair as she walked toward the back of the house, her back straight, a cane left hanging off the back of the sofa.

Left to his own devices, Scott took a look around from the threshold. The front door of the old farmhouse was near one corner of a large, high-ceilinged living room stuffed with comfortable-looking furniture, area rugs, soft throws, and lots of books. Stairs rose up the wall to his right. He debated the wisdom of spending the night in Cooper's old room; better take the sofa and let the ghost have his territory all to himself. Ten minutes alone was all Scott needed. He wasn't kidding about getting a good run in reverse and slamming on the brakes. One engine, delivered. One haunted driver, outta there.

"Just in case you're thinking what I think you're thinking," Cooper drawled with a get-even grin, "your truck ain't running so good again. Might as well take your bag in. My room's top of the stairs, second door on the right."

"Don't go to any trouble for me," Scott said sarcastically. He was tempted to slam the front door in the ghost's face, but experience had taught him it was useless.

"Oh, no trouble," Grammy responded from the other room. "I'll just heat up some leftover chili. If I know Maggie, she'll be flying in here any minute."

Scott enjoyed watching Cooper's face segue from a get-even grin to out-and-out horrified. This was too good to let slide.

"Say, Coop, isn't Maggie your daughter?"

"She's supposed to be in Chicago."

"I take it you two don't see eye to eye."

"Just like her mother, that one." Cooper scowled. "Too hard on a man. They never understood what I was doing, how I was seeing to their future."

Scott tossed his Stetson onto the top of the coatrack. "My truck better run like new come morning."

Ten minutes later, he'd confirmed that the truck indeed would not start. He stood on the porch, beer bottle in hand, duffel bag at his feet, and seriously considered going for his emergency pack of smokes. He'd bought them at the start of the road trip. They'd been riding on the dash ever since. They called to him constantly, mostly when Cooper was visible and verbal, which was too damn often to suit him.

He hoped Maggie could see Cooper; he looked forward to watching her light into him. It'd make the whole trip worthwhile.

"What's that noise? Crickets?"

"Spring peepers," Cooper answered.

"What's that?"

"Tree frogs."

"Fine, don't tell me." Scott took a swig of beer. He'd refused it at first, until he'd seen the look of longing on Cooper's face when Grammy had offered it. Yes sir, coming to St. Louis just kept getting better and better.

"How's that taste?"

Scott smacked his lips and sighed with pleasure. "Prime stuff. Too bad you can't have any."

The ghost grumbled.

"You know what would top this? Chocolate chip cookies. Your mom know how to make those?"

He wasn't surprised when Cooper didn't answer. Talked when he shouldn't, wouldn't talk when it'd be useful. Just downright cantankerous.

"Nice of your mother to offer me your room," Scott said, intending to add insult to injury. He expected Cooper to change his mind and tell him to stay the hell out of his room, but he didn't.

The peepers stopped abruptly, as if all were on the same switch. Seconds later, sirens pierced the ensuing silence, wailing closer until finally three squad cars roared down the street. Light bars flashing, the cops braked around his truck, raising dust as they hemmed it in. Grammy shot out onto the porch about the same time they killed the sirens. He was pleased to see her looking less haggard than when he'd arrived. She'd brushed her hair and donned a pretty pink sweater and stretch pants.

"Your granddaughter's a cop?" Scott asked hopefully. If not, he figured he was about to lose his beer and miss out on a good home-cooked bowl of chili, not to mention getting shoved up against a patrol car with his legs spread.

Grammy *hmph*ed. "It'd be cheaper for her if she was."

A zippy little red Mustang, top up, slid to a stop six inches from the rear bumper of the last squad car. The red paint was splashed and dripping from barreling across the creek at the head of Cherry Lane.

A lovely wisp of a creature popped out; straight blond

hair, flashing green eyes, wearing a suit the color of pearls.

"Goddammit, Maggie." The cop riding drag rounded on her, leaving Scott to the other two. "I told you to let us handle this."

So, this is Maggie.

"You're afraid of *her*?" Scott whispered to the ghost as the cops approached the porch.

"I ain't afraid of nobody," Cooper snarled. But his gaze shifted away to the tree line.

Shiny, shoulder-length hair bounced with agitation as the delectable Miss Cooper darted between bumpers on impossibly high heels. Her suit had to be top-of-the-line, the way it flowed with every inch of her body as she charged across the narrow lawn. Worry creased the delicate features of her face. Eyes flashed a mix of fire and anger, and promised revenge if he'd so much as harmed a hair on Grammy's head.

The uniformed cop body-blocked Maggie at the bottom of the steps. She didn't stand still for that, though, not this exquisite creature. She dodged and darted and peeked around the uniform, shouting, "That's him!" and "Grammy, are you all right?"

To think Cooper could have sired someone so pretty, so utterly enticing, was beyond comprehension. Scott would have told him so, too, but conversing with a ghost in front of three cops who were partial to Maggie couldn't possibly play out in his favor. Besides, after seven long, *long* weeks of abstinence, everyone else was about as noticeable as wallpaper. Grammy and the officers faded into the background, taking care of business as Maggie climbed the steps.

"*You*," she said with recognition.

Fame had many benefits. The fact that she already knew who he was would make getting to know her a whole lot easier. Being the daughter of a champion, she probably followed the circuit religiously. Women didn't throw their bras and panties at him, but he'd been known to autograph a few.

She was dressed professionally; he extended his hand in like manner. Women enjoyed that sort of thing.

"Nice to meet you," he said.

The fire didn't leave her eyes. In fact, it had a hot, searing edge to it that didn't bode well for their first meeting. She didn't even hesitate as she topped the last step and advanced on him, though she was a good head shorter. "You owe me five hundred dollars."

"Excuse me?" He tucked his hand safely away. For a second, he entertained the idea that they'd met before, that money was somehow involved and she had a legitimate claim he'd forgotten. But those green eyes? Uh-uh, no way he'd forgotten her.

"You picked a helluva time to hit the wall," she said.

A lesser man would have run. Not Scott Templeton. He'd stared death in the face more than once. No way a little slip of a woman like this could back him against the house.

Maggie approached high-and-mighty Scotty Templeton with the full intention of getting him off her grandmother's porch and on his way within the next sixty seconds. She'd allow an extra thirty solely due to the duct-taped cast on his foot. It wasn't that she had no sympathy for his plight, but Grammy was, at times, too gullible for her own good, and Maggie needed to be in Chicago.

And of course he was at fault for hitting the wall seven weeks ago and costing her a bet.

"Ah," Scott said with a grin. His hazel eyes twinkled back at Maggie with a ray of understanding, and a crease dimpled one cheek as he stood his ground and deciphered the debt she'd accused him of owing. "A betting woman."

"No," she said flippantly. "I *like* giving away brand-new radar detectors."

Scott's lips puckered into a low whistle. "Nice one, five hundred dollars."

She circled around, putting herself right where she needed to be, between him and the door. "That includes the speeding ticket I got because I had to rely on an old piece of crap."

"Just out of curiosity, what did you stand to win?"

"Certainly not you on my grandmother's porch. Nice of you to stop by, though." She picked up his duffel bag and thrust it into his arms. It was like hitting a brick wall, no give at all.

His smile was lopsided, both amused at her attempt to push him off the porch and unabashedly interested in turning a less-than-stellar first meeting into something more. Like most drivers she'd met, he displayed a Texas-sized ego in that department.

"Much as I'd like to," he said without a shred of regret, "I can't leave."

"I've got three cops with me," she said, implying that they'd haul him away, given the word. Only then did she notice they were taking their leave.

"Bye, Grammy. Bye, Maggie," they said as they headed for their respective patrol cars.

"Geez," she said flatly, fisting one hand on her hip. "You guys are cops, you're supposed to have a clue." She'd gone to school with two of them; Bobby'd sat behind her in sixth grade, and she'd dated Chris in high school. He was her best friend's brother.

"Sorry, Maggie. Grammy says she invited him to stay."

Scott's duffel punctuated that as it hit the floorboards behind her.

Bobby snapped his fingers as if he'd just remembered something, like his *duty*, and approached the porch. When he pulled a notebook out of his pocket, Maggie was pleased to see that he was going to get official.

"Mr. Templeton, I almost forgot. Could I get your autograph for my little boy?"

Maggie growled with frustration and made no attempt to hide her annoyance as she trotted down the steps for a personal chat with the other two. "Look, guys, Grammy doesn't know him from Adam. I need to go to Chicago and I can't leave her here alone with him."

"She's an adult, Maggie," Chris explained patiently. "It's her house. She invited him. There's nothing we can do."

Maggie turned to appeal to her grandmother's good sense, but caught only a glimpse of the older woman's back as she darted indoors.

"Fine." She folded her arms. "Better confiscate his beer bottle for fingerprints, then. You know, just in case our bodies are missing when you get around to checking back in three days."

"Shoot, Scotty Templeton went to Webster. I played against him in the Turkey Day game. We don't need prints."

Maggie threw up her hands. Who could argue against a local-boy-made-good, former football jock?

"Call us if you need anything else, though."

"Yeah, right."

"And for chrissake, slow down!"

Abandoned by the cops, who examined the load in the back of the pickup and proclaimed it "bitchin'" before they left, Maggie had no choice but to handle this herself. She took a deep breath and slowly turned back to Scott, rooted up there on the porch. A cool breeze ruffled his dark hair and dislodged a lock to fall over his forehead, threatening to distract her. He probably paid big bucks to have it styled to do exactly that. She stiffened her resolve.

"You can't stay here."

"Grammy invited me."

Maggie gritted her teeth at his familiarity. She quickly brushed off her aggravation, though, in favor of an approach that might work better.

"Fine," she said matter-of-factly, remounting the steps

to gain equal advantage. "I think you'll find our dogs aren't quite so gullible."

"Dogs?" He glanced around pointedly.

"Big ones," she said. "Huge. A hundred pounds each. I don't know why we keep them, they're half wild anyway. Someday they're liable to eat somebody whole."

"You mean those three mongrels cowering under the porch?" Scott snickered.

"Highly unlikely."

"Well, let's just see, shall we?" He whistled, but got no response. Then he clapped his hands, called, "C'mon, boys!" and whistled again. "C'mon! Time to eat."

They *whined*.

Maggie leaned over the rail just in time to spot the big, black, hairy one duck its head back under the porch. She turned on Scott. "What did you do to our dogs?"

"He didn't do anything." Grammy returned to the threshold with neither cane nor limp, and for heaven's sake, she'd changed out of her pajamas, too. "Chili's almost ready. Come inside or I'm closing the door. I can't afford to heat the whole darn neighborhood."

"Look at her," Maggie said gently, trying to appeal to Scott's sympathies. "If she were your grandmother, would you want a stranger sleeping in her house?"

"He's not a stranger," Grammy said, waving her hand dismissively as she gave up on their rushing to supper. "He's an old friend of your father's. Come in when you're ready, then."

"He's not old enough to be an old friend of my father's," Maggie retorted as the front door swung shut behind Grammy.

Maggie glared up at Scott. His lips were cocked with amusement. This had to be new, a woman hell-bent on getting rid of him. He probably saw it as a game.

"I'm harmless," he said with sincerity. "Really. I just have to deliver that engine"—he indicated it with a nod of his head—"and then I'll leave."

"Great." She stepped aside, giving him full access to the stairs. "Have at it."

"Truck won't start."

"That shouldn't be a problem for you."

"See, I'm delivering it for . . . Well, sort as a favor for your dad."

With a large sweep of her arm, she indicated that the entire front yard was at his disposal.

"It should go in the barn," he said.

"There's no room."

Scott cocked his head, as if listening to another voice. "There's more than one barn."

He was observant, Maggie'd give him that. "They're both full of junk. Junk that my father collected his entire life. Plus more junk that he's had *delivered*"—she surrounded that with finger quotes—"over the years."

Scott looked astounded. "Really? I'm not the first?"

Satisfied now that she knew exactly how to get Scott away from their front door, Maggie grinned. "Follow me. Just let me change my shoes first."

She stopped by her car to change into Keds, and while

she was there, she grabbed her phone and wireless earpiece.

Scott kicked the front tire and said, "Looks low."

"The ground dips there."

The main barn stood two hundred feet away from the house, to the side and back. The slightly downhill track was seldom used, but the clay had been so packed over the years that not much grew along it; sparse weeds, a little spring grass here and there that would die in the heat of summer.

Scott trekked behind her the whole way. Maggie turned around once to see how he was doing—maybe she should have driven him that far in her car—but he hobbled along in his cast just fine, grinning to himself. She caught him studying her backside, so she didn't ask what he found so amusing.

The large barn door wasn't any easier to slide than the last time she'd been out there a couple of years ago. Scott leaned in close. Heat poured off his body as he reached over her head and sent the door flying to the right. He massaged his arm afterward.

"It doesn't get used much," she said, meaning the door.

"It's nothing. I just took the cast off a week ago, and it's still stiff."

"You took it off?"

"It was time."

"Wow." Maggie flipped on the overhead lights. "Hometown hero *and* a doctor. Whenever do you find time to race cars?"

The interior of the two-story brick barn was cold from the long winter and so stuffed with her father's "collectibles" that they couldn't take more than two steps inside. Lamps, dishes, toys, tractors, tools, lanterns, political statues, neon lights, stereos, Christmas ornaments—you name it, it was in there. Horse collars, for God's sake. And that's just what she could see from where she stood. Besides all that, there were the mystery boxes, their flaps still folded or taped shut, stacked here and there with no regard to order or structure. Heavy boxes smashed the ones below, tilting them to crooked angles. Shorter stacks had boards across them, forming tables upon which more crap was piled.

"Good Lord," Scott said in awe.

"Yeah. A highway-variety antique mall gone awry."

"Is that a path through there?"

Maggie shrugged. "Maybe."

"Cooper sent all this here?"

"He accumulated most of it himself. After he died, Grammy used to say there was a chain letter going around that said, 'If you don't want ten years of bad luck, buy any old piece of junk and drop it off at number 3 Cherry Lane.'"

"What do you think?"

She looked him square in the eyes, impressed that he wasn't intimidated by her. Vexed, but impressed. "I think Grammy made it up. I think this is how she doesn't deal with his death. I think if there's a chain letter out there, she started it."

"I didn't get one."

"Yes, let's get back to you. Fifteen years of additional junk, and now you show up with an engine, of all things." She tipped her head and studied him. "Everybody else just left. Why aren't you leaving?"

"Like I said, my truck won't start."

"I'm sure you've been taking engines apart and putting them back together since you were twelve."

"Ten, but that's beside the point."

A dimple appeared when he smiled; just one, just on the left side. When Maggie found herself studying the other cheek to see if a second would appear, she almost slapped herself.

"It won't start again until there's a spot here for that engine," he finished, and she had no idea if he'd said anything in between.

"Right." Dimple aside, if he wasn't going to take responsibility, Maggie wanted nothing to do with him. "I'll bet you can have a sizable spot cleared in a couple hours."

"With a little help, I can be done before supper."

She was just about to tell him she'd let him in the house to eat when hell froze over, but the *ka-ching* of her cell phone interrupted.

"Maggie, just calling to make sure you'd left." Her boyfriend, Kevin, lived in Chicago. Besides her interview tomorrow, they had big plans this week. He'd be so disappointed if he knew she'd been delayed.

Maggie stepped aside for some privacy. "You know me," she said with a chuckle. "Get out of St. Louis before rush hour."

With luck, she'd be back on the road within the hour, so what harm was there in a little lie? She'd drive faster.

"Great, I'll wait up. How's Grammy?"

"Still being a pill. I'll tell you all about it tonight."

"I'll give you a massage," he said, and disconnected.

Maggie regretted that she wasn't there getting one right now, and she quickly closed the gap between Scott and her again. "Tell you what. You get that engine out of your truck in the next ten minutes, and I'll pack a nice hot meal for you."

He was holding a box he'd plucked off the floor, searching in vain for an out-of-the-way place to move it to until his gaze shifted to her. "Like I said . . ."

"In this suit? Not a chance." She headed toward the house without turning her back on him because, really, he was a lot bigger than she was, and in spite of the cops knowing him, she didn't. "Oh, I don't know what you did to scare the dogs away, but I doubt it works on recluses."

Scott froze, right after extending his arms so the box was nowhere near his body. "I hope to hell you mean old men who live alone and don't shave for months on end."

Maggie grinned. "Only if they have eight legs, segmented bodies, and violins on their backs."

As Scott hobbled to his pickup for a heavy pair of gloves, he muttered very unflattering things to Cooper about his daughter, ending with "Jesus Christ, she acts as if I *want* to stay. Not that I'd mind getting to know her a little better, mind you, because I gotta tell you, I'm a leg man, and she's got legs up to—"

"Keep your goddamn hands off my daughter." Cooper loomed close and scowled at Scott, who walked right through him.

"Shit, Coop, don't do that! It freaks me out."

"Maggie's too good for you."

Scott pulled leather gloves out from under the seat and shook them at the ghost plaguing him. "Maybe. But once I deliver this baby"—he patted his prize engine—"you're outta here, remember? She'll give me her number or my name's not Scott Templeton. Now don't make me walk through you again. I have stuff to move."

He hobbled back to the barn and strode through the door to find the nicest ass poking up in the air, encased in a tight pair of put-your-hands-right-here jeans. Weeks of abstinence aside, it was a very nice ass. It took an extra moment to corral his thoughts and realize Maggie was struggling to lift a box too heavy for her.

"Whoa, wait a minute, let me help you with that." Scott rushed forward, pulling on the gloves as he went. He added his pair of hands to safe territory, the cardboard box. When he and Maggie straightened up, they were close. Very close; only an eighteen-inch box separated them. "I thought you weren't going to help me."

"Are you kidding? I can't leave until you leave, and I have to leave. So no matter how much Grammy asks you to stay, no matter how much you want to stay, you have to go."

"I don't want to stay."

"You don't?"

"I didn't want to come here in the first place."

"Then why did you?"

"Your father—"

"Is dead," Maggie snapped, giving Scott his first inkling that she was not as open-minded as her grandmother.

"No kidding."

"Save your breath," the ghost grumbled from atop a tall stack. "She'll never admit I'm here."

Pressing the matter sure wouldn't win him any points, so Scott bit his tongue and helped Maggie with another box.

Cooper took advantage of the silence, not that he wasn't prone to butt in any other time. "I can't believe my mother saved so much. I mean, I expected her to, but still, I can hardly believe it. My fortune's still here."

Fortune, my ass. Scott tuned him out. He'd much rather talk to Maggie. "Why are you keeping all this stuff?"

"Not me," Maggie said. "I don't keep stuff. I don't collect things." She made a face, as if the very thought of collecting anything left a bad taste in her mouth. "As a matter of fact, I would love to get rid of it. I put myself though college as an auctioneer. There's nothing like taking a full auction hall and watching it empty in front of your eyes. Going once, going twice, bang the hammer, and by the end of the day, completely cleared out." As Maggie paused in her work, a little shiver of pleasure rippled through her, obvious even to Scott as it punctuated her words.

His gaze roamed the contents of the barn, his silence speaking volumes.

Maggie caught his drift and laughed lightly. "Why do you think I liked what I did? It was vicarious pleasure, believe me, because I grew up with this instead of a father. My mother was married to *this* instead of a man. Which is, I'm sure, more than you want to know."

Blushing from revealing too much, she bent over and tackled another box, one more her size. Scott didn't help, but gave her the space she sought.

"This needs to be sold," Cooper said, looking as if he'd pass out from the excitement. "Every bit of it. Ruby should be in college. Lord knows, that girl needs some direction. And Ma's not getting any younger. She can move into one of those retirement places."

Scott had two boxes in his arms, nowhere to put them, and someone else he'd much rather listen to. "Hey, Maggie, is there room up in the loft for any of this?"

"Nope. Loft is full."

Cooper turned pensive.

Scott knew that look; he turned his back on the ghost. No way he was getting trapped into anything else. He quickly, desperately kicked several boxes into one another, crushing them into a smaller stack. Anything to clear more space fast.

"Okay, I think that's enough room to get it in here. Maggie, I hate to run, but if my truck starts, I need to get on the road."

This was rushed and lame, but he didn't want to leave without her number and he didn't dare dawdle. Better to meet her again in ghostless territory.

"You think maybe I can call you sometime?"

"Only if you don't mind my boyfriend punching you out."

Cooper stepped closer to Scott. "You can forget dumping that engine without a hoist. And after that, Ma could use some help. She's an old woman. A strong guy like you—"

Scott wheeled on the ghost, jabbed his finger at it, and roared, "Don't even think it. We had a deal."

Anger at the ghost didn't prevent Scott's noticing that Maggie'd stopped moving things. Empty-handed, she inched toward the big door, cutting him a wide berth.

"Don't leave," Scott begged. "Don't leave me alone with him."

Maggie's gaze darted around the interior.

"Come on, your grandmother knows he exists. She must have told you."

"You think you're talking to my father?"

"Mostly he's talking to me. He wants— What the hell do you want, Cooper?"

Cooper smirked, as if he'd won. "I guess it all needs to be appraised first. Wouldn't want Ma to get cheated."

"He wants—" When Scott turned, Maggie was already halfway out the door. "He wants all this appraised and sold so your grandmother can go to a retirement home."

"Grammy? Get real." Maggie stalked out, cutting him a sideways glance.

God, he hated that look. He barely knew her, and that look meant he wasn't ever likely to.

"You know what I said about fixing you a hot meal? Forget it. You know what Grammy said about you spending the night? You can forget that, too. Drop the engine in here if you must, but then leave."

"My truck won't start."

"So walk."

"It's getting dark."

Maggie paused ever so slightly, just long enough to toss parting words over her shoulder. "Good thing you have a truck to sleep in, then."

"It's supposed to get down to forty tonight," he called after her.

She didn't even slow down. She'd been enticing earlier, charging at him in her skirt and heels. He was used to women rushing toward him. Maggie was the first one who couldn't wait to get away.

Damn, he needed to stay until morning and try this again. But as soon as he talked her into giving him her number—and he would—he absolutely had to get away from the friggin' ghost.

 *Chapter 3*

Cooper's laugh was annoying as hell. It grated on Scott's nerves. Every time he heard it, he wanted to grab him by the throat and throttle him. Pretty damn hard to do to a ghost, though.

"You ain't doing so well, son."

"A little less audience participation would help," Scott shot back. He kicked a cardboard box, found it relatively solid, and did the only thing he knew Cooper wouldn't like. He sat on it.

"What're you doing?"

"What's it look like? I'm taking a break."

Scott crossed his arms, daring the ghost to just try to make him get up and work. Too bad the cigarettes weren't in his pocket. He could have tapped one out, real slow. He could have taken his time lighting it, real cool like. He could have blown smoke in Cooper's face and laughed when he tried to inhale.

Dang, he had to start carrying those.

"A break? You haven't even been working. You been hitting on my daughter the whole time."

"You call that hitting on her?" Scott snickered. He'd been jacked around enough to give as well as he got.

Or as well as he could to someone who wasn't alive. "I haven't even begun to hit on her."

"You stay away from her."

"Hey, man," Scott said, affecting an innocent shrug, "if the truck won't run, I can't leave. Can't get much simpler than that."

With irritation still his prime objective, Scott stretched his legs out in front of him, crossing his good ankle over the cast. He grinned at the ghost and leaned against the stack behind him for effect, but that was a mistake. It wasn't sturdy enough, and he tumbled awkwardly into a jumble of boxes. If Cooper hadn't doubled over in laughter, Scott might have gotten up. As it was, he wiggled his back and shoulders into a more comfortable spot and closed his eyes, feigning all the comfort of snuggling into a feather bed.

"Wake me when the sun comes up," he said.

"Fine. No skin off my nose."

Within minutes, the ghost was off in deeper regions of the barn, not so silent as he moved things around. No telling what he was looking for. No way Scott was asking.

The peepers worked up to a full chorus, their volume rivaling that of any cicadas Scott had ever heard. It was kind of nice, actually. A man could sleep pretty well to that. Unless he got hypothermia in this frigid barn and wandered off to the river in the middle of the night.

He wouldn't mind wandering into the house and running into Maggie. He wondered how serious things were with her boyfriend in Chicago. She wasn't wearing an engagement ring. She hadn't said, *Sorry, I'm in a relationship*. Looked like open territory to him.

"Sweet Jesus, it's worse than I thought."

Scott's eyes flew open.

Grammy was bent over him, her brow wrinkled with concern. "Did she hurt you? Can you get up?"

He quickly shoved several boxes out of the way so he could stand up and dust himself off. One rattled like broken china. With any luck, Grammy was a little hard of hearing.

Standing a good foot shorter, Grammy tipped her head this way and that as she looked him over. Scott wasn't quite sure what that was all about until she said, "Maggie came in in such a snit, I was afraid she'd clunked you over the head and left you to the wild animals."

Scott grinned at the idea of Maggie trying to clunk him anywhere. "Nah, I was just taking a break to annoy Cooper."

"Lawrence, you mean?"

"Yes, ma'am."

"He likes to be called Cooper?"

Scott shrugged. "He never said one way or the other."

"Lots of people used to call him Speed, but I always liked Lawrence. Sounds more dignified. Anyway, seeing as you're fine, come on to supper and bring him with you."

"Do I have to? Bring him, I mean."

"I need you to get some answers for me. You know, be our go-between."

"But Maggie—"

Grammy took him by the arm and started for the house.

"Now don't you go frettin' about my granddaughter. I know she can be a handful once you rattle her focus, but that's good, healthy spirit." She winked up at Scott with pride. "She got that from me."

Halfway back to the house, Scott wanted to be clear on something. "Does she sneak up behind people and clunk 'em on the head often?"

Grammy muttered, "Don't I wish," and from her tone, Scott thought it wise to leave it at that for now.

When he entered the warm, homey kitchen, the Mother Goose cookie jar couldn't have been more noticeable if it had jumped up and down on the counter and started dancing. Surely Grammy wouldn't put store-bought cookies in a nice old jar like that. Scott washed up at the sink, anticipating dessert, sniffing the air for a clue as to chocolate or peanut butter—or hey, in a pinch, oatmeal raisin would do—but all he could identify with any certainty was chili. He'd just sat down to a steaming bowl of it, smothered with onions and grated cheddar, when Maggie joined them. She was mid-conversation, hands-free and wireless, talking to someone about the need to leverage his assets more efficiently, but quickly signed off.

Maggie glared at him, and both fists landed firmly on her hips. "I made myself perfectly clear—"

"Mr. Templeton is our guest," Grammy said softly, as she set another bowl of chili on the table.

After that, Maggie didn't berate him anymore, but the way she yanked out her chair said plenty. She sat ramrod straight, primly almost. If a woman's gaze could sling darts, Maggie was adept.

She probably thought she was scary, but Scott only noticed nicely rounded breasts thrust forward and passion flaring in the depths of her green eyes. He was smart enough to keep that to himself.

Grammy seated herself opposite Scott. "Where's Lawrence now? Should I pull out a chair for him?"

Scott perused the kitchen, puzzled but pleased to see it was just the three of them. "That's odd. He's always around for meals."

Grammy *hmph*ed in a typically maternal fashion, clearly put out. "I told you to bring him."

"He doesn't listen," Maggie chimed in.

"That's for sure," Scott agreed.

"I meant *you*."

"I listen just fine." Scott grinned, pleased Maggie was still talking to him. He couldn't pass up the opportunity to show her how well he listened. "Your boyfriend still expecting you this evening?"

"Of course not. I called and explained how stubborn you are." If possible, Maggie sat even straighter and raised her chin in challenge. "You owe me a massage, too."

"Mind if I eat first, darlin'?"

"I didn't mean *personally*."

Scott held the fiery gaze in Maggie's eyes. Didn't matter how hard she glared at him, he wasn't giving in first. He couldn't help grinning, which made her glare harder, which made him grin more. She had a hint of chili sauce on her bottom lip. It was up for grabs whether he'd dab it off with a napkin or his own lips.

"If you two don't mind, I'd like to know if my son has finally sent me a message." Grammy broke Maggie's concentration, which rescued Scott from reaching out and make a complete ass of himself.

"That reminds me..." He forced himself to stop staring at Maggie; no sense giving her the upper hand. Instead, he addressed Grammy's request. "When Coop saw all the stuff in the barn, he couldn't believe it. He said it ought to be sold."

Grammy's gaze narrowed on Scott, then Maggie, then flitted back and forth, not about to let either of them off the hook. A black-and-gray marbled cat wound itself around Scott's good leg and meowed for something. He doubted it was chili, and even if it was, the cat wasn't getting any of his.

"He said to tell me that?" Grammy asked.

"No, he just said it. You know, just shook his head at the mountain of stuff in there and said it needed to be sold. All of it."

Grammy's lips thinned ever so slightly, as if she was displeased but didn't intend to show it. "Is this some kind of trick?"

Taken aback, Scott and Maggie both shook their heads in quick denial. He didn't know how Maggie felt, but personally, Scott was shocked to be accused of such a thing.

"My Lawrence worked so hard to collect everything. Maggie's been after me to get rid of it since she turned sixteen. But, Scott Templeton, I'm surprised at you. You seemed like such a nice young man. Hardly the type to try and fool an old lady." Grammy sniffled.

Scott felt like a heel, even though he'd done nothing.

Maggie was quick to pat Grammy's hand. "I'm sorry. I had nothing to do with this. I knew we shouldn't have let him in."

"Hey!" Scott objected, sick to see the hurt in Grammy's eyes. Desperate to redeem himself, he said, "There's more."

Grammy folded her hands in her lap and very primly said, "Go on."

"He said Ruby should be in college."

Grammy's lips twitched, and then she hooted. "Our Ruby?"

"She could study clothing design," Maggie said, rushing to her sister's defense. "Or cosmetology. I offered to help her with tuition, but she says she can do better out on her own."

Grammy pressed her lips together firmly this time, as if she wanted to add something uncomplimentary to that, but wouldn't, not in front of an outsider.

"Anything else?" she dared.

Scott debated the wisdom of continuing. Everything so far had gotten him in hot water.

"Oh, go on," Maggie said, grinning. Probably thinking he'd really put his foot in it, and then Grammy'd send him packing.

Grammy waited patiently.

"Okay," Scott said with a long sigh. "But only because you're making me. He said with the money you'd get from selling everything, you could look into a nice retirement home."

"Leave my home?" In an instant, Grammy looked as old and tired as when she'd first opened the front door.

"That does it." Maggie slapped her hands on the table and made a big to-do about getting to her feet. "I'll be in my room. Loading my gun in case Mr. Templeton can't find his way out."

She'd barely exited the kitchen before Scott rushed to apologize. He hadn't forgotten how much his own grandmother had been attached to her home; he just hadn't been thinking.

"Grammy, I'm sorry. I didn't mean to upset you. I just wanted to be honest about what Coop said."

"Retirement home," Grammy scoffed. She pushed her bowl away, leaving her supper untouched. She sighed and stared in the general direction Maggie had taken.

So did Scott. "Uh, she doesn't have a gun, does she?"

"Oh, don't worry. She'd never go out and buy one on her own."

That settled, Scott tasted the best chili he'd had in years, but with both women upset, it lost some of its appeal.

"Although," Grammy said with a hint of a smile. "Lawrence bought a lot of different things. No telling what Maggie found out in that barn."

Maggie cracked open her bedroom window for fresh air, curled up on the window seat, and kept watch. Her room was dark, so Scott couldn't see her if he looked up, but she'd know the moment he left the house.

Interesting how deferential he was to Grammy. When Grammy'd pouted about his suggestion to sell everything, he'd looked as if he'd tear his heart out and give it to her if she'd just smile again. A man didn't fake that, not the hurt she'd seen in his eyes. It probably would be perfectly safe if he knew she planned to leave town tonight, but a vision of herself on the nightly news, saying, *He seemed like such a nice man,* was enough to keep her cautious.

Speaking of which, how long did it take to eat a bowl of chili, anyway? She'd sit here another five minutes, but that was it.

The lights were still on in the barn. The dogs milled about nervously just outside the open door, occasionally charging it with a rousing bark, then backing off. Chances were a raccoon or opossum had a home in there. Shoot, as seldom as anyone went inside, both barns probably'd been colonized by any number of animals.

The spring peepers' chorus covered the sound of Scott's footsteps, but once he was in the yard where she could see him, Maggie went on alert. He headed for the barn; she raced downstairs and locked up for the night.

Grammy had just finished kitchen cleanup. She folded the dish towel in half and draped it over the edge of the sink to dry. "Did you really tell him to sleep in his truck?"

"He's just a stranger, like everyone else who's ever

brought something by," Maggie said reasonably. "I don't recall you inviting them to spend the night."

"He's a race car driver."

"Please, that says something in itself, don't you think?" Through the mullioned window in the top half of the door, Maggie watched the dogs turn away from the barn and charge Scott. "Have you fed the dogs yet?"

"They're more interested in whatever's in the barn."

"Is he feeding them? He's feeding them!"

"He asked if he could take them some treats." Grammy joined Maggie at the window. "For heaven's sake, I've never seen them quite like that before. What are they doing?"

"It looks as if they're . . . *blocking* him?" The dogs were big, a good eighty to a hundred pounds each. They leaned, jumped, and shoved against Scott; he swayed through them like a drunken sailor on leave. Once he entered the barn, the dogs went back to skulking and barking. "Geez, they're useless."

"They just don't take well to Lawrence. My goodness, look at that man work. He lifts those boxes like they're empty."

Maggie tried not to stare. When she noticed Grammy grinning at her with a speculative sparkle in her eyes, she flung herself away from the view with a snort of disgust.

"So what are you going to do now?" Grammy asked.

"Wait until he goes to sleep. Then I'll drive to Chicago, catch a nap, and go to my interview. If he's still here when I'm done, I'll drive straight back."

Grammy's face fell, à la kicked-canine déjà vu. "You're still going?"

"Yes, so please don't start moping around again. When he gets up in the morning, you can say I just ran out to the store or something, that I'll be back any minute."

"Oh, he doesn't scare me."

"Yeah, that's what worries me." As long as the topic had been raised, Maggie pressed for what she'd wanted for years. "He's right, though, about selling everything in the barns. That's a fire hazard out there. With our luck, it'd go up in flames when the lines are down, and we wouldn't be able to call the fire department."

Grammy sighed. "I'll think it over."

Maggie ran outside without a jacket and moved her Mustang so she wouldn't wake Scott later when she started it. Then there was nothing left to do but curl up again on the window seat in her bedroom and wait.

When observing his every move involved a pair of binoculars, she rationalized that she was just waiting for him to do something that would give her grounds to call the cops.

Peering at him had absolutely nothing to do with watching him doff his jacket and work in his shirt.

Fine-tuning the binoculars for the best view had nothing to do with admiring the strong back and well-muscled arms it took to lift some of those boxes.

Absolutely nothing.

While Scott shifted dirty, dusty antiques for a couple of hours, the ghost went off and pouted at the news that his mother had balked about selling everything. Previously, Scott would have said the ghost's absence was the highlight of his day. Now that he'd met Maggie, though, it came in a distant second.

Was there as much substance there as he suspected? Maggie was as protective of her grandmother as he'd been of his. Anyone could call 911 and send the cops to the rescue. How many people almost beat them home? And then canceled their plans and stayed? She had something going in Chicago, something important. Cooper had said so. Her whispered phone conversation had said so.

And yet . . . she was still here.

He worked up a sweat, shed his jacket, and kept going until he'd moved, mashed, and relocated enough stuff to make a sizable bare spot, starting at the door and going in about fifteen feet. As long as he had to wait until tomorrow for a hoist, he might as well make a home for the engine away from the weather, away from where people who came after him would stack who knew what on top of it. Come morning, he'd put it down nice and easy, then barricade it with a protective wall of sturdy boxes.

Finished with that, he retired to the passenger side of the truck, where there was more room to catch some sack time. The ghost followed and resumed making a pest of himself, carrying on endlessly about this collectible and that collectible, and how their value must have soared by now. It was all terribly boring.

"I wish you'd quit moving around," Cooper complained every fifteen minutes until Scott could no longer ignore him.

"I'm trying to stay warm." Scott stamped his feet and rubbed his gloved hands briskly over his thighs. If that annoyed Cooper, so much the better. "You remember what it's like, being cold?" he taunted.

"You should have a hat. A hat blocks a lot of heat loss through your head."

"It's on the coatrack."

"Don't do you any good in there."

"You know, if I have to have company, it should be someone who *has* body heat." Scott reached for the door handle.

"Fixing to go get it?"

"I'm gonna take a leak, do you mind?"

"Be careful the dogs don't bite it off." Cooper cackled and added, "Oh, never mind. It's so cold, you'll be lucky if you can find it."

"At least I have one."

The dogs didn't make an appearance, which was too bad. Scott was seriously considering inviting them to sleep in the truck. They couldn't be any more annoying than Cooper and had to be a heck of a lot warmer.

He thought he saw movement in the house, which was mostly dark except for some dim lamps or night lights. He glanced at last year's Rolex. Ten-thirty wasn't all that late. Maybe Maggie was still up. He really needed that hat.

Maybe she was in her nightgown. Which meant she'd be annoyed as heck to answer the door at night, but

Maggie in a snit would be better than no Maggie at all. He rapped lightly on the front door, and after a minute, a little harder. Finally she opened it.

No nightgown. She'd changed, all right, but now she was in black from head to toe, sweater, jeans, socks, and shoes, much as a person would do if she didn't want to be seen. But that was crazy. She was in her own house.

"Hold on a minute," Maggie said into the cordless phone, then lowered it, reacquainting Scott with the perfect bow in her upper lip. Lord, he wanted to cover it with his mouth in the worst way, but she said, "It's late, Mr. Templeton," and glanced past his legs.

"They're under the porch again."

She *hmph*ed, too, but more delicately than her grand-mother. "What can I do for you?"

"Sorry to bother you this late, but I left my hat on the rack inside, and my head's cold."

"No problem." Maggie handed him his Stetson, keep-ing a wary eye on him and the door as she retrieved it, which made him glad he hadn't asked to go in and get it himself. "Did you make enough room in the barn?"

"I think so."

"Great." She added a bit of advice around the edge of the door as she eased it closed. "You might not want to wander around in the dark. With the dogs on the loose, the coyotes generally keep their distance. But tonight"—she shrugged—"well, I don't think they'll at-tack, but I can't promise."

Scott grinned all the way back to the truck, even as a

cloud passed over the sliver of moon and plunged the yard into an inky blackness. He settled back into the truck with Cooper and said, "Yes sir, that is one saucy woman you almost raised."

Two women living more than shouting distance from their nearest neighbor—obviously they scared uninvited visitors by whatever means they had at hand. If they wanted him to think they had bodies scattered around the property, well, he didn't see how talk hurt anyone.

"How old was she when you did the one-way?"

Coop grunted. "'Bout fourteen, fifteen maybe." Not being sure how old his daughter was when he died told Scott worlds about him as a father.

"I still can't believe you're afraid of her." Scott parked his back in the corner, stretched his legs all the way to the pedals on the other side, and tipped his hat down over his face.

Come morning, he'd do what he'd come here to do. Then he'd get Maggie's phone number. He should be on the road well before noon. Fontana, the next race in the Rolex Series, was in a couple of days. He could show up there, downplay the whole ghost thing, blame it on drugs or injury related to the last crash, and maybe land a job driving again before hell froze over. If he didn't freeze first.

"If I tried the key now, just to run the heater, would it start?"

"I'm not cold."

"Yeah, didn't think so."

Time ticked by. Every few minutes, Cooper asked Scott

if he'd seen this vase or that lamp or a box of something in particular. Owls hooted, one nearby, one farther away in response. A pack of coyotes barked and yipped, their chorus punctuated with long, flat howls—so Maggie hadn't been kidding about them.

"Is she the violent type? I mean, is that why you're afraid of her?"

"How many times I gotta tell you, I ain't afraid of nobody!"

"'Cause if she is . . . You know, if she, say, dresses all in black and sneaks out here with a gun and shoots me in the head, well then that engine's not going anywhere in the morning."

Cooper laughed for ten minutes. Then he was quiet for five, which was just about a record. Scott had just nodded off when the ghost said, "I been thinking about the problems an auctioneer's gonna have."

Lord, please, if Maggie gives me her number, if I've ever been good a single day in my life, make her the kind of woman who doesn't take after her father.

The ghost nudged Scott when he didn't respond, just to make sure he was listening.

"They like to auction stuff off in lots, you see. So he's gotta understand that when he goes through the barn and finds one corkscrew, for instance, it don't mean that's the only one there is. I mighta picked one up in Kansas City, another in Des Moines, like that. There could be a hundred corkscrews in there, maybe more, and I doubt any two of them are in the same box. You following me?"

"She'd give me a blanket if I asked for one, wouldn't she?"

"There's quilts in the barn."

"No way, man," Scott said. "Not even if they've been bagged in plastic."

"Wuss."

"If a ghost recluse bites a ghost—"

"No such thing as a ghost recluse."

"How do you know? I bet they hide real well."

"Think about it, Templeton. A train can run right through me and nothing happens."

"A house that size . . . she'd have one to spare." Scott sat up straight, settled his hat, and reached for the door handle.

"Don't listen to me, then. Go ahead, bother her, see if I care. Make her mad. Won't get her number then." Cooper smirked, very satisfied with himself.

Outside, the air wasn't as frigid as Scott expected. In fact, it was warmer than inside the truck. "Damn ghost," he muttered, then thumped on Maggie's front door.

She was beautiful when she threw the door open, even with her hair mussed on one side and a crease on her cheek. She raised her arm as if to check a watch and seemed put out to find she wasn't wearing one.

"Do you know what time it is?" she snapped.

His hand shot out of his sleeve so he could check. "Eleven-thirty."

She grinned, though he could tell she was trying hard not to. "Championship watch?"

"Yes, ma'am. If it weren't for your father, I'd have a pair."

At the mention of her father, Maggie's posture stiffened. "You knocked on my door to tell me that?"

"I was wondering if you have an extra blanket."

"Wait there." She shut the door this time.

Coyotes yipped again, closer now. Scott wouldn't have thought much of it, except for Maggie's earlier warning. He moved restlessly under the porch light until she returned and handed him a large stuff bag.

"It's a sleeping bag. You just shove it back in there in the morning."

He tucked it under one arm. "Thanks, I appreciate—"

With a wicked glint in her eyes, Maggie plopped a throw pillow on top of it. "Thought I'd save you another trip."

Her cheeky grin warmed him to the core, and he was halfway through a sincere "Thanks" when she shut the door.

"Appreciate it. See you in the morning." He hobbled off the porch with a stupid grin on his face, not even noticing Cooper at the bottom of the steps until he'd passed through the cold spot.

"You really need all that?" the ghost criticized. "It don't look that cold."

"How would you know?"

"It'll take up half the truck."

"Like you care?"

"I'm just thinking about you, son. No sense you being uncomfortable."

"Since when have you— Look, if you had my comfort in mind, you'd shut the fuck up and go away. I mean it, Coop. I can't sleep with you talking all the time. You're worse than a dripping faucet."

"Well, why didn't you say something?" Cooper scratched his head, looking just a smidgen distressed. "I think better when I do it out loud. See, used to be when I needed to work through something, I'd do it under a hood. Nothing helps thinking like an engine and a tool-box."

No way Scott would admit he understood.

"Can't do that anymore, so I took to running off at the mouth, I guess. Come on, I got a better place for you to sleep."

Scott followed him around the side of the house, lagging behind because the ghost might not have to see where he was going in the dim moonlight, but Scott sure as heck did. In back of the house, Cooper pointed at a concrete garden gnome.

"Look under there."

Scott tipped it to the side. Cooper whisked out the old skeleton key and headed down narrow steps. It was so dark at the bottom, Scott never would've found the keyhole, but Cooper didn't seem to have any trouble. Nothing happened, though.

"It's painted shut," Coop said. "If you can muscle it open without scaring my family, you can sleep in there."

"In the cellar? Like what, a bad dog?"

"Close as I can recall, the furnace puts off a good deal of heat."

"Make way. Coming through."

Scott felt his way down the steps and put his shoulder into the crease. He didn't want to frighten Maggie, though.

"Wait. Is there an alarm system?"

"Yeah. They're under the front porch."

 *Chapter 4*

Shortly after sunrise on Tuesday, Maggie and the dogs stood beside her formerly dependable little red Mustang. The front tire wasn't just a little low. It wasn't debatable whether she could drive to the nearest service station and have it repaired. It was so flat, the rim rode the street.

Of all the rotten luck.

If she hadn't nodded off last night waiting for Scott to fall asleep, she'd already be in Chicago, near mass transportation. But *nooo*, she had to be stuck in the boonies debating whether to change the tire or summon a taxi to the airport.

She squelched her first impulse, which was to kick it. Instead, she muttered expletives that had never before crossed her lips. It was a colorful stream she'd heard many times behind the wall, back when she and her mother used to follow Pop on the racing circuit. She'd always giggled when one of the mechanics let loose because someone nearby always tried to cover her ears. It felt really good right now to express *exactly* how she felt.

She called Chicago.

"Finally!" Kevin answered with a breath of relief.

"You know I don't like how fast you drive, but today it'll pay off."

"Let's hope I can fix the car fast, too."

Big groan. "Now what?"

"Don't worry. Nothing major, just a flat." Maggie brushed black dog hair off her pearl-colored skirt, which she'd have to change out of first. She waited for Kevin to say something encouraging, but he didn't. "I can change it. I should be on the road in less than an hour."

"Maggie, if you're going to be successful, you have to act successful. A road service package came with your car when you bought it—call them. That's what they're there for."

"But I—"

"Maggie," he overrode her with a not-so-patient sigh. "You should have been on the road fifteen hours ago."

"Geez, don't worry about it. I can still make it."

"Okay, honey, I'm sorry. You know I just want everything to go well so we can be together every day."

"I know. Me, too. See you in a few."

Maggie called road service, then entered the house more slowly than when she'd left, dropping her coat on the back of the sofa on her way to the kitchen. She needed coffee. Lots of coffee.

In the kitchen, she found Scott on the far side of the room with his hand in the cookie jar—literally. Startled to find him in the house, Maggie stopped short.

"Whoa, hometown hero, doctor, *and* lockpick? Your mother must be very proud."

Scott grinned sheepishly, said, "Coffee?" and popped

a chocolate chip cookie into his mouth. Holding his hand over his heart, he murmured compliments to the cook and thanks to the angels. "I swear, if Grammy were my age, I'd propose. You didn't say if you wanted coffee."

"You couldn't have heard me if I did." Maggie made light of his being in her kitchen, but was savvy enough to keep the table between them.

"I had a cookie attack." Scott shrugged, as if to say, *So sue me.* He poured a steaming mug and held it out. When she didn't rush forward to take it, he set it on the table and poured one for himself.

"You broke into our house."

"Correction." He dug into the front pocket of his jeans and slid a skeleton key across the table; Exhibit A.

"So?"

"It's to the cellar door."

"Uh-huh." She knew exactly where he'd gotten it, because she'd tried the same thing a long time ago. "And how many of those relics did you go through in the barn before you found one that fit?"

Scott looked wounded. "Man, you are one suspicious woman. Coop showed me where it was." He *tsk*ed and shook his head at her. "Really, under the garden gnome? You might as well invite the burglars in."

"Coop. Right."

"He says he didn't talk all the time when he was alive, but since he never shuts up now, I find that hard to believe."

Since Scott hadn't robbed them blind while they slept or butchered them in their beds, Maggie figured it was safe to sit at the table and warm her hands around the mug. He was drinking coffee out of the same pot; she figured hers was safe to taste. Big mistake.

"Oh God, that's good. Add coffee making to your list of talents."

"Darlin', everything I do, I do well." Scott winked and popped another cookie into his mouth.

It was the wink that did it, that took away any innocence, that turned a simple murmur over a homemade cookie into a low, sensual hum of another nature entirely. It made Maggie think of dark bedrooms and long, steamy nights. Bare skin and urgent touches. Whispered endearments. *Moans*, for God's sake.

She affected naïveté, gulped coffee, and swallowed hard.

"Well, except for dealing with your father. I can't seem to get a handle on that." Scott stared at her, eyebrows raised expectantly.

"Dear Abby's just a letter away."

"Come on," he begged, sliding into a chair across from her, his arms sprawled across the table as if closeness bred helpfulness. "He was your dad. You have to give me a tip or two before you leave."

"I can't leave with you here, remember?"

Scott smiled indulgently as his gaze roamed over Maggie's suit. "You mean you can't leave if I know you're leaving, but you can sneak out in the middle of the night so, just in case I'm a lowlife, I'm left guessing when you're coming back. Hey, I know how these things work."

Maggie figured the truth probably was written all over her face. "Like I said, I can't leave with you here."

"So help me out with your father, then. He's driving me nuts. I could handle it if he didn't talk to me, but he's so irritating that I answer him back and, well, suffice it to say that my friends were not amused."

"Ran for the hills, did they?"

"Darn near broke the sound barrier." One corner of his mouth tipped up. "Can't say I blame them."

"You couldn't prove it to anyone."

Scott grimaced and sipped his coffee. "Not for lack of trying."

"So why think I believe you?"

"Oh, I don't know." He flashed his one-dimple grin. "Maybe hundreds of strangers delivering antiques to your door?"

Maggie sipped coffee to die for and wished she could believe him. If her father truly *had* sent Scott, she wouldn't have to hang around. Pop had been inattentive, but not stupid or cruel. He wouldn't send a con man or a serial killer to their home.

"Trouble is," she said, "I have no reason to believe it's my father you're dealing with."

Scott sat back in his chair. "You're expecting some-one else?"

"I'm not *expecting* anyone."

"Go on, ask me anything about him. I'll tell you everything I know."

Maggie laughed at his audacity. "That's not proof. You could be talking to anyone."

"What?" Scott's eyes twinkled with amusement. "You think he's an imposter?"

"I think *you* wouldn't know the difference."

"So . . ." He shrugged as if what he had to say next was unimportant, but Maggie knew better. "If you're not afraid of a challenge, try me."

His confidence gave Maggie pause. "If you want to convince me that my dead father is here"—her tone implied his lunacy—"have him tell you something about me that you couldn't possibly know."

He weighed the options. "Like what?"

"Surprise me."

"That could take a while," he stalled. "Sometimes he's ornery and won't answer."

"Uh-huh." Maggie glanced around the kitchen pointedly. "I don't see you asking."

"He's not here right now."

"Of course not," she said, taking care to keep it light. No sense tipping her hand. "You should go find him."

He glanced at the door. "Ahh. You're going to lock me out, aren't you?"

She affected an oh-so-innocent smile and pocketed the skeleton key. Scott sighed with resignation.

"I'll need sustenance," he said. "Coffee and cookies."

"Knock yourself out." She grinned to let him know she meant that in the most literal sense.

She did lock the door behind him. Then she arranged for an engine hoist to be delivered before noon, because she knew that no matter what, Scott wasn't leaving without his truck. In fact, she probably should change into jeans and help, just to speed him along. At this point, there was still a chance she'd make her interview.

Grammy breezed into the kitchen, breaking into Maggie's musings with a trilling "Good morning!"

She was more herself today, in a light green sweatshirt that sported spring robins tugging worms from tufts of grass. Maggie's mother was into theme dressing, too. So was Ruby if you considered Goth a theme. The closest Maggie wanted to get to theme dressing was matching her earrings—to each other.

"My, it was good to hear voices in the kitchen again this morning," Grammy said. "Where's Scott?"

Maggie held up the skeleton key. "Apparently he slept in the cellar."

"Well, I did invite him." Grammy hummed to herself as she opened the refrigerator and took stock. "Will he be back for breakfast, you think?"

Maggie sighed. "I think he's like a stray cat. Feed him once and he's pretty hard to get rid of."

She'd just explained her unsuccessful night and this morning's flat tire when Scott thumped on the door. Grammy sprinted across the room to let him in. The biggest scowl this side of Texas softened to a nice smile as Scott bent down to accept Grammy's grateful hug.

"It's just so wonderful you found the key! Now I can restock the water jugs without carting them up and down so many steps. There's fewer out back, you know."

"Glad to help," Scott said, sounding as if he meant it.

"Though Maggie'll be gone, and it'll take an old lady like me"—Grammy's voice wavered ever so slightly—"all day just to carry them up the back steps."

Scott hadn't seen all of yesterday's performance, so he had no idea the lengths Grammy could go to to get what she wanted. Maggie didn't clue him in. As long as he was available when the hoist arrived, he deserved whatever her grandmother dished out.

"I hope the spigot isn't rusted shut. I don't have the strength I used to. Arthritis, you know. Of course, it's not so bad in my right hand . . ."

The poor man had no idea what he was up against. Within seconds, Grammy steered Scott toward the cellar to carry out her semiannual restocking of potable water. Emergency guidelines recommended one gallon per person per day, which wouldn't have been so bad, but Grammy preferred to have thirty gallons on hand at all times.

"Don't just sit there," she said to Maggie.

"But—"

"Show him how it's done."

"But I have to watch for road service."

"Nonsense! I'll see them or they'll come to the door. Now get out of that suit and help him."

"I can't believe I caved," Scott said.

Even after he'd carted half a dozen assorted picnic jugs of water out of the cellar and into the backyard, he was still dazed by the speed with which Grammy had gotten her way. It wasn't that he wasn't used to dealing with an elderly lady, but Grammy's technique put his grandmother's to shame.

At least Maggie was working with him. He didn't get to enjoy her long legs in a short skirt anymore, but there were other perks. Running up and down the steps had warmed her enough to strip down to a spandex T-shirt. Eight-plus pounds in each hand showed off nice definition in her arms.

Still, to let a little old lady wrap him around her finger with such ease!

"I must be out of practice," he groaned.

"It was cute, though, how you pretended to put up a fight."

It didn't make any sense to correct Maggie if she thought he was cute, so he let her think it.

The suit and shoes had fooled him yesterday. This wasn't some gal who spent every minute in high heels and a nice desk chair or one who needed everything done for her. No sir, the fact that she was no stranger to physical work rounded out the package quite nicely.

He followed Maggie up the outside steps again, eye level with low-riding jeans and a tush that begged to be touched more each trip. Coop was leaning against a tree, scowling at him, but he kept his distance and held his tongue for a change. Scott didn't give a flying fig if the ghost didn't like him staring at his daughter. Maggie was too delectable to ignore.

Her phone *ka-ching*ed. She glanced at it, but didn't answer.

"Your boyfriend?"

"Mr. Stevens. I send my high-maintenance clients to voice mail and get back to them when I have time to hold their hands."

"If they're high maintenance—"

"It's that or tell them I'm not at my desk, and believe me, they don't like hearing that. Pour those on the forsythia, would you?"

Scott was at a loss until she pointed. "Why do you store water, anyway?"

"We're on a well. When the electricity goes out, so does the pump. It's nothing for a few hours, but two years ago an ice storm knocked out our power for five days."

"That's what hotels are for."

"Hotels are for nomadic race car drivers." Maggie upended her jugs, letting the water soak the roots around the shrubbery.

"Did I hear you mention road service?"

"I have a flat."

"Oh, that's *right*." Scott kept his grin somewhat under wraps, lest Maggie take offense and dump the next jug on him. "It was low yesterday, wasn't it?"

"Too hard to let that pass?"

"Oh yeah." If road service didn't have it changed by the time he was ready to leave, he'd do it for her.

They continued trooping up and down the stairs, emptying and refilling jugs. Scott carried two gallons in each hand and made it look easy. The last time he could remember struggling to impress a female, he'd been in high school.

Did boy-girl stuff ever change? He could race a car around fifty others on the toughest courses, but when it came right down to it, he stooped to the basics: showing off how much he could lift.

If this didn't work soon, he'd attempt three in each hand. Or take his shirt off.

Grammy didn't know whom to thank for Maggie's flat tire, but if she knew who'd dropped the nail or screw, she'd treat him to dinner every night for a month. Now if the hoist would only come later, much later, Maggie would feel she had to stick around. She'd miss her interview, which was only a formal prelude to a job change. She'd reschedule, of course, but if they put her off for, say, a month, she might—please, God—break up with that boyfriend of hers by then.

Grammy didn't even want to refer to him by name; it might make someone think she approved. If he lived here in St. Louis, it might be different, but he didn't, and she couldn't be fond of anyone who'd take Maggie away. Well, except for a vacation. Or a honeymoon.

If road service was prompt, the rental place had to be considered express. Grammy's hopes faded as she and Maggie stood on the front porch and watched the hoist arrive.

"What'd you do, tell them the pope was here?"

"Next best thing," Maggie replied with a satisfied smile. "Scotty Templeton."

Grammy eyed her granddaughter with dawning realization. "Is that right?"

"Mm-hm." Then Maggie blushed and got flustered. "Stop that. I didn't mean it that way."

"What do they call that? A Freudian slip?"

"More like an imaginative grandmother."

"Hey, I'm not the one comparing him to the pope."

"I only meant that he's famous and, yes, I dropped his name to get better service. For his sake."

Grammy patted Maggie's arm and said, "Whatever you say, dear. Let's go out to the barn and keep an eye on him."

"I'm sure he can move the engine just fine without me."

"But it's very heavy. What if he drops it on his foot?"

"He won't drop it."

"He'd be trapped under it with no one to help."

"Then call 911."

"I'd be so frightened, I'm afraid I'd faint." Grammy fanned her face with her hand. "He'd have to do like that guy in the desert and amputate his foot to get free."

"It was his arm, not his—" Maggie bit her lip in an effort not to laugh, but Grammy knew she had her. "Oh, never mind. I'm coming."

God bless Dr. Phil. If it weren't for him, Grammy might not have understood the finer points of manipulative shenanigans. Who knew!

When Scott hobbled out to the front yard for his truck, it started right up, which, sad to say, just lit Grammy's suspicions afire. He *seemed* like a nice young man, but when it came right down to it, he hadn't done a thing to convince her that Lawrence was there. Maggie was right. They'd only met him yesterday; she should be cautious.

Still, he was better than what's-his-name, whose five-year plan called for *talking* about getting engaged in two years and *talking* about having babies in five years. A man like Scott would distract Maggie, bust into her narrow focus, show her another side of life. An exciting side. Maybe she just needed to be shown what she was looking at.

Over the years, people had been in a hurry to drop stuff on the porch and run. Maybe *hurry* was too tame a word, as many hadn't even bothered to ring the bell. Scott, on the other hand, gazed at the engine sadly as he hoisted it out of the truck bed.

"Aw, look at his face," Grammy said, pleased when Maggie did so. Now if she'd only *see* him for the fine specimen of a man he was.

"You ladies stand back now," Scott warned.

Grammy wasn't above laying it on thick. "Looks like he's leaving his dog at the pound. One he raised from a pup and took everywhere with him."

Scott spread a tarp on the ground and settled the Hemi gently into the space he'd cleared. He even patted it. What next? He'd hug the darn thing? Kiss it good-bye? He didn't even notice when his truck died.

"Grammy, do me a favor? If you decide to sell this, give me a call, will you?"

"Soon as I know what my son wants." Grammy spotted a new path through the collectibles.

Scott watched Coop's mother drift into the depths of

the barn, her fingers caressing objects along the way as if searching for latent messages. He'd like to be able to say something to make her feel better, but he had his own problems.

He took one long, last look at the greatest classic engine he'd ever owned. Maybe the greatest he'd ever seen.

No sense lingering, though. He had to get the heck out of Dodge before Coop knew what was up. He'd already missed Homestead-Miami. If he showed up for practice at Fontana without a ghost sabotaging every effort to win a spot on a team, surely he'd be behind the wheel in no time, racing for the checkered flag.

He was done here except for getting Maggie's number. Hell, he'd take his chances with her boyfriend. Not many men could hold a candle to a racing champion.

"Maggie?"

She wasn't watching him anymore. He glanced around. She'd neither gone into the barn, nor had time to make it back to the house. There was only one place left—his truck.

He'd like her inside, on the seat. Didn't matter if she wanted a ride back to her car, all the way to California, or a more personal good-bye. Any of the above meant she'd give him her number without a lot of fast talking on his part.

Instead, Maggie was standing on his front bumper, the hood open, half her body underneath, bare skin visible between her shirt and jeans.

"What the hell are you doing?"

"Trying to get it running again. If you leave right now,

I think I can make my interview. If I don't make any stops."

"And if the cops don't pull you over. Get your hands off my—"

"Oh yeah, that reminds me—I'll take your radar detector, too. In lieu of a new one." Maggie's hands flew over connections, checking them with knowledge and finesse. Seemed she'd learned a few things from her old man. "In fact, you can waive the whole five hundred dollars if you get this thing running in the next ten seconds."

Scott felt hair stand up on the back of his neck, and it wasn't lightning. It was worse.

"If it doesn't start, there's only one reason why, and you won't find it under there. Now get down before you mess something up."

When Maggie made no move to cease and desist, Scott plucked her from the bumper and set her down, then dashed behind the wheel and turned the key.

Nothing.

"You said you'd leave as soon as the engine was in the barn." Maggie extended one arm toward the barn. "Ta-*daaa*."

She was almost too cute to take seriously, but Scott nevertheless stood up on the running board and roared, "Cooper!"

Instead of the ghost making an appearance, Grammy rushed out of the barn, looking very determined. "Oh, thank goodness. I was afraid you'd already left. You still haven't talked to Lawrence for me."

"Some other time, Grammy," Maggie snapped. "He has to leave. *Now*."

"But . . . this may be my only chance. Who knows if they'll ever both be here at the same time again?"

No way the waver in Grammy's voice was catching Scott off guard again. He doubted Maggie'd fall for it, either. But if the ghost didn't uphold his end of the bargain really soon, well, Scott didn't want to be the one torn limb from limb by these two women.

"I'm not a young woman anymore, you know. I can't go to my grave not knowing what happened on that racetrack."

"Cooper! My truck!"

A darting movement on the other side of the truck caught Scott's eye. It was Maggie, headed toward the front end again. Lord only knew where she'd gotten the wrench in her hand, but hell'd freeze over before she'd use it on anything of his, especially since nothing was broken. She'd just stepped onto the bumper again when he wrapped one arm around her slender middle, plucked the wrench from her grasp, and sent it flying.

She kicked and wiggled and squirmed, and he enjoyed holding her close before setting her on her feet, at which point she socked him in the arm. Not a half-bad punch, really. He sure wouldn't want her mad at him.

Scott took one look at Grammy, couldn't decide whether she'd sabotage his ride to keep him there longer—it *could* run in the family—and slammed the hood. That should stop a little old lady unless she was into shooting out tires. Maggie was a bit more difficult to handle. Not that he minded handling her. In fact—

A crash inside the barn alerted them to Coop's whereabouts.

"I'll get him," Scott said. "Can I trust you to leave my engine alone— What am I saying? Of course I can't. Come with me."

Maggie crossed her arms and grinned, daring him. Scott grabbed her hand and pulled her along, keeping her beside him as they closed in on an increasing amount of racket.

"Careful," she warned, her tone way too serious to actually be serious. "Could be a rabid raccoon."

"Recluses, man-eating coyotes, rabid raccoons. Lord, woman, anything else and you'd need a wildlife permit."

"I'm just warning you, if it runs at us, I'm climbing up your back and letting you deal with it on your own."

Scott tripped over his own feet on the climbing-up-his-back part. Maggie snickered.

"What? There was a hole there."

"Right. Best be careful, then. Groundhogs get as big as basset hounds around here."

"Groundhogs," he mused with a grin.

"Hey, there's no telling what'll get you in here."

The mission to find Coop came to an abrupt end when a ratty, mounted doe head tumbled from the top of a heap and landed at their feet, blocking the way.

Tongue in cheek, Maggie said, "See?"

Grammy caught up just as Scott spotted Coop squeezing between stacks of boxes. "Hey, Coop, start my truck, man."

The ghost's face was transformed with excitement. "I can't believe this. Is it *all* here? Every bit of it?"

"Could there *be* more? C'mon, man, you promised."

"Ask her."

Hope grew in Grammy's eyes as Scott relayed the question. "He's talking to you? Right now?"

"Yes, ma'am."

"Ask him what—"

Coop shouted so loud, Scott missed Grammy's question. "He kind of wants you to answer him first, ma'am. If you don't mind."

"I couldn't part with any of it."

Still keeping his distance, Coop whooped with joy. "Even what was here before I died?"

"I think she was perfectly clear on that. Can I go now?"

"Even my Lemon Twist 'Cuda?"

Scott generalized that. "He wants to know if there's a yellow muscle car in here."

Grammy looked thoughtful. "Yellow? Oh, I don't remember anyone delivering a car. I think I'd remember yellow. What about you, Maggie?"

"Well, Pop had a yellow 'Cuda, but I don't know what happened to it."

"Even if it was here," Grammy elaborated, "these barns are a prime target on senior prank night, if you know what I mean. Why, a moose head showed up in the principal's car three or four years ago. I don't know if it came from here, but they sent it back to us anyway."

"Hot damn!" The ghost danced around and up the

mountains of junk he'd accumulated, uninhibited by a need for secure footing. "This is even better than selling my collectibles. Son, you know what the Hemi alone is worth. Imagine when it's reunited with the original body. Why, I bet it'd bring a couple hundred thou."

"I'm sure any auctioneer would check into that."

"*Then* people wouldn't make fun of my collectibles. *Then* they wouldn't call it junk no more. Ruby could go to college. Maggie could start her own business. My mother could live in one of those newfangled communities, with trips to the mall, and bingo in the evenings . . ." Coop's dancing came to an abrupt halt. "The 'Cuda isn't where I left it, though, and I can't find it under all this stuff. Everything has to go. Right away."

"Great," Scott said. "They'll hire an auctioneer just as soon as Grammy's convinced that you're Lawrence."

"Oh, *please*." Maggie tapped the toe of her sneaker in the dust and angled her wrist up in front of Scott's face so he could see time fly. *Her* time.

"Come on, man, hurry up. I gotta leave so Maggie can get to her interview."

"Leave?" Coop feigned confusion.

"Oh no," Scott said with a restrained laugh of denial. "No, no, *no*. We had a deal."

"I can't trust any Tom, Dick, or Harry to drop that Hemi back in the 'Cuda."

Scott felt Maggie's gaze burning into him, and he wasn't even looking at her. He took a step toward the ghost with a sense of urgency, but that was as close as he could get without a ladder.

"News flash," Scott announced. "If you don't let me leave immediately, your daughter's gonna kill me, and then where will you be?"

"You idolize that engine as much as I do, Templeton. I don't trust nobody but you to handle it." Coop brushed his hands together, signifying a done deal. "That's it, then. You're staying."

Chapter 5

Scott was speechless. Royally pissed off. It was bad enough the ghost was ruining his life, but now he was messing with Maggie's, too. Everything about her radiated regret. It hurt to watch her slump onto a crate and tug her cell phone from her belt. She stared at it a moment, as if debating the wisdom of her next call, then heaved a heavy sigh and speed dialed.

Whatever he said now was bound to be wrong, so he went with simple. "You heard, then?"

"No, but I got the gist of it." Curling forward, Maggie's forehead dropped to rest on her palm.

At least she wasn't digging a hammer out of the junk and charging at him, though he'd feel less guilty if she did. Losing his job had been bad, so he understood how she must feel, losing her carefully planned and scheduled chance to move up.

Coop, *the jackoff*, hadn't hung around to see how badly he'd hurt anyone. Grammy had wandered off again, navigating around stacks of antiques, making her way deeper into the barn, searching for her elusive son. Scott was left to deal with damage control. As he saw it, he had two options, one no better than the other.

He could walk away. The interstate was less than five

miles. He could thumb a ride to California, but the ghost would just follow and ruin any chance he ever had of racing again. Or reveal himself to Maggie and make *her* do what he wanted.

Except Coop was afraid of Maggie. The question was: Why? And how could Scott use that to their advantage?

The second option was to stay and hunt for the 'Cuda, but without a lot of help and tons more room to store stuff, well, Maggie didn't have that much time.

Scott snapped his fingers and announced, "I have a plan."

He sounded excited, but with Kevin going off in her other ear, Maggie had more important things to deal with. She'd known this phone call wouldn't be pleasant, but for a boyfriend, Kevin was sorely lacking in any effort to assuage her hurt over the whole unfortunate situation.

"Go ahead and leave," Kevin urged. "I'm sure everything'll be fine."

"How can you say that? You've never even met him."

"Grammy's comfortable with him, isn't she?"

"But I'm not."

"She invited him; he must be okay," Kevin cajoled, as if Maggie would buy it the tenth time around any more than she had the first.

Again, she tried to explain the ins and outs of letting a total stranger into her home. "But we don't *know* him."

"Scotty Templeton's famous. Everybody knows him."

It wouldn't help matters to tell Kevin what an insensitive, head-in-the-sand, hero-worshiping jerk he was today. Cutting her losses, Maggie firmly said, "I'm going to call Personnel now and reschedule," and Kevin snapped, "Good luck."

It wasn't entirely his fault. He didn't believe in ghosts, so she'd never told him she used to have one of her very own, long ago.

Personnel put her on hold three times. While Maggie waited to reschedule, Scott paced a short, alternately excited and agitated route on the narrow path between head-high jumbles and stacks of boxes. She had no doubt he was angry with somebody . . . no, some*one* without a body, but she didn't know whom. She hadn't seen or personally heard from Pop's ghost in thirteen years; didn't seem likely he'd come back at this late date. Surely by now he was wherever spirits were supposed to go when a body died.

She'd heard the racket in the barn, stuff being moved, shuffled, thumped from one stack to another. A wild animal would have dug into a hiding place and held it, frozen in place, watching silently until everyone left. It wasn't a raccoon, opossum, fox, or anything else alive making that noise.

So . . . if they were dealing with a ghost, what did Scott have to be excited about?

A woman finally returned to the line. "Miss Cooper? I checked with one of the interviewers, and he said someone will call you when the team members' schedules permit them to reassemble."

"Do you know approximately when that will be?" She'd have to request more time off work.

"It could be any day."

Today was Tuesday. She had the rest of the week off; maybe they'd call back in the next couple of days. Even if Kevin didn't work there, it was a good advancement for her. She transferred to the head of the committee's voice mail, where she left a personal apology and an assurance that she was still very interested in the position.

There, it was official. Since Scott had shown up yesterday, she'd dreaded missing her interview. Now it was irrevocably canceled. If his truck miraculously started right this instant, she still couldn't make it on time. In fact, if she hadn't been so wrapped up in *leave, leave, leave* before, she would've realized that even an hour ago was too late. Driving a hundred miles an hour flat out, door to door, just wasn't a viable option.

Scott lowered himself onto the crate beside Maggie. His hip bumped against hers, stayed close, and suddenly a close-minded boyfriend and troublesome ghost didn't seem so important.

"I'm really sorry," he said in a matter-of-fact, no-bullshit tone that was too up-front to be anything but honest. He dangled his arms across his knees, setting his I-have-a-plan excitement aside long enough to pay respect to her problems. "Did they say how long?"

"Maybe this week. Maybe not."

Maggie didn't bother to scoot away, to break the contact where their legs touched. Truth was, Scott's warmth and strength felt good; something tangible to hold on to in the face of the intangible. And there was something else . . . She sniffed the air.

"Do you smoke a pipe?"

"No, why? Oh, the smell. Obnoxious, isn't it? It sort of follows Coop around, more so in closed spaces. Can I borrow that?" His outstretched hand indicated he wanted her phone.

She sniffed the air again, said, "It's kind of nice, actually," and handed her phone over without a second thought as to whether he wanted to make a local call. The same insensitive, hero-worshipping jerk had put her on his cell account months ago, so Scott could call China for all she cared.

"Jeremy? Yeah, man, it's me," Scott said.

Darn, probably not China.

"Wait, wait, don't hang up. I promise I won't mention the you-know-what . . . Yeah, I'm here in St. Louis. Got in yesterday . . . I'm staying with a friend."

He grinned at Maggie, and she didn't think about socking him in the arm again. When he was done here, would they be friends? Would she ever bet on him in a race again without remembering his strong, hard thigh brushing hers on this crate?

"I'm calling because I could use some help. No, no, it has nothing to do with a ghost, I swear . . . Because we're brothers, that's why."

Once Scott secured Jeremy's commitment, he made two more calls. On both of them, as soon as he said "'Cuda," he could barely spit the address out fast enough, so Maggie knew they were gearheads. When he started to dial a fourth person, she snatched her phone back.

"Just how many people are you planning on inviting to *my* house?"

"The quicker we go through this stuff, the faster we find the car."

"I only got the gist of it, remember?"

"Oh, right. Sorry, I forgot. Well, *now* Coop won't let me leave until I find the 'Cuda and drop the Hemi back in. He says it's the original pair. He believes they're worth more together than separately, and"—he shrugged reluctantly—"I have to say he's right on that count."

Maggie mulled that over. Sure sounded like her father's grass-is-greener tune, and if more money was all he was after, then he was still the same sorry excuse for a father he'd always been. "The Hemi—is that the same engine he won the championship with?"

"Yep."

"What about that car? I mean the actual body?"

"Probably wrecked, or he'd be having me find it, too."

"And he hasn't wised up yet? He still thinks all this will make us rich?"

"Seems so."

What the heck—her father's ghost or not, Maggie'd been trying to get rid of this junk for years. "Fine, but both barns are packed to the gills, and you can't just form a line of your friends to move boxes outside. What if it rains?"

"That's why you're going to arrange trucks? Maybe a

warehouse and an auctioneer?" He smiled smugly, confident she'd acquiesce.

"And if Grammy doesn't agree?"

"Hey, she wants an intermediary, she has to make some concessions." Scott's smile segued to that irresistible one-dimple grin, which made Maggie smile back. If he turned that on Grammy, she'd agree in a heartbeat.

She kept that to herself and said, "Proud of your little plan, aren't you?"

"Wait'll you hear the rest of it."

"It better involve a way to appease Kevin."

Scott glanced around cautiously, then lowered his voice to a deep whisper and held out his hand. "Maybe we'd better talk somewhere else. Come on."

It surprised Maggie that she didn't hesitate to press her hand into Scott's. He pulled her to her feet, which would have been a good time to let go, but she didn't. She walked beside him out of the barn, marveling at how a man's grip could be so firm and so gentle at the same time. In comparison, Kevin's was, well, neither. Bland, maybe, though she'd never thought that of him before. He was always so determined, so opinionated, so decisive. Those all sounded like good traits, so how come Scott's grasp felt better? Stronger. Gentler. By the time they reached the kitchen, she'd forgotten they'd been discussing a plan.

Just inside the back door, Scott spun her around to face him and leaned close. He was going to draw her into his arms and kiss her, and she knew she'd kiss him back, not because she was mad at Kevin for being insensitive, but because she was staring at Scott's lips and wondering if they were firm and gentle, too.

"How do you keep him from bothering you?"

Maggie blinked, puzzled by the question and no kiss.

"He doesn't come in the house," Scott said, his tone a mix of urgency and bafflement. "He keeps his distance—I've watched him actually move away from you. You and Grammy can't hear him or see him."

Maggie laughed. "Oh, you mean the ghost."

Scott released her arms and straightened up, letting his hands ride on his belt. "Why is he afraid of you?"

"Oh, I doubt—"

"Whatever you do to make him leave you alone, I want to be able to do it, too. You help me get rid of him, for good, and whatever it takes, I'll help you smooth things over with your boyfriend." A hint of distaste crossed Scott's face, and Maggie couldn't help herself.

"What? You're going to call him up and talk dirty for me?"

The horrified look in Scott's eyes was priceless. "Don't make me do that."

Maggie laughed so he'd know he was off the hook, but he didn't seem totally reassured.

"Is that what he likes?" he asked.

"I was thinking the shock value might make him forget he's mad."

Scott grinned then, his dimple back in place and deeper than ever. Hazel deepened to cocoa as his eyes darkened with a devilish gleam.

"Well, I'm a man. Talk trashy to me, and I'll let you know if it's working."

"Why do I think that'll accomplish nothing?"

Scott stepped closer, sending Maggie's heart into a thumping mass, especially when he lowered his voice to an intimate level and said, "I promise it'll accomplish a *lot*."

Desperate to restore a sense of normalcy, Maggie reached around him and snatched the kitchen phone off its base.

Scott groaned and backed off. "Don't make me listen."

"Listen? Oh no, buster. You said you'd smooth things over."

Scott slumped onto the nearest chair, his elbows resting on the table. Maggie dialed; Scott's head dropped into his hands. An answering machine picked up and went through its spiel about leaving a message, but he couldn't know that.

"Well, hello," Maggie said into the phone, torturing him with her most sultry voice.

Scott groaned and hunched lower.

An elderly gentleman picked up and drawled, "Ike Seibert Auctioneers and Appraisers."

"Ike, it's me, Maggie Cooper." She quickly covered the social niceties with her old mentor and friend, strolling around the kitchen as they chatted their way around to the topic that interested them both.

"So," Ike said, "are you finally going to empty out that barn?"

"Two barns, remember?"

"It's been a long time, Maggie. You still have all that?"

"And then some. You still interested?" He'd seen the contents years ago and asked to be remembered when the time came.

"I can stop by tomorrow morning," Ike said. "If that's all right."

"I'll count on you for lunch."

Maggie returned the phone to its base and jumped slightly when Scott stepped up behind her, because she hadn't heard him move. He leaned close. His warm breath teased the bare skin on the side of her neck.

"Darlin', I hate to be the one to tell you this, but men have a whole different idea of talking trash."

Maggie grinned. "Really?"

"First you need to cuddle up real close, like this." Scott's body didn't plaster itself to her backside, but darn near, and scorched her nonetheless.

"But, um . . ." Her voice cracked, and she cleared her throat. "He's not here."

"Figuratively, Maggie. If you pretend you're this close, you'll sound this close."

"I will?"

"Sure. Hear how your voice has changed? How it's deeper? Softer. Sexier."

Scott's hands touched the backs of Maggie's wrists and slowly smoothed their way up both arms to her shoulders. He teased; she tingled. He dipped his head and nuzzled her hair aside, just below her right ear. His breath was warm, the touch of his lips on her skin as delicate as a butterfly's caress.

The back door flew open. "There you are!"

Maggie ducked away from Scott, embarrassed to be caught so close.

Grammy's face glowed with excitement. "I smelled Lawrence's pipe tobacco. In the barn. My goodness, I'd know that blend anywhere. You have to come with me right now and talk to him."

Grammy grabbed Scott by the sleeve and didn't wait for his assent. As he was tugged out the door, he looked back at Maggie. He mimed a little boy being dragged to the woodshed by the scruff of his neck, and he made her laugh.

She'd had no business encouraging him. Anticipating his touch.

She slapped the back of her hand and said, "Bad Maggie."

For two hours, Grammy was tireless. With great excitement she'd say, for example, "There, over by the mermaid lamp," and Scott would walk, squeeze, wiggle, shove, or climb his way to a gaudy old mermaid lamp, only to say, "He's not here, Grammy." A whole off-season of working out hadn't prepared his body for all this twisting and turning.

"Are you sure?" she asked. "Call him again."

"He's ornery, not deaf."

Maggie tried to talk Grammy into taking it easy, but there was no stopping her. She ordered Scott onward, sending him this way and that to check around the U.S. Army Air Corps box, which turned out to be toy lead soldiers; to an autographed photo of Clark Gable; a box of children's books; a banjo-shaped barometer that forecast rain; and on and on.

She pushed herself too hard. Maggie tried several times to make her sit down, but Grammy shooed her away.

Finally she began to show her age. Her pace slowed. Her back curved. She wrung her hands. Her attitude slid from "Over there!" to "Why won't he talk to me?"

"I promise I'll ask as soon as I find him." Worried about Grammy, Scott finally put his arm around her shoulders and steered her gently toward the exit, even when she resisted. "You know him better than I do. What do you suggest?"

"I guess he's beyond a whippin'," she grumbled.

"If not, I got dibs on giving it."

Grammy *hmph*ed.

"You go on back to the house and let me try on my own, okay?" But as soon as he released his hold on Grammy, her forward momentum stopped.

Maggie slid into his place, said, "Grammy, we missed lunch. Scott must be starving," and swept her away.

Alone, he had no trouble finding Coop. He didn't even have to look.

"What the hell did you think you were doing?" The ghost lit right into him. "Couldn't you see how tired my mother was getting? She's not a young woman anymore, you know."

They were a quarter of the way into the huge old barn. Scott cleared off a chest freezer and tossed several folded and plastic-bagged quilts on top. He stretched out on his back, letting his muscles relax and his vertebrae settle back into some semblance of alignment.

"You listening to me, son?"

Unconcerned with how pissed off the ghost got— actually, *relishing* how mad he could make him—Scott cocked one knee and propped his casted foot on it. "Got any smokes on you?"

Hit with a barrage of small items, Scott raised his arms in self-defense and laughed. Fortunately nothing was large enough to do him bodily harm, no hammers or lead pipes, which made him wonder if the ghost had limited strength. If their positions were reversed, he sure as hell would've thrown something larger than the copper ashtray he plucked from the air.

"Hey, thanks, man," he said, resting it on his chest. "There's a pack in my truck, right outside the door. Mind getting them for me?"

"Up yours."

"Why won't you talk to Grammy, Coop? She's a nice old lady. I think she just wants some answers."

"I can't answer her questions right now."

"Because, let me guess, you're a horse's ass?"

Coop paced a circle around the freezer, which was disconcerting because he kept passing through objects. Scott shook his head and tried to resign himself to that oddity. He couldn't make the ghost stop being a ghost, and he didn't want to give Coop the satisfaction of knowing he was driving him *nuts*.

"I can't help wondering why I'm still here," Coop said. From the look on his face, he thought explaining the ins and outs of his situation was beneath him, but he'd attempt it for Scott's sake. "You know, why I haven't 'passed.' It's always puzzled me. I used to think it was 'cause I didn't do enough to ensure my family's future. I wanted both girls to go to college, you see, to make a better life for themselves. I know that don't make no sense, 'cause look at all the men who die without leaving their families nothing, but I thought maybe things were different in my case, so I kept working at seeing to their future."

Scott looked at Coop and spread his arms wide, indicating the mountains of junk surrounding them.

Coop's lips thinned, his grin reluctant. "Yeah, I know. I think I outdid myself."

"I think you outdid several selves."

"So the question remains: Why am I still here? I used to talk to Maggie. She'd always been so levelheaded, I thought she might know. That went nowhere. But now that I look back, I think I was on the right track. I think maybe I'm supposed to settle something with her. Or Grammy or Ruby."

"Uh, gee, then maybe *talking* to Grammy would've been a good start, don't you think?"

"Are you crazy? How can I pass now? I'm this close to seeing my 'Cuda restored." A minute distance, if Coop's thumb and index finger were an accurate indication. "If there's anybody on earth that can understand that, it's you, son."

"Yeah, she'll be a beauty, all right. I can see myself now, driving her down the street—"

"You?" Coop loomed over Scott, making him feel pretty vulnerable lying there on his back. "Other than putting the Hemi back and making sure she runs, you keep your goddamn hands off my 'Cuda."

Scott held the ghost's gaze and raised his hand in the air, mimicking Coop's finger-to-thumb measurement. "Should you be using language like that? You know, *this close* to passing and all?"

Looking mad enough to spit, Coop grabbed the nearest item at hand and threw it. When Scott laughed at the ghost for hitting him with a naked brunette Barbie, he got two more hurled at his head.

"Make fun of me if you want," Coop fumed, "but I'm staying till that car is restored. And if working things out with my family is what I'm s'posed to be doing instead, then I'll just keep to myself when they're around. And I'll thank you very much not to lead my mother on like that again."

"Me lead her on—that's rich. Take some responsibility, man. If you need to tell her something, then tell her."

"No. I don't want to pass before I see my 'Cuda again the way she's meant to be seen."

"You're a jerk."

Scott rested his forearm across his eyes. Maybe Coop'd take the hint and go away. Permanently.

"Scott?" Maggie's call came seconds later from the vicinity of the barn door.

Coop stalked off, as much as a ghost can stalk. He swore as he went, which enhanced the image.

Scott jackknifed up for one last jibe. "Who's running and hiding now?"

"Not running, son. Not hiding. I'll be keeping my eye on you."

"Scott? You in here?"

As long as Maggie was joining him, Scott would rather be where he'd been than up to his neck in musty boxes. He resumed the supine, cast-over-cocked-knee position that had started to ease the crick in his back.

"Back here, Maggie. To your left."

When she strolled over and noticed him clutching one brunette and two blond Barbies to his chest, she stopped and put a hand on her hip. "I don't know, Templeton. Think you can handle three at once?"

"I'm innocent. They attacked me. I was just lying here, minding my own business . . ." He patted the freezer to substantiate his story. Also as a subliminal invitation.

"Yeah, that's what they all say." Maggie stepped closer and touched the freezer. "I remember this. Grammy used to send me out here when she needed meat."

Scott twisted, popping his back. "I don't suppose there's any traction equipment stored out here? I think I pulled something."

"I think you're pulling something now."

"No, seriously." He flipped onto his stomach and suggested what might seem to be a safe spot, not too high, not too low. "Feel it. There's a knot right in the middle of my back."

"Nice try." Maggie tested a couple of boxes as stools

and found them wanting. She eyed the quilt-padded freezer. "Is that as comfortable as it looks?"

He scooted over, but not all the way to the edge. When she boosted herself up and her rear bumped against his hip, he figured the ghost better get lost if he didn't want to see his daughter seduced right there among all his collectibles.

"It's great on the back," he encouraged.

Maggie raised her knees to pivot.

"Careful, though. The plastic's slippery." Scott was fully prepared to stop her from tumbling off whether she needed it or not. He'd put his whole body into it.

Sneakers landed by Scott's shoulder; not what he'd expected. Maggie's head came to rest way down by his feet, where she scrunched the quilt into a makeshift pillow. With a cheeky grin in his direction, she said, "Ah, that's pretty good."

So, you miss one opportunity, you get another. Scott turned onto his side, propped his head on his raised hand, and scooted closer to Maggie.

"Hey, watch the cast, would you? The last thing I need is a black eye."

"Maybe you should turn around. You know, to be safe."

She didn't take the hint, and he didn't push. Not that this would sound like an accomplishment any other day of the year with any other woman, but less than twenty-four hours had gone by, and he was at least lying beside Maggie.

"Don't let me stop you," she said.

With one finger, he started tracing shapes on her jeans, just above her knee.

"I meant talking to Pop."

He stilled his hand, giving her no reason to brush it away. "You know he's here?"

Maggie cocked one knee in the air as Scott had earlier, and rested her other ankle on it. That dislodged his hand from her thigh, but presented with that brain-deadening view, who the hell cared?

"Grammy's right; that's his pipe tobacco. So what's he doing?"

"Looking for a machete, I think. If you find my head on a platter, you'll know who did it."

"I don't want to bruise your ego, Templeton, but your head in here with all this junk—who'd know?"

"You have any mummies in here?"

"I think Grammy would've mentioned it. Geez, the piles look taller from this angle."

"Hey, I have an idea. Why don't you call some of your friends to lend a hand, too?" He hoped like hell they'd be women, not those cops. "My buddies'll work longer if there's beer or women involved. Preferably both." When Maggie didn't say anything right away, Scott nudged her and said, "Hey, you awake?"

"They're all busy." She sat up abruptly, as if the thought of being anything other than awake next to him was too close, too intimate. "You mentioned helping each other—"

Scott coughed loudly, cutting her off before she could

say too much. He pounded his chest and said, "I think the dust is getting to me." Catching Maggie's gaze, his slid around the interior, hinting that they couldn't count on being sans ghost in the barn.

She nodded in understanding. "Let's get some fresh air."

 *Chapter 6*

Because the dogs trotted peacefully alongside Scott and Maggie toward the house, Scott figured Coop wasn't nearby. He wasn't taking any chances, though, as the sometimes-lingering aroma of pipe tobacco was an unreliable indicator. He'd wait to discuss how to get rid of a ghost until after they were safely inside, away from prying ears.

It was pure magic to have Maggie walking beside him. The ground had a gentle slope here, a dip there; from time to time, her shoulder brushed against his arm and made him that much more aware of her. As if he needed help. A country boy he wasn't, but by the halfway mark, he'd learned to spot which terrain would ease her toward him, and he slowed the pace so he could enjoy it longer.

A gentle breeze carried a floral scent his way—a surprise, since they were walking through grass, not flowers. Besides, he'd figured Maggie for a vanilla woman, probably just a carryover from the baking aroma lingering in the house.

He leaned toward her when she wasn't looking and sniffed to see where the scent came from—maybe her shampoo—but he couldn't tell without crawling all over her. Sounded like fun, but it was a tad early for that.

Maybe tomorrow.

He'd promised to help with her boyfriend. Why? He had no idea, except he was desperate for help and it seemed the quickest way to convince her. Other than that, he ought to have his head examined.

"If you want to smooth things over with Kenny—"

"Kevin."

"Right." As if he cared. "You should call him."

"I was kidding earlier. You know, about talking trashy."

"Too bad." Scott felt just the tiniest bit guilty grinning until Maggie responded with a little smile of her own.

"You wanted to help with that?" She sounded mildly curious.

"Rehearsal's always a good idea."

"Clear-cut advice would be better."

"That's easy. Men are like cars."

Maggie groaned. "Please, no 'Top off our oil once in a while or we don't run so well.' I've heard it."

She was absolutely adorable, working a PG-but-suggestive little hand gesture into that. Only a single man who hadn't been with a woman in too many weeks to count would read anything into it, but there you had it.

"I'm not doing phone sex," she said.

"That was the last thing on my mind." *For the other guy.* "Look, men want to be needed. Men want to fix things. Kermit—"

"Kevin."

"—probably just got mad because you took care of

everything and didn't let him help. So my advice to you: Tell him you need him."

Maggie jammed her hands into her jeans pockets. Scott understood it wasn't because they were cold.

"What?" he said.

"*That*'s how you're going to help me patch things up?"

"Hey, you can't work things out if you're not talking. Take the first step. If he's half a man, once he hears you apologize, he'll turn right around and do the same. Trust me. Relationship saved."

Maggie's sideways glance clearly said she suspected he'd been living on another planet. "And you've been in a committed relationship how long?"

"Why, Miss Cooper." Scott slipped his arm around Maggie's shoulders, loosely, as they neared the porch. "You're flirting with me."

She pushed him away playfully. "How on earth did you read flirting into that?"

"You said the R word. You're trying to find out if I have a girlfriend."

She shook her head and looked exasperated, but she was smiling, too, so Scott figured he was doing okay.

"I already know you don't have a girlfriend."

"I knew it—you Googled me last night."

"Are you kidding? You'd drive a woman crazy before the R word even dawned on her."

Scott laid his hand on the small of Maggie's back as they ascended the porch, their steps perfectly timed on each tread. If the apology to her boyfriend worked, he might not get another chance to touch her. That didn't seem fair.

"Okay, I think it's safe to talk now," he said as they entered the kitchen. He closed the door firmly and double-checked it, though if Coop wanted in, no door would stop him. "Now tell me, how do I get rid of him?"

"Well, I'm no expert . . ."

"I'll try anything."

Maggie pulled a sharp knife out of the block on the counter, and Scott said, "Uh, short of killing myself."

"It usually only takes one finger. Sometimes two."

When Scott crossed his arms so all ten fingers were safely tucked away, Maggie was able to suppress a burst of laughter for all of one second, maybe two, before she gave him reason not to bolt for the nearest exit. "Get the roast beef out of the fridge, would you? I thought I'd slice some for sandwiches while we talk."

"I knew that."

"Uh-huh. Do you always think women are going to hurt you?"

"Grammy says you clobber people."

"I do not! Honestly, the things she comes up with."

Maggie punctuated with her hands as she spoke, the knife waving around like a conductor's baton, so Scott carefully plucked it from her grasp and said, "If you don't mind, I'll slice while you dispense with the ghost-busting advice."

He shifted the roast to the table, out of Maggie's range just in case she didn't like the way he carved. The marbled cat sat at his knee and looked hopeful. It tried an insistent meow, but after the last seven weeks, Scott excelled at ignoring *insistent*.

"I've been thinking," Maggie said. "If Pop's ghost is still here after, what, twelve or thirteen years, maybe he has a good reason."

"Maybe he needs a manual. Let's put him out of his misery."

"You're sure you want to rush into this?"

"Who's rushing? Another week and we'll be celebrating our anniversary."

"Okay, then," she said with resignation, moving around the kitchen, getting the rest of their lunch together. "It's pretty basic, really. When you have a ghost you don't want, you have to tell it to go away."

"Hey, if Coop didn't understand 'Get the you-know-what out of my life,' I don't see how 'Go away' will work."

Maggie'd just joined Scott at the table with bread, chips, and condiments, so he caught her wince.

"What?"

"Cussing at him won't help," she said. "Keep it simple, like 'I want you to go away and leave me alone.' Maybe more than once. And you might have to tell him he's dead and doesn't belong here."

"He knows. He said he's not ready to pass—his term, not mine. He's determined to see the 'Cuda restored first."

He must have gotten a little carried away with the knife and the roast because Maggie nudged him with her foot and said, "Killing the steer again won't help."

"Oh. Yeah. You sure I can't swear at him?"

"No swearing, no yelling, just 'Go away.' Otherwise . . . I can see it now." She held her hands up, squared off like a frame. "You, driving a ghost-white car around the track. Your new, though somewhat pale— Is he pale?"

"Not so much."

"Your new racing partner on the roof. The numbers, maybe 66 or 99, painted to look like a pair of eyes. Scotty Templeton, the talk of the racing circuit." One corner of her lips tipped upward as she tossed two simple words back at him. "Trust me."

"Oh, that was low."

Maggie took a deep, sweeping bow. "Thank you very much."

"But I'll try it anyway, that's how desperate I am. And if it doesn't work, I saw something in the barn that might. I'll need help, though."

"What is it?" she asked, looking a little wary, Scott noticed.

Good; he had her attention.

"Tonight," he said cryptically. "After dark. Bring a candle."

It rained the rest of the afternoon, usually just a drizzle, but at times hard enough to hear on the roof. The damp weather compounded the chill still lingering in the barn from the long Midwest winter. Scott managed to keep warm by moving things. His friends and brother would arrive to help tomorrow, but he might be able to stumble upon the 'Cuda yet today.

"You're dead," he said every minute or two, which was how often he glimpsed the ghost. Coop was uncharacteristically silent. Maybe this was working. "Go away."

"You're cussing in subtext," Maggie said.

"What?"

Thank God she didn't use vibrate mode on her phone, or he'd never know whether she was talking to him or answering a call. For someone who was supposed to be out of town, she sure was connected. Efficient, too; she handled most clients' concerns in a few minutes.

"I can feel it," she said. "I'm sure Pop can feel it."

"What you feel is him standing over there laughing at me."

Maggie gasped. "The nerve!"

"You'd be more believable if you wiped that smirk off your face."

"Sorry, can't help it."

"I didn't smile when you called Killjoy and told him—"

"*Kevin.*"

Knowing exactly how to avoid a fight, Scott flashed his dimple. Maggie tried not to smile in response, but didn't have much success. The fact that she could smile at all after Kevin repeatedly refused to answer her calls wasn't wasted on Scott. She'd left a series of voice mails after lunch, beginning with a nice apology, as prescribed, progressing to a curt message to call her back, almost ending the last message by questioning his parentage, but Scott grabbed the phone from her before she could get it all out.

When he moved, the ghost caught Scott's eye.

"You're dead. Go away."

Maggie groaned again, louder this time. Definitely frustrated. "You're like a dripping faucet. Just when I think you've stopped . . ."

She was documenting loose, stand-alone items with a digital camera and a tape recorder. Grammy hadn't been kidding when she'd claimed Maggie was focused. Her efficiency and thoroughness were remarkable as she itemized things large and small alike.

"Late nineteenth-century child's bicycle, sixteen-inch detachable driving wheel. Early nineteenth-century tea chest, tortoiseshell, silver-plated knobs, two interior compartments. Nice condition."

"Are those worth anything?" Scott asked.

"I haven't kept up, but ten years ago, on a good day, the tea chest would have brought about four hundred dollars."

Scott glanced around at thousands of boxes, maybe hundreds of thousands of items, and did some quick math. "Hey, not bad."

"Don't get excited. I'm afraid this tea chest is the exception." Maggie's gaze skimmed over boxes sealed with tape, boxes with their flaps tucked in on themselves, and boxes without any tops at all. She moved on. "Concrete garden gnome, painted, eyes closed, about 1960. Geez, what was he thinking?"

Scott enjoyed the cadence of her voice, the expertise with which she worked. He should be half so focused, he realized, as he suddenly noticed Coop again. The ghost was observing Maggie, and Scott had slacked off in the banishment department, a condition he quickly rectified.

"You're dead. Go away."

Maggie clapped her hands over her ears. "Enough!"

She reminded him of the drama ghost, but not so much that he couldn't grin about it. "Boy, the nut didn't fall far from your family tree."

"What's that mean?"

"You take after your father."

"He's holding his ears, too? If I were you, I'd give up."

Coop laughed at him again, then mimed a man dangling from a noose. It was an outstanding impression, since he could hover a foot above the floor and kick his feet. Scott took that to mean the ghost was giving him just enough rope to hang himself, but how, he wasn't sure. He still had a backup plan the ghost wasn't privy to, but was determined to give Maggie's method a fair try first.

"You're dead. Go away."

Covering her ears again, Maggie staggered and threw herself backward onto a sturdy trunk. "I never said to go on and on and *on*," she wailed. "Give it a rest."

"Hush." Scott turned to the ghost. "You're dead. Go away."

Still supine, Maggie uncovered one ear. "Have you stopped?"

"If it bothers you, go back to the house."

"Yeah," she said, perking up. "I could help Grammy with supper."

"There's an idea. When should I come in?"

"When you're quiet?"

"You know, you're a lot funnier than your father. I was going to say it's too wet out for you to come back for me, but after that comment, I think I'll let you."

"I can call you. There's a phone jack by the feed room."

"There's rooms in here?" Good Lord, junk he hadn't seen yet.

Maggie rose to her feet as limber as a dancer. Scott wasn't quick enough to offer her a hand up, but managed to touch her anyway under the guise of brushing dust off her shirt. He worked his way down her back until she glared at him, took him by the hand, and led him toward the front of the barn. Hell, she could glare all she wanted, but as long as she held his hand, he'd follow her anywhere.

Maggie extended her arm toward a mountain of trunks, boxes marked "China" and "Books," and an apex of dining room chairs and one faded Red Flyer sled. Setting the big items on top made no sense, but what in here did?

"The feed room's behind that. You'll recognize it because it's full of old tools."

"Then why don't you call it the tool room?"

"The jack's on this side of the wall. As long as you're moving stuff, if you can get back there and plug in the phone, I'll ring you when we're ready. You can come in sooner, though. *If* you're quiet."

Scott nudged a bottom trunk near what appeared to be an edge of the stack, but with this many years of disorganization, it was hard to tell. He was testing the likelihood of shoving his way through when a nameplate bounced off his head and landed at his feet.

Maggie snapped a picture. "Brass nameplate, S.S. *Titanic*, approximately thirteen inches."

If this had hit him on the head and fallen at his feet before a race, Scott would've run the other way. "Think someone's trying to tell us something?"

"Maybe."

"A little small, isn't it?"

"Could be a replica made to scale. Or off a lifeboat. Or somebody's idea of a joke."

Scott caught Maggie's eye to give her fair warning. "I'm going to say it again."

"*Ten seconds.*" She sprinted for the door.

He gave her five. "You're dead. Go away."

"Son, I mighta croaked, all right, but you're getting downright annoying."

Forget being helpful; it was time to bait the blasted ghost. "Did you check out those garages yet?"

"Oh, *now* you're talking to me?"

Scott shrugged as if he didn't care. With Maggie gone, he could start on the area they'd need tonight. He wanted it to be just right. Coop kept his distance at first, then curiosity got the better of him.

"What garages?"

"The ones Grammy was talking about at lunch," Scott ad-libbed. "Oh, you weren't there. Guess I should've passed this on to you earlier. She remembered something about your wife paying off a debt with a car? Sound familiar?" He paused a beat, as if he cared, before he continued. "She thought it might've been the 'Cuda. You sure you didn't hear this?"

"Who'd she say?" Coop asked eagerly.

If Coop was like most gearheads, this would work, and Scott and Maggie could have the barn to themselves this evening. Scott thought, *What a sucker,* and feigned perplexity. "I'm not sure exactly. Did somebody do some work for you who didn't get paid before you died?"

"Not *that* much."

Scott shrugged with unspoken meaning. Coop vanished on a fruitless 'Cuda quest, leaving him to clear an area for the night and turn out the lights.

"One candle isn't very bright," Maggie said. "Are you sure we can't turn on the lights?"

She paused inside the big sliding barn door, Scott just behind her. The sun had set while they'd eaten supper in the kitchen with Grammy, and although the rain had stopped, there was no moonlight to speak of.

"That would ruin it," Scott said very near Maggie's ear.

"I'm not sure it's wise to have a candle in a barn."

"It's in a jar. Now face forward, that's right, and let me steer you."

Bundled up in a turtleneck and leather jacket, Maggie

still felt heat where Scott grasped her shoulders as he urged her deeper into the dark barn. Supporting the candle she'd liberated from the emergency cellar stash, Maggie proceeded slowly down a high-sided, narrow path that hadn't been there this morning. Scott shadowed her. No guiding was necessary; a radar-challenged bat couldn't have taken a wrong turn in this tunnel. He kept his hands on her anyway, which was oddly comforting and distracting at the same time.

"Nothing better jump out at me," she said.

"The dogs'll warn you first." All three had tagged along, romping, panting, sniffing. If anything wild was in there, it wouldn't dare move and give itself away.

"How far back are we going?"

"Just a little more. Okay, turn to the right now."

The small candle didn't shed much light, but it sure lent an eerie feeling to a recently cleared eight-foot circle, its periphery bound by irregular stacks. In the center sat two oak, straight-backed chairs. Facing each other. No more than a foot apart.

"This isn't some devil-worshipping thing, is it?" she asked.

"Yeah, like we need one of those, too. Have a seat."

Maggie sat, holding the candle on her lap until Scott pulled up a brass smoker's stand to set it on. She scooted as far back in her chair as possible, knowing his knees and hers were never going to fit in that tiny space without a lot of touching. Not that that sounded bad, no, not at all. But what else did he have in mind?

"A séance?" she guessed.

"Are you psychic?"

"No."

"Then we're not having a séance." Scott slipped into the other chair, but there was no knee jostling, at least not the kind Maggie'd expected. He simply straddled hers with his in a no-nonsense grip. "Comfortable?"

Her gaze roamed the circle and ended on the man in front of her. "Not entirely."

"Ready?" Scott reached under his chair.

"I don't know. What're we—?"

He plopped a board onto their conjoined laps.

"A Ouija board," Maggie said with surprise and a measure of relief.

Some people swore they were dangerous to mess with, but Pop had collected at least a dozen of them and nothing bad had happened yet. No books flying off shelves, no doors slamming, no getting pushed down the steps.

Frowning at it, Scott rotated it ninety degrees, first one way, then the other. "Is there a right way for this to go?"

"Read the directions."

"We don't need directions. I did this as a kid, didn't you?"

"Where's the planchette?"

"This thing?" In his hand was a smooth maple planchette, nearly triangular, with rounded angles and a circular viewing window in its middle.

"That's it." It was a nice old set, Maggie noticed; in good condition. "Is there a box?"

"We don't need the directions."

"It's worth more in the original box."

"Oh. Yeah, it's over there. Let's focus on this now instead of the collectibles, okay?"

"And we're doing this because . . . ?"

"We're going to ask the spirits to help us send Coop on his way. You know, guide him to the light or whatever they do."

"Uh-huh." Maggie tried not to sound doubtful, because, well, why rain on Scott's parade? If Pop was still here for a reason, their playing with a talking board certainly wouldn't get rid of him, but she could be a good sport. "Who goes first?"

"I can't believe you never did this. We do it together. Put your hands on here, like this."

Scott demonstrated an elbows-bent, fingertip touch, as if playing a piano. Maggie copied him. Not only were their knees touching and their fingers close, but their bodies were angled toward each other. If he lost his balance, she mused in a flight of fancy, his lips were likely to land on hers. Who knew what would happen after that? He could blow her five-year plan out of the water. Not that it was her plan to start with. In fact, some parts needed blowing out of the water.

"Earth to Maggie."

"Mm, sorry."

"Okay, now that you're back, we start by moving this around in a couple circles to warm up. And, oh yeah, I'm supposed to announce that we only want good spirits, no bad ones, and if we get bad ones, we're supposed to mention Jesus because the devil can't stand to be around Jesus."

"Good Lord, where did you get that?"

"Hey, that was the inside scoop when my brother and I did this."

"Please tell me you were kids at the time."

"Concentrate. Follow me."

Scott led off by pushing the planchette in a clockwise circle around the board, three slow loops that wouldn't have warmed up an ant. Maggie's knees sure were warm, though. A table might be more level, more stable, but not nearly as much fun. After a minute, it dawned on her that so much silence in a huge barn wasn't natural. The dogs had left.

"How will we know if we get a bad spirit?" she asked.

"We ask for good ones."

"And they cooperate out of the goodness of their hearts?" Maggie snickered. "Oops, guess they don't have those."

"I forgot to mention: Doubters have to get purified."

She stifled a laugh by pressing her lips tightly together and hoped he was joking—about all of this.

"Okay, now that it's warmed up, we ask simple questions, follow the planchette around, and take note of whatever letters or words it stops on."

Maggie squinted at the dimly lit board. "One candle isn't going to cut it."

Scott sighed, which didn't make her feel the least bit guilty.

"I mean it. I can't see all the letters."

"Okay. Don't move, I'll be right back."

Maggie was left with cold knees and the board while Scott foraged up a piano bench and a dry, dusty, three-candled hunk of greenery once disguised as a Christmas centerpiece.

"You went to auctioneer school," he said. "Is this worth anything?"

"Absolutely."

"I mean more than fifty cents in a garage sale."

"Seriously, Scott. One thing I learned is that, as a professional, you have to think about this from all angles. I mean, what if you're caught in a blizzard and need kindling? Think what you'd pay for it then."

"Ouch. I can't believe you had me going there." He plucked one of the hot-summer-in-a-barn wilted candles from the centerpiece and used it to light all three off the candle in a jar.

Maggie looked forward to feeling Scott's legs against hers again, but she wasn't prepared for him to sit down, reach his hands behind her knees, and pull her hips forward on the seat. Any closer and she'd be feeling him up with her kneecaps.

"There, that's better," he said, clamping his thighs to hers.

Once Maggie remembered to breathe again, she admitted it was. To herself.

"Hands on," he ordered. "Okay. Quick warm-up." After once around the board, Scott said, "Here goes. Is anyone here?"

The planchette, with their fingers lightly on board,

wandered around for ten to fifteen seconds, then stopped on the YES.

"Are you pushing?" Maggie asked. "Because it feels like you're pushing."

"Me? I thought that was you."

"I'm following."

"It was never this strong when I was a kid. Okay. Next question: Who are you?"

"Are you supposed to ask that?"

"It's polite."

"Who made up these rules? Did someone channel a bunch of ghosts and ask for the ten commandments of Ouija-ing?"

"Light touch now, it's moving, it's moving. M...E..."

After the second letter, the planchette stopped, and Maggie and Scott both held their breath.

"Could be initials," she said finally.

"Could be a smart ass."

"Maybe you'd better tell it again that we only want good spirits."

"It knows. Next question: Did you ever live on this plane?"

Maggie figured, *Whatever,* and kept her mouth shut. As long as the spirits didn't read her mind and spell out shame on her for enjoying Scott's legs holding hers captive and double shame for wondering how to get his hands back on her for even a second, she was okay.

A low hum made Maggie jump, which made Scott jump. They laughed self-consciously.

"Thought I'd try my phone on vibrate tonight," she said.

"Don't answer it."

"Ooh, maybe it's a modern spirit. Maybe the board's too slow, so it's calling instead."

Scott shook his head with resignation. "Nothing's going to happen unless you at least believe something's *possible*."

"I *believe* I'll answer my phone."

This was her business line, after all. Just because she'd planned to be out of town didn't mean she couldn't answer a quick question after hours. The thing about working with really rich people was that when they wanted an answer, they generally expected it *now*.

She checked the display. "Well, doesn't that just figure."

"The spirits have caller ID? Come on, let it go."

"It's Kevin. I've been waiting for him to call, re-member?"

"Yeah, and how many voice mails did that take?"

Maggie narrowed her gaze at Scott, ignoring the nig-gling thought that he might have a point in favor of the larger picture. "I thought you were helping me patch things up."

"A little hard-to-get never hurt anyone. Come on, let's get rid of our number one problem. As soon as Coop is gone, everything'll fall into place and go back to normal."

He was right. Reluctantly, Maggie let the call go

to voice mail. Two Ouija questions later, the phone beeped.

"Geez, he left that long a message?" She wasn't sure if that was a good sign or a bad one.

Scott's legs squeezed hers as the planchette and their fingers darted to NO, but she couldn't remember what the question had been.

How come Kevin never did fun stuff like this? Aside from his not believing in ghosts, how come he'd never cleared a spot in the barn for a little one-on-one? How come he never clamped his thighs around hers and tried to make her concentrate on one thing while feeding her fantasies of a totally carnal nature? How come being in a small room with Kevin didn't heat her up as much as being in a large barn with Scott?

There was something about being next to Scott that was comforting and energizing at the same time. A real puzzle. Maggie'd always loved puzzles. Games she could take or leave, but puzzles held her focus until she conquered them. That's why she was good at wealth management. She looked at investments and her clients' money as big puzzles to be deciphered and sorted and solved. Fit the pieces together, build a solid base, and expand.

The puzzle of Scott was only one of those darn phero-mone things. Had to be. What she and Kevin had had been built over two years. Scott was just a distraction. A hot one, too. She took her hands back long enough to shimmy out of her leather jacket.

"You want to ask the next question?" Scott asked.

Not while you're here. Resisting the urge to fan herself, Maggie said, "You're doing fine. Go ahead."

"Did you notice how strong it's getting? Maggie?"

"Uh, yeah. Strong."

"I can't wait to tell Jeremy about this."

"Is he your brother?"

"Uh-huh, three years younger." The planchette doodled on the board, not touching any letters. "I think we're boring the spirit. Next question: Can you help us send Lawrence Cooper on to wherever spirits are supposed to go after people die?"

The planchette darted to NO.

"Well, that was definite," Scott groused. "Why not?"

Nothing happened.

"That's odd. Let's just make a slow circle to get it going again. Maggie?"

"Ready when you are." Ready, yes; concentrating, well, maybe not on what Scott wanted her to concentrate on.

"Clockwise, remember?"

"I'm ready."

"So move."

"Hey, you're stronger than I am. You have to move, too."

"Me? I'm trying. Are you trying?"

Maggie raised her hands. Scott pretended to be unable to move the planchette long enough and hard enough to make Maggie laugh.

"You think this is funny? You try."

He raised his hands. Maggie resumed her touch on the indicator again and wiggled it around, proving he'd been faking it.

"Hm, maybe the spirit's getting tired," Scott said. "I hear this works better if we get naked."

"You'll work better if you don't make any more suggestions like that."

"It's for the sake of science."

"Next question."

Scott's devilish grin persisted as he settled his fingertips across from hers. "Next question: How do we get rid of Coop?"

The planchette suddenly vibrated.

Maggie snatched her hands away at the shock of it. She stared at the board, then Scott. "Whoa, how'd you do that?"

"That never happened before." He stared at the board with excitement, seemingly unaware that he was rubbing his fingertips together.

Maggie knew just how they felt—tingly. They both glanced around as if there could be some logical answer, like Grammy standing behind them with a remote control in her hands, laughing at the joke. Since that didn't happen, their gazes gravitated as one, back to the board bridging their laps.

Leaning forward so only Scott could hear, Maggie whispered, "This really works? I thought you were kidding."

"I was," he whispered back.

"Ask it another question then."

Scott appeared thoughtful for a moment before wiggling his fingers and looking at Maggie, meaning, *Hands on*. She stared at him. He stared at her. Together, in unspoken agreement, they inched their fingers forward, tested the planchette to find it still, vibrationless. They settled in for another tour around the board.

"Are you a good spirit?"

YES.

"Can you help us send Lawrence Cooper to a better place?"

In the blink of an eye, the planchette went from room temperature to scorching. Maggie and Scott snatched their hands away. She wasn't sure what to do next, other than stick her fingers in her mouth to soothe them, but Scott, being a guy, reached out to test it.

"Careful," Maggie warned. "You could bake a pizza on that."

He got close.

It sparked.

"Holy *shit*." Scott jumped to his feet and stuck his singed finger into his mouth. Maggie clamped a hand down on the board to keep it from flying off her lap. No sense damaging a perfectly good antique.

The dogs charged into the circle, barking madly, racing around wildly.

The planchette sizzled like a bundle of Fourth of July sparklers, and the whole secluded area suddenly brightened like a camera flash. Scott's face registered shock. No way Maggie was accusing him of tampering with the toy this time.

"Do you think—?"

"I think maybe we've done enough for one night," Scott said. "We should put it away. We can try again tomorrow."

In response, the board on Maggie's lap burst into flames.

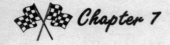

Chapter 7

One look at an unconfined fire, and Scott's scars jumped to life, involuntarily reacting to a driver's nightmare.

Flames blazed out of the Ouija board, licking wildly from corner to corner. Maggie sat there in shock, motionless, unsure which way to move, her arms stretched out to the sides to avoid getting burned.

A professional driver's instinct was to unbuckle everything and get the hell out. With great effort, Scott tamped down that instinct. He applied boot to board and sent it flying away from Maggie.

How was he supposed to know it'd land on a damn wreath? A wreath that flared up like the dry tinder it was. Sparks flew every which way, some landing on the nearest boxes, many of which were as old as the antiques inside.

The ghost, who'd been laughing himself silly, stopped abruptly.

Scott almost grabbed Maggie and ran. But this was no small, confining race car. There was room to maneuver here and a lot of investment at risk, so he stripped off his denim jacket and beat at the flames. He grabbed Maggie's jacket, too, and did double duty with it in his other hand. Within seconds, though it seemed longer, every last spark was out. It wasn't hard to be certain because they were now in total darkness. At least he thought they were still a *they*. Unless Maggie had cut and run, which would have been the smart thing to do, but he hoped she hadn't. It wasn't every day he got to beat out a fire and save a woman.

"Maggie? You all right?"

"I have to hand it to you, Templeton. You sure know how to show a woman an exciting evening."

If she were hurt, she'd be crying. If she were mad, she'd be screaming at him. Sarcasm was good.

"How about you?" she asked, closer now.

"Just peachy. Where's the candle? The one in the jar."

"It fell over." Maggie's hands landed on him with a light touch. She patted her way across his chest—*sweet Jesus*—and latched on to his arm.

All in all, not a bad evening. Hell, when he stopped to think about it, he'd saved the whole damn barn.

"If you think that was exciting," he said, "wait'll you see us try to find our way out of here. I don't suppose your dogs fetch flashlights on command or have Seeing Eye degrees."

"God, you're smart."

Ouch.

He liked the way Maggie's hands wrapped around his arm. His muscles were rock-hard, guaranteed to make a woman feel safe and protected. He almost flexed to heighten the point. "Hang on tight. I'll lead us out of here."

"Leave? I'm not leaving." Maggie's grip tightened, and Scott felt rigidity spread through her. "I am too friggin' *angry* to leave."

Uh-oh. But then Scott realized she wasn't facing him.

"Is he here?" she asked.

"That board didn't ignite on its own."

"That's what I figured. I don't know where you are, Pop. I don't know why you're still here, but you can't stay. You can start a fire, but you can't put it out? Geez, you're dangerous. You're dead. Go. Away."

When Maggie turned back to Scott, he knew she was ready to go, but now he was getting an earful from the ghost. He watered it down some and said, "Coop says he's needed here a little longer."

"No," Maggie said firmly, loud enough to be heard in every corner of the barn. "Mom doesn't need you; she's married and starting a new life. Ruby doesn't need you. I don't need you. No one here *needs* you. No one here *wants* you. You're dangerous. You're dead. Go. Away."

She took a step, nudging Scott to begin their exit. He found the perimeter of the circle and started forward. A second later, something happened to Maggie's legs, because she plunged downward and dangled from his arm so fast he couldn't have stopped her even if he could see her. He lowered her the rest of the way, then reached down in an attempt to scoop her up. He'd always had good aim in the dark. Unerring aim. It was a well-honed skill for a bachelor.

"Hey, watch it." Maggie brushed his hand off her breast.

Nice. Soft. A handful. He'd been without sex so long, he was surprised he could concentrate on the fact that she'd fallen and wasn't, in fact, trying to drag him down and have her way with him.

He heard her stumbling around and said, "What's going on? What're you doing?"

She cursed quietly. "I found one of the chairs."

Scott couldn't help laughing. He had no idea why. Maybe relief. Maybe Maggie's dry comment. "Maybe you should just sit in it while I go turn on the lights."

"It'd be safer." Her hands landed on him again, though, and this time when they wrapped around his arm, she snuggled her whole body tightly against his side. "See if you can miss the hurdles this time, okay?"

He thought about yelling for Coop to turn on the lights, but that didn't sound nearly as cozy as inching out of the barn with Maggie plastered up against him. Her breast felt almost as good against his arm as it had in his hand. He took it really, really slow. By the time they exited, she'd be really, really grateful.

It wasn't until they reached the door and he turned on the outdoor floodlight that he noticed Maggie was limping. Big time.

"What's wrong? Did you get burned?" Scott successfully scooped her into his arms this time and frantically shouted, "Dammit, Coop, get out here and start my truck!"

Maggie rubbed her thigh. "Anybody ever tell you you have a kick like a mule?"

"It never came up before— What are you talking about?" Her jeans were a little charred, but as close as they were now, he could see it was only superficial damage.

"You *kicked* me."

And here he'd thought he'd done so well. "Sorry, it seemed the quickest way to get the board off your lap. I'll rub it for you."

"Oh my God, do you ever stop?" Her complaint was tempered with laughter as he carried her to the bed of his pickup.

"Sweetheart, I haven't even gotten started."

Men did this in the movies all the time, carried women in their arms and still managed to open doors and turn down beds. Scott only had to support Maggie while he laid their jackets on the truck bed. Easier said than done. He couldn't give up once he started, though. She looked at the truck, looked at him, and grinned a little knowing grin that said, *Yeah, let's see if you blow this, too, Templeton.*

"Afraid I'll drop you on your ass?" he asked.

"You notice I'm hanging on to your neck?"

"That's because you like me." By propping one foot on the bumper, he was able to support her bottom and spread their jackets as a cushion.

"My jacket!"

Any hope of grateful kisses and thigh massages was eradicated as Maggie propelled herself out of his arms and held her jacket up in the light. It was pretty scorched, especially the lining. She tipped her head sadly and made that little sound of dismay that all women know how to make. No matter how Maggie meant it, it was designed by nature to make a man feel so bad, so low, that he'd move heaven and earth to fix whatever was wrong and make it right again.

There was only one way a real man could handle this. Even though it was all the ghost's fault, Scott hung his head and said, "I know. I owe you a leather jacket, too."

Was it any wonder he couldn't sleep that night? Maggie'd given Scott her mother's old room, so either she thought he was good for the jacket or realized ruining it hadn't been an option.

Insomnia wasn't new to Scott. When interviewed by the media about pre-race jitters and how they'd slept the night before, all the drivers shrugged off the question and parroted the words, "It's just like any other job. You get up, you go to work, you get the job done."

Uh-huh, sure. As safe as bagging groceries. As if a field trip into a wall didn't hurt a helluva lot more than dropping a can of soup on your foot. As if crawling out of an upside-down car meant he wouldn't have a crick in his neck because he was just doing his job. As if more than the tiniest percent of Americans had good reason to wear flame-retardant underwear to work.

A smoke used to help, so shortly after midnight, Scott crept down the stairs and outside. The peepers were in full swing, and his poor, dead truck was under scrutiny by a humongous raccoon.

Not that he knew what size one was supposed to be, but this guy had to be the king of all of them.

"This isn't St. Louis," he muttered. "It's Wild fucking Kingdom."

The coon lumbered off, not toward the trees, but into the barn, which made Scott think a chain-mail suit might be a good investment when he started poking around in there again.

"You're lucky it wasn't a skunk," Coop said.

Scott glared. "If I were lucky, you'd be gone."

"You know the answer to that."

"You're dead. Don't you get it? Warranty *expired*."

"Give it a rest. I'm staying, and you're gonna search that barn till I get what I want."

"That coon's got teeth, man. And claws—I saw claws. If you want me in there again, you need to be scaring everything out."

Coop glared back. "Haven't had much luck with that lately."

Scott grinned. "Got yourself in hot water with Maggie, didn't you?"

"Don't make no difference. I gotta do what I gotta do."

"Yeah, me, too. I've been giving that some thought. I can finish the season and then come back and put your car together."

"No."

"What's the rush? You're already dead."

"Don't mean I'm senile. We had this discussion already. I won, remember? And in case you ain't figured it out yet, I always win."

Scott's smokes weren't on the dash. What the coon hadn't destroyed was scattered all over the seat and the floor, along with dirt and hair. He sagged against the quarter panel, desperate enough to consider sweeping up tobacco and rolling it in an old charge receipt. Who cared about a little coon fur, anyway?

"You know, Coop, if I were really lucky, you'd be a distant memory and my truck would be drivable." To even the score, he couldn't help adding, "And I wouldn't be assigned to a bed *across the hall* from your daughter."

"I thought that might be a problem. I got a solution."

"Dying to hear it."

"Answer your phone."

Scott's mobile, missing for weeks, *vroom*ed inside the truck like a miniature engine. He saw no reason to pick it up now. More important—should he tear off a piece of receipt or just roll the hell out of a whole one?

"Well answer it!"

"Like I want to talk to anyone you know? Get real."

"It's no one I know, son. You delivered my engine, I'm returning your phone, simple as that. Go ahead, pick up your messages. I'm sure they'll take your mind off Maggie."

Only one thing could do that.

"A job? Somebody needs a driver?" Scott practically dove through the window and plucked his phone off the seat. As he waited to access voice mail, he said, "Fully charged? Way to go, Coop. Think you can make that a permanent condition?"

"Just listen to your messages."

"*You have 252 new messages.*" Scott glared at the ghost. "Swear to God, if I missed out on a driving job because of you—"

"*First new message.*" The digital spiel was followed by soft, sultry Sherri cooing, "Scotty, honey, I know you must be in terrible pain. Call me when I can come over and make it all better.

"*Next new message.*" "Scotty, I know you won't be able to get into your tux for my award ceremony tonight." Patti wasn't as sultry, but she made up for it with boundless energy. "How about I bring a bottle of champagne over afterward and we have our own private celebration? Call me.

"*Next new message.*" Scott began deleting them halfway through. Sooner when they started turning nasty. "Really, Scotty," Janet snapped after the first fifty were erased. "It's not like you broke your dialing hand." The one after that mentioned breaking it for him.

Not one single voice mail about cars, races, auto parts, or interviews? Nothing from his agent? In seven weeks?

Not a chance.

"Aren't you gonna call them back?" Coop asked, clearly befuddled.

"Dream on."

"I thought you'd be happy."

"No, you thought I'd be out here all night return-ing calls instead of thinking about creeping across the hall and crawling in bed with your daughter. You're an obsessive-compulsive, control-freakin', sorry excuse of a ghost."

Coop shrugged. "Sticks and stones."

Scott pocketed his phone. Maybe if he hid it in the house, Coop couldn't tamper with it. Maybe not every racing team owner on the face of the planet was pissed off at him for not returning their calls. *Maybe* there was still one who'd try him again. You never knew. Drivers got hurt, on the track and off. They got sick. They need-ed to be replaced. It felt good to know he was the pick of the short list.

"Don't look for me too early tomorrow." Scott winked at Coop. "I think I might sleep in, if you know what I mean."

"Dammit, Templeton—"

Scott turned his back on the ghost. "You're dead. Go away."

Maggie was trying to kill him, for sure. Scott returned inside via the kitchen and found her bent at the waist, her head in the refrigerator, her ass encased in tight black pants. It begged to be touched. It screamed, *Handle me, I'm yours!*

He weighed his options. Double-cheek, cupped-hand grasp for maximum effect, or single in case she was skittish? Since she might have a sharp object in hand, he opted to go with a simple pat on her right cheek and a suggestive question.

"You ready for that thigh massage?"

She whooped and jumped forward before he could squeeze, and from the sound of jars crashing inside the fridge, she banged into a shelf, too. The marbled cat sprang out over her head, kangarooed off her back, skidded across the table, and headed for parts unknown. Maggie spun around, rubbing the top of her head, glaring daggers.

Only she wasn't Maggie. Same height, same curves, but this young woman had short, raven-black hair streaked with burgundy.

"Ow-w-w." Following an initial wince, the brow-pierced siren gave him a long, slow once-over. "Oh-h-h. I'm guessing, since you're not wearing a stocking over your head or throwing me on the floor, you're here for Maggie."

Scott's impulse was to back away, but being a gentleman, he stayed to apologize for accosting a strange woman in the middle of the night.

"Shit, I'm sorry."

She smiled regretfully. "Me, too. Have you been sneaking in long?"

"No, I, uh, I'm staying here for a while."

"Man, I should go away and come back more often."

"You must be Ruby." It was an easy deduction: platform combat boots, red eye shadow, and an elaborate black spiderweb drawn across one side of her face. At least Scott hoped it was drawn on. Since the brow piercing wasn't a ring or a ball, but a sooty black spider, he wasn't sure.

He liked the black suede bustier. Man oh man, he hoped Maggie had one of those and that she'd wear it for him.

"And you are?" Ruby prompted.

"Oh, I'm sorry. I'm Scott Templeton."

"My sister and a race car driver?" Ruby made a face and laughed. "No way."

"You might be right. Grammy invited me." Thankfully, Ruby poked her head back into the fridge while Scott explained his presence, thus giving him the opportunity to get his wits about him so he could look at her again without staring at her spiderweb.

"You want anything?" she asked.

Maybe it'd help him sleep. "Sure. Whatever you're having. Unless it's the cat."

She came back with a handful. "Pitas, tzatziki, and sprouts. I don't eat meat."

The cat meowed plaintively from the doorway. Scott couldn't stand it; he had to ask. "Why was he in the fridge?"

Ruby laughed. While it was a nice enough laugh, similar to Maggie's, it didn't do anything for him. Did that mean he wasn't sex-starved? Well, no, that wasn't possible, because he was, but did it mean that when it came to Maggie, something more was going on?

"He was on my shoulder until you goosed me. And 'thigh massage'? *Please.* If that's your code for sex, it's not going over Grammy's head."

"I need a code?"

Ruby placed everything on a tray and headed for the main part of the house. Scott didn't know what tzatziki was, but since Ruby didn't eat meat, he felt confident that it wasn't some critter she'd killed in the backyard.

Ruby glanced back over her bare shoulder. "Well, come on. You can tell me more while we eat."

Scott hid his cell phone in a kitchen cabinet before he followed her to the dining room. Right past the table. Through the living room with perfectly good coffee table. Up the stairs, past Maggie's door, and halfway around the second floor, where Ruby opened a door to reveal a narrow set of stairs leading up.

This couldn't be good.

"I, uh . . ." Sprouts were bad enough, but Grammy, or maybe it was Maggie, had mentioned that Ruby lived in the attic. That probably meant sitting on her bed to eat. With her. He knew a wreck waiting to happen when he saw one, and this one looked to be a doozy.

"Come on," Ruby said, looking back at him. "I don't bite."

At the crack of dawn, the birds began chirping and going about their spring nest-building activities. Grammy was only a beat behind them. Her agenda was slightly different, but no less urgent.

My, but guilt was a heavy burden. Sometimes she went for days on end without thinking about it, but that wasn't a relief, as then she felt even more guilty for forgetting about it. This circle had to end, one way or another. It was Wednesday already. Surely today was the day she'd get to talk to Lawrence. If his death wasn't her fault, she needed to know.

Fifty years ago, when he was nine months old, her only son had been hell on wheels. She'd put him in his toddler walker; he'd propelled himself around the house for hours on end. He wasn't done until he was done. There was no waiting him out, and it took two adults to catch him. She and George, God rest his soul, laughed and exclaimed over how cute and persistent Lawrence was, and bought him a little yellow pedal car for his birthday. What were they *thinking*? The furniture and interior walls were in mortal danger. They banished him to the yard. To this day, if you knew where to look, you could see the ruts he'd worn into the ground.

Now that Lawrence was back, Grammy couldn't wait to talk to him, but she had to rely on Scott, and he wasn't up yet. She couldn't very well barge into the bedroom and wake him. He might not wear pajamas. He might kick the covers off when he slept. She'd wait until eight.

She'd send Maggie.

Not that she'd ever seen either man naked, but you only had to glance at what's-his-name to know that once Maggie got an eyeful of Scott, she'd realize what's-his-name's shortcomings. He was too narrow in the shoulders, too smooth of face. No way he had enough testosterone to make him any fun in the bedroom. Maggie deserved better. She deserved Scott.

But enough about them. Today was her day.

Lord only knew why, but she wanted to look her best for Lawrence. She spent time on her hair and topped her jeans with a pretty peach sweater embellished with matching beads. After that, she went downstairs and brewed a pot of coffee. Not for Lawrence's sake, of course, but the aroma would waft up the stairs, wake Scott, and get this whole show on the road.

Maggie was the next one down to the kitchen, but not until eight o'clock. Her hair was combed, maybe, but that was it. Grammy was about to explain the finer points of grooming to catch a man of Scott's quality when she noticed something amiss.

"Why are you limping?"

Maggie chugged a glass of orange juice before she rasped, "Because I've got a bruise the size of Texas." She pulled open the front of her floor-length robe, showing off a large black-and-deep-purple patch on the outside of her thigh.

Grammy gasped. "Lord, child, what happened to you?"

"Scott kicked me."

"He *what*?" Grammy's blood turned icy.

"He had to. The fire was spreading."

"What fire?"

"In the barn last night."

"The barn!" Grammy rushed to the window, afraid to find her connection with Lawrence had turned to ashes overnight. It was still standing, though. "Lord almighty, girl," she said with her hand over her heart, "don't scare me like that."

Maggie limped to the table, rekindling Grammy's anger. And here she'd been cooking sausage links for that bum!

Hmph. "Sit down. I'll make us some breakfast while you explain just how you got hurt."

"I need coffee first."

With little sleep behind her, Maggie couldn't find the energy to explain anything without caffeine. Grammy set a steaming mug of coffee in front of her, along with a gelled ice bag. That figured. She might play old and helpless when she wanted her way, but she'd do anything for someone in pain.

"I still think his license plate stands for some kind of demon," Grammy groused.

"Speed demon," Maggie acknowledged.

"You said Spider-Man."

"I was trying to calm you down."

Maggie settled in the chair knowing that, in twenty minutes, she'd be more alert and her thigh would be numb. Then she could talk. Then she could *think*. After breakfast, she'd hunt up her old reference book on ghosts, because Pop had to go, today, before somebody got seriously hurt.

Something nagged at her, though. She'd forgotten to do something; she just couldn't remember what. All the commotion last night, the fire in the barn, Scott carrying her in his arms. His chest solid and hard against her. His arms solid and strong around her.

Yum.

Shoot, she'd forgotten to listen to Kevin's message.

And he hadn't called to wish her a good morning, so he must be really mad. That wasn't nearly as upsetting as it would have been two days ago.

"Morning, ladies," Scott boomed as he entered the kitchen with a lively step.

The screwdriver in his hand was barely a blip on Maggie's radar screen as the twinkle in his eyes rivaled the dimple for her attention. A man had no right to look that good in the morning when she felt this crappy. Especially one as virile as he. It wasn't fair.

"How's that look today?" The twinkle was a sure sign that Scott was hoping for more show than tell as he plucked the ice bag off her leg.

Maggie yanked it out of his hand and put it back.

Grammy poked him in the ribs with the fork.

Scott jumped away from both of them, moving pretty fast for a guy with a broken leg. He backed toward the door, studying them suspiciously, keeping a particularly close eye on the fork. "Maybe I'd better come back later."

"Did you need something?" Maggie asked, covering a yawn.

"Garlic. I just remembered that Ruby said it's good for repelling ghosts."

That woke her up a little. "You talked to Ruby?"

"Yeah, she came home last night. We had a snack and sat up late talking about a lot of things. She suggested putting a clove or two in my pocket."

No snide comments about how Ruby dressed, no

snicker when he said her name. Maggie was intrigued. Grammy even lowered her fork, but she still glared at him before she returned to the skillet. And she kept an eye on him.

"Mm, sure smells good in here." Scott inched his way back into the room with a lot less overt enthusiasm.

"What's the screwdriver for?"

"Oh, I found a lock in the barn. Old, but perfectly good. And I thought since you ladies insist on leaving the key to the walk-out outside, you might like a little security up here." His gaze rested on Maggie when he said, "I found everything else I needed in the *tool* room."

Sure enough, there was a deadbolt on the cellar door. Maggie waited to see if that earned Scott some points back from Grammy, but she was holding firm.

"Have some coffee," Maggie offered, wishing he'd made it.

"Thanks. I could smell it all the way upstairs."

"And tell us more about Ruby."

Scott lifted a couple of cookies from Mother Goose, fixed a mug for himself, and topped off Maggie's before taking the chair closest to her. That put his back to Grammy, which, under the circumstances, Maggie thought pretty brave.

"My buddies are coming to help today," he said. "Did you invite any of your friends? I'm just asking because when I brought this up yesterday, you never mentioned anybody."

"They have jobs." She used to talk to Kelly and Stacie every day, but time had slipped away in the past year or so. "You were telling us about Ruby."

"Oh yeah. She got in, oh, about twelve-thirty or one, I guess. She was getting a snack together when I came in from taking a walk."

"In the middle of the night?" Grammy scoffed.

Maggie mimed smoking; Grammy nodded that she understood.

"I wish. Your raccoon ripped up the whole pack before I could get to it."

"Did she scare you?" Grammy asked.

"She sure as hell did." Scott chuckled, not with humor, but in relief that he'd escaped unharmed. "You people need bodyguards around here. Mask, claws, evil damn eyes. I'm surprised the dogs let her be." He shuddered.

Grammy pulled a rolling pin from the drawer. The ice bag thudded to the floor as Maggie jumped between it and Scott's head.

"He meant the raccoon!"

Startled, Scott studied them over his shoulder. "Of course I meant the raccoon. Who'd you think I meant?"

"Some people make fun of Ruby," Maggie explained.

"Hey, she's okay. Nice kid. Her designs are really sexy, but her taste in food's a little strange." His shudder appeared genuine. "Some cucumber-yogurt thing. With sprouts."

Grammy settled into silent, if wary, approval. She

probably wouldn't poke Scott with the fork again anytime soon, but Maggie wasn't giving the rolling pin
back, just to be safe. Grammy might not like Ruby's
Goth getups, but she took it to heart when other people
judged her for it.

"Anyway, we got to talking about me and the ghost,
and she says there's a book around here about how to
live with them or get rid of them. I sure as hell hope
it's not out in the barn. All she could remember was the
garlic remedy."

"We don't have garlic," Grammy said decisively.

"Sure we—" Maggie began.

"No garlic."

"But we always have—"

Grammy banged the fork on the edge of the skillet,
repeatedly, making quite a racket until Maggie gave up.
"Scott's going to help me talk to my Lawrence, and then
maybe we'll have garlic. Not before."

Scott squirmed in his chair. "Well, I'm afraid that puts
us in a bad place, because Coop's afraid to talk to either of you before we find his 'Cuda, and I can't force
him."

"Afraid?" Grammy said. "Of what?"

"He thinks he's supposed to tell you something."

"Oh! I knew it, I just *knew* it."

"But he's afraid he'll disappear to wherever ghosts go
when they're done here, and he doesn't want to leave
until he sees the engine back in his 'Cuda. You raised
one stubborn sonofabitch, Grammy."

"Don't I know it."

"We can't afford to wait," Maggie said. Couldn't afford to have Pop hanging around, playing with fire. What was to stop him from doing more damage? What if he got it in his mind to mess with something else, like someone's brakes? No two ways about it, he was dangerous and had to go. Today.

Grammy drew herself up tall and straight. "You two leave my Lawrence alone, you hear? Find that car he wants so bad. And when you do, if he still won't talk to me, I'll have it hauled to a junkyard."

Scott choked on his coffee.

"They'll turn it into a pancake. I'll pay them if I have to."

"Oh, Pop won't like that," Maggie warned. "He won't like that at all." Scott's life would never be the same. Heck, *her* life would never be the same.

"Damn, Grammy," Scott said in awe. "You're one tough broad—and I mean that in the nicest way."

Grammy tipped her chin in acknowledgment. "Be sure you tell him what I said. Every word."

"Hallelujah! Yes, ma'am." Scott jumped to his feet, rubbing his hands together in anticipation.

Now that Scott's attention was focused elsewhere, Maggie was more than a little surprised to feel pangs of—what?—jealousy? That was just stupid, really, because Pop was dead and she was here.

But as Scott ran out the door without a backward glance, Maggie wished he were running toward her.

 *Chapter 8*

"Good Lord," Ike said as he and Maggie picked their way back to the big sliding door that afternoon.

The rail-thin, white-haired auctioneer wasn't commenting on the three bikers who'd arrived a few minutes ago, wearing dark visored helmets, black leather jackets and chaps, and heavy boots. Grammy'd charged out onto the back porch, shotgun in hand, but backed off when Scott hugged one and shook hands with the other two. They'd retreated to the barn, discussing how to cover the most ground in the least amount of time in their quest to find one Lemon Twist auto body. It wasn't as if it could be hidden in a box. Then again, it couldn't be anywhere but on the bottom of a pile, either.

Instead, Ike's comment referred to the dusty, mildewy, two-hour perusal of both barns.

"You certainly have a lot of collectibles. I've been in the business four decades, and I've never seen such an extensive collection."

"It's me, Ike," Maggie replied in a dry tone. "We had tuna sandwiches in the kitchen, remember?"

He puffed on an inhaler, his only defense against years of dust and mildew. "Okay, what I can see is eighty percent junk."

"I think you're being generous."

"It's hard to tell when so much is boxed up. You still don't collect anything?"

"Nope. Still doesn't make any sense to me."

Ike plucked the small *Titanic* nameplate off a box. "This could be off one of the lifeboats."

"Or not."

"If it is, it could bring about ten grand."

Ike handed it to Maggie, who looked at it with an odd mixture of hope and reality. So, something in here might be worth more than a few hundred bucks. "That'd be good news. Maybe after expenses, Ruby'll get that new car she needs."

"Any idea what Grammy paid for it?" Ike laid the nameplate on a box.

"Nothing." Maggie debated the wisdom of this, but she finally explained Pop's penchant for collecting. And delivering. "Don't look at me like that. It's all true."

"Why didn't you tell me years ago?"

"Please, I was sixteen and trying to appear professional. I didn't think 'I want to sell everything my dead father is collecting' met the criteria." When Ike didn't reply, Maggie got a little worried and said, "What? Is something wrong?"

Ike led the way back toward his van. "I hate to tell you this, Maggie, but I don't have the staff to handle this size account right away."

"It's the ghost thing, isn't it? I knew I shouldn't have—" Maggie didn't bother to finish; Ike was laughing.

"Oh, Maggie, I've dealt with ghosts before. No, it's

not that. This is a big job. A *big* job. I hope you're not in a hurry."

"Actually, I am."

"Well, I'd rather not do this, but I can recommend another house."

"I don't want someone else. But I have it on pretty good authority that there's a classic car in there somewhere, and I need to start moving stuff so I can get to it."

"Your good authority is your father?"

Maggie nodded.

"That's why Scotty Templeton's here?"

"Yep." Maggie cocked her head and looked at her old mentor in a new light. "I didn't know you were a racing fan."

"You were so mad at your father years ago, I was afraid to mention it."

She toed a clump of spring grass. "Sorry."

Ike smiled indulgently. "We were all teenagers once. How about I check the schedule and get back to you?"

Scott and the bikers could be heard calling to one another in the barn.

"In the meantime, seems as if you have lots of help, so how about I lend you a warehouse and see what I can do about scheduling?"

Scott stepped back to examine a medium-sized box, wishing he could check every side of it, but in this jam-packed barn, that was the exception, not the norm. Years of dust clung to it, but under that, he could see it originally had contained a toaster oven. Odds were, it didn't now. He kicked it—with his boot, not his open-toed cast—and jumped back.

Daryl, an old high school buddy, backhanded Jeremy on the shoulder and said, "What the hell's the matter with your brother? I've been stacking boxes nice and neat, and what's he doing? Kicking things."

"Something rattled," Scott said in his own defense.

He had to admit, though, for a guy carrying an extra thirty pounds and wearing a stupid red bandana tied around the top of his head, Daryl had accomplished a lot already. He had a knack for knowing where to start and what to move. And then what to put on top of that. He didn't just move a pile, he selected boxes from here and there and built a wall solid enough to lean on. An engineer at heart; who knew?

"You mean rattled, as in broken china?" Daryl asked.

"I mean as in a rattlesnake."

"Man, how many rattlesnakes you ever heard?"

"Hey, there was one once in the infield."

"*Viperidae victimae.*" Bruce strode around the edge of Daryl's wall like a longshoreman with a large box on each shoulder. At least he wore gloves, but any fool carting boxes that close to his neck ought to be in something more spiderproof than a Harley-Davidson T-shirt.

Daryl snorted. "*Reptilus flatus.*"

Latin scholars they weren't, but back in high school, they'd been hot for a couple of Catholic girls. They hadn't gotten the girls, and the Latin suffered, but maybe it helped them both through law school.

"It was *alive*," Scott snarled.

"Yeah," Bruce agreed. "Before it was run over."

"Hey, it rattled. You know, if something crawls out of one of those boxes and bites you on the neck, you're driving yourself to the emergency room."

"If something bites me on the neck, you're out one donkey. In fact, I'm having serious doubts there's a 'Cuda in here at all."

"You mean he lied to us?" Daryl asked.

"My information is that's it's here," Scott said.

"Your information comes from a dead guy."

Bruce stopped working and stared at Scott. If this wasn't Speed Cooper's barn and at least *likely* to have a 'Cuda in it, he wouldn't have stayed to begin with. Now it was beginning to look as if he might desert and take Daryl with him.

"Maybe we need to negotiate a trade," Bruce proposed, which wasn't as bad as Scott had feared. You never knew what a lawyer could come up with.

"Beer," Daryl suggested.

"Women," Jeremy said.

"Even better, my time for yours," Bruce said.

"*Our* time," Daryl corrected.

"Yeah, our time."

"Looks like you got a rebellion on your hands, big brother." Jeremy looked more amused than sympathetic.

Scott needed these guys and about twenty more gearheads. Or a ride off the property. They'd probably hold him up for one of his cars. Resigned, he said, "What do you have in mind?"

"What d'ya think, Daryl?"

"Quid pro quo, man."

"Yeah, just what I was thinking. Scott, ol' buddy, we have a proposition for you. How about, in exchange for us working here with you, you spend an evening with us at Gateway?"

Gateway International was the racetrack across the river. It had everything Scott missed. The noise. The smells. The action. *Team owners.*

Scott narrowed his eyes, sensing a trap. "You can take that much time off?"

"We own the firm."

"We have *flunkies*," Daryl added with a big grin.

"So what's the catch?"

"No catch. We run an outreach program to get illegal street racers off the streets and onto the track. Trouble is, we're not reaching enough of them. Having the famous Scotty Templeton on board could be a good draw."

"It's a long way from street racing to endurance racing," Scott said realistically.

"Can't hurt."

Maybe he could slip away without the ghost noticing. "You going tonight?"

Bruce grinned. "Tomorrow soon enough for you?"

"All *right*. Let's get back to work then, shall we?" Scott rubbed his hands together briskly, anticipating his return to the track, not sure who'd made the better deal.

He returned to the work at hand, his mind neither on what he was doing nor marveling that his friends had matured into responsible citizens, but on how soon he could sway a team owner to give him another chance.

He'd completely forgotten why he was kicking boxes until the rattle startled him to full attention.

"There, did you hear that?" He searched over his shoulder for corroborating witnesses. Instead he got Jeremy with a bemused expression on his face. "You heard it, right? It's a snake."

"*Christ*. Move over." Jeremy shouldered his way past him and nudged each of the boxes until he found the one that rattled. He dragged it to an open spot and tore it open.

"Careful," Scott warned.

The fool kid stuck his hand in without looking first. He snatched it back out fast enough, though.

"Uh-huh, see what I'm saying," Scott said, feeling somewhat vindicated. Even Bruce and Daryl were curious and stepped closer to watch. "You guys don't know the things I've seen prowling around here. Big things. Hairy things. Critters with claws and teeth."

Jeremy plunged his hand back into the box, snatching it out several times, timing his moves, jumping around, circling the carton for the best vantage point, hoping to present himself as a difficult target. If he kept at it, Scott was going to have to step in just to save the idiot.

"Maybe you'd better leave it," Scott warned.

"Wait, wait, I almost got it."

"What the hell is it?"

"*Arachnid fierceus*," Bruce said, which made Daryl snicker and come back with "*Homo sapiens wussus*."

Scott said, "Close it back up. We'll take it out to the woods and open it there."

Jeremy paused, hand arched in mid-air before making his final grab for the snake.

Scott muttered, "Oh, damn," hooked his cast around his brother's leg, and took him down for his own good.

"No, wait, I almost got it." On hands and knees, Jeremy lunged across Scott's legs for the box.

Scott tackled him and crawled over him to get there first. He began to rethink the wisdom of cutting off his arm cast when a sharp pain stabbed through his wrist, slowing him down just enough that his kid brother got the upper hand—now there was a first—and grabbed the box. He stuck his hand in again.

"Got it! Careful, careful, everyone back." Withdrawing his fist, Jeremy twisted and lunged at Scott, who was still hanging on to him. "Gotcha!"

Jeremy held his prey aloft and guffawed like a man who'd had too many beers already today, then shook it—in reality, a small bubble gum machine—so hard that the balls rattled against the glass jar with sharp cracks.

It was a stupid toy; the kind you'd buy for a kid at a heritage theme park because it was a handmade pine base with a Mason jar and it demonstrated how people amused themselves before MTV. Scott glared at his kid brother, snatched the toy away from him, smashed the jar on his cast, and proceeded to feed him dried-up gum balls. It wasn't easy; he got as much dirt in Jeremy's mouth as anything else. They rolled around on the floor, tumbling over and over, six-year-olds at heart.

"You fight like a girl," Scott said, laughing. Not a very original insult, but it was the only kind he'd hurl at his brother since their grandmother had whipped them both for calling each other *pussy* and *dickhead*.

Jeremy was doing a pretty good job of reciprocating with the gum balls, nearly shoving one into Scott's mouth while he was jeering. They got all tangled up, arms and legs wrapped around each other, dirtier than they were clean. Nothing slowed them down until they tumbled against a pair of trim black boots.

"You boys having fun with the antiques?"

Scott craned his neck to get a view of Maggie, hands on hips, staring down at them. In his favor, he had his little brother pinned. "Well, I—"

"He's trying to kill me," Jeremy growled. Taking advantage of the distraction, he threw Scott over and regained the top.

"You no good little—" While Scott was getting tired and his arm wasn't holding up too well, he did manage to save face in front of Maggie by toppling his brother over once more, setting him firmly on the bottom. He held him there with his forearm on his neck. "Had enough?"

Jeremy croaked, "No," and was struggling to one-up him once again—yeah, like that would happen—when Maggie landed firmly in the middle of Scott's back and said, "Enough!"

More air whooshed out of Jeremy than him, so that shut Jeremy up and held him still long enough for Scott to enjoy Maggie straddling him from behind. Now if he could only figure out how to flip over without dislodging her.

Jeremy kept struggling to upset the balance of power. Maggie's palms landed on Scott's shoulder blades. Her added weight gave his sore arm a break and kept Jeremy pinned.

"You're not getting up until you both promise to quit breaking things."

"Help me out here," Scott whispered in Jeremy's ear, hoping for a little mercy. "To the left on three."

"Wait—"

"*My* left. Three."

It wasn't smooth and pretty, but Maggie did end up beneath Scott, and he did manage to get prone on top of her.

"Ow," Maggie breathed, pushing against Scott's chest.

Sensitive to the fact that no woman would want a man between her legs with his buddies looking on, Scott maneuvered to the side, though he kept his casted leg thrown over one of hers. No sense giving up everything. To her credit, Maggie neither wrapped her free leg around him in ecstasy nor rudely dug the heel of her boot into the back of his thigh to hamstring him.

Instead she rubbed the side of her head. "What did I hit?"

Scott tossed the pine base aside, leaned on his elbows, and murmured, "Better let me check."

He stripped off his glove and edged a bare hand beneath her softer one, cupping her head as Jeremy and the guys got bored and wandered off. Maggie's hair was as silky as it looked, so fine and straight that golden strands slid beneath his palm and wisped through his fingers. She didn't close her eyes, sigh with pleasure, or do any of the things that, in his experience, indicated he was making headway.

"Is this working?" he whispered, easing his body higher up hers. Enjoying every inch of her along the way.

Maggie held Scott's gaze quizzically and slowly shook her head. He hoped like hell that was an invitation for stronger medicine.

"Maybe this then."

He might race cars hell-bent for the checkered flag, but Scott had learned long ago that women didn't appreciate speed the same way men did. To them, anticipation was an aphrodisiac. He took his time. He admired the golden specks in her green eyes as he leaned in ever so slowly and finally pressed his lips near her temple. Gently, but not tentatively.

"You're off target, Templeton."

He grinned involuntarily, a sure sign that he was starting to like sassy. "Patience. I'll find it."

He soothed her with butterfly kisses in that oh-so-sensitive spot right next to the eye. He trailed them down her cheek, his lips caressing skin that not only looked as smooth and flawless as a supermodel's, it was. This was no cover girl beneath him, though. No skin and bones here. Maggie was as delectable to pin as she had been to watch. She'd be a real handful, when he got that far.

Down, boy. Anticipation.

Thinking about what his hands would be full of was not conducive to *slow*, so Scott corralled his thoughts and nibbled the corner of her lips. He followed with his best kiss, noninsistent yet hungry, guaranteed to melt the toughest woman into puddles of longing. Right on schedule, Maggie's eyes fluttered closed. Right on target, Scott moved in, wrapping himself around her, pulling her close, enveloping her, cuddling her. Finally her lips moved softly, tentatively beneath his.

Yes!

He sensed a need in her, a deep, indefinable yearning. Not a simple *want*. Not a *desire*. Those he could fix; just give him thirty minutes. No, this was something more basic, almost as necessary as breathing, but he couldn't put his finger on it.

And he wanted to.

Christ, he'd never tried to make love to a woman and think at the same time. He wasn't sure it was even possible.

Maggie's lips moved beneath his. Her kiss grew stronger, more insistent, hotter—

And then she sputtered. Or spit—he wasn't sure.

"Geez, what *is* that?" she complained.

Scott was about to defend his technique when he noticed the streak of grime running from her temple to her mouth. A band of brown and pink. Gritty looking. It couldn't have come from anywhere but him.

Hell.

Licking her lips, Maggie sputtered again. She stared at his face. "What've you been doing, eating the barn floor?"

He swiped at his own cheek and came back with a

smear of brown dirt and crumbled up colored gum balls; definitely gritty. Trying to salvage the closeness he'd built between them, he licked the tip of one finger and made little tasting sounds.

"Cherry?"

Maggie laughed at his noises and pushed against his chest. "Eat all you want. We used to keep pigs in here."

Hoping to rescue the mood, Scott rolled off and wiped his face with both sleeves. "How's that?"

"As long as you don't intend to get your face anywhere near mine, it's fine."

Scott sighed. He needed water, and spitting on his sleeve to wash his face just wasn't going to cut it. Besides, the ghost was closing in, his face set in stone.

"Might as well come meet the guys then."

"Oh, not just yet." Maggie sat up and held out her cell phone. "I forgot to call Kevin back last night and, well, you're supposed to be helping me, so I thought you should listen to his message first."

 *Chapter 9*

At one minute to five on Thursday, Maggie's cell phone broke the calm in the barn with a lively chirp. She went from a sane woman with an armful of collectibles to a novice juggler who suddenly had too many items in the air. Breakable items. Possibly valuable items.

She crouched. She grabbed. She shuffled. Everything was saved, her thigh throbbed where it was bruised, and still she managed to check caller ID.

Area code: *Chicago.*

She'd been on pins and needles waiting to hear back from Personnel before her week off was completely used up. Her reputation was impeccable, her clients couldn't be happier, and she had a killer résumé, but as careers went, canceling that interview at the last minute was suicidal.

She landed on her butt on the dirt floor and still pulled off a professional, competent "Maggie Cooper." No wonder they paid her so much.

She felt nothing but relief and anticipation as Sharon in Personnel identified herself. She wouldn't be calling if it wasn't good news.

"We spoke earlier," Sharon said. "The interview team is reassembling in four weeks."

Not exactly on fire to meet her, Maggie noted, vacillating between irritation and relief as she committed the pertinent details to memory. Four weeks from yesterday. Seven A.M. She glanced at her wrist out of habit; no watch to orient her as to the current date. Where'd she leave it *this* time?

"You should know, we don't often reschedule." Sharon was about as warm as a Midwest hailstorm. "This is ample notice. Mr. Frye *strongly* suggests you not miss this again."

"I'll be there."

Wild horses wouldn't keep her away. She'd drive up a day early. Wait, she'd already tried that. She'd drive up two days early. Kevin wouldn't mind. Scott had been half right about apologizing; she'd tried it and Kevin had forgiven her, but he hadn't apologized back.

"Your interview?" Scott asked.

"Four weeks." That'd put her at Kevin's overnight. Why did that feel less than perfect?

She could go into the office tomorrow to offset an extra day, but then she looked at Scott and she didn't want to go back early. Geez, how fickle was that? She and Kevin were a *couple*. They had a history, for God's sake. Before he'd been hired away and moved to Chicago two months ago, she'd had a key to his condo. Grammy'd quit expecting her to call when she spent the night out. China patterns had taken on new importance.

"Sorry my being here's messed things up for you, interview wise. I was thinking, maybe if I autographed some copies of my book for you to take to the committee, it'd help smooth things over? I can write a personal apology in each one."

"I don't know if they even like racing."

"Doesn't matter. A signed copy of a book impresses the hell out of people. If they're not into racing, they'll put it on their desk and use it to impress clients who are. I can get some passes to Indy, too . . . autographed photos for their walls . . . whatever you think'll win them back over to your side, just name it."

Maggie would have teased him about having a big ego, except he wasn't exaggerating. People used to push and shove just to get near Pop. They'd been downright rude if they thought they could get their picture snapped standing next to him. Oh, and what they wouldn't do to get one with their arm around his shoulders!

So instead of some snappy comeback, she said, "Thanks. I'm sure they'd like that." After all, putting "I'm sorry" into writing—in a book that was likely to be passed around for lots of people to witness, or on a photo that would grace an office wall for years to come—wasn't something lightly given.

Scott took a swig out of a water bottle and wiped his mouth with the back of his hand. He noticed her staring at him. No points there; it was pretty obvious. He held out the bottle. "Want some?"

Maggie started to say no, but after yesterday's fiasco, drinking from the same bottle might mend any hard feelings; a picture-is-a-thousand-words way of saying, *Okay, so you don't disgust me.* So she did.

"Sorry about spitting at you yesterday."

Scott grinned, flashing his dimple. "My fault entirely."

"It was nothing personal."

He stepped closer. "Can't say the same for my actions."

Whew, was it hot in here or what?

"I've been thinking about going over to Gateway tonight," Scott said. "What say we make it a celebration? In honor of getting your interview."

Maggie laughed, thinking only a gearhead would equate going to a track with celebrating. "Sorry, I'm fresh out of mosquito repellent."

Scott looked a little puzzled and scratched the back of his neck. "Is that some new polite way of saying you'd rather spend the evening with your girlfriends? Or washing your hair? Because if it is, okay, I get it, especially if it's friends. But if it's not, here's the deal."

She wasn't at all swayed by Scott's ensuing explanation of Bruce and Daryl's outreach program to get illegal street racers into legal drag racing.

"Praise it all you want," she said. "But I remember the days when we called that place The Swamp."

Scott leaned close; Maggie almost missed what he said, and not just because he was whispering, either. "So if you're free, I thought we could discuss you-know-what on the drive over."

They couldn't very well sit in the barn and plan how to oust Pop; he could be sitting on their shoulders and they wouldn't know. Sometimes she smelled his pipe tobacco, sometimes she didn't. They couldn't discuss it in the house, either; if Grammy knew they weren't patiently waiting for Pop to answer her questions, there'd be hell to pay.

But the racetrack?

"I don't know." While she didn't care to ever see a track again, she was pretty sure she wanted to spend more time with Scott. "I thought you couldn't leave," she said, buying more time to think it over.

"My truck won't run. We'll take your car."

"And, um, you know . . ."

"He's keeping a close eye on Jeremy and Ruby at the moment." Scott's low chuckle told Maggie that anything that made Pop unhappy made Scott happy. "So now would be a good time."

"But I've been working out here all day. I'm filthy."

"Yeah, a racetrack is such a clean place."

Maggie sighed. Did she really want to tag along and talk ghostbusting just to get ignored once they got there? Once Scott got near high-powered engines and burning rubber, well, she knew men and cars. She'd been *weaned* on men and cars.

Scott treated Maggie to dinner at a nearby Steak n Shake, then they hit the highway headed east—*hit* being the operative word.

"Anybody ever tell you you drive like a crazy woman?"

Maggie'd found the ghost book that morning, and Scott thumbed through it now with slow deliberation, as if he rode with low-flying pilots every day. He had all he could do not to grip the dashboard and scream.

Amused, Maggie turned her head and looked at him.

"Eyes on the road! Eyes on the road!"

"Geez, do all race car drivers have these control issues?"

"I don't know—how many have ridden with you?"

"Two so far, and I have to tell you, Pop was a lot better passenger."

"You probably paid more attention to the speed limit with him on board." The hell with it; he gripped the dash. If he wasn't careful, he'd start roaring at her the way the team owner did at him. Thank God she was at least a *good* driver. "Wait a minute, didn't your dad die before you turned sixteen?"

Maggie winked. "No cops on racetracks."

She was cute when she smiled. Too cute; Scott almost forgot his life was in danger. Almost forgot the two double steakburgers and chocolate malt cartwheeling in his stomach.

"You ever wonder what it'd be like to open her up all the way?" he asked.

"Sure, but there's nowhere here to do that."

"Yeah, this isn't a *racetrack*," he said pointedly.

"You're very tense, aren't you?"

"I'm about to *die*."

"Oh, you are not. Calm down and quit leaving dents in my dash."

He forced himself to release it.

"Seat gap," Maggie said next.

Scott eased himself back in the seat.

"There, isn't that better?"

"No."

"Maybe if we talk."

"No!—pay *attention* to the *road.*"

"I can do both." Her phone *ka-ching*ed. "Hello?"

"Bull*shit,*" Scott said. He yanked the headset out of Maggie's ear and barked, "She'll call you back," into it before he tossed it into the glove box. She glanced at caller ID to see who it was, and he grabbed her phone and threw it in, too.

"That was my mom."

"Then she'll understand."

"Well. Okay."

What more *could* she do? Fight him for it while she was driving? Obviously she had more sense than that. At least when he crashed on a track, he was in a well-built car, strapped into a custom-fitted seat, and covered head to toe in fire-retardant underwear. With an ambulance on hand.

"So," she said. "What'd you find in the book that we can try?"

He stared at the book, reorienting himself to the possibility of life after riding with Maggie, then opened it to a random page.

"*'Ask the ghost to leave,'*" he read. "Yeah, right. Been there, done that. Moving on. Oh, here's something. *'One tried and true method of getting rid of a ghost that you don't want in your home is to toss rice all over the kitchen floor before you go to bed at night.'*"

Maggie snorted. "You don't want to mess with Grammy over her floor."

"Wait a minute, let me finish. *'Your bothersome ghost will pause to count the grains of rice.'*"

"Why?"

"Hush. *'Ghosts aren't very good at counting, so yours will repeatedly lose track and have to start over again.'*"

Maggie started laughing, but Scott kept reading.

"*'Simply sweep up the grains of rice in the morning, and repeat the next night until your ghost gives up and leaves.'* How will this work? Coop doesn't even come in the house."

"How will it work *period*?"

Maggie was right; throwing rice on the floor to confuse Coop was downright stupid. Now gears, maybe . . .

But why the hell would a ghost stop to count something? He turned the page at the same time the windshield-mounted radar detector beeped and flashed a text message. Maggie slowed down; Scott took a welcome breath.

"Okay, let's try another," he said, more relaxed now that they were going the speed limit. "*'One surefire way to repel a ghost is to paint the door to your house red.'* Where'd you get this book? The whole damn barn is red brick."

"Maybe the author never ran into a color-blind ghost. Next."

"I'm skipping ahead. Let's see what other 'tried and true' and 'surefire' ways there are. *'Reacting to a ghost provides it with energy and makes it more powerful. A vital step in ridding your home of a ghost is to decrease its energy. Do not recognize its presence. Do not react to any noises or appearances that it makes. Do not talk to it or even about it.'* Yeah, this is good. Coop hates it when I ignore him."

"There must be something more proactive that we can do."

Scott turned another page. "Graveyards—oh, *this* oughta be good." He read to himself at first because he was tired of reading dumb stuff aloud. "Listen," he said after a few sentences. "I think I found one. This sounds doable."

"'Bout time." Maggie checked the radar detector display and her mirrors, then said, "Here we go."

Out of habit, Scott also checked the display. "Hey, I thought you said your radar detector was a piece of crap."

"That's my new one. You like it?"

"It's just like—" Three hundred fifty dollars was *not* a piece of crap. "It's *mine*."

"You owed me, remember?"

"So you stole it?"

Scott wasn't sure which was more distracting, Maggie's devilish smile or the way she hammered the gas and said, "Hang on."

The Swamp had grown into a full-fledged international raceway when Maggie wasn't looking.

Pop never drag raced, but he'd known a lot of guys who did, and since he had a knack with engines and transmissions, many of them let him experiment on theirs. Long before she reached ten, Maggie figured out that "going to the track with Pop" didn't really include Pop, whether it was the quarter mile or the oval. Didn't mean she didn't hope things would change, though. He was there; she was there; he might actually trip over her in the pit and notice her someday.

Never happened.

Back then, Gateway was a simple drag strip with a nightclub on the far side. While it had grown up and joined the rest of the racing world, it was still near the river, still pocketed in mosquito-breeding wetlands.

Maggie doused herself with repellent and offered the bottle to Scott.

"It's *April*," he said, as if it was too early in the year for the little monsters.

"Uh-huh."

"You live with coyotes, raccoons, God knows what else—hey, by the way, you owe me a pack of smokes—and you're worried about a few tiny insects?"

"Tiny?" she scoffed. "These are *Illinois* mosquitoes. If you're not going to use it, hand it over. Any bites I get swell up like marbles."

Scott dabbed a few drops on his neck and arms. If Maggie were a bloodsucking insect, she'd land on him anyway.

"Mosquitoes don't like smoke," he said. "Maybe you should stand downwind of the burnout."

"Oh, goody. A picnic for my lungs."

Drivers routinely wet their tires before a race, then spun them on the track, building heat, making them sticky. While it meant better traction, it put out great mounds of vile smoke. Years of that produced a lingering, burning rubber stink that tickled Maggie's nose and dredged up old memories. She pushed them aside.

"I forgot my pen," Scott said, looking around the nearly empty lot.

She thought she must have heard wrong. "You have a special pen?"

"Hey, I won it. People like getting autographs with a championship pen."

"Championship *pen*? What'd you win—a Soap Box Derby when you were eleven?"

"Ten, but that's beside the point." Scott's gaze was playful and as soft as a caress, warming Maggie in spite of the chilly breeze. "What can I say? I hang on to things."

"You don't have two barns back home full of crap, do you?" If he did, she'd break her no-speaking-to-Pop rule and beg him to send Scott packing.

"No."

Talk about déjà vu—a second after they were spotted, Maggie was elbowed aside by two dozen teens in jeans and tees in their quest to surround Scott. They were mostly of driving age, vying to meet him, shake his hand, get his autograph, *any*thing. It was pure redundancy when Bruce spoke over the commotion to make a formal introduction.

"Here he is, just like I promised. Scotty Templeton, winner of three championships and last year's Rolex 24."

A husky, buzz-cut teen in grease-stained khakis grabbed Scott's wrist and held it aloft so everyone could admire the championship watch.

"Bet you wouldn't sell it," someone said.

"I'm aiming to collect them," Scott answered with a competitive wink.

Maggie groaned to herself. On the plus side, he'd spent several days in the barn and hadn't mentioned ever collecting one thing in there, so maybe it was only really expensive trophy watches he wanted.

Bruce clowned a dejected look as he, too, was elbowed aside. "Did I mention we went to high school together?" It earned him a couple of grins.

Maggie knew how it felt to get overlooked. She started to empathize, but amazingly, Bruce just let it roll off.

"Okay, here's what I thought we'd do," Daryl announced. "Since some of you are going to race for the first time tomorrow evening, we'll cover the start again, get you comfortable with the Christmas tree, get questions out of the way, and then Scotty can take over. You can ask him anything you want about any aspect of racing. Sound good?"

Just as she'd thought, Maggie would be left to amuse herself. She got a few curious glances from the girls, but other than that, she was just someone who'd come along for the ride, someone who had a dozen years on them, plus a diploma, a degree, and a profession. In other words, a totally grown-up and boring adult. Might as well go back to the car and return her mom's call.

"Hey, before we start," Scott said to the teens, "I know

some of you are here just to watch your friends, but if you're at all interested in this sport, the lady with me is Maggie Cooper." He extended his arm toward her; a dozen curious stares followed. "She grew up in racing. Her father was Speed Cooper."

Maggie's gaze searched out Scott's, wondering if he was as impressed by knowing Pop as he sounded. From the slow, seductive glow in his eye when their gazes met, she'd say not. In fact, he looked as if Pop and this crowd were the furthest things from his mind right now and she was the most important person there.

It was unsettling. Sweet, though. Too bad for him, dropping Pop's name didn't get much reaction, let alone enthusiasm.

"He had more championships than I do," he added.

Okay, there was some interest, from guys and girls alike, though it was the latter who stared at her the longest. It'd be rude to go back to the car now, so Maggie resigned herself to hanging around a track one more time.

The dozen nonracers who'd come along to watch scattered in small groups over three of the bleacher seats by the start line, while the racers slated to run in the next day's event delved into the preliminaries: the ins and outs of tech inspection and obtaining armbands.

"Good grief, we'll be here all night." The young woman beside Maggie pulled her dark hair into a ponytail, then reached into the cooler on wheels at her feet. "I'm Alyce. Want a Dr. Pepper? I have plenty." For a teenager, she assessed Maggie with a very old-soul gaze.

"Yeah, thanks."

From there, Alyce handled general introductions, but Maggie still felt like the outsider she was because no one else had much to say—not to her, anyway. The teens huddled in small groups and chatted among themselves, though they did make sure the bags of chips and pretzels made the rounds.

The first mosquitoes weren't shy. Within minutes, everyone was tipping sodas with one hand and swatting with the other, Maggie included, and all she could think was *Boy, Scott's going to be sorry he didn't apply more repellent when he had the chance.*

Salvatore, huddled with another boy two rows below Maggie, turned around and asked, "Is it true? Scotty collects cars? How many's he got?"

Great, someone trying to draw her in, and she hadn't a clue.

"We just met a few days ago," she said with an apologetic shrug. She didn't want to make the kid feel she was brushing off his interest. "Cars, huh?"

Scott a collector—well, that figured. What gearhead didn't see value in every spare part he got his hands on?

"Fifty, I bet," Salvatore said.

Clay shoved Salvatore's shoulder, the way guys do when they get their facts wrong. "Thirty. I read it in *People.*"

They stared up at Maggie again, as if she'd settle the argument.

"I'll ask."

Thirty? That was a fanatic, not a collector. Was she nuts to feel some interest in him?

Must be; she felt herself take an emotional step back before she could even decide whether she wanted to.

When the racers moved onto practice starts, the smell of fresh, burning rubber from a screaming burnout catapulted Maggie back to childhood. She wrinkled her nose.

"Look, my earplugs match my shirt," Amber bubbled with way too much cheerleader potential. She had the figure and the bouncy ponytail; all she needed were the pom-poms. She'd tagged along with her boyfriend to-night because that's what fifteen-year-old girls do when they date gearheads with licenses.

Amber's unrestrained enthusiasm vibrated through the whole seat, right over to Maggie, who lost track of the proceedings in front of her.

Thirty cars. At how much a vehicle? Buying a car didn't mean you got a whole one. Sometimes Pop just got a body, or a tranny, frame, engine, whatever. Some were to collect; some were for parts.

Maggie knew what she wanted in life. More impor-tant, she knew what she didn't want. Scott wasn't just another race car driver or a gearhead, both of which were bad enough.

No, he had to be a collector, too.

It was fortunate she'd come with him tonight. Her path was clear.

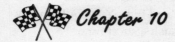

Chapter 10

There was only one way to get through the rest of the evening before Maggie drove Scott home and dumped him at his truck. Only one way to put him out of her mind, because sure as shooting, he kept creeping back in. Maggie turned her attention to the teens around her.

The boys were discussing the benefits of part-time jobs so they could afford to take dates to their proms; tickets, tuxes, and limos were just a small part of the expense. The girls took that as a challenge and loudly discussed the price of dresses, shoes, jewelry, and getting their hair done. Maggie bit her tongue about being able to support a third world country on the total, which she prayed was grossly overinflated.

Sunset came and went. The breeze kicked up and clouds hid the stars. They'd be lucky if it didn't storm before they left. On the plus side, the mosquitoes took a hike.

Maggie hunkered down for the duration, learning things about Scott as she watched the class. Things she was better off not knowing. She watched the kids bombard Scott with questions. They wanted to know all about endurance racing, how it affected the drivers as well as the cars, how many tires were allotted per race, what it was like to be on a team, and so on. He answered patiently; they listened attentively. It was clear they looked up to him. His friends respected him. You couldn't say much better about a man in such a short time.

Near the two-hour mark, Maggie grew restless and sore from sitting so long. Alyce passed around a huge pan of brownies.

"Anybody else?" Alyce asked after the pan had gone around once.

Maggie couldn't remember which name went with which girl, but the size two brunette in the hot-pink spandex top licked chocolate off her fingers and said, "Ooh, Matt's coming, gimme one for him. I swear," she said, laughing and shaking her head, "he is so tuned in to desserts."

A collective groan passed through the group.

"What she means," Alyce explained quietly to Maggie, "is that he's tuned in to *her* having dessert. Hey, isn't that Scotty in the car with Tim?"

At the starting line, Scott was, indeed, sliding into shotgun position in the near car. Maggie thought the poor guy had to be in serious racing withdrawal to climb into a vehicle with an inexperienced, lead-footed teenager.

The Christmas tree started its red-to-green blink sequence downward. Both cars rumbled loudly. When the final light glowed green, they surged forward, more or less together, the drivers displaying less than stellar reaction times but lots of eagerness.

Burning rubber, screeching tires, roaring engines—nothing had changed. There was the old familiar shudder, a deep rumble really, that centered in Maggie's chest, vibrated harder and harder against her ribs, then passed over her as the cars roared by on the other side of the fence. Not just a little vibration, either, like the planchette. This was a deep, thumping bass, so strong, so powerful, it was hard to imagine why it didn't shake human hearts out of rhythm.

Maggie'd never felt such a sensation anywhere but at a racetrack. And, darn, it felt just a little bit . . . *good*.

That just wasn't right. What was the matter with her? She'd hated trailing after Pop when she was a kid. She'd hated the long days and nights away from home. She wanted to ride her bike over to Kelly's or Stacie's house and play. She wanted to hang out at the public pool and get a killer tan. She wanted to go to camp and make key chains and beaded necklaces and hemp bracelets. But if they stayed home, there was no money for the thousand simple things all kids want to do. Pop had won championships, all right, but there were "investments" to pay off, and "deals" that couldn't be passed by.

A sudden swerve on the strip jerked Maggie's attention back to the two cars in front of her. Someone may have yelled—it was impossible to tell over the roar of the engines—but there was no mistaking Alyce's tense grip on Maggie's shoulder as the red car on the far side swerved toward Tim and nearly collided with his silver Celica. With Scott in it.

At these speeds, not a good idea. Tim overcorrected, nearly took out the fence, overcorrected *again*, and finally straightened it out.

Maggie let out her breath, surprised to have stopped breathing. As often as she'd seen similar drama over the years, it should've been as common as blinking. Must be because there was no crowd, no officials; more like street racing, but without interference by and dangers of normal traffic.

It couldn't have anything to do with Scott being in the car.

Well, sure, but just because she knew him, right? Not because she felt anything for him. Not because he'd tackled her and rolled on the floor with her and kissed her. And, oh God, what'd she done? She'd *spit*. How mature. But she'd apologized.

More important, so had he. Unlike Kermit.

Maggie reined in *those* thoughts as Alyce laughed and said, "I bet Tim was *so* nervous having Scotty in the car with him."

Maggie grinned, remembering Scott's white-knuckled ride with her, but she probably shouldn't share that.

In the excitement, Maggie hadn't been aware of Hot Pink getting up to meet her boyfriend, but now she was climbing back to her spot on the bleachers with her head down.

"Is she crying?" Alyce asked, her tone fiercely maternal and protective.

The tall, willowy girl next to Hot Pink nodded, then gave her a hug, which Maggie thought was sweet.

Unexpectedly, she felt a hole inside herself, as if her old girlfriends were missing. She felt a sudden urge to call them, but her phone was back in the car.

"That jerk," Alyce said. Maggie had no right to ask, but that didn't stop Alyce from explaining. "Every time he sees her eating, he warns her about getting fat."

"She wears a two, for God's sake," Amber bubbled.

"I don't care if she's a twenty-two, it's not right for him to say things like that." Alyce extended her leg and nudged Salvatore and Chuck with her foot.

"We told her before," Chuck said. "We've all told her."

"She's right," Salvatore said to Hot Pink. "Why do you put up with that?"

Hot Pink sniffed. "He's under a lot of pressure."

"See? She's never gonna get it," Chuck said.

Alyce booted him in the back of the head, then bumped shoulders with Maggie and said, "Scotty's looking for you."

Maggie's gaze darted to the well-lit track, certain that Alyce was grossly mistaken. No way that warm grin was for her, even if it did make her pulse skitter alarmingly. No way he could work the cars and still take time for her. A smile in this direction at this time could only mean there was something fantastic behind her, like a spare high-powered engine. Impulsively, stupidly, she checked over her shoulder.

Nothing but bare bleachers.

By the time she'd recovered enough to smile back at him—they could, after all, remain friends, right?—

the moment that could have been theirs was past. A pretty young girl jumped out of her car, launched herself onto Scott's chest, and darn near wrapped her legs around him.

"Your sister?" Maggie asked Amber.

"How'd you know?"

Alyce snickered and turned away.

"Just a guess."

Scott's grin turned lopsided. Like a doting big brother, he set the girl at arm's length and patiently listened to a glowing blow-by-blow of the quarter mile she'd just run. She chattered nonstop and stuffed a piece of gum into her mouth all at the same time, then laughed and offered Scott one, too. He declined at first, then with a playful glance in Maggie's direction, he changed his mind.

Maggie's breath caught in her throat as Scott quickly blew a huge bubble and winked at her.

Okay, she got that. No engine. Her.

She was coming to terms with that, letting it wash over her and warm her, letting it erase some of the loneliness she used to feel when she watched Pop, when Scott unexpectedly sucked in the bubble and broke out his dimple-accented smile. He was thinking about their sticky kiss in the barn, she just knew it.

Was he thinking of doing it better?

Well, not from over there, he wasn't. And he probably wouldn't come over here and try it in front of all these people, because who knew what kind of rumor that would send through the racing world.

If he did, she probably shouldn't spit at him this time. Even if he did collect things.

But under the circumstances, she definitely wasn't kissing him back.

They drove home in a thunderstorm, tucked into the Mustang like two travelers sheltering in a common cocoon. Much to Scott's relief, Maggie drove conservatively through the pouring rain, slowing to thirty like everyone else.

He didn't remember a lightning show ever being so awesome. Brilliant, jagged bolts flashed from cloud to ground, glowing against the inky sky like multitendriled vines shooting down to earth. Other flashes sizzled within the massive clouds overhead, darting from one to another, lighting the sky and outlining the heavy cover. They were headed against the storm, but from the looks of it, they wouldn't be driving out the back door anytime soon.

Scott couldn't imagine anyone he'd rather be with. Maggie'd been a real trouper at the track, chatting with the kids instead of keeping to herself, and they'd certainly seemed to like having her there. Tim's girlfriend had even hugged her before they'd all dashed through the rain to their cars.

She'd been aware of him, too. When he'd blown his gum into a bubble and winked at her, she'd looked surprised at first, and her slow smile told him that she knew exactly what he'd been thinking.

Was *still* thinking.

Maggie hadn't winked back, but hey, they'd spent more hours together in three days than most couples had after weeks of dinner dates and clubbing. She knew he got up in the morning rarin' to go, brewed a killer pot of coffee, and had a respectful fear of poisonous spiders. He knew she slugged around in her robe until she'd had coffee, was game to attempt new things, and got a kick out of trying to scare him with talk of wild creatures.

Several things weren't lost on Scott. Maggie hadn't raced off to see Killjoy even after determining that it was safe to do so. She hadn't turned away when he'd blown that bubble to remind her that they'd been in each other's arms on the floor of the barn and almost enjoyed it. And there was no possible explanation for her spending this evening with him at the track except that she, too, understood the inevitable.

He'd been staring at her legs and her body and her pert smile for hours on end since Monday. He'd enjoyed every syllable of her sassy banter. If he wanted to be really noble, he could say he admired the way she respected Grammy and Ruby, but while that counted down the road, it sure as heck wasn't foremost on his mind.

Sex was.

Definitely time to move forward.

Grammy could be a deterrent, though. Women were funny that way. Put an older relative in the house with them, and they got shy in the bedroom. Especially the passionate ones.

I should be so lucky. For putting up with Coop, God owed him a passionate woman.

"What?" Maggie said, risking a quick glance his way when lightning flashed and illuminated the inside of the car.

"I didn't say anything."

"I know, but you're grinning."

"And you said you weren't psychic."

As if on cue, lightning flashed again. There was no counting the seconds to the next thunderclap to see how far away the storm was; it was right there, hitting with a loud boom, then rolling on and on.

"This storm's really bad," Scott said when the rumble passed momentarily. No sense letting a perfect opportunity go to waste. "We could stop somewhere for the night."

"Do you hear . . . ?"

Shit. *Now*? The *ka-ching* from the glove box was barely audible. Where was the next thunderclap when he needed it?

"Yeah, that's mine," Maggie said. "You mind getting it?"

Scott retrieved the phone and checked caller ID. "Grammy," he said, and connected with a friendly hello.

"I hope you two aren't driving in this," Grammy barked.

"We're going slow."

"*Maggie let you drive her car?*"

"I offered—" He didn't get to correct Grammy's mis-assumption.

"She never lets anyone drive her car. Try not to wreck it."

Ouch. "Yeah, she loves you, too. Good night." Scott disconnected before he gave in to impulse and ordered Grammy to bed. With earplugs—for the thunder, of course.

"She always calls when I'm out in bad weather. Her or Mom. Sometimes both."

"I hope the storm doesn't keep her awake." Or better— that it was loud enough and long enough to drown out Maggie's orgasms. Two or three, at least.

"She feels better if I promise to wake her up when I get in, so she knows I'm safe."

The phone *ka-ching*ed again.

No way Scott was making that promise, so he answered with, "We're together. We won't wake you when we get in."

Instead of Grammy, though, a male voice said, "Who's this?"

Too late for caller ID. From the curt tone, it had to be Killjoy who said, "Never mind. Is my girl there?"

My girl. Scott gritted his teeth. If only he could send the next lightning bolt through the phone to zap Killjoy on the other end, he could write this off as a good day. Too bad that wasn't possible; he'd have to handle him another way. A little less permanent, but nonetheless rewarding.

"It's storming here," he said. "Maggie needs both hands on the wheel right now."

"Who is it? Give me my headset." Maggie reached for the glove box. Scott batted her hand back onto the steering wheel. "I'm right here," she shouted over another rumble of thunder, "but my phone's been *kidnapped*."

"Give her her goddamn headset."

"Let me guess. Kenneth?"

Scott heard "*Kevin*" in stereo.

"Ooh, watch that truck, hon. He's going way too fast for this weather," Scott said, not because Maggie needed the advice, but because it'd put the other guy off. "Hey, it's really tough driving right now, Kev. Maggie'd be safer if I just relay a message."

"You're letting *her* drive? What are you, nuts?"

"What do you mean, am I nuts?" The trick, Scott knew, was to sound sincere. "Maggie's doing a fine job. I feel perfectly safe with her driving."

"Yeah, well, considering you crashed when there weren't any other cars around, I guess you would."

What *was it* with everybody?

Scott snarled, "I'll tell her to call you in the morning," and turned the phone completely off.

Maggie muttered something about who was nuts and who wasn't. Didn't sound complimentary.

"Doesn't think much of your driving, does he?" Scott said.

"Oh, and you weren't screaming on the ride over?"

"But I adjusted. I was calm enough to read. I'm guessing Kermit wouldn't be."

Maggie grinned instead of correcting him, but not for long. "We always argue over who's going to drive."

Scott took great pains to look as comfortable as if he were sitting on his own couch. Ten minutes after leaving the highway, Maggie turned onto Cherry

Lane. Monday's slow-moving creek had turned into Thursday's gushing stream.

"Whoa, hold up," Scott warned. "That may be too deep."

"You want dry feet, hold 'em up."

He started to raise them before he spotted the depth marker and realized she was kidding. "How much clearance do you have?"

"It comes up fast," Maggie said, "but I've got a couple inches left. Good thing we're not a half hour later."

"Yeah," Scott said flatly. "Or we'd have to turn back and go to a hotel. Wouldn't that be a shame?"

Maggie eased the Mustang across the stream, avoiding a splash stall. At least the rain had slowed enough to turn the wipers down. "We've got company."

In the gravel drive, Maggie pointed the headlights toward the barn, but didn't venture onto the old track, which appeared soupy enough tonight to swallow her car whole.

In this area, Scott expected "company" to be wildlife. In his defense, he'd been programmed all week to expect no less. Frogs that lived in trees—hell, why not fish as big as cats, then? An odd variety that came up from the river in thunderstorms and walked on tail fins. Turtles the size of hubcaps. Maybe even water moccasins the size of boa constrictors. Anything but humans.

But human, they were. The lights were on at the barn, inside and out. Three cars and two pickups stood outside, grouped as if they'd arrived in a pack.

Well, why the hell not? May as well throw a party the way his night was going.

"You don't think Grammy'd try her hand at a Ouija party, do you?"

"Not tonight. She plays bridge on Thursdays, and *nothing* interferes with that."

"Die-hard player, huh?"

"Gentleman partner." There was humor in her voice. "Milton Bradshaw. Grammy wouldn't miss her evening with him."

Hot damn, no Grammy on board tonight.

Maggie leaned forward and peered through the rain and darkness. "I don't recognize any of the vehicles."

"That white monster belongs to Tate Nevins."

"*The* Tate Nevins?"

"Could there be two? Not if there's a God. And I bet I know what they're all doing here."

"Not looking for the 'Cuda." Incredulity marked Maggie's voice. "How—"

"Bruce and Daryl wouldn't talk if you staked them out in the infield."

"Most men would consider that a treat, wouldn't they?"

"Not in July. How about Grammy?"

"She'd do anything to get out of the infield. Heck, I'd give up my own mother to stay out of the infield."

"Do your clients know you're this easy to side-track?"

"My clients don't push my buttons."

"I push your buttons?" Scott grinned, happy in the

knowledge that he was having *some* effect on her.

"And I'm not sidetracked. Grammy doesn't want anything to interfere with talking to Pop, so in answer to your question, I'm sure no one heard about the 'Cuda from her."

"Kenny, then?"

"Never!"

"Did you tell him finding it's a secret?"

"Well, not exactly."

"And doesn't he know people who like to invest in things? Collectors, maybe?"

Lightning strobed through the clouds and showed Maggie chewing her lip. "I'm pretty sure he doesn't know Tate Nevins."

"It's only a matter of degrees." Scott reached for the door handle. "No need for both of us to get wet. I'll get rid of them."

"Make it fast or the creek'll be too high."

"Oh, trust me, they won't be here another five minutes. Wait up for me, okay?"

Maggie twisted in her seat, the way a woman does to kiss a man good-bye, which Scott was thinking about only because of his dry spell. He was too surprised to take advantage of it, though, before she leaned into the back to search the floor. She was close, though. As close as she'd been all evening.

"What're you wearing?" he asked, sniffing quietly.

"Uh, the same T-shirt and jeans I left with," she said as if he were a dope, which he probably was. "Anything else you have to imagine on your own."

Wrong thing to tell a horny man. Scott smiled and said, "I'm imagining nothing."

"Figures."

"But I meant perfume."

"Oh. I don't wear any. Darn, where'd it go?"

He closed in on her shoulder and sniffed again. "It's something flowery. I remember smelling it as a kid, but I can't quite place it."

"If it's honeysuckle—"

"That's it!"

There'd been a heaping vine of it on his grandmother's fence. He and Jeremy used to pull the flowers apart and lick off the tiny drops of nectar. In his present state, it wasn't good to think about licking, because his sex-starved imagination progressed to visions of pulling Maggie's shirt out of her jeans and running his tongue over her skin, searching for drops of anything.

Christ, if he didn't get laid soon, he'd go insane.

"It's probably my conditioner. Darn, it should be here somewhere."

Summoning an impressive amount of self-control because he hadn't laid a woman in a car in years and didn't intend to relive his high school conquests, he said, "What are you looking for?"

"My umbrella. You're going to need it."

"Don't worry about it." He reached for the door handle. The cold rain would do him a world of good right now. "Unless you think I need it to fight off thunder-crazed coyotes."

"Nah, they like their men dry."

"I'll be sure to get extra soaking wet, then." The light came on when he opened the door. Maggie couldn't miss his suggestive wink when he gave in to the simplicity of the predictable line: "You can help me change."

He ducked out of the car before she came back with something pithy. If he had to be away from her for five minutes because some fools thought they could trespass on private property, then he wanted her to be thinking about him and nothing but him until he walked through her door.

The temperature had dropped at least ten degrees with the storm. Hell, if he got wet enough and started shaking—he chattered his teeth to see if it was possible for a person to fake that; it was. When Maggie saw that, what could she do but put her arms around him?

Maybe she'd march him right into a hot shower.

He'd need help, of course.

 *Chapter 11*

Tate Nevins was a small, freckle-faced redhead with an ego the size of Jupiter. He stood in the glow of the floodlight outside the barn, feet planted wide, a blue-and-white umbrella emblazoned with the words *Team Nevins* to keep him comfortable. Funny he'd picked one four feet in diameter; beneath it, he looked like a pinhead.

"Time for you to leave," Scott said.

The jerk *smirked*.

No sense wasting his breath. Or his time. The open toe on Scott's cast was oozing mud from the hike to the barn. His foot slipped around inside it, and the whole thing felt as if it were stretching.

Scott reached into his truck and laid on the horn to draw everyone out where he could dispense with them all at once. While a couple of trespassers wandered near the entrance and glanced in his direction, they quickly returned to the hunt and left the talking to Nevins.

Couldn't blame them. Given the opportunity, he didn't want to be around the swollen-headed braggart, either.

"Last chance," Scott said. "Round up your friends and go."

"A '71 'Cuda in pristine condition—it's a national

treasure, Templeton. You can't keep that to yourself."

"*If* it's here, it belongs to the Cooper family."

Nevins pulled a face. "It'd be like . . . like finding a video of the Kennedy assassination and keeping it in your basement."

"Yeah. Right."

Looked as if he'd have to throw them out one by one. After weeks on the couch, he had enough pent-up energy to get the job done. It'd be like a tune-up, so he'd run smooth the rest of the night. Maggie'd appreciate that.

Scott strode past Nevins and was just about to enter the barn and start with the biggest guy when one hopping mad ghost stormed out and said, "Rainin' like a sonofabitch, ain't it?"

"Either make yourself useful or get the hell out of my way," Scott snarled.

"The creek's getting high," Coop said. "Make them leave. *Now*."

"I don't see you helping."

"I threw stuff at 'em—I did." Coop scratched his head. "They made jokes about ghosts, but it didn't stop 'em none. And after the Ouija fire, I didn't think I should mess with the big stuff. No sense burning the barn down."

Scott towered over the ghost for a change. "Let me make one thing perfectly clear. I'm going to get rid of them for *Maggie*, not because you want me to."

"But—"

"Shut up, I'm not finished."

He didn't get to, either. Inside the barn, a man shouted, "Holy—!" A heavy thud was quickly followed by a string bean of a guy hurtling out of the barn, yelling, "Run for your lives!" as he threw himself into a silver pickup and gunned it in a sloppy circle, showering a halo of soupy mud over Scott and everyone else before he tore out of the yard.

"Don't look at me," Coop said. "I was standing right here the whole time."

"Yeah, like that reassures me." Scott figured he owed someone a treat for terrorizing the chickenshit. "What do raccoons like to eat? Besides cigarettes."

"Anything. Dog food, people food, an entire garden . . ."

The hasty departure had the rest of the 'Cuda hunters looking a little nervous. Nervous was good. Skittish was even better.

"Say, Coop, instead of just standing there, why don't you—"

Nevins interrupted what he obviously saw as a one-sided conversation between Scott and thin air. "You were a good competitor once, but damn, Templeton, you're losing it. You need to see somebody."

Scott planned to. She came up to his chin and smelled like honeysuckle. And she might not wait all night.

"I'm still a great competitor, you no good, trespassing sonofabitch. Now get the hell off this property before I show you just how far gone I really am."

Nevins's cronies fell into a half circle behind him. Scott didn't know if they were planning a discussion, a fight, or a Tupperware party, and he didn't much care. One way or another, they were leaving. He stepped forward, ready for anything—except the entire area dropping into blackness. Can't-see-your-hand-in-front-of-your-face blackness.

For a bunch of guys banded together for a little illegal trespassing and thieving, they started to sound pretty nervous.

"What the—?"

"Hey! My umbrella—"

"You guys feel that?"

Seemed Coop had figured out how to cause a little mayhem after all. Another minute and they'd be squealing like little girls at a slumber party. The next lightning flash highlighted them making a beeline for their vehicles, checking over their shoulders as they ran.

Vehicle doors slammed, one after another. Engines gunned. Headlights blazed. Spinning tires flung mud everywhere as they sought traction, and then Scott was alone in the dark. With luck, the creek was still passable and nothing was blocking the road; the way the wind had picked up, anything could be down.

"Coop? You around? I can't see a darn thing."

"Funny. Don't bother me none."

"C'mon, man, I'm soaked. The least you can do is lead me to the house."

"Barn's this way."

"My clothes are in the house."

"So's my daughter."

"Say, that's right. You think she'll hold a flashlight for me while I get out of these wet clothes?" Scott said, laughing because Coop was so angry, he was flinging mud. "Christ, man, if those little pantywaist mudballs're the best you can do, you need to work out."

He was still laughing at the ghost when he realized why Coop was trying his darnedest to distract him. There was a small spot of light between them and the house, slowly coming closer. At first he thought Coop might have called in backup, but it turned out to be a flashlight.

Maggie's coming for me. She knew it was too dark for him to find his way back to the house. She'd thought about him.

Yes!

"Time for you to get lost, old man."

"Why should I?"

"Cavalry's coming. I'm about to be saved, and you don't want to see it."

Maggie struggled to hold her umbrella steady as she slipped and slid in the muddy yard on her way to the barn, aimed a flashlight in front of her, and talked on the cell phone all at the same time. If the wind picked up more, she'd have to forgo the umbrella. Her path was crooked as she sought traction on clumps of tender grass instead of slopping through the mud, but it was a losing battle.

Ruby was on the phone. She'd called to report that

she was safe at a friend's in Webster for the duration of the storm and wouldn't be home tonight. She sounded happy about it.

"Anybody I know?" Maggie asked, thinking maybe the Goth guy Ruby'd gone out with a couple of times before the convention. Hey, maybe she liked guys with pierced tongues.

"Jeremy Templeton," Ruby said.

"Scott's brother? You just met him."

"And I had the best day. We went to the zoo. Do you know how long it's been since a guy took me to the zoo? Never. The goats tried to eat my skirt, and he bought me a hot dog."

"Hell-o-o, you're vegetarian."

"I can make exceptions. He's so kind and sweet."

"He's a *biker*."

"Okay, he's kind and sweet in a macho sort of way," Ruby giggled.

No, she *gushed*. What was next? Pale pink nail polish and bleached hair?

"I'll bet Scott's the same way," Ruby added.

"I don't know. I barely know him."

"Kevin's not."

That was true; Kevin wasn't. Last week, Maggie could've seen him telling people that she, his "long-standing significant other," was the daughter of a race car champion. He'd bragged to his coworkers, soon to be *their* coworkers, that she was smart and funny and pretty, and a force to be reckoned with in the wealth management game.

"He's probably grouchy as an ol' bear because you aren't doing what he wants," Ruby said.

He'd probably already relegated her to "someone he'd once dated" and told everyone from the president to the filing clerk that she was unbelievably gullible. So gullible that she'd been duped by a stranger on her doorstep into poking through a barn full of junk to find an old car that probably didn't exist. It'd be a wonder if they'd still interview her.

"You deserve better, Maggie. You could have kind and sweet in a macho sort of way, too, you know."

"Why are you laying this on me now? I need to get Scott and get out of the rain."

"It's the storm," Ruby said. "I'm not scared or anything because, well, we are who we are . . ."

Storm drills were yearly occurrences in the Cooper house. Grammy'd lost her home and sister in a tornado when she was ten. She'd been prepared ever since, and anyone who lived with her darn well better be prepared, too.

"And it got me to thinking," Ruby said. "A tornado *could* hit tonight, and I *could* die tonight, and what if that happened before I got a chance to tell you that you're a wonderful person and that Kevin's not the right man for you?"

Maggie slipped, flinging her arms out to catch her balance. Only another fifty feet to Scott, who, head to toe, was covered with a dark, muddy film. Except for his wide smile, which almost lit up the night. It certainly lit her up inside.

"Oh God, now I've gone and upset you," Ruby said into the silence. "I didn't mean to. I'm sorry."

"I'm not upset. A little confused maybe." There, she'd said it out loud. Time to deal with it.

"Aw, Maggie, that's understandable." This from her sister, who normally was neither comforting nor maternal.

"Since when do you get to be the big sister?" Maggie asked.

"Since I want you to be happy. Call me in the morning and let me know how it goes, okay?"

"Nothing's *going*."

Ruby laughed. "It is if he's anything like his brother."

"I'm confused, not out of my mind."

"You will be when he kisses you. Just remember— you're not engaged or anything."

"Hello? Hello? You're breaking up."

Ruby shouted, "I said, 'Wait'll he kisses you.'"

"Ruby? You there?"

Maggie ignored her sister's repeated promise that a Templeton man was God's gift to women and let her think the mobile company broke the connection.

Everything around her was silent, save the whoosh of branches as the wind whipped them about. No tree frogs tonight. No coyotes howling. No owls hooting. No coons wrestling the bungee cord on the trash can.

Despite the mud caking her shoes and splattering the backs of her jeans, Maggie felt an unexpected wave of nostalgia at the thought of moving away. She lived right in the heart of St. Louis County, a stone's throw from the Meramec River. The grocery store was five minutes away; the mall, ten; live theater, fifteen or twenty; and downtown about the same, depending on her route. And still, deer and turkey frequented her yard. Hawks and vultures soared overhead. The neighborhood was thick with pretty little bluebirds and yellow finches.

She'd started out teasing Scott with threats of wildlife because, well, it was easy to do. While that was so much fun in itself, it also turned out to be a fond farewell to the many animals she'd grown up with.

Maggie suddenly realized she hadn't outgrown this place as much as she'd thought. Besides, she liked the people she worked with, VPs and coworkers alike. Most important, Grammy and Ruby were here. This was where her mom would return to visit.

So why the heck was she planning to move? For herself, or because Kevin had left and thought she should, too?

Still, the job in Chicago would be a big boost to her career. It was only a few hours' drive away. She could get home often.

"Who's there?" Scott held his hands up to block the light as Maggie closed the gap between them.

She stopped a few feet away, just in case he had a notion to grab her and give her another dirty kiss. "Let me guess. You thought disguising yourself as a creature from the Black Lagoon would scare the big bad men away?"

"I must've dropped the soap," Scott said with an air of befuddlement. "I can't find it."

Puzzled by his illogical reply, Maggie watched him

pull his shirt out of his jeans, then up over his stomach and ribs, showing off an increasing amount of well-honed torso. She raised the flashlight, illuminating each new inch of skin along the upward trail as the shirt finally came off and the rain started to make tracks through the thin streaks of mud on his skin. She hadn't completely lost her mind; she wondered what the heck he was up to, but that set of pecs—*wow*—would make any woman forget her name. Even a nun.

So what chance did *she* have?

"There's no hot water." Scott tipped his head back, letting the rain shower over his face.

He rubbed his hands through his hair, just as one would shampoo. One wrist was narrower than the other, atrophied from weeks in a cast, and he had a scar on his left shoulder the size of her cell phone. His teeth started to chatter.

"I'm so cold."

"Maybe you should, uh, put your shirt back on." *Please don't.*

"Oh. Okay." He picked it out of the mud and tried stepping into it as if it were a pair of pants. That, of course, didn't work. Once he had one foot partway in a sleeve, he hopped in small circles and kept trying.

Maggie's light wandered over wide shoulders and broad back, highlighting a good deal of smooth, well-tanned skin and—*Lordy*—muscles, muscles, muscles. If he wanted to make an ass of himself and wear his shirt on his butt, who was she to complain?

"Can I go out and play after I'm dressed?"

Being prepared covered a lot of first aid instruction, including recognizing the confusion that accompanied hypothermia. Maggie was considering how she'd warm Scott up when she caught him peeking at her. It was not the peek of a confused man.

So, the faker wanted to play.

"Oh, poor baby," Maggie cooed. "You look sooo cooold."

Scott shivered, but all in all, did a really good job of pretending to be discombobulated.

Maggie opened her arms. "You poor, wet thing. Come here, I'll warm you up."

Hunched over because his cast was stuck in his sleeve, Scott hobbled closer.

"Wait," she said, infusing her voice with sudden urgency when he was no more than a hairbreadth from falling into her arms. "Oh my God, what's that on your arm?"

Scott froze momentarily, then broke character. This time when he hopped around in the mud, he slapped furiously at his arm, and his other foot became tangled in his shirt, too. He shouted, "What? What is it? A recluse?" and "Something bigger? How many legs does it have?"

No hypothermic confusion there; just pure Scott.

"Don't just stand there! Do something!"

"If you insist."

Maggie aimed her foot at his hip. Tangled up the way he was, it took very little pressure to topple him, and over he went, arms and legs windmilling, body sliding in the slippery mud. It tickled her that she'd bested him. She laughed with joy.

Scott rose to his knees with a mighty roar.

She had a head start; he had a clumsy cast to slow him down. Maggie tossed the umbrella and ran.

She would've made it to the house first—if she'd quit laughing and if he'd had casts on both legs, maybe. Within yards of the porch, Scott tackled her high and took her down. To her surprise, they rotated in the air and she came down on her back, on top of him, held tightly to his chest by the circle of his arms as they slid several feet across wet grass and mud.

Maggie heard whoops and shouts of glee and more laughter, and realized it was both of them. Playing. In soggy wet grass in the middle of a thunderstorm.

And it was fun.

Scott rolled Maggie over and kissed her, radiating a vitality that held her like a magnet. She heard sirens instead of bells, and it was so wonderful that she arched her body against him and breathed him in, sighing as if she'd found safe port in a storm.

When Scott lifted his head and propped himself on his elbows, Maggie yearned to study his face, but the flashlight was on the ground. She could feel him staring at her, though, as seconds passed.

"What?" she finally asked.

"Just waiting for you to get it over with."

"What?"

"The spitting."

She grinned up at him, and taking his head in her

hands, she pulled him down for another taste. His lips were cool against hers. Smooth, no grit this time. And contrary to his caveman tackle, he didn't force his tongue down her throat but nibbled his way across her lips, taking small tastes, warming her in regions he wasn't touching. Not yet anyway. One second she was catching her breath, the next she was breathless with anticipation.

Maggie broke the kiss when the tornado sirens registered on her brain and the world started spinning. Her first thought was *Dorothy, here I come*, but then she was suddenly on her feet and Scott's hands were all over her, steadying her, turning her, pressing the flashlight into her hand, pushing her toward the kitchen door.

"Inside," he barked. "Hurry."

Whole trees were in motion. Rain blew sideways and pelted her face.

"No," she said. "The cellar." She pulled the opposite direction.

"It's just a watch, right? The shower's closer this way."

Scott was winning the tug-of-war until Maggie braked harder and said, "We're past the watch stage; it's a warning. And there is no shower."

"Huh?"

"No electricity, no pump, remember? No pump means no water, no shower."

"But I'm . . ." He looked down at himself.

Maggie shone the light over him, head to toe, though considerably slower along the whole path in between.

Laughter bubbled up inside her again, and she said, "Yes, you certainly are."

He swiped a streak of grime off his chest. "Got a good downspout?"

"You *want* to stand out here and get harpooned by a tree branch?"

"Rinse me before they take my picture?"

"What picture? We have a compost pile behind the barn for people too dumb to take shelter."

Maggie led the way down to the cellar, and they closed the door against the storm. Both of them were dripping, though she looked and felt like a drowned rat next to a bare-chested Adonis. Scott didn't seem to think so, because no sooner was the lamp lit than he wrapped his arms around her and slowly, seductively, recaptured her lips.

"You're soaking," he said between kisses, pulling the hem of her tee upward. "Don't want you to catch a chill."

She raised her arms without thinking about it, until the shirt was off. Scott's hand felt along the back of Maggie's bra, and his Rolex felt cold against her skin.

"Your watch," she said, thinking he'd be so disappointed if it got ruined from the water and mud.

"It's been through worse."

"Take it off, I'll—"

"Never."

"Ooh," she said saucily. "Afraid I'll run off with it?"

"Does this hook in front or come off over your head?"

She reached between them and unhooked her bra. He

pulled her tightly against his cold, wet chest, mashing her breasts into mounds against his pounding heartbeat.

It felt heavenly. It felt right. He held her tightly, as if she might have any thought of wanting to leave his arms. He nuzzled her ear and murmured, "God, you're so warm."

"You fake confusion again and you'll be out in the rain, Templeton."

"Sleeping bag."

If he hadn't been so ardent when he uttered those two words, she might have thought twice about what she was doing. But Scott was breathless with passion and purpose, and at the thought of sharing a sleeping bag with this man, Maggie's insides flamed hot enough to light wet logs.

He back-walked her across the dirt floor. Thigh to thigh, wet denim rubbing against wet denim.

They unstuffed the bag. Maggie thought they were laying it out together until Scott reached around her and cupped her breasts with his hands. In a heartbeat, they were on the bag, Maggie on the bottom, Scott beside her and on top of her, eagerly running his hands over every inch of exposed skin until one landed on her belt buckle.

They were about to get down and dirty as Maggie never had before, and suddenly she knew they'd been leading up to this, talking around this, for days. That deep down, where she couldn't hide from the truth, she'd known she wanted him all along. *Needed* him. His touch, his kisses, everything.

"Wait." Scott raised himself off her.

Maggie missed the weight of him on her, against her.

He came right back with the flashlight. "I want to see you."

"Yeah, I'm so attractive right now."

"Well, I don't know. Let's look."

He straddled her middle, so there was no dodging the beam or his intentions. Maggie slicked back her drowned-rat hair.

"Leave it. It's beautiful," he said, setting the light on the floor, pulling her hands away and kissing her fingers while he studied her.

Too intensely, she thought. As if he were trying to see inside her head and read some subconscious message, when all she wanted to do was rip the clothes off his body and see if he was as much fun as touching him promised to be.

Smeared with a thin coat of mud, he still looked pretty darn good. All over. Maggie tugged her hands free and reached for him, eager to feel him against her again. He ran a finger tenderly over her skin, from temple to chin.

Then his hand fell away. His grin faded.

"Ah, damn," he said.

"What?"

"I can't . . ." He looked down.

"Why the heck—" Bewildered, Maggie glanced at her breasts. They were a little muddy, maybe, from sliding through the yard with him, but nothing gross. "Swear to God, Templeton—"

"It's not you. It's me."

She looked him in the eyes and reached for the front of his jeans. "Anything I can do?" she asked with wicked thoughts racing through her mind. *So many choices.*

"No!" Scott practically threw himself off her.

Shocked, Maggie couldn't move.

"You got any games down here?" he asked.

The house could blow off the foundation, and she'd still lie there wondering what had gone wrong. He wanted to play *games*? He'd have to be mortally wounded to play games *now*.

Although . . . There was that one burn on his shoulder, maybe more. There'd been car crashes, on the track and off. He could have other injuries.

"*Ohhh.* Sorry." It probably was rude to glance at his groin, but also second nature.

"It's not what you think."

Then he'd *better* have other injuries. "Pin the tail on the *jackass*?"

"You're pissed."

"Really." Pissed was good; it kept tears at bay. If she lost that advantage, she'd be a blubbering fool.

Sitting on the floor, Scott wrapped his forearms loosely around his knees and made a perfect picture of a man who was proud to work with his hands and get dirty and crawl into a woman's bed at night. Only he wasn't crawling into hers, and she felt naked in front of him. The light didn't shine far enough to locate her bra or T-shirt, so she sat up and mirrored his position, covering her bareness with her knees.

"I'm fine," he said, and she knew that he knew what she was thinking. "It's not that. But when I saw you in the light . . . Ah, Maggie, I'm getting dirt all over you again, only this time it's mud and it's half the yard." It sounded like an apology. A serious one, too; no dimple. "Look around us."

She lifted her chin and held his gaze.

"Maggie . . ." He held out his hand, seeking hers.

She pulled hers out of reach. "I'm listening."

"I don't want our first time together to be in a cellar on a dirt floor. You deserve better."

First time? She'd never seen or heard *Scotty Templeton* and *long-term relationship* used in the same sentence. Fast cars, fast women, even faster conquests; she should count herself lucky.

But she didn't. Not just now. Unless—

"Define 'first time.'"

He grinned then. "Told you it wasn't what you were thinking."

He inched forward until her legs were squeezed between his, and his arms looped around her knees, too. The backs of his hands brushed against her nipples, and his thumbs made lazy circles over the sensitive skin there.

"It should be your best time ever," he said, holding her gaze with an earnest steadiness. "You should wake up in the morning looking forward to an encore, not a musty cellar with a head-banger ceiling, not spiderwebs and mold, and clay that's as hard as concrete. And you should lie in my arms thinking, *Sure, he's a race car driver and annoying as hell, but who knows? We might have a future. Let's take it a day at a time and see.*"

"I look that bad with a little mud on my face?"

He leaned close and kissed the tip of her nose. "You look beautiful with mud on your face. I was raised better than that, though, and I feel like scum knowing I put it there."

Maggie squinted at him, as if she'd be able to see into his head and get some clue what was going on in there. "Are you playing hard to get?"

"Not my style."

"Do you think it'll make me want you more?"

He took her hands in his and seemed to have trouble coming up with words.

"Because," she said, "it's working."

"Maggie, I— It is?" A slow grin lit up his face. Then disappeared. "No, really, that's not what I'm doing." Then returned, dimple and all. "You want me anyway? After everything I said about the cellar and the dirt floor and—"

"I especially liked that 'annoying as hell' part. It's sexy when a man can admit his faults."

"Hell, if you think that's sexy, I've got a whole laundry list of faults."

He rose to his knees, looming over her for a moment like some mighty god out of the sea before easing her backward onto the sleeping bag.

"Besides being annoying, I'm wishy-washy. One

minute I resolve not to make love to you on the floor, the next I can't keep my hands off of you. I'm not sure I'm what you need—"

"God, you're all talk."

He laughed against her skin. "See, told you so."

A few feet from Maggie's head, hanging on the wall, Scott spotted tools. Not what he should be noticing with a half-naked woman in his arms, except that, in a way, it was exactly what he needed. One tool looked as if it'd cut through anything. "Wait here. Don't move." He could feel Maggie's gaze follow him as he crawled to the wall and grabbed the cutters.

"Should I be worried?" she asked.

To his relief, Scott could tell she was still teasing.

"Wait," she said, rolling to her side when she saw what he was doing. "You shouldn't—"

Scott winked at her as he dug into the wet cast with the enthusiasm of a man who didn't want to lose the mood. "I'm a doctor, remember?"

"Scott, no, wait. What if it's not healed?"

"You know how many broken bones I've had?" He didn't wait for her answer. "More than any doctor patching me up, that's for sure. Don't worry, I know what healed feels like." He tossed the plaster aside and wiped the mud off his leg with Maggie's shirt.

They helped each other out of their wet, muddy, stiff jeans, the heat between them doubling with each new inch of skin revealed, with each second apart, until finally they were naked together. Maggie lay before Scott, feeling his gaze caress her skin from head to thigh.

"God, that looks awful," he said, barely touching the large, multihued purple bruise with the tips of his fingers.

Maggie shivered in anticipation of more. "It's nothing."

"You sure? 'Cause I could kiss it and make it better."

"Come to think of it, I can barely move."

Scott said, "I suspected as much," and dipped his head until his lips touched her discolored skin.

Soft. So soft.

The bruise wasn't big enough to take more than a few seconds. In no time, Scott's lips began to wander, higher, then lower, then higher again until Maggie didn't care what he did, as long as, *please, God*, he did it right damn soon because she didn't know how much longer she could stand his delicious, tender touch, which was growing more insistent, more demanding by the minute, until she grabbed him and pulled him and finally his body covered hers.

She tried to wait. She tried to meet his needs before he entered her, but apparently turning into a moaning, mindless blob *did* meet his needs, because while Scott never hesitated, Maggie felt an intensity in him that she hadn't suspected, almost as if he were giving her a part of himself that she instinctively knew he'd never shared before, that he wasn't accustomed to sharing with anyone. And she accepted it and tucked it away in her heart to analyze later.

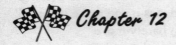 *Chapter 12*

What the hell was wrong with his face?

Scott tried to smile and utter a decent good morning when he and Maggie woke in each other's arms hours later. His lips barely moved, but that wasn't the worst; his cheeks were as stiff as a fucked-up transmission, and when he felt his face, he discovered an itchy, cracking mask of dried mud.

Apparently Maggie hadn't kissed all of it off, though not for lack of effort, he thought, working on another grin with no success.

"Shit. Why on earth would anyone pay for a mud facial?"

Maggie lifted her head from his chest, looking fabulously satisfied if he did say so himself. In the dim glow of the flashlight on the floor, she raised heavy-lidded eyes in his direction and assessed why he was talking funny.

She hummed lazy satisfaction, and when she nuzzled back into position, Scott thought she was going back to sleep—until her fingers unexpectedly wriggled into his ribs. He didn't disappoint in that department, either, as ticklishness was something he'd never mastered. Making him squirm was so much fun for her, she worked her way south, learning other spots that finally cracked the mask with weird popping sensations, until her hands reached the old burns on his left thigh and abruptly stopped.

Maggie pulled away suddenly, and when she stood up, Scott felt a cold chill pass through him that had nothing to do with passing the stormy night in an old cellar. He cursed under his breath at his stupidity and mumbled, "Sorry."

He should kick himself. He should have warned her. He should have thrown the sleeping bag over his legs before they fell asleep, and he quickly did so now as the light level in the cellar came up.

Maggie's back was to him as she adjusted the oil lamp hanging from a rafter hook that appeared secure enough to hold it through an earthquake. Looking like a goddess of the night in spite of the dirt streaking her skin, she slipped into a long T-shirt out of her emergency stash, then kneeling beside him, she turned back the sleeping bag and feathered a whisper-soft kiss over one of the lowlights of his life.

"Bet that hurt," she said tenderly, not at all repulsed.

Scott was so astonished, he had trouble finding his voice, trouble keeping it steady so she wouldn't know how moved he was. Baring his soul didn't come easy to a man who never had to.

"Kinda. I was young and stupid and thought a few holes in my underwear were nothing to worry about." He had nothing clean to put on and didn't really care.

The rest of him looked way better than the scars, and look at the attention they were getting.

Idly, Maggie's fingers stroked the ruined skin. "Pop was scared of fire. He'd laugh about hitting the wall and walking away, but if one of the other drivers' wrecks caught fire, he'd clam up for weeks. Wouldn't say a word. Not to anybody."

"He never said—is that how he died?"

Maggie shook her head. "Head trauma."

"Now that I believe."

That prompted an easy smile, soft and gentle, and then she changed the subject. "You mentioned games earlier. We have a bunch stored in that old armoire over there."

"A whole armoire full?"

"Don't get excited; at least half of it's Ace bandages and splints. Gauze pads. You know, first aid stuff. When Ruby and I get tired of games, Grammy makes us practice. It's tradition."

It wasn't an assortment of games that sent a spark of excitement shooting through Scott, that drove his heart to thump erratically in his chest. "Well, at the time I suggested it, I was looking for something safe to do with my hands. Now I'm getting better ideas. I bet Ace bandages make good handcuffs."

Maggie smiled behind lowered lashes and picked at a piece of his cracked mud mask. "Dirty old man."

"Hey, this dirty old man votes we play Monopoly and make love in every hotel we put up."

"Naked men don't get to vote."

"Okay," he said with a put-upon sigh. "You pick."

"Naked men who're covered in mud and talk funny don't get to play, either."

"Are these rules written down anywhere?"

"They evolved over the years. Don't break your other leg on the steps when you go get cleaned up."

"You don't like me dirty?"

"I like all your joints limber," she answered with a promising wink.

According to the small weather radio, it sounded as if another storm was about to hit. They'd be here awhile yet, as the radio continued to broadcast watches and warnings for flash floods, hail, and high winds in St. Louis County and all other counties to the south and west for fifty miles. Time for lots and lots of variety—games, first aid, or otherwise.

Outside, Scott used two gallons of stored water to wash down, and he did it lightning-fast because the temperature had dropped again. He spent as much time on his Rolex as anything else. Might seem stupid to most people, but then most didn't get it, didn't understand why he never took it off. They didn't understand the years of hard work that led up to the weeks of logistics that boiled down to twenty-four hours of timing, luck, and teamwork that resulted in an elite championship. He shared that with men and women who worked equally hard and had become close personal friends.

For some reason, it was easier for people to understand a Super Bowl ring than a championship watch. With Maggie's background, though, Scott knew she got it.

It was so cold, he was almost embarrassed to go back inside. There were spare clothes in those tubs in the cellar, but had he thought to bring something out to use as a towel? *Nooo*, of course not, because when he'd stood up bare-assed in front of Maggie, all he could think about was how not sexy it was to be hunched over so he didn't wonk his skull on the low ceiling and fall unconscious at her feet. Lying at her feet didn't sound so bad, but the unconscious part would ruin it.

Giving in to the inevitable, Scott executed a charging hobble through the cellar and up the stairs, only to find the door locked from the other side, thanks to him, so he followed with a running hobble down the steps and through the cellar again, out around the outside, and in through the kitchen door.

"Hey, gimpy, bring some juice," Maggie called through the floor.

He opened the cellar door. "You want some clothes?" *Like Ruby's bustier?*

"Got some."

"Figures."

They probably stored them in Ziploc bags according to season. Extra shoes, too, no doubt, whereas when he returned in jeans and a sweater, he was also barefoot because he'd left Indy with one boot and a cast.

Too bad he hadn't gotten to pick out Maggie's dry clothes. He wouldn't have selected the old navy blue sweatshirt and baggy jeans she had on now, but even in them, she still looked as delectable as the first time he'd laid eyes on her. Her hair was wet and clean, so she'd done the outside wash-down, too. And she was braless and cold, which knocked the sexy quotient up another thousand percent.

Besides the requested juice, he'd scooped up the cat, his cell phone, and the bottom half of Mother Goose.

"Hey, Mom, it's me. I got your voice mail," Maggie was saying. "I'm so glad to hear you're having a good time. Everything's fine here. Really fine. Can't wait to talk to you."

Scott figured he'd be the main topic.

Maggie signed off before dipping her hand into the decapitated fowl. "Mm, cookies. Great idea."

She hummed a little moan of satisfaction when she bit into it, reminding Scott how she'd moaned with mindless pleasure, whispering his name over and over in his ear while he'd moved inside her a couple of hours ago. It had been nice, better than nice, hands down the best of his life, but he got the feeling it was also just a tad shy and reserved. He hoped like heck it was because it was their first time together. If there was more passion burning beneath the surface, he couldn't wait to ignite it.

"Anything look like fun?" Maggie gestured toward the armoire. Scott ambled over to check it out.

"I feel like the hunchback of Notre Dame," he said.

"Cuter, though."

Boxes and boxes of games, and Scott would bet a new set of tires that none of them was sex-related. He looked at them. He looked at her. "Tradition, huh?"

"This or first aid."

He could be patient when it was worth his while. "Monopoly."

Maggie made a face. "You said that before."

"Can't beat a classic."

"Yeah, if you like to collect property and hotels." She swiped her next cookie right out of his hand with an impish grin and took a bite. "You just want to be the race car. How about Jumanji?"

Scott shuddered. "Wild animals. Besides, Jumanji just sounds like Ouija." He emphasized the J's. "No thanks. Risk."

"Collecting countries and armies. Why?"

"Let's leave the ghosts out in the rain, okay? Lie, Cheat & Steal."

"Collecting votes."

"That's like a dirty word to you, isn't it? Okay, what's Wide World Travel, then? That sounds different."

"Collecting cargoes."

Scott groaned. If she wanted to play games first, fine, but they'd better get on with it fast or he was going to eat all the cookies, succumb to a sugar high, and pounce on her. "I see Twister."

"I don't mind, but it's Animal Twister."

"You got a simple deck of cards in there?"

"Hm," she said, poking around the boxes. "They're missing."

"Yahtzee."

Maggie shook the box, heard dice, and glowed when she said, "All right, we're in business."

They sat on the sleeping bags with the Monopoly

box upside down between them as a tabletop. Maggie kicked off her flip-flops, which were as scarlet as her perfectly pedicured nails. She had a toe ring, too; Scott saw a flash of gold before she folded her legs and tucked her feet underneath.

"What're we playing for?" he asked. They each had a scorecard and a little pencil. In addition, the cat climbed in his lap, so he was doubly glad he'd put on jeans.

"You have to play for something other than points?" Maggie asked.

"Sure, that's what competition's all about."

"I don't know. Sometimes when we're down here more than a day, we play to see who has to restock. But I guess we could play for cookies."

"Nuh-uh." Scott drew Mother Goose close.

Maggie stared him down. "It's those or canned peaches, canned tuna, and crackers."

"Damn, I hope we're not stuck down here for days."

"It's a spring storm, not the second Ice Age."

"You might run out of clothes."

"Doubt it."

"You might have to dig into Ruby's stash for extras."

"You probably think she lounges around the cellar in an underwire bustier."

"A man can hope."

Maggie would've tempted the devil himself when she grinned real slow and said, "You're on. If you win, I'll look in Ruby's bag." She dropped the dice into the cup and shook it.

Scott wasn't born yesterday; he knew the finer points

in making a deal. "And if you find a bustier, you'll put it on."

"Yes."

"And you'll play at least one game without putting anything on over it."

"I'll bet you negotiate your own racing contracts."

"Yes or no."

"Depends on what you'll do if I win."

"Name it."

"Carte blanche?" she said with raised eyebrows, which made Scott think twice and say, "As long as it doesn't involve animals."

"You like Ashes."

The cat purred in Scott's lap. "Oh. Well, he doesn't look at me and think, *Dinner.* So what do you want if you win?"

Maggie chewed the inside of her lip while she thought it over. "You know that ghostbusting idea you read about going to the cemetery?" When he nodded, she said, "I don't know, sounds creepy to me. If I win, you go alone."

"Deal." He snatched the cup away from her as if the world might end if they didn't get the game going. He rolled five boxcars. "Yahtzee!"

The marbled cat sprang onto the upturned Monopoly box, and because the dice scattered like mice in all directions when he landed, he kept pouncing in circles on the sleeping bags.

Scott thought the cat's antics were hilariously funny until Maggie said, "Where? I don't see any Yahtzee."

* * *

The violent thunder and wind outside was nothing compared to the storm raging within Maggie.

Kevin vs. Scott.

Always right vs. not too proud to admit that Pop had Scott in a bind.

Self-centered vs. thoughtful enough to install a lock for Grammy and rescue the cat. Maggie'd been scratched for her trouble one too many times. As far as she was concerned, Ashes could weather a storm wherever he chose.

Settled vs. racing cars and chasing rainbows.

Sensible and practical vs. collector. She knew without asking that Scott had at least one garage and possibly a basement full of parts. It was in the job description. If it were anything else, Maggie maybe could learn to overlook the collecting part because how many vehicles could one man accumulate? A dozen? Maybe two? Compared to two barns full of everything under the sun, the amount wasn't a problem. But his whole life revolved around cars, and *that* set off warning bells.

Scott hadn't ignored her at the track, though. Not only had he caught her eye from time to time, he'd gone out of his way to introduce her to others so they could help her pass the time.

As a result of this pro-and-con quandary, Maggie's thoughts were not on Yahtzee. Her rolls sucked. Her choices were illogical. She didn't get her bonus points. Scott rolled two Yahtzees, counting the one the cat messed up, so she not only lost, she got stomped.

On the surface, her losing wager appeared to put her in a bustier *and* in a cemetery, but while Scott had been washing up outside, she'd been sorting through the tub of clothes. Ruby had sweats, tees, underpants, and nothing else in her bag. Scott might have won, but for nothing. And there was another thing—Kevin would've fumed, while Scott, in contrast, asked if she'd negotiate his next racing contract.

She was almost too tired to play the next two games, but she'd never laughed so much with a man and didn't want to quit.

"Tired?" he asked when she yawned.

"I can't even remember what we played the last game for."

Scott pushed the box off the sleeping bags and stretched out on his back. "You agreed to come to my next race."

Maggie snickered. "Yeah, that happened."

Scott held his arm wide, his shoulder beckoning her head, but she had to get up and adjust the oil lamp.

"You want to check your voice mail once more before I put this out?"

"Nah, I think it's useless. Coop must be messing with it."

"So use my number. He won't know."

"Really?"

"Sure, if it'll help you get another job."

It came out of her mouth so easy, and yet sounded strange to her ears. To Scott's, too, because he lifted his head and said, "Lightning struck you, right? And yet you look perfectly normal."

She plunged the cellar into darkness.

"If you fall on me, you have to be the pillow."

"That's how you and the fence bunnies play it, huh?"

"It's tradition. I know how much you value tradition."

God, she loved his sense of humor. It outweighed everything in the "pro" column combined. He was right, too. She *was* traditional, and for her that meant one boyfriend at a time. She had to do something about that.

According to the radio, the dangerous part of the storm had passed without a tornado touching down, and yet neither mentioned retreating upstairs to a large bed with a softer mattress. Instead, Maggie lay on Scott's chest and wiggled into a comfortable spot, no longer concerned with sleeping.

"What did I lose last game? For real."

"I lost." Scott pulled her sweatshirt over her head. "I'm bringing you coffee in bed and cooking breakfast."

Maggie finally talked to her mother, live, on Friday afternoon. She'd abandoned Scott in the barn in favor of curling up on the window seat in her bedroom while her mother relayed tales of scuba diving on the Great Barrier Reef one day and sleeping on a sheep ranch the next. It was such a relief that she'd finally met a man who shared his life with her, and Maggie told her so.

"Life with your father wasn't so bad. Did you ever need anything you didn't get?"

"Well, not *necessities*," Maggie admitted. "How'd you manage that, anyway?"

Her mother chuckled softly. "Easy. I went out to the barn and got something and sold it. He never noticed."

"Really? Did you ever sell a car?"

"Yes."

"And he didn't *notice*?"

"If he did, I just said it got moved or had stuff put on top of it. It wasn't as if he'd go look for it."

Maggie suddenly had the most awful thought. "It wasn't yellow, was it?"

"All of them were yellow."

"*All of them*?"

"Three, as I recall. Your father had a thing for yellow cars. Don't know why."

Good heavens, what if the 'Cuda had been sold already? What would happen when they emptied the barn and found no car? Would Pop let Scott off the hook, or send him on a bizarre, long-term, cross-country treasure hunt for months, maybe years on end?

"If it helps any, the cars were in the new barn," her mom said. "I think."

The cemetery Scott and Maggie visited on Friday night was small, old, and guarded by a creaky wrought-iron gate, but no fence. Low clouds exacerbated the dreariness of the place, tucked into a nearly forgotten acre behind a Catholic school, not ten minutes from the house. Bundled into sweats and jackets against the poststorm chill, Scott led the way as they followed their flashlight beams between rows of tilted and cracked headstones.

"1861," Maggie said behind him. She'd been reading old dates off the markers since they'd entered. Many were worn and illegible. Some were tall and ostentatious. 1861 was the oldest so far.

"Is your father buried here?"

"No."

"Too bad. I was hoping he'd see his gravestone and take the hint."

The ground was soggy. The spring bulbs were beaten down, resting on sodden leaves.

"This wouldn't be so creepy during the day," Maggie said.

"We were busy."

Ike had put some people together, scheduled an auction for the following weekend, and sent staff to help Maggie move more of what she continued to call crap. Scott had spent the day reglazing second-story windows busted in the storm and moving antiques. He'd also made some calls, mostly leaving messages using Maggie's cell as his new contact number.

Now there was something remarkable. From a woman who hated racing, who nursed a grudge because her old man was a lousy father who preferred cars and tracks over his family, who depended on her phone to stay in touch with her clients, the offer was totally unexpected. And greatly appreciated.

An owl rose out of the darkness, so close they could hear the flap of its wings and feel the breeze stir on their faces. Maggie ducked and jumped closer; Scott was more than happy to put his arm around her and hold her protectively against his side.

"I think we interrupted his dinner," he said.

"Eww. If I step on anything dead, you're finishing this mission on your own."

"You're not so brave away from home, are you?"

"He caught me off guard. The bats don't scare me at all."

"Bats?" he scoffed good-naturedly. "You don't give up, do you?"

"They're just coming out of hibernation. Haven't you seen them flying around?"

"Those are birds."

"Birds sleep at night. Sheesh."

"An owl's a bird."

"Okay, birds who aren't owls sleep at night."

"You mean those things darting around?" He searched the night sky now and couldn't find any, but he'd seen them in the headlights when they'd parked.

"Uh-huh."

She *could* be right. "Maybe we should just dump this dirt and go."

Maggie laughed at his sudden hurry; Scott didn't mind in the least. As a matter of fact, he wasn't sure which he liked more—her eyes flashing with fire when she was mad at him or the way laughter purred out of her like a well-tuned engine.

They decided to do the job right, though just what that was was open to debate. The book was sketchy on directions.

Their first hurdle had been how much dirt to dig out of the front yard to transport to the cemetery. The book said "some" from alongside the walk leading to the main door. "Some" could be spoon-sized or a whole shovel full. Since he didn't want Grammy stepping in a hole, he'd scooped a sandwich-sized amount from an area where she wasn't likely to step.

The second hurdle was choosing the cemetery. They didn't want one so close that Coop'd find his way back—Scott couldn't believe he was thinking this was reality, but desperation at having his life controlled by a dead man justified stranger things, he supposed—or one so far that it'd take all night. Because Scott had better things to do with Maggie than traipse around crooked headstones.

The third hurdle was figuring out where they were supposed to leave the dirt they'd brought. "Throw it into the cemetery," could mean just that, literally, or it could mean throw it on a grave. And if the latter, whose grave? How far in? How old? Did gender matter?

The fourth hurdle showed up before the third was resolved. Flashing red and blue lights cut through the darkness. Vehicle-mounted spotlights blinded them.

"Maggie? Is that you?"

"What, Jethro and Bubba don't recognize your Mustang?"

Maggie elbowed him and held her hand up to block the light. "Chris?"

"Come on out."

"Dump the dirt," Maggie said quietly to Scott, and

he untied the plastic grocery bag from his belt and up-ended it.

"Freeze! He's dumping something!"

"Hands in the air! Hands in the air!"

"Step away from him, Maggie! *Now!*"

"Oh, for Pete's sake. Chris—"

"Show me your hands! Let me see your hands!"

"Above your head! Above your head!" a second cop shouted.

Scott raised his hands and muttered, "Do *not* tell them why we're here."

Maggie turned to him, her normally sassy and stubborn eyes now green pools of confusion.

"If you do, I'll be needing that white race car you were describing the other day—you know, the one with the ghost eyes—because sure as shooting, everyone's going to hear about Scotty Templeton, ghostbuster."

"You'd rather have them thinking you're dumping drugs and calling in the lab boys? Because 'Scotty Templeton dumps mysterious substance in abandoned cemetery' sounds a lot worse than 'ghostbuster.'"

The cops were almost on top of them, guns drawn, still calling out orders in duplicate.

Scott raised his arms higher and pasted a patient smile on his face. "Fine. But we're telling them it was your idea."

Half an hour later, Scott was swearing for the ump-teenth time that he was not with a satanic cult and that the young, dead opossum was left by an owl and not part of a ritual sacrifice. As evidence, there was no blood or fur in the grocery sack. It bore no evidence of a rodent's struggle to escape.

Maggie swore up and down, again, that they'd brought dirt to the cemetery to fill in a hole that Grammy said she'd seen on Pop's grave, but they hadn't been able to find it, so they'd just dropped the dirt and were ready to go home when they'd been *blinded* by the cops' spotlights.

They swore this in front of not just Chris and Bobby, but in front of every cop who stopped by to lend a hand, which was copspeak for checking out the loonies Chris and Bobby had apprehended in the graveyard. Most of them left shaking their heads. Scott wasn't sure if that was pity for him and Maggie or for their fellow officers.

"Come on, guys, you know Maggie," Scott pleaded. "Look at her. Her nose is turning blue, she's so cold. Let's call it a night, okay?"

Another call came in, and it must have been more urgent, because Chris looked him right in the eye and said, "I'll be watching you," before they rushed to their patrol cars.

"Think we dumped the dirt in the right place?" Maggie asked when they were alone.

"I think we need a better reference book. You ready to go home?"

"Yeah."

"Okay if I sneak into your room tonight?"

Maggie grinned up at him with longing that mirrored Scott's own desire to show her how much he needed her. "Oh yeah."

* * *

Maggie drove home like a bat out of hell, as usual. Scott, leaning as close as his seat belt would allow, played with her hair and teased the sensitive spots on her ear until she giggled and said, "You're distracting me."

"Must be; you actually slowed down."

Wrong thing to say; she leaned on the gas.

"So, what's the fastest you've ever driven?" he asked.

"A hundred ten. You know out west, where the highway goes straight forever and you don't see another car for miles? Out there. It was embarrassing, really."

"You got stopped?"

She snorted. "I was passed by a *delivery* truck. Going uphill."

"Ever think of racing? Following in the old man's footsteps?"

"Puh-*lease*."

"Now wait, think about it for a minute. I mean, you know, you like to drive fast. You've got the history, the background. It's a real rush. And there'd be no delivery trucks to show you up."

"Yeah, couldn't allow that." Maggie tipped her head toward Scott's hand, and he took that as a sign to stroke her some more. "I wouldn't want to race, though. I'd just like to drive as fast as I want for a long time, without worrying about tickets or someone crashing into me or forcing me into the wall."

Maggie slowed to a crawl on Cherry Lane. It wasn't wide enough to receive county maintenance, and the potholes played havoc with suspensions. As she pulled up to the house, she said, "Did you move your truck?"

"In my dreams."

"Seriously, look."

Sure enough, his big black behemoth sat in the side yard, right smack in the middle of the track to the barn; lights on, all four doors and the hood open.

Scott's hand fell from Maggie's hair and he snapped to attention. "Maybe it's Coop's parting gift."

"I'd pull up closer, but I think the ground's still too soft."

"His way of saying good-bye?" Man oh man, this meant he could leave in the morning.

"If it is, he doesn't mind running your battery down to do it."

"He likes having the last word. Come on, let's check it out."

Maggie was out of the Mustang right behind him, and as they hurried to the pickup, she slipped her hand into his.

Okay, maybe not *tomorrow* morning. Why rush off if he didn't have a driving job yet? He could take a day or two to make fresh calls, touch base with some old buddies, a few team owners—

He lost his breath without warning and gasped for fresh air that wasn't there. "Oh. God. Did something die?"

Maggie sniffed the air. "Manure."

"*Damn.* I used to pick stalls at Valley Mount. No way that's manure."

"Pig manure."

Scott gagged. "Oh shit."

"Yeah, that's another word for it."

How could she grin like that when he was about to *die*? But worse— "No—my truck! It's in my truck."

Scott dropped Maggie's hand and rushed up to the door thinking, well, nothing, because who could think through that stench? It took away his breath and clogged his brain except for one powerful, overriding message: *Get. Back.* And he did; he reeled backward, bumping into Maggie as he went.

"That does it," he swore. "I'm fighting dirty now."

Maggie peered around him. "Eww, on the driver's seat. That'll be hard to get out."

"Get out? *Get out?*" No way that stench was coming out. He backed farther away from the truck, pulling Maggie with him, holding one hand over his nose and mouth. "You think they'll take that seat at the dump?"

"That's a little drastic, don't you think?"

"Beats torching the whole thing."

"Where are you going?"

"To bed."

"What about your battery?"

"I'll have it replaced."

He stopped only because Maggie slipped her hand out of his, and he didn't really want to leave her. Heck, he wanted to cuddle up in bed together for the entire night, but she'd gotten some harebrained idea and was actually walking *closer* to the truck. Then circling the truck. A real glutton for punishment.

"You're not human," he said, maintaining his distance.

She reached in through the passenger side and shut off his lights. "We had pigs, remember?"

"You get used to that? Oh wait." Out here, it made sense. "You had a pet pig, didn't you?"

"Arnold, just like on TV." Maggie brushed her hands on her jeans, and with just enough light coming from the back porch, she looked mighty fine walking toward him.

"What happened to him?"

"He fell in love with the neighbor's sow and moved out. They promised not to eat him, so I let him stay there."

"You romantic, you."

Side by side, they stared at the pickup.

"What if he's not really gone?" Maggie said. "What if he's just getting even for the cemetery thing?"

"Please, don't even think it."

Maggie slipped her hand into his again, and hers was so soft and warm, it reminded Scott what the rest of her felt like. Heaven. He leaned in close and whispered, "Come on, let's go to bed."

Laughter bubbled out of her and her nose crinkled when she said, "God, there's nothing sexier than a man holding his nose when he says that."

He leaned close to her and laughed with her and thought, *No way I'm helping her patch things up with Killjoy. She's too good for him.*

 *Chapter 13*

Monday morning, Scott lazily cracked open one eye to find sunbeams inching through the window, landing on a bedside table stacked with color-coded file folders.

What a waste of good sunshine. Give him a race car and a track any day, but not paperwork. Charts, files, graphs—dang, it wasn't enough that Maggie walked around with a phone in her ear all day; she took her work to bed with her at night, too.

Not last night, though, he thought, his chest puffing up with pride.

Scott blinked and rolled to his side and looked around until his gaze landed on a stunning vision in blue. Maggie was poised in front of a wall mirror in a curve-hugging dress and jacket, very professional-looking if anyone wanted his opinion, applying mascara to lashes that he'd discovered were naturally long and sooty. Her week off was over; it was back to the office today. She looked ready—hair shiny, jewelry simple, and no two ways about it, high heels did something for a woman's legs, even when they were as perfect as hers to start with.

"Christ, people think I have a dangerous job."

The intimate warmth in her answering smile seriously

jeopardized her getting to work on time. "What?"

"How do women walk on those?"

"We start young."

He rested his hands behind his neck—the better to keep from pulling her back under the covers—and enjoyed the show as she slicked on lipstick next. Through the closed door, Scott heard the cat hiss at something in the hall. He was pretty sure he knew at what, but it'd take more than that to distract him.

Coop had started coming into the house. Scott wasn't sure just when he'd started, and Maggie and Grammy didn't know it yet, but to someone as tuned to this particular trouble as he was, the evidence was irrefutable. If either of them ever went into his room, they'd think he was the biggest slob this side of the Atlantic. He kept the door closed and tried not to scream obscenities every time he changed clothes, which took longer and longer because Coop not only tossed the room, he smeared toothpaste and shaving cream where toiletries weren't meant to go. He liked to turn the light off and throw the room into pitch blackness when Scott had one leg halfway into his briefs, too.

Maggie put the final touches on her lipstick, then turned around to face Scott and check the contents of her purse at the same time. "You want my car today? If we can sneak you out of here?"

"Seriously?"

"Drop me off, and it's yours until five."

He was antiqued- and ghosted-out, for sure. After he'd shoveled and hosed the worst out of his truck and had it towed to the dealer for whatever manure remedy they deemed necessary, he'd spent the weekend following several pages of advice in the ghost book.

He hung every mirror he could lay his hands on in strategic spots in the barn and in his room because a ghost was supposed to be scared of its own reflection; Coop had accumulated a *lot* of mirrors.

He rang a bell in every corner because that was supposed to repel ghosts, too. There was no expert on hand to say whether the four corners of the barn were the only ones that counted or if every corner made by every stack of junk needed attention, so he went for safety and rang it all over the place until Jeremy threatened him with bodily harm and took it away. There were other bells; good Lord, if a person wanted to collect bells, they came in all sizes in everything from glass to metal. He'd left well enough alone after Jeremy hid the first one, though, because Maggie refused to come back to the barn unless he promised.

Mornings had been a little tricky, sneaking back to his own room without running into Grammy or Ruby, though Scott suspected Ruby knew where he was spending his nights. She slept right above them, and while they hadn't yelled the rafters off, really old farmhouses weren't built for keeping secrets.

Half an hour later, Scott was up and dressed in jeans and a sweater, one sleeve still wet where he'd rinsed off mouthwash and tried to dry it with a hair dryer, until the dryer suddenly quit. He stood inside, watching out the front window as Maggie doled out treats to the dogs by the Mustang. When it appeared that Coop was busy elsewhere, Scott slipped out, limping now instead of hobbling. Just to be safe, he ducked down in the passenger seat.

It was a mild spring morning, a nice day to enjoy the sun instead of digging through an old, dim, dusty barn. After four inches of rain, the grass was greener, the air fresher, and new leaves were growing by leaps and bounds. The peepers were back in full voice.

"Have you ever seen a tree frog?" Scott asked, straightening up as they left Cherry Lane behind and wound uphill to Big Bend.

"Sure, they're cute little things. Sometimes they climb all the way up to the bedroom windows."

Even if he believed her, he had better things to do in the bedroom than look for frogs on the window.

Maggie was more patient on the rush hour drive into Clayton than anytime previously, but it was still a wonder the cops didn't lie in wait for her.

"Any idea what you're going to do today?" she asked.

"Worried about your car already?"

"Nah, I'm running a tab for you. You wreck it, I'll just add it on."

As a running joke, this one could last the rest of their lives. Scott was surprised to find the thought didn't twist his gut into sharp knots and propel him into a panic attack. Pleasantly surprised.

"How is it on gas? Coop demagnetized my credit cards."

"Full. You need cash? Take some out of my purse."

Borrowing money didn't set well with Scott, not from Maggie or anyone, but he'd been getting by in Jeremy's running shoes and really needed his own.

"Got enough for a pair of shoes?"

"Mm, better take a credit card."

He tried to remember if he'd ever so casually lent a woman his credit card, and knew he hadn't. After the circumstances under which he and Maggie had met, he felt privileged to have earned her trust. There was no way he mistook her for a woman who was easily duped.

"You're sure?" he said.

"I can use the extra income. You know what loan sharks charge these days?"

"Not offhand."

"That's okay. I'll make a few calls and find out."

Maggie parked in front of an office building in downtown Clayton, out of traffic's way, but instead of getting out or kissing him good-bye, she twisted the mirror toward her. Scott watched in fascination as she made a ponytail, turned it into a fancy twist, nabbed a clip off the console, and opened it with her teeth. When she was finished with her hair, she made a face at her reflection and turned to him.

"The mirror's too small. How's it look?"

"Great, just like before."

"I used to wear it down, but Kevin says this is more professional-looking."

"Oh-kay."

Her gaze darted between him and the mirror. "Don't you think?"

Scott leaned in and kissed her before he said, "I thought you looked lovely and professional before, and you look lovely and professional now."

"What was that?"

"What?"

"That was a *peck*."

He leaned back. "You didn't like that?"

"If I were a bird I might like it."

"If you were a bird, you wouldn't be wearing lipstick."

With a wicked glint in her eye, Maggie pulled out the clip and shook her hair loose. "This stuff stays on all day. Kiss me right or you don't get the car."

Maggie had achieved none of her goals last week, not a single one. She should feel like a failure, but how could a woman fall in, uh, *start* to fall in love, and feel like a failure? Not possible.

Dressed in her favorite blue Armani, eager to get the day done and meet Scott out front, she floated into the office with her briefcase and two thermoses of heaven.

"May I help you? Oh my gosh, Maggie, I didn't recognize you this early," the receptionist teased. Sarah was the darling of the office, barely twenty, with a killer smile and long, curly red hair to die for, and still she was as sweet as could be.

"It's this new coffee," Maggie said, breezing by

Sarah's desk. "I brought enough for everyone."

Vanessa did a double take at the copy machine and scrutinized Maggie over the top of her reading glasses. "Mm, girl, it's not coffee putting that glow on your face, or Starbucks would be charging a hundred dollars a cup."

"Maggie's glowing?" Paige popped out of her office. "Kevin must have done something right. Wait—he proposed early!"

Quentin rode his chair to the doorway of his cubicle, as far as the phone cord would stretch. "Someone proposed?"

David's bald head popped over the top of his cubicle. "Oh, goody! Can we have a shower? I always wanted to attend a bridal shower."

"Down, boys and girls. I haven't seen Kevin." Maggie made a no-nonsense beeline for the coffee bar. "Come on, you have to taste this. Everybody. I swear it's the best I've ever had."

Paige leaned close to Maggie and whispered, "We still talking coffee?"

"*Ye-es*."

"You haven't seen Kevin?" Paige asked. "Red cup's mine. I thought you were spending the whole week with him."

"Yeah, well, something came up at home."

"Mm-hm," Vanessa hummed, holding out her mug. "Told you it wasn't coffee. Just half, honey, I already had enough caffeine this morning. Though from the look of things"—she was eyeing Maggie's hair, which she hadn't worn down in, oh, forever—"it's not just caffeine's got you up this early."

"I've always been a morning person."

Paige hooted.

Vanessa said, "Girl, you've been dragging your butt in ten minutes late for the past year."

The coffee worked immediate magic, producing a couple of *Oh my God*s, enabling Maggie to keep the status of her love life to herself.

"Where on earth did you get this?" Quentin asked.

"You ground your own beans, didn't you?" David said. "Do you keep them in the freezer?"

Maggie shook her head. "A friend made it, I don't grind my own anything, thank you very much, and I couldn't leave town because, well . . ." There had to be a way to keep the story short and simple. "There was this guy who brought something to the house, see, and he stayed, and, well, he makes the best darn coffee, doesn't he?"

"Shoot," Vanessa said, sauntering away with hers. "If I had a man at my place made coffee like this, you wouldn't see me coming in here fifteen minutes early."

"If you had a man at your place," David said, "you wouldn't come in here at all."

"You're right. I'd tie his butt to the kitchen sink."

"Yeah, after you tied him to the bed."

Everyone but Maggie and Quentin drifted back to cubicles and offices.

"Seriously, nice to see you back to your old self,"

Quentin said, hoisting his mug in salute before he also returned to his desk. "Thanks for the brew."

In spite of having kept in touch with some of her clients by phone over the past week, Maggie had a ton of messages waiting for her. When the third guy in a row said, "Wow, I didn't expect to hear from you before ten o'clock," she sat back in her chair and wondered how everybody could be so wrong. She *was* a morning person. Even when she was a kid, she'd always been the one waiting on the neighbor kids to get up so she'd have someone to play with.

It bugged her to the point where she accomplished little more than spying out her door. When Quentin took a coffee break, Maggie strolled out to the counter under the guise of doing the same.

"Any left?" she asked, buying time, because as friendly as everyone in the office was, they didn't often get into deep personal discussions. Or was that just her perspective? she thought, miffed to be second-guessing herself.

"That nectar you brought—no. Same ol', same ol'—yes." Quentin was holding the carafe, so he poured for her, too.

"Q." *Where to start?* "We've been friends a long time, right?"

"Let's see. Thomas is four now, so I'd say four or five years is about right."

"Well, I've been thinking, you know, about what you said before. And I was wondering, what did you mean about being back to my old self?"

"Oh. Nothing, really." He shrugged, paid too much attention to sugaring his coffee and nervously fiddling with his tie.

Maggie was patient, though; no ducking her when she wanted an answer!

"It's just that I keep hearing the same message, and I'm not sure what everyone's talking about," she said, keeping her voice low so as not to invite everyone into a let's-tell-Maggie-how-it-is encounter group.

Growing thoughtful, Quentin said, "When I started here, you used to have a kind of a glow. I don't know what you'd call it. Feisty, maybe. Sassy. Whatever. You knew what you wanted and you went for it, Maggie. And we all respected that—we still do. Respect you."

He glanced around, still looking for escape, so she said, "But I don't go for it anymore?"

"No, I'm not saying that exactly. I don't know. Over the last year, year and a half, you seemed to close down a little. As if a light inside you went out. Oh," he hastened to add, "you're still professional and great at what you do and you never let work slide, you always stay later than anyone else—"

Maggie held up both hands to stop his cover-my-ass rambling, then smiled and patted his arm to reassure him that she wasn't going to commit coworker carnage.

"Thanks." When Maggie strolled back to her office, Quentin was still fiddling with his tie, probably wondering whether he'd been too honest.

She hadn't thought about Kevin much over the weekend, but now she couldn't help wondering if he'd seen these same changes in her. She speed dialed him.

"I miss you so much, baby," he said right off the bat.

No tingle at the sound of his voice. No jump in her heart rate. Stunned, Maggie realized there never had been. If Kevin had made her blood boil, she'd never have looked twice at another man.

Oh, he was a great guy, paid lots of attention to her, advised her selflessly, was practical and steadfast. But was that enough? He'd be there for the birth of their children, have time to teach their son how to ride a bicycle, and would neither live dangerously nor run his car into a wall before their daughter brought home her first boyfriend.

"You're not still mad at me for missing the whole week?" Maggie asked, though she suddenly realized she didn't care if he was.

"I was a jerk. You couldn't help it. You probably have a lot to catch up on after a week away from your desk, so maybe I can get away soon and come see you next weekend. Unless they send me to Europe—that's coming up any day now. So how would that be? Would you like that? We could do something different. One of the guys was telling me how he and his wife took a riverboat trip up the Mississippi."

Maggie was glad Kevin kept talking because she couldn't find the words. She couldn't say, *Yes, that sounds exciting, I can't wait.*

She wanted Scott; she knew that much. But even if, God forbid, he walked away after what she'd had with him, after having her eyes opened, could there ever be anything between Kevin and her again? Would she even want that?

"Kevin—"

"Or we could book a romantic weekend at a B&B. I heard about one that includes a hot-air balloon ride. Oops, other line, baby. We'll talk later, okay? Love you."

It was just as well. Maggie needed time to think. All misgivings aside, did she have Scott? He hadn't committed himself.

Worse, even if he had, until he was free to pick up and leave whenever he wanted, she wouldn't really have him at all.

"In the name of the Father, I bless this barn," Scott said.

"I don't know," Maggie said, sounding uneasy to him. "You're probably going to hell for this."

"It's what the book said to do. In the name of the Father . . ." Truth be told, the theatrics Scott was going through were partially due to how cute Maggie was when she got irritated with his endless verbal repetition—prayers, if you will—or worried about his mental health.

"*In nomine Patris,*" Daryl intoned behind him, then took a swig of beer.

"*Dominus vobiscum,*" Bruce added.

Maggie shook her head. "All of you. Straight to hell."

"*Ad infinitum.*"

Scott had picked Maggie up after work again today, then driven straight to a local church and filled a small bottle with holy water. She'd kept a lookout, as if they were doing something wrong and lightning might strike them dead on the spot.

It was Maggie's night to cook. They'd had dinner with Grammy, who was put out with her gentleman friend.

"Milton says I have to let go of the past," Grammy complained. "He says I have to get on with my life."

Scott figured advice on Grammy's love life was better handled by the two Cooper granddaughters, so he'd retired to the barn and started sprinkling holy water. Again, the instructions were vague. To him, "sprinkle at every door" carried the possibility of meaning every lid of every trunk and box that the ghost could hide in, and he thought maybe he should open the ones he could get to, so he'd been very busy. Eventually, everyone except Grammy joined him.

Maggie's granddaughterly counsel hadn't taken long, and once she'd come out to the barn, she stayed nearby all evening, keeping him company, going through boxes and labeling the contents on the outside with a red marker. She didn't take a break until her phone *ka-ching*ed.

"Kevin *again*?" Daryl said to Scott. "Geez, can we say 'controlling'?"

"Hey, tell her, not me." The more people who told her, the sooner she'd figure it out.

"Somebody needs to do something about him." Ruby stared at Scott so he wouldn't miss the point.

She had no idea what she was asking.

Scott continued sprinkling. "Look, I knew a woman once who fell for a guy like him. I felt just like you."

"So what'd you do?"

"Strapped him in my car and took him on a ride he'll never forget. Showed him what it was like to have no control, to be at someone else's mercy."

"Scared him, huh?" Ruby grinned.

"He wet himself."

Ruby hooted approval. "I'd like to see Kevin wet himself."

"Then he packed up and moved out."

"Great. She was rid of him."

Scott grimaced. "Not exactly. As soon as he talked to her again, she took his side. She claimed *I* was controlling and jealous, and married the bum. So, can I do anything? Can any of us do anything? Some things, yeah, like Daryl expressing his concern, but when it comes right down to it, Maggie's responsible for herself. All I can do is be here for her." Hoping he'd spelled it out plain enough, he returned to anointing corners. "In the name of Jesus, I bless this barn."

"Oh, I know another one," Bruce said. "*Christe eleison.*"

"What's it mean?"

Bruce shrugged and looked at Daryl, who shrugged, too.

"I'm not saying it if I don't know what it means."

"Shoot, man, it's a prayer. It starts with Christ. It has to be good."

"I'm still not saying it."

"I'm getting me another beer then."

"Yeah," Daryl agreed, following his law partner out of the barn. "Me, too."

Jeremy and Ruby decamped next, dragging rusted, peeling metal lawn chairs outside where they could hold hands and talk, listen to peepers, and admire the stars. Bruce and Daryl had brought a cooler. Scott figured he was lucky anybody'd gotten any work done this evening.

"I banish all spirits from this barn . . ."

"You're getting hoarse," Maggie said. "Want a soda?"

"Yeah, if you're going that way," he said, thinking, *Finally*.

Maggie's retreat gave Scott his first opportunity to get the tapes he'd bought that afternoon. He'd chosen them over CDs because he wanted them to look old, as if they'd been in the barn a long time. He tore off the wrappers on *Does He Control Your Life? How to Tell*; *Regain Control of Your Life*; *What's Best for You;* and half a dozen others, then scratched up half the cases, threw away the rest, and tossed the cassettes into a box in the area in which Maggie'd been working. If she overlooked them, he'd come up with another idea.

He couldn't tell Ruby earlier, but he wanted to help Maggie see that Kevin was just what Daryl had said, controlling. He had to handle it carefully, though, delicately, or he'd be guilty of the same thing.

That accomplished, Scott returned to ghostbusting. The freezer was next. He set all the quilts aside, but not too far because maybe he could con Maggie into taking a break when she returned. He tried to lift the lid and found it stuck, so he put his back into it and forced it, then dipped his fingers into the holy water in preparation for spritzing the inside.

That's when he saw it staring up at him. Two eyes. Wide open. Unblinking.

Human.

"Holy—" The lid slipped from his fingers and fell with a loud thud, and he hoped Coop felt it when it smacked him on the head.

Only . . . that might not've been Coop. Coop would be sitting up, right through the lid, laughing that stupid, obnoxious cackle of his for scaring the bejesus out of Scott. He'd point his finger at him and laugh himself silly.

Scott eased the lid up for a second look. And not just a crack, either, but all the way so he had a little more light, because if there ever was a time he needed a spotlight, this was it.

Was that—? No, of course not. Why would there be a corpse—and a vaguely familiar-looking one, at that—packed in straw in an old chest freezer in Maggie's barn?

Unless . . .

Grammy?

Maggie?—no, no, not Maggie. She'd mentioned a gun, of course, but that was just a bluff.

Wasn't it?

Of course it was. He'd seen Grammy with a shotgun. Maggie'd mentioned burials in the compost pile. He wouldn't put much past Coop, either before or after he died.

But a body? Surely there was a logical explanation.

Yeah. Right. Geez, no wonder the string bean had run for the hills.

Figuring a little holiness couldn't hurt, Scott was spritzing the corpse for good measure when Maggie returned. He closed the lid slowly, scrutinizing her face and demeanor for any sign of fear or apprehension. Or, oh, *guilt.*

"It took longer than I thought," she said with a warm smile. "They just have beer in the cooler, and I had to go— Why are you looking at me like that?"

"Just thirsty, I guess." Scott chugged the soda too fast, which of course made him belch.

"Yeah, that's attractive." Maggie tucked her hair behind her ear, then returned to her task, crouching by the boxes, opening another one to inventory. "Have you seen Pop at all this evening?"

"I don't think so."

He drained the can and squashed it in his hand while he debated the etiquette of finding a corpse in a woman's freezer. A woman he'd slept with and made love with and hoped to steal from her boyfriend. Attachments such as that put a strain on the traditional responses, he thought.

Should he call 911? Should he talk to Coop first? Give him a chance, if he knew anything, to explain? Because maybe Maggie had no idea what was packed in straw in a chest freezer in her barn.

"I'd sure like to talk to Coop," Scott said, raising his voice to carry to every brick corner.

"You shouldn't," Maggie warned.

"This time . . . I think it'd be all right."

She sat back on her heels and studied him. "You feeling okay?"

He bobbed his head noncommittally.

She grinned up at him and said, "Drank that soda too fast, didn't you?"

"Hey, Maggie, you've got company." Bruce strode in, followed by Maggie's two cop friends. In uniform, and not looking any happier this time than last. Man, if they were here to question him again about the cemetery, they couldn't have picked a worse time.

"Hey, guys," Maggie said with a welcoming smile, not at all put off by their stony expressions. "What's up?"

"We're here to search for a body."

Scott's stomach twisted into knots. If this was payback from the ghost for the dirt and the mirrors and the bell ringing and the holy water, Coop ought to realize he was messing with his daughter's freedom.

"Great—the more, the merrier," Maggie said gratefully. "We've been looking for days—"

She obviously had no idea how her words could be misconstrued, so Scott inched out of the cops' line of sight and tried to give a heads-up to his buddies by miming and charading, *Dead body in the freezer*. He wasn't sure if they understood.

"—and frankly," Maggie continued, "I think we're all getting just a little tired of it. Did Kelly come with you?"

"You're aware there's a body in here, then?"

"Well, sure. You might want to change into old clothes first, though. Everything's pretty dusty."

"Maggie . . ." Scott warned.

"Don't say another word," Bruce said with cool authority, and Scott thought with relief that he'd gotten the message after all, even though from looking at his face, you couldn't tell one way or the other. "Miss Cooper meant an *auto* body, officers. A car. We've been searching for one since last week."

The officers' expressions were unreadable. Scott didn't think they were buying it, but that could be just because he'd seen what he'd seen.

"Seems someone reported seeing human remains in here a couple nights ago, and this"—Bruce waved the official paperwork—"is a search warrant."

Maggie chuckled. "Right."

"He's not kidding." Daryl took it from Bruce and passed it to Maggie.

She rose slowly, skimming the document while Scott wondered how many fingerprints he'd left on the freezer and if he could erase every last one of them by sliding his butt along the edge, because sure as hell, his were the ones they'd find.

"Oh, for heaven's sake." Maggie thrust the document back at Daryl, but her focus was on the cops when she planted her fists on her hips. "If there was a dead body in here, don't you think we'd all *smell* it?"

Scott's gut clenched tighter when both cops turned

without hesitation toward him, and Chris said, "Not if it's in an air-tight freezer."

Bobby eyed the nondescript plastic bottle in Scott's hand and, swear to God, his hand slid toward his revolver. "What do you have there?"

"Water." Scott chugged it and smacked his lips. "Thirsty job."

Bobby didn't look as if he believed him, but instead of pursuing that, which would have been nice, which would have been a relief, actually, he said, "Step aside, please."

Scott put as much distance between himself and the freezer as he possibly could without getting handcuffed for leaving the scene of a crime.

As Chris lifted the lid and said, "Ah-hah," Maggie said, "Oh my God—that?"

"Maggie—" Scott warned again, thinking that tomorrow he'd be visiting her in lockup if she didn't heed his warning.

But did she? Nooo, not Maggie. Instead, she said, "*That*'s what you're here for?"

"Not another word," Bruce cautioned.

"You mean like, What took you so long? It's only been in there five years."

Bruce and Daryl just about fell over each other to get between Maggie and the law and to keep her from further incriminating herself, short of clamping a hand over her mouth.

"Maggie, as your attorney, I have to advise you—"

"Oh, get out of my way." She brushed Bruce aside with an impatient huff. "My attorney, my butt."

"Please, listen to him." Scott took Maggie by the arms and dragged her back, while Bruce advised in hushed, lawyerly tones what her rights were and why it was to her advantage to keep her mouth shut.

"Sweetheart, please listen to him," Scott begged.

"But—"

"Because I don't know how often I'd be allowed to visit you in prison."

Maggie looked taken aback for a moment, then her face lit up with a slow grin. "You'd visit me in prison?"

"Yeah, I always wondered how those conjugal visits work."

"Uh, Maggie. A word here?" Chris said.

She evaded Scott and his buddies, scowling at the latter—unjustly, he thought, since they only had her best interests at heart. She joined the cops by the freezer and peered inside.

"So how does he look? Did he hold up?" she asked eagerly.

Scott wouldn't have believed it if he hadn't seen it, but Maggie reached in and poked around as if she touched dead bodies every day.

"Maybe I should have used more straw," she said.

"Oh man," Bruce groaned. "She's cooked."

"You're lawyers; *do* something."

Bruce's look was a little sympathetic, but mostly questioning if Scott had gone both blind and deaf in the last three minutes. "In case it's escaped your notice, there are two cops witnessing every word she says."

"I wondered where you'd put him," Chris said. "Let's stand him up and see how he looks. I'll get his head."

Scott thought he must have misunderstood until Daryl whispered, "Witnessing, shit. The guys *with guns* are *in on it.*"

Until a few minutes ago, Scott's main goal in life was to get back on the racetrack. Now it appeared he'd be better off figuring out how to stay alive. Though he had trouble wrapping his mind around Maggie having anything to do with offing someone. Especially him.

Maybe not so her partners in crime, however. The ones with guns.

"You got any ideas?" Bruce whispered.

"Run like hell?"

 *Chapter 14*

Maggie watched carefully as Chris and Bobby lifted the body out of its straw bed. Technically, it was only the top half. That's all there'd ever been.

"Let's take it over by the door where there's more light," she said, eager to examine it.

In this light, it looked pretty darn good, but she doubted it'd hold up to scrutiny. The freezer used to work, back when she'd laid him in it, but it was old and cranky and looked as if it had bit the dust during a warm spell, because he was a little wilted around the nose and ears.

Jeremy wandered in with Ruby, took one look at the half body, and announced, "Ladies and gentlemen, Elvis has entered the building."

It wasn't the best wax likeness of him, though as far as looking alive went, it was good enough to fool most, including Scott and his buddies, who started laughing like demented fools, slapping each other on the shoulders and pointing fingers. In short, unable to speak in full sentences and yet trying to make the other two look more foolish. It was the only reason Maggie'd liked it enough to try to preserve it.

"God, I'd forgotten he was left here," Ruby said.

"I never was able to track down a stolen wax figure," Chris said.

Maggie and Scott hung back as everyone else talked at once and carted Elvis toward the bright spotlight outside.

"So," she said.

"So."

"Penny for your thoughts?"

Scott tipped his head a little bit sideways, the way he always did when she wasn't sure if he was going to tease her or kiss her. "I'll tell you on our first anniversary."

She smiled, slow and easy. "Define 'first anniversary.'"

Even though the light was less than optimum, it couldn't hide Scott's dimple when he said, "That would be where you wake up one morning a year from now, and you're lying in my arms, thinking how lucky we are and how every time is the best time."

"Every time can't be *the* best time."

"Sure it can." He shut the freezer and lifted her onto the edge and nudged her knees apart so there was no space between them. "Because we're going to practice. A lot."

Scott's ragged voice sent ripples of heat through Maggie, and she smiled softly, even as he nibbled at her lips and she breathed him in and wanted more. "A whole year, huh?"

"At least."

"Well, okay then."

She didn't care that they were in a dusty old barn

where Pop might be around or someone might walk in. They could practice half a best time now, and the other half later, after everyone left. And they were about halfway through their halfway when someone walked up silently and stood behind Scott and cleared his throat. Repeatedly.

"Sorry." Chris looked more amused than apologetic as he thrust his cell phone into the narrow space between Scott and Maggie. "Kelly wants to talk to Maggie, and she won't take no for an answer." Kelly was his sister.

Maggie looked at Scott with a mixture of longing and regret. And promise. "Remember where we were, okay?"

She accepted the phone, a little concerned Scott would take offense as Kevin did when her friends called, back when they used to call, but he didn't seem to. Which was good, because even though she was concerned, she had no intention of not talking to Kelly after not hearing from her for months.

"No problem," Scott said, easing away, allowing the night air to touch Maggie, to cool her body where he'd just been heating it up so well. "I'll just go check on Elvis."

"Chris says you have a new boyfriend," Kelly said in her ear. God, it was good to hear her voice again, the abrupt change of focus smoothed over by the warm cloak of old friendship, almost as if the months hadn't passed. "So, you want to get together?"

Maggie had so much to tell her. "Sure," she said eagerly. "Come on over."

"When?"

"Now."

Kelly whooped, said, "Hallelujah! I'll pick up Stacie on my way," and disconnected.

There it was again, that welcome-back attitude. Maggie still didn't understand what the heck everyone was talking about, but she knew how to find out. Kelly'd tell her—if there was anything to tell.

"Is there any more pepperoni?" Chris, still in uniform, was seated at the foot of the kitchen table, which had been extended to its full length for the late-night pizza party. It spanned the entire room, from sink to wall, and while it could have seemed crowded, it spoke more of camaraderie and reunion.

In honor of his resurrection, Slightly Wilted Half Elvis had the head seat. A series of exclusively nonwilted Elvis tunes poured in from the living room CD player, the rowdier songs prompting occasional hip gyrating, not necessarily harmonious duets from the guys.

"Hey. Down there. At this end." Chris raised his voice over the other ten, and yet, Grammy noticed, this still didn't distract anyone except his sister. "Pass some pepperoni this way, would you?"

"Mushrooms okay?" Kelly asked.

"Don't Be Cruel," Chris retorted.

The girls groaned; the guys hooted their approval. In seconds, everyone jumped back into various ongoing conversations.

Kelly picked up the last piece of pepperoni-and-mushroom pizza and took a bite. "Mm, God, that's good. Here, Maggie"—she nudged her with her elbow—"pass this to Chris."

With the kitchen as busy as it was, Chris didn't notice Maggie, too, take a bite before passing it on. But Grammy did. She sat midway at the table, reveling in the collective energy of these lively twenty-somethings as they devoured an assortment of six large Cecil Whitaker's pizzas, cheese bread, salad, and drinks. And stories! Oh my, it was so much like old times, it warmed her heart. Maggie and Ruby always enjoyed bringing their friends home, whether it be for slumber parties or impromptu get-togethers like this. The only thing better would be if Milton were here, but the cranky old goat had it in his head that she should quit worrying about getting answers from her Lawrence and get on with life.

Hmph.

If mingling with these youngsters wasn't getting on with life, she didn't know what was. The cranky old goat actually preferred a sedate game of bridge.

Double *hmph.*

Good thing he wasn't here, then. He'd never be able to handle four or five conversations going on at once, some of which not only crossed the table, but zigzagged. Pizza was passed, drinks were poured. Conversations flowed like river water; always moving, never the same, swelling as they went, parting into branches and coming back together again. High school. Jobs. Relationships.

It had been a while since they'd done this. Maggie'd

been so tied up in Kevin that she'd lost sight of what she enjoyed most, and Ruby's friends, of late, thought it was cool to "hang" in her attic room. It made Grammy feel better if she pictured them wearing capes and hanging by their heels, which, looking at some of them, probably wasn't too far-fetched.

She wasn't worried about Ruby, though; she'd outgrow it. But Maggie, well, she was like a rose bush that needed a shot of fertilizer, and if the heat in Scott's eyes meant anything, she'd likely be getting one soon.

Although, from the way Maggie smiled back at him, she might have already.

Darn that Milton for missing this party, Grammy thought, fanning herself with her napkin. Someone should set the cranky old goat straight.

"Hey," Chris complained when the edge of crust finally reached his end of the table. "What's up with this? Where's my pizza?"

"Oh, hey, man, was that yours?" Bruce asked around the last bite. He tried not to laugh, but everyone else was.

Putting on his best cop face, Chris dropped the crust to his plate and squared his shoulders. "I'm not Barney Fife, you know. I've got bullets in this gun and I want pepperoni."

It didn't take but a second for all those who still had some in front of them to pluck it off their slices and toss it at him. He grinned good-naturedly as he collected the circles and said, "I knew this gun'd come in handy someday."

"I hope that's not Too Much," Maggie said. Ruby and Stacie leaned across the table and high-fived her for the Elvis title match.

Grammy, feeling very proud and maternal and having no one else there to share it with, leaned toward Scott and said, "My granddaughters grew into nice young women, didn't they?"

The hungry gaze he leveled on Maggie wasn't in the same vein.

"Landsakes, I wish my Lawrence could see them now. He'd be so proud. Not that he had anything to do with it, mind you," Grammy added.

Ashes hissed and leaped onto the counter by the sink.

"Eww," Stacie said, pulling a face, glancing at the food on her plate with new insight and a bit of disgust. "You never used to let him up there."

Grammy was too surprised to yell at him, but Ruby did, and Maggie tossed an empty soda can into the sink, the racket of which launched the cat right off there with an offended yowl.

"Damn, this is good pizza, isn't it, guys? Mm-mm," Scott hummed around another bite.

Grammy agreed, though she wondered why Scott started talking over everybody. Maggie was watching him with a crooked, knowing grin, which could mean anything from *I'm making you wash the dishes tonight* to *You can eat pizza in my bed anytime.*

Grammy pressed her ice-cold glass of beer against the pulse in her neck.

"Outstanding," Scott boomed. "Spicy sausage and—

what is that? Oregano? Sticks-to-the-roof-of-your-mouth cheese. Crispy crust. *Smells* good, too."

With his back arched and his tail puffed out, Ashes retreated under the butcher block, and to Grammy's surprise, Scott turned to her and picked right up where they'd left off, in as normal a tone as before.

"So, Coop wasn't around much when Maggie was growing up?"

Mm-hm, he's interested.

Grammy felt comfortable answering because the others had resumed their own conversations; she and Scott could talk privately. "Lord, no, he was always chasing the next dollar. I don't know why my daughter-in-law put up with him until the day he died, except she just loved him so much. Grass is greener. Pie in the sky. The next 'sure thing.' Everything was a 'sure thing' to my Lawrence."

The cat flattened his ears and hissed.

"Now what's got into him, I wonder. Maggie, hon, do we have more pizza?"

"Mm-mm, I can *smell* it," Scott said, his voice again rising above the others.

Maggie'd stashed some in the oven to stay hot, and she laughed at Chris's hopeful look when he said, "Pepperoni?"

"Ooh, sorry," she said. "Sausage and Canadian bacon."

Chris's face fell. "Your phone's blinking."

Ruby hissed, "Shh," and from the way Chris jumped, he'd been kicked under the table, too.

Maggie checked her phone. "It's voice mail."

"Probably a client," Ruby said.

"Probably not important," Stacie said.

"You should get it later," Kelly said.

While Chris and Bobby nudged the women to find out what was going on, Maggie stared at her grandmother and waited.

"What?" Grammy asked innocently.

"You're the only woman here who hasn't told me what to do. I thought you may want to get a word in before the conversation picks up again."

"Treat Me Nice?" Grammy said in upspeak. She glowed when everyone applauded her, because she hadn't joined in before.

A lot of mothers and grandmothers would go to bed and leave the kitchen to the kids to party in, but not Grammy, and Maggie was glad her grandmother got along so well with her friends and felt comfortable with them, and vice versa. Life was good. Until recently, very recently, she'd forgotten to take time to notice.

Scott cleared his throat. "Want me to check it?"

"Yeah, thanks." They didn't want Pop to know that she'd given him the number to use for racing stuff, and from the way the cat and Scott were acting, she was pretty certain Pop was present.

Ruby whispered, "If it's Kevin—"

"Ruby," Maggie warned.

"Oh, fine."

"Honestly, I don't know what everyone has against

him." Maggie yanked the hot pizza out of the oven and set it in the middle of the table. "Kevin's kind. He's hardworking. He's focused."

"He's moved away," Ruby said with a smirk.

"He invests twenty percent of his salary."

"He wants everyone to know it . . ." Kelly muttered.

Maggie scowled at her because, really, Kevin was careful about growing his asset base and diversifying his equity investments. Very informed. Anal about research. Seemed no one here cared about those qualities. Not tonight anyway.

Grammy *hmph*ed.

"He has good taste."

"Would he give up his home and job for you?" Chris asked.

"He's generous."

"He bought you a car," Scott said, the phone still to his ear.

"There. See?"

"It's 'more appropriate'—whatever that means." Scott listened to more, then disconnected to relay the message. "There's no need to thank him, and you have up to two years to pay him back."

"*What?*"

There were a lot of *ooh*s and *uh-oh*s around the table. Everyone who'd known Maggie longer than a week sat back, as if she might start throwing things. Which she never did. Almost never. Scott, Jeremy, and Bruce picked up on the cue and eased back in their chairs, too.

"He said that?" Maggie ground out through tight lips.

Scott held out the phone. "I saved it."

"Good one," Grammy said as she nudged him, and Maggie said, "I saw that."

Daryl, who'd ducked out to the bathroom, came back to a whole different dynamic than when he'd left. He took his seat, and when no one else spoke, he looked around and very obtusely said, "Did I miss something?"

"She's All Shook Up," Bruce murmured.

Bobby, also in uniform, opened his mouth to add something, maybe another title, but changed his mind when Maggie snarled, "Kevin wouldn't do that."

"Yes he would," Kelly and Stacie said together.

Maggie would've sworn she'd never arched her eyebrows in her entire life, but she felt them go up now. She was the only one standing, and she looked at her best friends and very definitively said, "You have something you want to say?"

Bruce murmured, "*Sanctus excrementus,*" and the men grabbed pizza and beer and charged out the back door.

Chris and Bobby ran back in for Half Elvis. "Evidence," Chris murmured. They heaved him out of his chair and ran out with him tucked under their arms like a battering ram.

Stacie blew out a harsh breath. "*Men.*"

"No guts," Kelly said.

Grammy nodded in agreement.

"They took all the sausage," Ruby whined.

"Hell-o-o, you're *vegetarian.*"

Ruby sighed loudly and looked at Kelly and Stacie when she said, "I hope you guys know what you're doing."

"How could they?" Maggie snapped. "They haven't been around for the last year."

"Year and a half," Kelly said.

"Yeah—why is that?" There, Maggie'd said what was on her mind, what had been bugging her since her girl-friends arrived this evening and everything seemed as it was before. Nothing was wrong. No one was mad.

Then where the heck had they been?

"Well, if you think back," Stacie said, and *darn*, she had such a reasonable, nonconfrontational tone that Maggie found herself paying attention. "Every time we tried to get together, you were always busy with Kevin. Helping him organize his files . . ."

"Entering stuff on his computer . . ."

"Setting up a spreadsheet . . ."

"I understand that stuff better than he does," Maggie countered calmly.

Her friends grimaced as one. Looking at them was like having double vision.

"Maybe," Kelly said. "Or maybe it was just Kevin's way of keeping you away from us."

Taken aback, Maggie plopped into her chair. "Why would he do that?"

"Yeah. Why?"

She didn't expect an answer, and if she got one, she didn't hear it because she was too busy thinking back.

"Come on, baby, let's get these files done and then

we can go out to dinner and a movie," Kevin had said on more than one occasion. As well as "Maggie, sweetheart, you can see your girlfriends anytime, but I really could use your help now," "It's for our future," and "Why don't you cancel your trip to the lake? I've got two tickets to Bermuda."

But she couldn't help thinking Scott must have heard the voice mail wrong, because Kevin wouldn't commit *thousands* of dollars of her money. Would he? There was no way to know except to hear it for herself, so she accessed voice mail.

"Maggie, sweetheart, sell that old Ford," Kevin's message began without preamble. "You want something new when you move up here. Something more appropriate. Something that'll impress clients. And—are you sitting down?—I found just the thing and bought it for you. No, no, don't thank me. And there's no rush paying me back. I can give you a good interest rate over two years."

Maggie figured she'd turned purple or steam was blowing out her ears when Ruby jumped out of her chair and said, "Grab the glasses!"

"The plates."

"The pizza!"

"Margaret Anne Cooper," Grammy enunciated.

"Don't worry. I'm not going to throw anything." Maggie rose abruptly, sending her chair crashing backward against the edge of the counter. "Not here anyway."

She stormed out the back door, across the porch,

across the yard, thinking, thinking, thinking.

What Stacie and Kelly said rang true, she had to admit. Grudgingly. And put together with the gentle messages she'd been getting from Grammy and Ruby for the past year, and the less than tactful comment Daryl'd made about how often Kevin called—but really, she wasn't sure that was a problem; they liked to stay in touch. What was wrong with that?—it all made sense.

But—and it was a big BUT—she'd had a few beers. She probably wasn't seeing the whole picture as clearly as she needed to. If they were right—and it was a big IF—she certainly hadn't been seeing it for the last year or more, and she shouldn't run right out and do anything rash tonight. Certainly not drive straight to Chicago and accuse Kevin of cutting her off from her friends. Because he hadn't really. Had he?

If he had, she'd let him.

But he'd bought a car? _For_ her? And he was going to charge her _interest_? If she still had the power of speech, she'd be shouting at the gall of that. He'd hear her in Chicago without benefit of a phone.

"Maggie, wait up."

The moment Scott touched her arm, she wheeled on him and said, "A friggin' _car_?" No way she was taking that. "Who the hell does he think he is that he can call my Mustang an old Ford anyway?"

"It's not that old," Scott agreed.

"It's the way he said it," she huffed.

Scott tried to pull her into his arms; Maggie was too

agitated to stand still or enjoy it. Another blame to heap on Kevin's head, that he could ruin this for her even when he wasn't here.

"Nice night. Want to go for a walk?" Scott asked gently.

"No," she huffed, thinking, *God, could I be that petulant?*

Scott's moonlit smile was crooked and indulgent and maddeningly understanding, though there was no way he could understand how vexed she was right now.

"You're never going to do anything a man ever suggests again, are you?"

"Damn straight," she snapped.

"I don't think I've heard you cuss before." When he touched her arm this time, she didn't pull away. "I know this because you were really mad when you met me."

Maggie bit her lip because Scott was humoring her out of her anger, and she wasn't ready to let it go. "Your point is?"

He wrapped his big arms around her and gently pulled her head against his shoulder. "Please don't ever get this mad at me. Swear to God, I will *never* try to control you."

She wedged her hands between their chests and shoved a whole two inches between them. Truth be known, that didn't feel good. She didn't want more space between them, but—and here was a term she never used, not even silently, but suddenly she needed to because it was such a good fit—she was just so *pissed off.*

There, that felt better.

She'd deal with Kevin tomorrow.

"I know you think I'm weak for letting it go on so long," she said, calming down.

"I never said—"

"Stop. Right there." She wiggled free then, stormed into the barn and back out again with the box of tapes she'd "found" earlier.

"Oh." Scott scratched the back of his neck in as guilty a maneuver as Maggie'd ever seen on a man. At least he wasn't trying to hide it. "What gave me away?"

"If you want something to look as if it's been around awhile"—she picked up a cassette and brandished it as an example—"you should check the copyright date."

"Ah. I'll make a note of that."

"Or here's a thought." Maggie tossed the box aside, caring neither where it landed nor what spilled out of it, and did exactly what she did care about, which was to step back into the circle of Scott's arms. "Don't do it again."

Rising to her toes, she pulled his head toward hers, slowly, until their lips met in a kiss so warm, so comforting, and at the same time so *hot*, that she knew she was where she belonged. Forget charging off to blow what's-his-name's brains out; this was where she wanted to be.

She wrapped one leg around Scott, and when he cupped her bottom and lifted her higher, closer, she wanted to stay forever.

"Let's go make out in the barn." Scott's voice was ragged, with a sense of urgency that made Maggie even hotter. Yet something nagged at her.

"Can't," she whispered against his lips.

"We have an audience here."

"Later." As much as she'd enjoy escaping to the barn with Scott, if she'd truly let someone walk all over her for months on end, it wasn't a habit she intended to continue. She loosened her grip.

"Darlin', if you wiggle like that again, we won't even make it to the barn."

Maggie chuckled against Scott's lips, though it sounded as much like a moan as laughter, and continued to unwrap herself from him until her feet were, once again, firmly on the ground. "There's something I have to do first."

"For God's sake, *what*?"

"Mend some bridges. With my friends."

"Oh. Yeah. Right." With each word, Scott loosened his embrace, just a little, until Maggie turned and, holding his hand until the very last second, slipped away.

While it was only a hundred feet back to the porch, it was a very long walk. The guys were gone, but the women had hung around. Kelly and Stacie waited patiently on the top step, arms folded, saying nothing, not even when Maggie reached the bottom step. They weren't going to make this easy on her, that was for sure.

But then, she didn't deserve easy, she guessed. Somewhere along the line, she'd lost her way. Lost her *self*. And without that, how could she build a new, healthy relationship? How could she share all of herself with Scott when she didn't have all of herself back yet?

"I owe you guys a huge apology," Maggie said on the

first tread, and proceeded from there as she climbed each one. "I don't know what was wrong with me. I don't know how I let this happen. I can't say it enough—"

At the top, both girls opened their arms until the three of them were sharing a hug that was long overdue. And tears; Lord, how the tears flowed down her face.

Maggie felt a hole inside her begin to close up and heal, a hole she hadn't known was there. How could she have let this space come between them? They lived two miles down the road, for God's sake. They'd gone through twelve years of school together. She thought about what it meant to grow apart from friends, and how she hadn't even realized she'd alienated them, no, *lost* them, until this evening, and how thankful she was that it wasn't too late to make amends.

This time.

No, it wouldn't happen again.

Maggie sniffed against Kelly and Stacie's shoulders and squeezed them tightly and bounced them a little when she said. "If I ever, *ever*, tell you guys I'm too busy to do something with you again, I hope you sit on me and knock some sense into me."

"Yeah, right."

She opened the hug and made steady eye contact. "You want me to put it in writing? I will."

Kelly and Stacie were sniffling, too, as they shook their heads. "I don't think that'll be necessary."

"You won't forget again. We'll test you."

"Often," Maggie urged. "Until I get it for sure."

"But right now"—Kelly nudged Stacie and glanced

over Maggie's shoulder—"we're the ones who have to go."

Maggie turned. Scott was leaning against one of the newel posts, looking all casual and sexy and flashing his dimple.

Stacie hugged Maggie quickly and whispered, "This one's a keeper," in her ear. Kelly did the exact same thing. Then both her friends hurried to Kelly's car and left for the night. But they left something behind, too.

Her.

Peace.

A sense that all was right with the world; at least her world, right here, right now. While it was a gift, it wasn't something they'd given her, but allowed her to—no, *helped* her to find again.

She wasn't finished, either.

She held out her hand to Scott, who winked up at her and, knowing the house rules, faked a yawn and stretched and said, "Christ, it's past my bedtime. See you ladies in the morning."

He took the steps in two strides, pecked Maggie on the cheek, and headed inside.

"Yeah, me, too," Maggie said with a grin she couldn't wipe off her face as she followed him through the door.

"Sounds good," Ruby said.

"Not so fast, young lady," Grammy barked. "We're gonna clean up the kitchen. Better yet, you and me and Elvis can sit out here awhile and talk and look at the stars." Chris and Bobby hadn't really needed Elvis.

Maggie caught up to Scott and took his hand, the one

not in the cookie jar, and at the same time glanced over her shoulder in time to catch Grammy's knowing grin.

"But I've got to get to bed," Ruby whined to their grandmother. "I have a date in the morning."

"Another hour won't kill you."

"An *hour*?" she said with a pout. "Shoot, I can't wait to be twenty-eight."

Chapter 15

"An hour," Scott whispered, his voice rough and ragged in Maggie's ear as he held her within his embrace, sounding eager even to himself, and trust him, he was barely paying any attention to himself. "That should be enough time."

He kissed the dampness from her cheeks. Her girl-friends were nice people, obviously had her best inter-ests at heart, and—what the hell, this wasn't the time to think about them, either. Except that they approved of him, and every smart man knew the path to a woman's heart was smoother if it went through her girlfriends.

He and Maggie were standing beside her bed, arms and legs and bodies entwined, and he couldn't believe Grammy wasn't going to storm up the stairs, shotgun in hand, and throw him out. That she actually *approved* of his being there.

He'd done all he could, all Maggie would allow him to do, to show her that he understood her need to be independent, to be her own person, not to be possessed or controlled by another. Whether it would be enough when she saw Kevin again remained to be seen. Whether she'd keep the strength she'd regained, that was the question. Over time, how much control had she given up? Did a person ever get it all back?

These were questions Scott had no answers to. He hadn't listened to the self-help tapes; he doubted Maggie would, either. She had a history of strong family ties and longtime friends to draw on, though, and he hoped those would be enough. They had to be, because what else was there for him to give her?

He knew where to start. He hooked a finger into the neck of her shirt, then pulled it off over her head and tossed aside her bra. When he leaned in and kissed the hollow of her neck, she sucked in a sharp breath and shuddered, her throat pulsing wildly against his lips.

"Wait," she whispered against the top of his head as he worked his way down.

He groaned an unintelligible reply against the valley between her breasts.

"The cat."

"Let him get his own girl."

"Listen."

Sure enough, the cat was in the hall, hissing and yowling and generally carrying on as if someone were out to kill him.

"Goddamn ghost." Scott reluctantly released Maggie and headed for the door, ready to do battle in the hall with her father because this time he was *really* going too far.

Maggie pulled Scott up short, saying, "Oh, let me," with relish. She didn't even bother to cover herself with her shirt, just yanked open the door and snarled, "You're dead. Get over it. Go away," down the hall.

There was a crash at the far end. A picture fell to the floor with a thud. And then something toppled over downstairs.

Maggie picked up the cat before she closed the door, and Scott wondered if the marbled fur felt as soft against her breasts as they felt against his chest.

"He's joining us?" he asked warily.

"Ghost alarm."

"Uh . . . how about how *alarmed* I am about his claws getting near my vital areas?"

Maggie dropped the cat, then tumbled Scott onto the bed and straddled him and ripped his shirt open, her grin sexy and wicked and promising far more than an hour of mindless, endless pleasure.

"Not to worry," she said. "Everything vital will be in my hands."

He lay back and let her show him just what her hands could do, and whenever he couldn't stand not touching her, he tried to reciprocate, only Maggie batted his hands away, moved back, and stripped off the rest of his clothes, and he felt her breath on his skin, warm and moist and insistent, her mouth on him, hot and wet and possessive, until he couldn't think anymore.

And then she moved up his body and took him inside her and rode him until he had nothing more to give, and she clutched him and gave herself up with small breathless cries that made him wish the night would never end.

Maggie let him hold her then, let him pull her into the curve of his body, keep her warm, and whisper God-knew-what against her skin.

* * *

Scott hadn't slept in in forever, and it looked like the perfect morning to do it on Thursday; dark and dreary outside the bedroom window.

Why the hell get up and keep searching for that damn 'Cuda, anyway? He'd get up later and wash another round of clothes—his last load for a while, because he was now out of toothpaste and shaving cream.

Maggie had been spending her days at her office. Ike's crew had begun in the second barn, repeatedly instructed to come find him if they tripped across anything in Lemon Twist Yellow. Jeremy picked up Ruby on his Harley early each day and didn't return her until dinner or later. Bruce and Daryl spent less time helping him each evening.

Not that Scott blamed them. Without a hint as to the 'Cuda's whereabouts, without a clue that it had ever even been there, who was to say if that annoying old ghost didn't have Alzheimer's? Whether he was making the whole thing up? Although what sick reason a dead human being would have to drive Scott's career into the ground, no pun intended, was beyond him.

So why get up?

Scott rolled over onto Maggie's side, though, truth be known, neither of them had a designated side. His favorite position was bottom, with Maggie draped over his chest, her head snuggled next to his, usually on the same pillow. He scrunched it up under his cheek now and inhaled the lingering scent of her shampoo.

Nine more hours, and she'd be back. Fourteen more

hours, and they'd be in this room again, together. And who had top or bottom then was up for grabs, because Maggie was anything but dull and boring.

Exciting maybe? Nah, too tame a word.

Passionate? Way beyond that, thank you very much.

Hot-blooded? Oh yeah, definitely. He liked that one.

As much as Scott wanted to see Maggie in one of Ruby's bustiers, as often as he'd had the opportunity to suggest it again since the night they'd spent in the cellar, he couldn't. The last thing she needed was another man changing her. Some women, you could make a suggestion or two. With Maggie, a woman who was just finding herself again, well, she needed a little time to do just that. After a while, when he'd know the difference between her doing something for him and her doing something *for* him, he might buy her one of her own. About two sizes too small.

With a vivid picture forming in his mind of Maggie stretched out seductively across a large mattress, her breasts spilling over the top edge of a snug bustier, Scott started to slip back to sleep, to dream about what a night that would be. He was just getting to the good part when his blankets went flying—ripped off, actually, leaving him bare-assed and chilly.

"Lazy, good-for-nothing . . ." Coop snarled.

"Glad you're here. We need to talk." Scott rolled onto his back and doubled the pillow under his neck, only to have it ripped away, too, so he substituted his hands and issued the first jibe that came to mind. "I think you broke a lamp downstairs last night. You know, when you were running for the hills."

"Thought you didn't want to talk to me no more. Thought you wanted me to go away."

"Yeah, well, that hasn't worked, has it?"

"Get outta my daughter's bed."

"Oh, I'm so scared."

"You should be."

"You won't do anything to me as long as that car's still missing. You know it, and I know it."

"So go find it," Coop roared. He jumped on the mattress, turning it into his own private trampoline.

"Stop. You're giving my dick whiplash."

Coop loomed over him and shouted, "You're lucky I don't cut it off."

"What? You don't want to be grandfather to my children?"

"Children—ha! That's a good one." Nobody could have been more surprised than Scott when Coop bounced down and sat on the side of the mattress, slouched with his elbows on his knees, and said, "You don't have any more business being a father than I did."

"Whoa. We're not gonna bond now, are we?"

"It's true. I was a lousy father. I didn't even know it till last night."

This was a whole new side to Coop, and Scott didn't have a clue where to go with it. Let him talk? Tell him he was right? Get the hell away from him?

"Do ya think Ma was right? I had nothing to do with

raising them girls? Sure she was. She and my wife were here for 'em. They raised 'em. Did a fine job, too, except for letting Ruby mark up her face like that."

"It's not permanent."

"No? That's good."

Shit, Scott hadn't meant to cheer him up. So when Coop said, "And the little stick figure thing on her neck?" Scott got to bring him back down with "It's an ankh. Permanent."

Coop hung his head.

Scott said, "I liked it better when you didn't come in the house."

"Too damn many mirrors in the barn."

"So that works?" Dang, he'd bring them inside!

"Nah. Those fine old frames should be worth more today, but I heard the auction people saying we'd be lucky to get fifty to a hundred dollars apiece. Hardly worth the trouble."

Geez, who knew? A depressed ghost. "Yeah. Too bad you can't kill yourself and be done with it."

The ghost sighed, but said nothing.

"This is a trick, right?" Scott said. "To make me feel sorry for you and haul ass outta bed? You know, everybody would've been happier if you'd just asked Grammy to look for your dang car. She'd get to talk to you. I'd be racing. You wouldn't be freaking out over Maggie and me."

Coop wrung his hands. "Couldn't. Maggie pointed out to me a long time ago that I was doing more harm than good by hanging around where Ma could see me. And she was right. Wish I'd known it was going to go on this long, though. I mighta handled it different. Anyways, it's Thursday. You're going over to Gateway tonight."

"You know about that?"

"I heard you on the phone."

"And you won't try to stop me?"

"You'll come back. Maggie's here." Coop shook his head and pushed himself to his feet, moving like a much older man. "Don't make me hurt you, son. I can't stop you from playing around, Lord knows I've tried, but you hurt Maggie and . . . Well, just remember, they can't convict a ghost." He shuffled to the door.

"I liked it better when you were depressed."

"One last thing. Tell her— Would you tell her I feel real bad for being a lousy father?"

"Do you even know *how* you were lousy?"

"Not being here. Not seeing to her future."

"Christ, don't they have therapists in the afterlife? It has nothing to do with money."

"Well," Coop said, scratching his chin, obviously stumped. "No use thinking on it now."

"Apologize to her your own self, then."

Coop's eyes narrowed with contempt. "God, but you're a hard-assed sonofabitch. What she sees in you, I'll never know."

"Then you haven't been paying attention."

The biggest rat Scott had ever seen growled at him that afternoon, and for something so simple and stupid as moving a box it was partial to. Scott instantly jumped onto the nearest pile and didn't stop climbing until he'd reached the loft, because rats could climb, too, couldn't they?

He wasn't an idiot. He knew it wasn't a rat. But the only opossums he'd ever seen were a lot flatter and tended to stick to the road, and *they*, he knew—the live ones, not the flat ones—could climb. Anything that sounded that ferocious had to have teeth to back it up, and he wasn't challenging it to find out how big they were.

There wasn't much to do up on the pile except look for a way down that let the rat keep its space. And now that its space had been violated and it was pissed off, it probably had a new space and would defend it to the death. Scott's, not the rat's. So Scott hung around where he was.

It wasn't but a few minutes later that he noticed light on the far side of the pile, which aroused his curiosity because he'd thought that was the tool room back there or he would've tackled this stack sooner. He poked and prodded his way through to find a large, cavernous space below, with a small, dirty, grimy window set in the brick. Hence, the light. And below that window, beneath all that dirt and debris, sat a large lump that could be . . . might be . . . yes, there it was. Yellow.

It was just a glimpse, really, where something had run across the hood and disturbed years of dust and who knew what the heck else, but definitely yellow.

Eureka!

Automatically, Scott reached for his phone to call

Maggie and share the news. If it'd been on his belt, he probably would have done just that, but the closest phone was down on the tool room wall, and before he figured the best path to it, he had a better idea, which was to climb down to the lump and check it out first. No sense getting Maggie all excited if it turned out to be a Pinto.

He shuddered at the thought.

The trick was to move stuff to make a hole big enough and stable enough to crawl through and down the other side without dislodging a carton or tin or trophy or sled or anything else large enough to dent the body, if in fact it was the 'Cuda. He could just imagine it sitting there more than thirty years, only to be the idiot who came along and damaged it. Oh, Coop'd love that.

The first box Scott lifted off the stack, he didn't know what to do with. Climb all the way down and set it on the floor? Then climb back to the top? He'd have to do that how many times? Forget the rat, forget the teeth, he wasn't doing it. He held the box out from the stack, opened his hands, and said, "Oops."

It crashed to the floor. Coop didn't come flying at him, demanding to know what invaluable collectible he'd just trashed, so Scott did it again. And again. And again, until he could move around without stuff shifting on its own. On his way down the far side, he had to toss a few small items back through the hole he'd just made. Still no sign of Coop, so probably he was in the other barn, keeping a close eye on Ike's crew.

Finally, Scott reached bottom.

Christ, a convertible. Coop hadn't told him that. Chrysler probably made, what, fewer than ten convertibles with the Hemi in 1971? Right height, right length to be what he was looking for. Still, it could be another muscle car.

Gently, so as not to scratch it, Scott ran his fingers through the dirt blanketing the hood.

Lemon Twist Yellow shone through the streaks he left behind. And with quad headlights, no doubt about it, this was the 1971 'Cuda that Coop had badgered him to find.

"Templeton?" Coop called.

Speak of the devil.

"You in here, son?"

Scott froze, barely daring to breathe as he thought through the situation. Yes, he wanted to share the good news, but did he want Coop to know about this today? He'd start making crazy demands, like working around the clock to restore it and get the hell out of Maggie's bed.

Scott didn't want to spend his nights anywhere *but* Maggie's bed.

He eased down to the floor and watched the minutes tick away on his watch. He wanted to call Maggie. He wanted to share the news with her first. When he dared move, he plugged in a leaf blower and blew the hood clean. When he dared climb out, he whistled up the dogs to make sure he was alone, called them over by the tool room, and lifted the receiver.

* * *

Maggie was elbow deep in computer files when she picked up on her wireless headset.

"I found it!" Scott shouted over the line.

"Whatever it is, I hope it's better than what I found. Junk. In my trunk."

"Oh, sorry. I forgot to get that out, didn't I?"

"I guess I forgot to stipulate that when you borrow my car you're not allowed within a mile of any other gearheads."

"I promise it's not junk, Maggie. It's prototype; one-of-a-kind engineering marvels from back—"

"Yeah? How can you tell under all the dirt and grease?"

"Trust me. Listen, did you hear me? *I found it.*"

Caught by the urgency in Scott's voice, Maggie leaned forward in her chair. "You mean—?"

"Yes! It's here, just like he said. I blew off the dust, and, Maggie, you won't believe how beautiful it is. It's mint. No, it's better than mint—it's like traveling back in time or something, it's so perfect. If you had a camera in this phone, I'd send you a picture. And that's not all."

Maggie sat back, laughing gently at Scott's excitement. "There's more?"

"Yeah. It may be nothing, but I found something else. Who was George Cooper?"

"My grandfather," she said, puzzled. She didn't get to ask why he was asking.

"Uh-oh, dogs're acting up. Come home as fast as you can. Well, not that fast, but you know what I mean."

* * *

Maggie made it home in record time and, still in suit and heels, ran past all three tail-wagging dogs into the barn. Not nearly in such a hurry to see an old car as the man who'd hunted it down.

"Scott!"

"Behind the tool room."

Half a dozen orange extension cords snaked past a pile of junk that defied the term *pile* at all, since it looked as if there'd been an earthquake since yesterday. They led her through a new canyon, into a generous garage-sized area, and terminated in six well-spaced work lights. And in the glow of those work lights sat one 1971 Lemon Twist Yellow 'Cuda.

"A convertible," she whispered reverently before she threw her arms around Scott's neck. Her exuberance was not because of the car, though being a guy, he'd probably misinterpret that. He'd done what Pop wanted. Then, when he simply could have dropped the engine into the body and run off to the nearest race, he hadn't. He'd called her instead. He'd waited for her. "I expected rust."

"Good thing the roof didn't leak." Scott lifted her off her feet and twirled her with excitement, making her laugh, then kissed her as if she'd been gone a month. "Oh darn, you didn't change. Well, not really," he growled as he nuzzled her neck, "but I'm all dirty."

"You sounded so excited, I couldn't wait. Let me look around." *Let me see what brought us together.* For that reason alone, the car was priceless.

"In those stilts? You'll break your ankle. Better hold on while I give you a tour."

He draped his arm around her shoulders; Maggie snuggled close to his side as he led her in a circle around the car.

"Shaker hood scoop," he said, as if she couldn't see it for herself.

"Uh-huh."

"Cheese grater grille. Elastomeric bumper group."

"Oh-kay."

"Show some respect. Chrysler made less than ten of these."

"Really? Well, that is impressive."

Not for the reason Scott thought, though. What impressed Maggie was that had someone at Chrysler not decided to assemble this particular car in 1971—say whoever was in charge had a hangover one day and decided it was a bad idea to put the Hemi in a bright yellow convertible—Pop couldn't have bought it. And if he hadn't bought it, he wouldn't have misplaced it, wouldn't have needed someone to find it. And then where would Scott Templeton be right this very minute?

Not holding her close as they circled the 'Cuda.

Not reciting its attributes in her ear in faux foreplay.

"Louvers on the front fender. Bucket seats—good for cornering, as you know. Perfect for the way you drive."

"You saying I take turns fast?"

"Sweetheart, you do it all fast."

She turned into him then and ran her fingers through his thick hair. "Not everything."

"Mm. True."

"Maybe we should initiate that backseat."

"Maybe you should take a closer look at it first."

Unwilling to release Scott's hand, Maggie bent at the waist and peered through the open window. "Eww."

"Yeah, leave it to the mice to find the most valuable bedding in the whole barn. It can all be restored, though, just like the top—dry rot, tires, too—but don't worry."

As if. "You're not going to quote wheelbase and tranny, are you?"

"Four-speed, with pistol-grip shift lever, and that's all I'll say about that."

"Good."

"This baby went from zero to sixty in five and half seconds."

"You can't turn it off if you try, can you?"

Scott didn't dignify that with an answer. Instead, he pulled her back to his side and led her toward the brick wall, and she let him, thinking if he wanted to look at every darn thing in the whole entire barn, as long as she could stay tucked beneath his arm, she'd gladly go with him.

"Look at that," he said. Sitting on a workbench against the wall was an old, wooden toolbox, too big and heavy for her to pick up. It was dark with age, scarred with all the bumps and bruises a toolbox gets over many, many years. "There, on the lid: George Cooper. Your grandfather burned his name into it. Pretty fancy, too. And look inside."

Scott lifted the lid to reveal tools, lots and lots of

tools, which he picked through as he listed them. "Flare wrenches, feeler gauges, spanner wrenches, open-end wrenches, calipers . . . And not just car stuff. Hammer, screwdrivers, level, carpenter's ruler . . ."

He looked like a kid in a candy shop with ten bucks in his pocket.

"Everything's clean. Oiled. He must've been handy. I don't know much about collectibles, Maggie, but I know old tools in this shape are valuable."

"Be sure to set them aside, then, so they don't go to auction."

"Maybe I should move them to the cellar so there's no mix-up?"

She gazed up at him in wonder. "They don't go in the cellar."

"Well, I could lock them in the tool room, if you have a key."

"They don't go in the cellar or in the *tack* room, because they go in your truck when you get it back."

He cocked his head, studying her to see if she was serious. "No way."

Maggie nodded, thinking, *All he's done—and he's never asked for anything in return except a little help getting rid of a ghost.*

"I couldn't," Scott said.

"Yeah, you're right. What was I thinking? Pop has so much use for them."

"They belong to you and Ruby."

"No, I agree, you're right. Forget I said anything. Ruby'd kill me. Just last week, she was saying how we ought to get out Grampa's tools and add another story onto the house."

"Okay, okay. I give up." Scott laughed and held up his hands in surrender, and Maggie could see how pleased he was. How honored.

One person doing the same job, day in, day out. One day of his life. *One decision.* It all came down to that. How many seemingly simple decisions did she make a day? At work, they were just ordinary, investment decisions, advice really, but would something she said or did steer the course of someone else's future? Someone alive. Someone not even born yet? Someone she'd never meet, even.

It was enough to make a person second-guess herself, about a lot of things, really. But not this.

"I guess Pop's tickled. I'm glad." He probably had been the best father he knew how to be, and you can't fault people for being the best they can be.

Maggie was happy that Scott was now free to leave if and when he wanted, and ready to be disappointed when he got around to announcing it'd be tomorrow morning. Or tonight.

"Coop doesn't know about this yet," Scott said. "I can't decide when to tell him. On one hand, I want to get it over with. On the other, it's not as if he hasn't reneged before."

Decisions.

Maggie smiled, in spite of the fact that already she was hurting because Scott was thinking of leaving. It was stupid, really. She hadn't wanted him here in the first place.

"You okay?"

She snapped out of it. "Sure. Why?"

"You look a little . . . preoccupied."

"Oh. It's nothing."

She'd known his reputation before she'd fallen into his arms, but she couldn't deny that she'd fallen head over heels in love with him, a race car driver, of all people. This wasn't the time to be pensive, though; there'd be time enough for that after he left.

Scott tipped his head in the way she'd come to love, where he studied her and thought about saying more. "How about we do dinner and Gateway a little earlier tonight? I have a plan."

"Your last plan nearly burned down the barn."

"Swear to God. No Ouija boards will be harmed."

"Okay then."

Maggie turned toward the canyonlike passageway so as not to give herself away when she smiled, because aside from the Ouija board fire fiasco, she really did like Scott's plans.

 *Chapter 16*

"C'mon, tell me," Maggie pleaded again as she turned off the highway and approached Gateway.

"*God.* Beg, beg, beg."

Scott tried to sound put upon, but he doubted Maggie was fooled. She'd been trying to wear him down since she'd changed into jeans and buckled into her Mustang. So far, it hadn't worked—not on the way to the restaurant, not through dinner, and not on the drive to the track. Not even when she'd threatened to make him walk home, sleep in the freezer with Half Elvis, and eat Ruby's tzatziki for breakfast, although the tzatziki almost got him.

It was a nice spring evening, finally, just right for jeans and tees. Once they'd left the highway, Maggie opened the windows and let in the breeze. Scott snacked on homemade chocolate chip cookies while Maggie continued to plead for more information.

"C'mon, Scott. Tell me."

"You'll see in a few minutes."

"You're driving me crazy, you know that, don't you?"

"Yeah, but if I told you, then it wouldn't be a surprise."

"What surprise? We're here. Good Lord, how many cookies did you bring?"

"I know. It's terrible. I've probably put on ten pounds eating these things. Want one?" He popped another into his mouth and proffered the Ziploc he'd filled from Mother Goose's seemingly endless bounty.

"Good, huh?"

"You have no idea. You know, not just anybody can make these things."

"No?"

"I tried. I used my grandmother's recipe and everything."

"Aw, Scott, you're not just anybody."

"That's right," he said with an attitude. "Hometown hero, doctor, lockpick, *and* cookie judge."

"Don't forget 'Cuda hunter."

"'Cuda *finder*."

"That's right."

Maggie, the minx, had distracted him. When Scott made the mistake of closing his eyes in ecstasy over another cookie, she snatched the bag right out of his hand and laughed an evil laugh.

"Wow, how do you win races with such sucky reflexes?" She dangled it out her window and shot him a smug look that had *leverage* written all over it.

"No! Wait!"

"Tell me."

"Careful. Careful." He unhooked his seat belt and eased toward her, thinking of the many delightful ways he could punish her if she dared—

She shot him a look. "Back off or I drop the bag."

He held his ground.

"Back."

He sat down, then played his trump with a smug look. "That's okay. Grammy'll make me some more."

"*Grammy* didn't make them."

"Ruby, then. Ruby likes me."

"Ruby didn't make them, either."

"No way— *You* made these? No, don't tease me."

Maggie bobbed her head, keeping a suspicious eye on him even as she watched the road.

"That does it. Stop the car. I have to get down on my knee and propose."

Scott hadn't figured Maggie'd call his bluff, but when she braked just inside the gate on the deserted parking lot and laughed with glee, darn if he didn't give serious thought to doing just that—proposing. Sure as heck, life never would be dull or dreary married to Maggie Cooper.

"Well, all right," Scott said, stepping out of the car, unable and unwilling to resist any challenge this woman threw his way. He finger combed his hair and straightened his T-shirt.

They hadn't talked marriage. Hell, they hadn't even talked commitment. Some women, after a couple of dates, dropped dumb hints like *If we had kids, I wonder which one of us they'd look like*. Or *If I have a son, I hope he has your eyes*.

Maggie'd never said anything even remotely along those lines, Scott realized as he rounded the hood.

Did that mean she didn't think them?

Wasn't interested?

Would laugh in his face if he dropped to one knee in a deserted parking lot?

Christ. Did he have to be the one to drop dumb hints? And if so, was this the time?

He found himself at her door all too soon. He didn't know what to do first, but he didn't have long to ponder it, as Maggie shook the bag of cookies to tease him and drove off, calling, "Have a nice walk," out the window.

Ah, what the heck. He'd eaten too many anyway. The walk'd do him good. And when he caught up to her, he'd kiss that sassy mouth of hers until she was so hot, she'd want to rip his clothes off.

That'd give her something to think about the rest of the evening.

Half an hour later, Maggie was dazed, and it had nothing to do with kissing. Scott hadn't charmed her out of her clothes, he'd charmed her *into* some—borrowed racing gear; suit, helmet, gloves, the works. Even a two-way radio with a headset.

Pit lane on the oval/road course track was like any other pit lane she'd ever been on, only right now it was empty, save the two of them standing between her red Mustang and a white Viper. Bruce had dropped it off a few minutes ago, just tossed the keys to Scott and said to have fun, unconcerned that, *knowing* that, he'd run it around the track as fast as it could go.

And boy, she was sure it would go.

"It's ours," Scott said, meaning the track.

"The whole thing? We can do the road course, too?" She'd driven on a track before—Pop's one and only attempt at bonding as she approached legal driving age. The speed was cool; the oval boring.

"No traffic. No cops. Zip up all the way."

"It's sticky." Maggie ineffectively tugged at the zipper tab. The shiny silver-colored suit seemed like overkill to her. She wasn't going to hit anything. There wasn't anyone else out here to hit her. Even so, she was dressed neck to ankle in a triple-layered, quilted suit. The epaulets on the shoulders were not for decoration, but intended to assist in emergency extractions.

"Let's see." Scott yanked the zipper upward for her without breaking a sweat. "Ride a couple laps with me first."

Maggie couldn't get into the Viper fast enough. It took Scott a bit longer to adjust Bruce's five-point harness to fit himself.

"You look nervous," he said at last.

"You're going to get even with me, aren't you?" She laughed when she said it, as if that'd make it untrue, when it did no good to hope such a silly thing, because of course he was going to get even. He'd probably one-up her, too.

Scott grinned and set the engine to purring. "Try not to leave fingernail marks on Bruce's dash."

Pit lane disappeared in a flash, literally. Gone. Somewhere behind them. Sixty on the highway gave a person time to look ahead, look around. Even eighty.

But eighty on a track coming up on a turn when you didn't have a brake pedal on your side was, well, unnerving. Forget fingernail marks on the dash; Maggie clenched the edge of the seat. No way she wanted Scott to know she was nervous. Scared.

Excited.

That lasted until they sped up even more and approached the next turn. Maggie stomped an imaginary brake pedal; Scott's foot didn't move.

"Not yet," he said as wind roared in the open windows. It was noisy, but cooling, and in full racing gear, anything cool was good.

"Now?" she said.

"Not yet."

"Now." If not soon, it'd be too late.

"In a second."

"*Now.*"

"Almost . . . almost . . ."

And finally he braked, but only briefly. They continued to fly, the Viper gripping the pavement as tight as a rail.

"How fast was that?" Maggie asked after the turn.

Scott grinned. "You didn't check?"

"I . . . forgot."

He patted her knee.

"Hands on the wheel!"

He laughed, and after a second, so did she.

"Okay, so you were a saint to ride with me," she admitted.

"That was slow. Ready for another one?"

Maggie's gaze shot ahead, but by the time it did, they were already in a turn, her heavily helmeted head forced to the right, and where they were going wasn't in front of them so much as already *here*, curving around to their left.

"Feel those g-forces?" Scott asked after two laps.

"Wow. Yeah."

"They'll wear you out before you know it, so we'd better get you behind the wheel."

She was so ready, she sprinted to the Mustang.

"Don't push yourself too hard," Scott instructed a few minutes later, leaning in Maggie's window as she buckled herself in. "If you don't get enough speed before you wear out, I'll take you around some more. Ready?"

"Dumb question."

"Follow me, then. Learn the braking points."

"Okay."

"Just listen to me over the radio. Don't try to operate it yourself. Concentrate on your driving."

The road course wound through the infield with both right- and left-hand turns, then used turns three and four on the oval. Repetitious, sure, but not like an oval, and Maggie couldn't wait to speed around it on her own. If Scott didn't stop with the tips soon, though, the evening would vanish before she had her fill. She glanced at her wrist in a blatant hint; because of the long sleeve, she wouldn't have been able to see her watch even if she'd found it and worn it, but it was the message that was important.

If Scott got the point, he ignored it. "You don't have all

the restraints I had, so you won't feel as secure. That's okay. Start slow. Just do what you feel safe doing."

"Nothing over a hundred?"

He just grinned and said, "Right." And then he had the nerve to reach in the window and test her seat belt.

"Last one on the track is a dirty rotten egg." Maggie eased forward until Scott got out of her face, then laughed as she roared off and he ran to the Viper.

"Swear to God, Maggie—" came over the radio.

"Oh, relax. I'm waiting for you." She kept it at sixty, allowing him to catch and pass her in no time.

"Just monitor the radio."

"Yes, boss."

"I'll watch you in the mirror. If you're comfortable and I see you're getting close, I'll speed up. But don't pass me, because I'm your barometer for when you have to brake."

"You think Bruce knows he has a little scratch on his bumper?"

Scott took the hint and sped forward. "You know the meaning of 'monitor'? As in 'both hands on the wheel.'"

"I'm a racing brat, remember? I cut my first tooth on a radio."

"Suddenly I have new respect for your father."

Maggie had no trouble hanging with the Viper on the straightaway. Well, okay, maybe a little. Hitting a hundred out west where the highway could run as straight as an arrow for miles on end was a whole different animal than negotiating a track with several turns. And in some places, just to nag at her, there was a wall only a few feet away.

Pop had hit a wall. More than once.

He'd died hitting a wall.

"You okay?" crackled over the radio.

"Sorry." She pressed on the gas and caught up to the Viper.

"Hey, don't be sorry. Be safe. And stop talking on the radio, that's my job."

"You asked."

"It was rhetorical. Unless you're not okay."

"You drive like an old lady, Templeton."

"Remind me not to argue with Coop anymore. I'm sure you gave the man enough grief when he was alive."

"Only when I saw him."

This beat highway driving all to pieces. So what if her neck and shoulder muscles strained to keep her head straight on the turns. So what if the steering wheel vibrated in her hands as never before. So what if she was trussed up like an astronaut on liftoff.

"Let me lead," she begged after a few laps.

Scott dropped back without argument, coasting beside her for a couple of seconds.

"Only one thing," he said on the radio, looking over at her. "If I say 'brake,' it's because you've gone too late and you have to do it *now*."

She nodded at him, because she heard the concern in his voice and wanted to reassure him. "Okay, boss."

"I mean it, Maggie."

"I know. Me, too."

The Viper dropped back, and suddenly Maggie knew how a pilot must feel on her first solo flight. Nothing in front of her but a road with no rules and no traffic.

"Next turn's to your right," Scott said.

"The thing about leading," she said, "is that people don't tell you where to go. And, oh, Scott."

"Yeah?"

"I can't drive and watch the speedometer." Much to her surprise. "Tell me how fast I'm going in the turn, okay?"

"Shut up and drive."

Maggie didn't quit until the sun went down and she was bone tired. Her helmet felt like fifty pounds. Her arms tingled from the vibration. Her back was stiff from bracing herself in the seat.

She was exhilarated.

"How was it?" Scott asked when she floated toward him, running her hands through her flat, sweaty, helmet hair. He'd quit fifteen minutes ago, announcing he was going in search of something, *anything*, to drink, for both of them. She found him behind the wall.

"I'm exhausted," she said, throwing herself into his arms. "But I still want to drag you into the garage and make love until the sun comes up."

She could tell by his laugh that he knew exactly how she felt, that she needed no more words to tell him. She could feel it in his kisses, the way he lifted her so she could wrap her legs around him and stay there for a good long while. Getting her tired, quilted-racing-suit legs around him was impossible, and Maggie laughed and went limp and slid out of his arms onto the ground.

Scott hunkered beside her, his dimple deep and sexy and begging the tip of her finger to trace it. "If this is your idea of making love until the sun comes up, I'm getting another date."

"In addition to me?" she said. "You couldn't handle it."

"Sweetheart"—he leaned down, all the way down, and covered her lips with his in a kiss so hot she almost forgot where they were—"there is no addition to you. You are my everything."

That did it; Maggie melted right then and there. *I love you* didn't always have to be three words. *I love you* was in Scott's eyes. It was in his kiss. His remembering what she'd said about speed. Renting the track for the evening so she could loose the speed demon within her and meet it face to face.

With a burst of energy, Maggie jumped up and took him by the hand and jogged into the garage, tugging at her zipper as she looked this way and that for a little privacy. Not that anyone else was there, but you never knew, and she wasn't one to go public. She had no idea where she was going, but Scott changed direction and pulled her along behind him, through a steel door, into a small office that had its share of ashtrays and greasy car parts and dented file cabinets, and just as she thought, *What the heck? Love a driver, love his world. Get over it already*, he led her through a door beyond that into a private office with, thank God, carpeting and furniture.

"Oh," she said, looking around with surprise.

"You like—"

Maggie turned to tease Scott about knowing where the good rooms were and found herself swept into his embrace. It was pure pleasure to meld her body to his, to feel his strong, hard planes against her curves, to kiss him deeply as she proceeded to carry out her promise to make love until the sun came up.

"Thought you'd like it," he said against her lips.

"No, *this*"—she wiggled against him, side to side, working her way down his body—"is what I like."

"It'd be a whole lot sexier without that suit."

On her way back up, she tugged at the zipper again, but either her fingers were too numb to hold it or it was stuck.

"Problem?" Scott drawled.

"Only if you want sex in the next ten minutes."

He might as well have said, "Hell yes," considering the speed with which he attacked her zipper, freeing Maggie to make good on her offer.

She peeled off the racing suit, quickly at first, then slower and slower as she watched Scott's eyes darken to pools of chocolate. God, she loved making love to this man. Loved how he made her feel sexy and important. Loved how they could laugh and tease and make love at the same time.

He reached for the hem of her T-shirt. "Sweaty clothes. Mm, bad for your health. Gotta go."

Sweaty clothes didn't slip off easily, and they kissed and laughed and tugged impatiently at tees and damp jeans and even damper underwear until they fell naked to the carpet, and when Maggie wanted on top, when she straddled him, Scott gave her the lead.

There was no taking time this evening. Adrenaline still raced through her body, and, free of all the restrictive clothing now, Maggie directed all that energy into making love to this man. Kissing, touching, nibbling, stroking him until he was too consumed to utter anything intelligible. And when she'd apparently driven him nuts enough, when he could take no more without plunging over the edge without her, he rolled her over and gave as good as he'd gotten, kissing every inch of her, his breath warm and moist on her skin, his heart pounding fiercely against her own as he plunged inside her. She moaned softly and clutched him, like a lifeline, as each thrust pinned her, willingly, to the carpet. She shuddered and writhed and rolled her hips toward him until she no longer remembered where they were or why they were there, only that they were together as they should be.

And only after long moments of ecstasy and release, of gasping for breath and waiting for her sweat-slickened body to cool in the air and her heart to slow to normal, was Maggie able to whisper, "How did you know?"

She pillowed her head on Scott's shoulder, wiggling to find a spot comfortable for both of them. His hand idly traced patterns on her back as her fingernails did the same over his ribs.

"You mean, how did I know this suite was back here?"

Maggie's head popped up. "Suite? As in bathroom-with-a-shower suite?"

"Mm-hm."

"Cool. But no, I meant how did you know I'd like flying around a track for an hour?"

"Two hours."

"Really? Oh yeah," she said, remembering the sun had set.

"You mean, given your prejudices against race car drivers."

She tweaked his nipple for that one and made him chuckle.

"I could see it in your eyes every time you drove your car," he said honestly. "The way you caress the steering wheel."

"I don't!"

"The way you slip into the seat like you're sitting on a lover's lap."

"Stop"—she laughed—"you're making this up."

"The way you stretch out your leg when you're pressing the pedal, like you're feeling up your date under the table."

Maggie raised up on her elbow and threatened Scott's nipple with her teeth. "Who needs a table?"

He just laughed and squirmed and said, "That's my phone," when it *vroom*ed. "You mind handing it over?"

"Get it yourself, bub."

"I would, but there's this woman holding me down, having her way with me. Even though I haven't recovered yet."

Maggie sighed as if to say, *Oh my, look what I have to put up with,* and got to her knees and crawled from her clothes to his clothes to more clothes until she finally located Scott's phone under a sock. She tossed it to him; he caught it with one hand.

She had better things to do than eavesdrop on his conversation, like investigating the shower situation and whether it was big enough for two. The bathroom was small, with a simple, utilitarian, walk-in shower. Towels were in the cabinet under the sink. What she was going to do with a wet towel when she was done, she wasn't sure, but you can't dangle a clean shower in front of a sweaty woman and expect her not to use it.

"Hey, Templeton." She leaned out the door, inviting company.

Scott was sitting at attention, his back to Maggie, saying, "How soon do you need me?" and "Casts? Oh yeah, they've been off so long, I forgot I had them," and "Sure, no problem. I can leave first thing in the morning."

Scott was so excited at the prospect of racing again, he hadn't heard her call out to him. Didn't know she was standing there. The roof could have caved it, and she doubted he'd notice except to make sure he had a path to the nearest exit.

Maggie closed the bathroom door and fumbled for the faucet handles. Didn't matter what temperature the water was. Hot would clean her. Cold would shock some sense into her.

What was she thinking? That love would keep him here?

Of course not; she didn't even want that. He had a job to do, same as she did. She respected that. He could fly home between races.

But would he, she wondered as water streamed over her head and down her body, and she forgot to do anything rudimentary, like soaping up. Would he? Scotty Templeton, racing champion, had his own groupies. Just because she knew he loved her didn't mean he knew he did.

I guess that's why women hold out for those three words.

Just because Scott loved her, it didn't mean he was willing to give up the fast lane. Just because she was willing to overlook a few extra cars sitting around their lives didn't mean he felt the same sense of commitment.

She'd come into this relationship with her eyes open. And damn if she'd let him see her cry when he walked away.

Chapter 17

Scott was too excited to sleep past sunrise on Friday. As usual, Maggie lay draped across half of his chest, her breath warm against his neck, and he closed his eyes for a few minutes and just enjoyed the weight of her. The steady beat of her heart against his. The soft drape of her hair across his neck. The smell of honeysuckle.

He could stay here forever, if not for the call of the track. Maggie'd understand; she'd known who and what he was the moment she'd laid eyes on him. She knew what made him tick. What was important to a man like him. What he had to do. What he needed.

She stirred when he slipped away. He gave her a pillow to hug so she'd sleep a little longer and let him do the things he had to do.

He made a pot of coffee, then slipped Ruby's keys off the peg by the kitchen door and slid into her older Taurus. Black, of course, with a huge spiderweb decal covering the rear window. She'd complained that none of the locals could get it to run right anymore. He drove it for a few miles to see what was wrong, then parked by the barn, where there were lots of tools on hand, and opened the hood.

"I miss doing that," Coop said, standing beside him. "I see you found the 'Cuda."

"Yep." Scott studied the engine, which was running rough enough for a baby to see there was a problem. He covered the fender, laid out tools, and leaned in to get the job done.

"Saw you pack your duffel this morning, too."

"That's right."

"Job's not done, son."

"I'll be back when the series is over."

"That wasn't the deal."

Scott gripped the wrench tightly, frustrated that it was useless to threaten Coop with it, though he sure as heck wanted to. There were other ways to get the ghost's attention now, though, and Scott knew it and wheeled on him and stepped so close he could feel the chill.

"Here's the new deal," he growled. "I don't torch the 'Cuda now. I come back to finish it later, after the series. *After* you talk to Grammy and answer all her questions. Take it or leave it."

"You couldn't do that. You couldn't take that piece of history and desecrate it."

"Ya think?" Scott's laugh was cold and hard, and surprised Coop enough that the ghost actually took a step back. "Listen to me, you ectoplasmic pain in the ass. The last thing my grandmother ever did was send me off to a race. She knew how much I loved driving and how badly I wanted a championship, and she knew I wouldn't go if I knew she was dying—that's the kind of woman who raised me. That's the kind of love a parent has for a child, you self-centered, selfish bastard."

Coop winced in response.

Bull's-eye. Scott pressed on, nailing the point home while he had the chance.

"She didn't live until I got home. Now, you self-absorbed prick, do you think *for one goddamn minute* that your car means one millionth of a fraction of what I felt for my grandmother? Do you think *for one minute*, now that I have a driving job, that I wouldn't torch it and go, because that's what she wanted?"

Coop, the ornery old goat, seized on what he mistakenly perceived as a weak point. "Don't you want what's best for Maggie?"

"Yes!"

"Then finish the car and sell it, so she can take the money and start her own business."

Scott threw up his arms. "Where did you ever get the idea that's what she wants?"

"From . . ." Coop sputtered for several seconds. "Because she works all the time. She walks around with that little phone thing in her ear and talks to clients, day and night. Total return and equity investments and global orientation. Small caps. Mid caps. Secular trends."

"So she likes to eat; doesn't mean she wants her own business. Maggie's been too busy wanting what everyone tells her she wants. She hasn't figured everything out for herself yet."

"Now, don't you go getting her into driving race cars."

"Hell, she knows what she *doesn't* want," Scott said

with a dry laugh. "Except maybe for Killjoy."

"Yeah, he's a sore excuse for a man."

Scott shook the wrench at the ghost. "Don't think this little bonding session's going to change my mind. I'm leaving. This morning."

Coop kicked at a rock near his foot, sending it rolling aside as he gave in and gave up. "Does she know?"

Scott had a favor to ask—hard to believe, because he didn't want to owe Coop anything, but he cared enough that he had to ask. "Keep an eye on her while I'm gone, okay?"

"Did you . . . Did you break my little girl's heart?"

"Unlike you, no. Maggie understands that I need to race. She knows I'll be back."

"You sure about that?"

Maggie woke up knowing Scott was leaving. She thought she was prepared, until she reached out and felt the cold pillow, the empty space beside her. She bounced out of bed, fully alert now and, she thought sheepishly, a little panicky, even though he'd said he'd stay until she left for work.

The door across the hall was open for a change, and she stepped in to find the room empty; smelled like a can of shaving cream, but empty. When she rushed back and looked out her bedroom window and saw Scott by the barn, her heart swelled, nearly bursting with the joy of knowing he'd kept his word; he wouldn't leave until she did.

Clearly, he was arguing with Pop; looming over an

unseen person, arms flying, wrench wagging. She debated whether to get ready for work first or just go slip her arms around him and say, "Repeat after me. You're dead. Go away." One glance in the mirror, though—ratty hair, puffy eyes—convinced her to hit the get-the-red-out eye drops and take a shower.

The smell of coffee drew Maggie downstairs before her hair was completely dry. Scott's duffel sat by the back door, under inspection by Ashes, who meowed plaintively and poked his nose into the two-inch gap where the zipper wasn't quite closed. Maggie bent down to secure it, lest Scott arrive in Laguna Seca with an unwanted cat in tow. Imagine Ashes springing out at him in a dark hotel room; he'd think it was a mountain lion.

The duffel wasn't quite full; there was room for a going-away present. The chocolate chip cookies were all gone, but there was a batch of double-chocolate chunk in the freezer. He'd probably like those. She tucked them into a hollow spot, along with a few good wishes on his next race, then made sure the cat couldn't get his nose in.

After last night, she had a clearer picture of why Scott loved racing so much, of the charge he got from it. Although, throwing in the danger factor of twenty or thirty other cars and allowing for the stupid factor ought to take away some of the thrill, not increase it. She knew firsthand how quickly the scenery changed, how rapidly the turns came up, one after the other, right and left, and—call her chicken—no way she ever wanted to negotiate all that with anyone else on the track at the same time. She had neither the reflexes nor the attention span for it.

Grammy rushed into the kitchen, turned on the water in the sink, and proceeded to flatten her hair. She was dressed in her old robe and flannel pajamas, and speaking of attention span, done with patience and determined to get her way.

"You forgot the cane," Maggie said indulgently.

Grammy whipped it out of the pantry. "Stand back and watch a pro."

"No. You can't."

"Outta my way. I still got questions need answering."

"Fine. But if Scott stays because of your pathetic don't-leave-me-I'm-an-old-woman act, I don't want him."

"Pants on fire, girl. You love him."

"All the more reason to let him go."

Grammy *hmph*ed and waved her hand dismissively in the air. "Sometimes you remind me of your mother. She never asked her man to stay, either. She always believed if you love someone, you let him go. Darn fool woman, if you ask me. Look what it got her."

A warmth spread through Maggie as her childhood complaints suddenly came clear in a very grown-up way. Pop always came back. Maybe with a car instead of a paycheck, but he always came home. "Guess that's where I learned it."

Grammy leaned on her cane, getting into character. "If you ask me, sometimes a man needs a little nudge making up his mind."

Maggie huffed with exasperation. "Do you do this to Milton?"

Grammy wouldn't quite meet Maggie's eyes.

"You do, don't you? Geez, Grammy, grow up." Maggie snatched the cane away from her. She wanted to be dramatic and snap it in two, but it was too thick to even try it, so she opened the back door and tossed it as far as she could out into the yard. "I'm going to tell Scott good-bye now. Don't you dare be looking like that when I get back."

Grammy sagged deeper into her ratty old robe. "Guess I'll get dressed then," she said, sounding pathetic even to Maggie, who knew the score. "I can wear sweats to go casket shopping, can't I?"

"Oh please."

That wasn't the response Grammy'd expected, so when Maggie started out the door, Grammy changed to stalling tactics. "What's in the grocery bag?"

Maggie saw right through her and put her arms around her, hugging her soundly to reassure her. She said, "Don't worry, I'm not leaving," then poured a mug of coffee and let herself out, closing the door noisily behind her so Grammy'd think she was angry and not dare follow.

Scott didn't see her approach, and of course standing next to a running engine, he couldn't hear her, so Maggie took her time and enjoyed the view of him, his strong body leaning in under the hood, stretching, adjusting something. He had great hands. She committed the sight to memory, to draw out in the days, maybe weeks, ahead.

Who would've thought she'd carry coffee out to such a man's man in the morning, kiss him good-bye, and send him off to a race? Certainly not she. Not in this lifetime.

Ruby's car ran smoothly under his touch, and when Scott finally turned toward her and flashed that dimple—maybe the last time she'd see it, ever—her heart purred just like it.

"Morning," he said, all smiles. He killed the engine, wiped his hands on a rag.

"Hi." She didn't think she'd be able to smile again, but her lips had other ideas. "I saw you talking to Pop."

"He's working up the nerve to talk to you."

"I don't want—"

"Give him a chance, okay? Just this once."

"We'll see." She handed him the coffee.

Scott sipped it, and over the top of the mug, said, "You trying to set a new style, Armani and Keds?"

"That's me, the cutting edge of fashion." She studied him for a long moment, relishing every detail, especially the way his hazel eyes sparkled when he teased her, and how the dimple would come and go, which just made it more noticeable. "How long can you stay?"

No, that wasn't right; that sounded as if she were plotting to change his mind. She'd meant to ask when he was leaving; ten minutes, twenty, an hour. She just couldn't say that word, *leaving*.

Good grief, give her a minute and she'd be hunting up that cane.

"Taxi's coming at eight-thirty." It'd take him to pick up his truck.

Out of habit, Maggie glanced at her wrist. Bare, of course.

"You know, I don't believe I've ever met anyone so hard on watches."

"I forgot to take it off until I was in the shower, and then I thought I set it on the flush box. It wasn't there this morning, though."

"It never is."

"I think it's Ashes."

"Yeah, time is so important to a cat."

Maggie wrinkled her nose at him.

"Tell you what," he said, leaning in to kiss the wrinkle away. "Until they put homing devices on watches . . ." He set his mug on the fender and took off his Rolex. "You won't have to worry about this getting wet."

"No! I couldn't." Maggie shook her head. Not his championship watch.

"Give me your arm."

Maggie didn't step back, didn't want to put more distance between them, but kept both hands firmly on the grocery sack. As if that'd stop him.

Scott slipped his steel-and-gold Rolex around Maggie's wrist. "There. Waterproof. Wear it in the shower."

Belatedly, she remembered to close her mouth. "I can't be responsible for a Rolex."

"Are you kidding? Have you lost anything else since I've been here? A shoe? A purse? A file folder?"

"Well, no, but this is too big. Too loose—"

"Your phone? Your earpiece?"

"No. But—" A championship watch was irreplaceable.

"Then trust me, you won't lose this, either. What's in the bag? Cookies for the road?" He looked hopeful.

Still reeling from his generosity, his . . . She wasn't sure what it was. A gift? A loan? At least he wasn't giving her two years to pay it off.

"Cookies?" Scott prompted.

"Oh." Maggie corralled her thoughts and handed over the bag. "You have a long drive. I thought you could use it."

Scott plunged his hand in eagerly, then stopped short and took a closer look inside. "My radar— I mean, *your* radar detector. I don't know . . . As long as you're not returning it, like a ring or something." He tipped his head and studied her for a moment. "You gonna slow down while I'm gone?"

Maggie's head bobbed in a nod, then she laughed and shook her head and said, "Probably not."

"I'd best hurry back then."

"Flying would be faster."

"Flying's for birds."

Scott set the bag aside and held his arms open, and Maggie stepped into them for a few last minutes to remember him by, for every last second she could get. She committed every touch to memory, his hands, his lips on hers, his strong arms cradling her against his chest, fingers running through her hair.

And when he didn't come back? She'd mail him his

watch. There was nothing for him to feel guilty about. No reason to give it to her if he wasn't going to be on her arm with it because once he returned to the track, once racing got under his skin again, took hold of him again, she couldn't be sure he'd find the time to even think of her.

Scott bent his head close. "I didn't mean to make you cry," he said tenderly, then kissed her cheeks to dry them.

Embarrassed that she'd gotten all misty and he'd noticed, she laid her forehead on his shoulder and blatantly lied. "Shampoo. You'd think I was old enough to wash my own hair, wouldn't you?"

"Wish I could stay and help you with the auction. First one's coming up real soon, isn't it?"

"Ike and I can handle it. You have points to make up." Maggie took a deep breath and raised her head, determined to let him go without making it difficult.

"You sure you're okay?" he said. "You don't look okay."

Her eyebrows shot up at that, and in a tone that any man knew meant he'd stepped in it, she repeated, "I don't look okay?"

"You look wonderful," Scott said, kissing her again. "I forgot about the shampoo."

"Uh-huh. Truth is, your mind's already on your new team and the next race."

"Sorry."

"No, that's all right. It should be. That's what you do, what you're meant to do. Your focus is what'll keep you safe. Don't apologize for it. Just come back safe."

"As soon as I can."

She eased out of his arms, holding his hand until the last second as she stepped away. "And, Scott . . ."

"Yeah?"

"Promise me something."

"Anything."

Their fingers parted. Maggie took another step. "Stay away from the wall."

Chapter 18

There was a big to-do in the media center at Laguna Seca. Microphones. Cameras. Old, well-established racing team. New blood.

Scott was the new blood, of course. And the vultures—he found himself thinking of animals at the damnedest times—the *media personnel* wanted to know how he was doing since his crash, how his head was—they didn't mean physically—and how he thought he'd do in tomorrow's 250. As if any driver ever interviewed said anything other than "I'm excited to be here, of course," and "Looking forward to doing my job to the very best of my abilities, as always," and "When the race is over, I hope we have a good day and take the checkered flag."

What did they think he'd say? That he'd been dragged kicking and screaming by a ghost into the wilds of the Midwest? That he'd met a woman who turned his world upside down and nearly made him forget that his grandmother had selflessly sacrificed her last weeks so he could do what he loved best?

God, Maggie'd even sounded like his grandmother when he'd kissed her good-bye last week. Only he missed Maggie a whole lot more. But he'd stayed focused.

When they weren't having phone sex.

"You want me to talk trashy?" Maggie'd purred when he'd told her how much he missed her for the zillionth time last night.

"Sounds good to me." *Absolutely.*

"What do you like?"

"Visuals."

"Body parts?" she asked with a restrained chuckle.

"If they're your body parts. You can start by telling me what you're wearing."

"I've never done this before."

"I'm a guy. Use vivid detail."

"Mm. Okay. I'm wearing a white blouse. It has a high neck. And I'm looking forward to getting out of it because it's kind of scratchy. I think it's giving me a rash."

Scott sighed loudly, and Maggie laughed outright.

"Have you *never* seen an adult movie?" he asked.

"Okay, I'll try again."

He could hear her try to be serious, but every other second, she'd snicker until finally she said she had it under control.

"I've got it now." Maggie lowered her voice. "I borrowed one of Ruby's bustiers today."

All right! Maybe she did have it. Scott was eager to get down to business and do his part.

"It's a little small on me, though," she said. "I'm spilling out of it."

Oh yeah. "Describe it."

"It's dark bronze, and velvety soft, with these cute little ribbons . . ."

Scott bit his tongue so he didn't bark at her when he said, "Tell me how you look *spilling out of it.*"

"You mean, mounds of creamy white flesh pushing over the top, etcetera?"

"Oh yeah. Exactly. Only slower. More detail."

"Pushing me up so high, you can see the edges of my areolas peeking over the top?"

Scott undid his belt. "What else?"

"I have on this little bitty matching thong."

He unsnapped his jeans.

"Barely more than a ribbon, really. Tied at the sides of my long, silky-smooth legs. It's so tiny, you can tell I just had a Brazilian wax."

"What's that?"

"That's everything, babe."

Scott swallowed hard. "*Every*thing?"

"Every last follicle." Maggie lost it then; she snickered. "Yeah, like I'd ever have *that* done. Can you imagine the pain?"

"Uh . . ."

"Take, for example, a guy. Spread his legs wide. Then pour hot wax all over his genitals and apply strips of paper. You with me so far?"

"Uh—" Scott tried really hard to picture doing this to a woman, not to him, and that was kind of interesting. But nooo, Maggie—the minx—persisted.

"Then when the wax sets up, you start ripping 'em

off. Pulling the hair out by its roots. One . . . by . . . one. And when you're done? You missed some, so you do it again. Let me tell you, if that's how they do it in Brazil, those gals are nuts."

"Well, I don't know about you, but I'm done," Scott said.

"Already?" She started snickering again and had trouble talking. "I'm just getting to the good part."

"Darlin', the good part is you're terrific in person. If you don't mind now, I'm going to walk down the street and buy a magazine."

"No, wait," she'd said, laughing. "I can do better."
She couldn't.

"Say, Templeton, you all right?" a man's voice crashed into Scott's fantasy.

He blinked at the reporter in front of him. Oh yeah. Media center. Publicity. Whew, he needed to head for St. Louis right after the race tomorrow, for a little one-on-one.

"Scotty," the reporter said, with a quick check of his notes. He was a narrow-faced little guy; reminded Scott of a rat. "You missed Homestead. The Ferrari Maserati 400 had the closest finish in Rolex Series history. How do you feel about that?"

On second thought, the rat was more like an opossum; looked kind of soft but had a helluva growl. Thinking about that helped Scott clear his head and get his act together.

"I feel good, Bob. As you know, racing puts quite a strain on the body, and we depend on each other, so

I wanted to be in good physical shape before I came back." Pleased with that response, Scott focused on another reporter for the next sound bite.

"Scotty, you were fastest in yesterday's practice session as well as today's fifteen-minute qualifying session. Did you think you'd come back after your hiatus and score the pole in tomorrow's race?"

"Hiatus?" Scott scratched the back of his neck. "Darn, I thought those were casts."

Polite laughter filled the room, and he let it die down.

He and Maggie talked by cell phone every day. She kept him up to speed on her job, evenings spent with her girlfriends, and Ruby and Jeremy's romance, which was progressing quickly. Jeremy'd asked Maggie's advice on buying Ruby a piece of jewelry since he was new to Goth stuff but didn't think a black widow ring was quite the tone he wanted to set.

She described how the barn was clearing out, the efforts she'd gone to to find out any history on Slightly Wilted Elvis. She put up a brave front, but Scott knew her well; when she got sassy, it just showed how much she missed him.

He told her about his new teammates and the car, problems they were fixing, how good it felt to be back to racing, but only when he was actually on the track. Otherwise, he spent more time missing her. Neither of them mentioned Killjoy; all in good time.

Right now, he wanted to call her and tell her about winning the pole position instead of answering questions. He hung in another five minutes before breaking free.

On his way out of the media center, Scott bumped into Tate Nevins, who kept his distance when he smirked and said, quite loudly, "So. Templeton. How's it feel to have a girlfriend with a body in her freezer?"

Several passersby drew up short at that.

Scott just grinned and kept walking as he quipped, "Yeah, they don't take too kindly to trespassers in Missouri."

Maggie spent hours at West County Mall with Kelly and Stacie, something the three of them hadn't done together in way too long. Because it was Saturday, they teased her mercilessly until she turned off her cell phone. They talked more than they shopped, laughed themselves silly catching up, and Maggie in particular bought way too much at one of the specialty shops, but they had the prettiest sky-blue, beaded bustier, and looking at it made her miss Scott.

Trying it on had her anticipating his return, dying to have him see her in it.

"Holy cow," Kelly said as Maggie modeled it for them.

"Yeah. Wow," Stacie said.

Maggie assessed herself carefully in a full-length mirror. Her jeans were snug, but not as confining as the bustier. "I don't know. Think I should try on a larger size?"

"No!"

They shopped until two, then went their separate ways. Maggie'd barely stepped foot out the mall doors when she powered up to retrieve her messages.

"Hi. It's me," Scott said, and Maggie's step slowed, as if she were afraid she'd somehow miss a word. "Just thinking about you and Slightly Wilted. Bet he's starting to look pretty good with me gone, huh? Look, I'll be tied up for a few hours in the garage, and then there's a drivers' meeting. I'll call you after that. Hope you're having fun with your friends. I miss you."

Just hearing his voice made Maggie feel warm and cherished. He called every evening, told her how much he missed her, asked how her day had gone, told her how much he wanted to crawl into bed with her, asked what she had planned for tomorrow, told her what he wanted to be doing in bed with her. That'd been going on for two weeks now. When he showed up again, *warm and cherished* was going to be *hot and ravished*.

"Ms. Cooper, this is Sharon in Personnel."

That put a brake on *hot and ravished*.

"We've rescheduled your interview. Tomorrow, one o'clock. You're expected to call if you can't make it. We won't reschedule again."

"Geez, what a bitch," Maggie muttered. She deleted it with a jab of her finger and went on to the next message before realizing today was Saturday, no one interviewed on Sundays, it must have been an older message, she'd missed her chance again, and *damn,* she'd already erased it.

"Miss Cooper, David Frye here." Head of the selection committee. "I'm looking forward to our interview tomorrow. I know it's short notice, but I hope you can make it."

Okay, no way she'd missed two old messages. Even her provider couldn't be that cruel.

"Hey, Maggie, this is Joan." Joan worked in Personnel for Maggie's current employer. "Kevin called and gave me your new address. How come you didn't tell me you were moving? Chicago—wow, can I come visit? Anyway, just wanted to let you know I've updated the files. Stop by next week. We have paperwork to do."

Maggie instantly thought of several words to describe Kevin, none of which she could say out loud. He'd been sent to Europe for a short trip, and kept his calls few and far between, but even so, Maggie'd tried to break up with him twice. He kept finding reasons to end the calls before she said the words.

Speak of the devil, guess who the next message was from.

"Sweetheart, I've been selfish. I've been mean. I know you're going through a tough time, and you're hurting, and you know what? After ten days away, well, it sure as heck made me see the light. You're going to miss your family when you move here. Your sister."

He'd never said "your sister" before without sneering.

"Your cat. What the hell—bring him with you. I know I've always said no pets, I know I haven't been patient with him in the past, but what the heck, a guy can change, can't he? Bring the cat when you come up for your interview. We'll bond, I promise. And one more thing. I know I said kids weren't in our five-year plan." A moment of silence. "What would you think about changing that? Call me."

Call him, nothing. Maggie drove straight home and packed her bag. She barely noticed the turkeys strutting through the yard or the riot of wild black cherry blossoms. It wasn't until she was on the highway, on her way to Chicago and that interview, that she discovered she'd picked up a passenger.

"Look out!" Pop shouted as Maggie swerved into another lane.

"Geez, don't do that! No wonder Scott crashed."

"He crashed 'cause he's ornery and he's got a temper."

"He does not." She looked at Pop with disbelief.

"Watch the road!"

"I am!" She turned her head and stared straight ahead. Good thing she could drive on auto pilot; watch traffic, check mirrors. "Scott said you wanted to talk to me. This isn't a good time."

"It'll have to do. And if I pass to the other side because of this, I'll be haunting Templeton till the end of his days," Pop groused.

That didn't make any sense. "If you pass—"

"I have friends."

Warning received, loud and clear. "Scott found the 'Cuda for you. So why are you still here? And why the heck haven't you settled things with Grammy yet?"

"I saw it," Pop said, seemingly taking no offense at her demands. Certainly ignoring them. "She looks fine, real fine. Good paint. No rust. No dings. Should bring a nice price. But that's not what I want to talk to you about."

Maggie pretended to concentrate solely on her driving; in reality, she was watching Pop out of the corner of her eye. With new perspective, too, since talking to Grammy. Mom always had professed loving him, even when she'd complained about not enough money, not enough of his time, not enough attention. Maggie hadn't believed her then—how could you love someone who drove you nuts? Who did what he wanted, when he wanted, with no regard for others? Who forgot his anniversary and his daughters' birthdays, but remembered the date of every piddling win?

Apparently, it was possible.

Not that much different from her putting up with Kevin's five-year plan. Man, if she had it to do over, she wouldn't waste her time. In fact, if Kevin so much as said "five-year plan" to her, she'd have to seriously knee something so far up inside him, there'd be no plan at all.

"Maggie, honey, I been studying on our relationship."

She snickered. Rude, but really, she was supposed to think he'd had this great revelation and turned over a new leaf?

"It wasn't very good. It was all my fault."

God, what was it with men today?

"See, I was raised to think the most important thing for a man was to make sure the family he loved had everything they needed. Physical things. Food. Shelter.

l his jaw, as if that'd help him
nyway, there was a flea market
ne of the towns I'd raced in. I
ng. So I went to that flea market
a little statue and brung it home

ally, a little shepherd and lamb.
dresser. Still not worth a dollar,

She smiled and got all teary-eyed
at the same time, and threw her arms around my neck
and, well." Pop cleared his throat. "We had you nine
months later. So, after that—"

"Enough!"

"This isn't about sex."

If it was, she was jumping out of the car.

"After that, I brung her more things. And one time, she
looked one of 'em up in a book at the library and told
me how much it was worth, and that's when the idea
hit me. Do you know how much valuable stuff people
mistake for junk—"

"Or the other way around," she muttered.

"—and sell for next to nothing?"

Maggie sighed heavily. "You haven't learned a thing,
have you?"

"Patience, girl, I'm not done. I been watching you
since Templeton came to the house. Seeing you through
different eyes. Seeing how you've blossomed. Picked
up with your old friends again. Made some new ones. I
can see now where someone who's the opposite of me

in some ways would seem safe to you. Seem like a good choice."

Did he mean Scott or Kevin?

Not that she cared. He'd made Scott crash. Forced him to give up his engine. Delayed and possibly ruined his career. Manipulated him into spending all his time looking for an old car. Tampered with his cell phone. Filled his truck with pig shit.

Ugh.

"And it occurs to me it may be my fault. It showed me that financial security ain't everything. That you got to raise kids to be emotionally secure, too."

"You've been watching Dr. Phil?"

"Ma turns it on. Anyways, I'm sorry I didn't make you feel like that. You know, emotionally secure. That I didn't tell you and show you that you're worthy of being loved just as you are. That you don't have to compromise yourself or 'earn' the love of a man the way Templeton"—he cleared his throat and stumbled over the rest—"the way he, uh, loves you."

Wow. Pop had never been a kidder, so Maggie didn't expect him to blow it with a joke. He really meant all he'd just said.

"You think he loves me?"

"Course he does."

Deep down, Maggie knew it, but it was nice to hear someone else say it. Except that someone else was dead.

"Call him and see," Pop said craftily.

"Talk to Grammy," she shot back.

"You missed the turn."

"No I didn't."

"Airport's that way."

"I'm not going to the airport."

"You can't drive to Laguna Seca in time. You'll have to fly if you're gonna see him race."

Christ. "You have a one-track mind, you know that? I'm not going to a race. I'm going to Chicago."

"No," Pop said with a long, frustrated groan. "Forget about Kevin."

"You know what? Much to my dismay, I've discovered I inherited some of your genes. Those people up there are making me jump through hoops for a job I'm no longer so sure I want. But one thing for damn certain? If I go out, I'm going out on top. I'm going to wow their socks off before I decide."

"He's no good for you."

"Pop!" It had started out as a nice apology, but you couldn't expect to turn a misguided man into an enlightened one just because he'd been dead fifteen years and once or twice listened to Dr. Phil.

"Oh, sure, you'll never want for money," Pop tried to reason with her. "Kevin'll be home every weekend. But where's the respect? Where's the passion?"

"You're dead. Go. Away."

"When you're with him, it's like you don't have any backbone."

"You want backbone? I'll give you backbone: Get your dead butt out of my car and go talk to your mother."

* * *

It was still dark out when the hotel started to shake. Alone in a single, in California, Scott rolled out of bed. Four A.M. He should have been thinking about how fast he could get to the track to see if it and the cars were all right. Instead, the present emergency shot his thoughts straight back to Maggie and the cellar, low light from an oil lamp, and intimate games for two.

He did have the presence of mind to multitask, grabbing his jeans and stepping into them while turning on the light and squinting against it to see if he could locate his shoes, because there'd probably be broken glass everywhere.

"Where you going?" Coop asked.

"*Shit.*" Another voice in the room was the last thing Scott expected. His foot caught in his pants leg and he hopped a couple of steps before he fell on his butt. The room was still, just as it should be. No earthquake; just an obnoxious ghost up to his old tricks, once again using the mattress as his own personal trampoline. "You're lucky you're dead."

"Let's not start that again. I'm dead. I know it. I ain't going nowhere. Now, you mind getting up from there? The flashing's killing me."

"Good."

"When did you start sleeping naked, anyway?"

"When Maggie kept stripping me. Sorry you asked?"

"Kevin's got her."

No preamble, just bad news, plain and simple. Scott's hair stood on end, much as it might have done in a real earthquake, only worse.

"What do you mean? He's at the house? He's drug her off to Chicago? What?" He shot to his feet and yanked his jeans on right.

"Worse. He called. She ran home from work and packed her bags. She left so fast, she didn't even write Ma a note. You gotta go after her."

"Are you nuts? My race is in"—Scott checked his bare wrist, then the clock—"eight hours."

"You have to go."

"There's a team counting on me. People depending on me."

"I'm counting on you."

Scott unsnapped his jeans. "Get off that bed; I need my sleep."

"Maggie's happiness depends on you."

"Then I shouldn't be so exhausted I fall asleep at the wheel on the hairpin, should I?"

Coop bounced on the mattress, slowly, hovering at each peak. The only way Scott was getting any sleep was to reason his way back into bed, and, shit, why'd the ornery old goat have to show up in the middle of the night?

"Maggie's a big girl, Coop. And focused, don't forget focused. It's not as if she's running off to get married."

The ghost swooped over him. "But what if that's exactly what she's doing? You have to stop her."

"No." Scott had his reasons. Good ones.

"At least call her."

"No."

"But—"

"Look, Kevin's always telling her what to do, what to think. You probably did the same thing, didn't you? Whenever you were around? Sure you did. I'm not going to repeat your mistakes. Maggie has to make her own decisions."

There, that sounded perfectly reasonable. No need to justify himself to a ghost, to share that he'd be on the first flight out after the race. It was only 112 laps; less than three hours start to finish.

But Coop wouldn't back off. "Have you told her you love her?" he demanded.

"She knows it."

"Are you sure? Did you say it?"

"I'm sure." Though, come to think of it, Scott didn't remember saying the actual words.

"Be very sure, son. You want Maggie to make her own decisions, fine. But shouldn't she have all the facts first? Shouldn't she know you love her? Because you can damn well bet Kevin's telling her. He don't play fair. No telling what lines he's feeding her. Right now. Go on. Call her."

"It's sneaky and underhanded."

"Now you're talking," Coop crowed. "I like that. Play on his level. Go on. Call. You're just leveling the playing field. You won't beg or nothing. You won't lie. Just tell her you love her. She'll make up her own mind."

"Shut up. You can't brainwash me."

"I'll do anything you want."

"Anything?" The word hung between them as they faced off. Not that it mattered one whit to him, but Scott would jump on that opportunity for Grammy's sake. "You'll talk to your mother? Answer her questions?"

Coop looked thoughtful, and not in a good way. More like thinking how he could back out of it. "But I wanta see my 'Cuda restored."

Scott spread his feet, crossed his arms, and waited.

"Oh, okay," Coop groused.

"When? And none of that crossing-your-heart bullshit."

"Today soon enough?"

"As long as you don't mind my torching the 'Cuda if you renege again."

Resigned, the ghost nodded.

Scott snatched his cell phone off the nightstand and punched M for Maggie. Not because Coop insisted, but because it was nagging at him that he might not have said he loved her. Not in three words. He'd said everything else. He missed her. Needed her. Wanted her. Wished she were here with him. Couldn't wait to see her again. But he'd made a habit of not telling women he loved them because, well, because he wasn't stupid.

Maggie would be the first. He needed to tell her.

He was connected after the second ring.

"'Lo?"

Definitely not Maggie. Her phone; middle of the night. Scott couldn't have hurt worse if Killjoy'd walked right into the room and shot him in the heart. He didn't even know if it was still beating. His whole chest felt numb. He could barely speak.

"Can I talk to Maggie?"

"You friggin' lunatic. It's the middle of the night."

"It's six A.M." In Chicago, anyway.

"If you want to talk to her, call back at a decent hour." Killjoy cut the connection.

Scott stalked across the floor, agitated that he'd been so stupid, so slow, that Maggie'd been so impatient. Pacing didn't help. The chair got in his way; he kicked it into the wall.

The occupant in the room to the left started pounding on the connecting door—his mistake, as Scott was still fuming over the severed connection, disgruntled because he'd played nice and hadn't told Killjoy what he really thought of him. The pounding continued until Scott yanked the door inward and snarled, "What?"

His balding, beer-bellied crew chief stood there in baggy boxers and nothing else, not a pretty sight as his fists rested on his hips and his gaze searched the room. "Sounded like trouble. Thought you might need help."

"Oh hey, man. Didn't mean to wake you," Scott said, meaning it. *Ghost strikes again. Part two.* He raked his hands through his hair.

"You alone? Sounded like a brawl."

"Not yet," Scott said, coming to a decision. He grabbed his duffel off the dresser and started throwing clothes into it.

"Hot damn!" Coop said, opening the drawers for him.

The crew chief blinked. "Going somewhere?"

"Family emergency."

"I hope to hell they live ten minutes from here and it's nothing more than a skinned knee, otherwise—"

"You know when the next plane to Chicago is?"

The crew chief studied the broken chair and battered wall before trying to reason with him. "Boss heard about you, you know. Heard you lost it after the last crash, couldn't be counted on. But I said, 'No, I've seen Scotty Templeton drive. I've seen him win.'" He shook his head, heavy with judgment. "Crying shame, that's what it is. You leave now, it's nothing less than professional suicide."

Scott pulled on a shirt and didn't take time to button it as he ran out the door. Grammy or Ruby would know Killjoy's address. He hoped. Maybe not; they didn't like him so much. But Maggie was organized. She would've given it to them in case of an emergency.

If going to see her right now and telling her he loved her wasn't an emergency, he didn't know what was.

 *Chapter 19*

Maggie set the receiver back in its cradle on the night-stand and debated what to do.

Ten A.M. in Chicago; eight in Monterey. Scott should've been up by now, but he wasn't answering, so probably he'd already left for the track. There were bound to be meetings before a race. Last-minute glitches to be addressed. What she had to say could wait. Laguna Seca wasn't twenty-four hours, like Daytona. It'd be over in less than three.

They'd talk then.

Scott had an hour in Denver to find a good cup of coffee and check his cell phone. He'd missed a call from a Chicago number that he didn't recognize. No message.

Killjoy calling to harass him about the early morning call?

Doubtful. Scott dialed it back from caller ID and got a switchboard; wrong number. He moved on to new messages.

Whoa, somebody call the cell police. A screaming, X-rated voice mail stated a clear and definite opinion on Scott's heritage and what he could do with his career. Had to be the team owner, but it was hard to tell. Scott had faced up to his responsibilities and stopped by the owner's suite on the way to the airport, and while the guy'd been visibly angry then, it was nothing compared to now that he was fully awake. He ended with a very clear "The only place you'll be able to race after this will be in Mongolia."

What'd they race in Mongolia? Yaks?

In contrast, Ruby's message was much nicer; Ike the auctioneer had called the house because he, too, had been unable to reach Maggie. If her phone hadn't made it all the way to Chicago, Scott would've worried that she'd had trouble on the highway, that she had gotten one ticket too many and been arrested. But it had.

On second thought, just because Killjoy was in possession of the phone didn't mean Maggie *hadn't* been arrested for speeding. She could've given her phone to him for safekeeping. It was possible she hadn't spent the night at his place after all.

Gee, which was worse—Maggie in bed with Killjoy or Maggie in jail?

Ruby requested that Scott pass on Ike's message when he finally talked to her, because in her opinion, it sounded important. She thanked him profusely for fixing her car, which she said now ran like a bat out of hell; looked as though the Coopers had another lead foot in the family. Her second message was a call back with Killjoy's address, plus information Coop hadn't shared. Maybe he hadn't known; with Coop, you never could tell. Anyway, Maggie's interview had been moved up, hence the impromptu trip. As for the location, Ruby said, "I know Maggie's mentioned the name a hundred times, but all I remember right now is *Something* Management."

Scott had no choice. When he reached Chicago, he'd head straight to Killjoy's.

"Hey. Coop." He found the ghost a few yards away, people watching, which meant watching people walk through him. At least he'd behaved himself on the flight to Denver. All the passengers within two rows had snuggled under blankets, but the ghost's ambient chill was unintentional. "I might need your help later."

"Am I getting thinner? You know, paler?" the ghost asked, staring at his hands with grave concern as he turned them this way and that.

"Focus, Coop."

"I heard you," he groused. "Whatcha got in mind?"

"Ruby doesn't know where Maggie's interview is. I have to go to Killjoy's. But he might not want to share."

"I can search his place."

"Yeah, me, too," Scott said, his jaw clenched. Killjoy could be seven feet tall and as wide as the door; no way he was keeping Scott from looking for Maggie. From telling her what he needed to tell her. "But I was thinking more along the lines of making him talk if she's not there but he knows where she is. You know, scaring the bejesus out of him?"

"Aw, Templeton, you saying you need me?"

"Don't make me puke." Teaming up with a ghost? What came next?

Ah, what the hell. Maggie was worth it. Scott just hoped she was around to hear what he had to say. And not through steel bars.

"Maybe they had a fight and you were just what-chamacallit." Coop turned pensive, then snapped his fingers. "Rebound sex."

"Don't make me hurt you."

There was a doorman. Security. Cameras. What?— Killjoy thought his clients might want a piece of him?

Scaling the side of the building from balcony to balcony was not an option.

"Hey. Coop."

"Aw, Templeton, you *do* need me."

"Shut up and start haunting."

Coop cupped his ear. "What? I can't hear you."

"For Maggie."

"Okay. For Maggie. But then I gotta go talk to Ma."

Scott watched as Coop warmed up with baby pokes and jabs at the doorman, who swatted the air around him. Just little offhand swats at first, as if an annoying fly had mistaken him for a garbage dump. Then bigger swats alternated with befuddled glances to see what could possibly be plaguing him and who might be watching his embarrassing predicament. Then came the flying leap after his hat, which Coop batted off his head.

"Think I can make him dance?" Coop said, cackling with glee.

He did, all the way down the steps and out onto the

sidewalk. The poor doorman was still pursuing his hat and swatting at nothing visible when Scott oh-so-casually strolled through the door and into the elevator.

Three o'clock. Of course no one answered Killjoy's doorbell. Why would he be here if Maggie was at his office?

His neighbor was, though. Lucky for Scott, a bright-eyed, great-grandmotherly sort of lady with packages galore stepped off the next elevator.

"Oh, you must be the courier," she said with relief. "Kevin was so worried the tickets wouldn't be here on time."

"Tickets?" Plural.

"To Las Vegas. You do have them?"

Kill me now; just get it over with. Scott found it hard to smile after hearing that, but he forced it. After all, he didn't really know why the jerk was buying tickets to Vegas. And even if he did, he couldn't give up now, not after coming so far, not when he hadn't told Maggie he loved her. He'd tell her, lay it all out plain and simple. He loved her, but it was her choice to make.

Not that he wouldn't argue if she didn't see the light. But there were limits a man shouldn't cross. He understood them well.

"Here, let me help you with those packages." Scott flashed his famous dimple and lightened the elderly lady's load, hoping she was a snoopy, loquacious neighbor of the worst sort. "I'm not a courier. Just a friend. Just in town for a couple hours and thought I'd drop in on ol' Kev. Sounds as if he's leaving, though."

Without so much to carry and keep track of, the neighbor tilted her head back and peered up at him, a stranger in her hallway. "Say, aren't you Scotty Templeton?"

As he followed her to her door, he tipped his Stetson and drawled, "Why, yes, ma'am, I am."

"Does Kevin manage your money? Because I'm considering consulting him on tax management strategies. How has he done for you?"

Lousy. "Actually, his girlfriend in St. Louis handles everything for me." Scott nearly choked on the girlfriend part, but a man had to do what a man had to do. And he had to get information, pronto.

She smiled softly. "Maggie? She's a lovely girl."

"You know her then?"

She unlocked her door and relieved Scott of the packages, setting them inside on a foyer table as she did so. "Kevin keeps me up to date. It'll be so nice to have another woman for a neighbor. Oh"—she covered her mouth with her hand when she realized what she'd said—"I hope I didn't let the cat out of the bag."

"No, ma'am. I guess I could drop in on him at the office. You don't happen to know where it is, do you?"

She did.

"Milton's right, Ma," Grammy's daughter-in-law said over the phone. In truth, Grammy had considered Maggie's mother a daughter since the day she and the two girls had moved in twenty-some-odd years ago. "You can't live the rest of your life waiting to hear from a dead man. It's not healthy, and you risk losing Milton if you do."

Grammy was on the cordless. As they chatted, she wandered out of the kitchen to get away from the dogs, who'd set up a loud ruckus on the back porch. It couldn't be Ike's staff making their hair stand up like that; they were busy holding the second auction off-property today.

She strolled down the hall, into the living room, where Lawrence's trophies stared back at her from the table in the far corner. She'd boxed up the older ones long ago; these represented his later years, the really big wins, and darn if they weren't starting to look like a shrine. Was it time to put them away, too? To clear all the old out of her life and make way for the new?

"Are you happy?" Grammy asked her daughter-in-law.

"You mean, was it worth it to risk my heart and love again?"

"Well, you know. Milton."

"Let's see. How can I put this delicately? *Yes*."

They said their good-byes, probably too abruptly, but Grammy needed to think, and she couldn't do that with someone talking in her ear.

Maybe Milton was right. Did she want a quiet, empty house after the girls left, for the rest of her life? She'd spent the last fourteen days angry with her Lawrence for leaving without talking to her, for disappearing without answering what all boiled down to one simple question, for not doing the one thing she wanted.

Whatever had made her think things would change?

She'd pack this stuff away and give the room a good spring cleaning, she decided with firm resolve, ticked at herself for thinking maybe, just maybe, she imagined a whiff of familiar pipe tobacco. After the cleaning, she'd buy a new dress, get her hair styled, put on some lipstick, and invite Milton to dinner. She might even raid the cellar stash for candles.

Yes, that all felt good. Felt right. Grammy felt herself moving faster now, lighter on her feet, until Ashes, who'd been sleeping on the back of the sofa, suddenly hissed. No little prissy house-kitty, those-dogs-better-stay-outside hiss, either. Ears horizontal, mouth open wide, lots of pointy teeth showing, right out of a Stephen King movie. He saw something. Was watching something.

Or some*one*. He leaped off his perch and darted halfway up the stairs. He peered through the rail and emitted a long, low yowl.

Grammy focused on the same doorway Ashes was watching. "Lawrence? Son, is that you?"

"Didn't want to scare you," he said, drifting into the room.

Speechless for a moment, Grammy's hand flew to her chest, and her mouth dropped open. "Oh my, it is," she finally said with a grateful sigh. Tears welled up in her eyes, and she just felt so silly about that. How many mothers got a second chance like this, anyway? She should be downright grateful. And not waste time.

"You don't know how long I've waited— Well, I guess you do."

"Sorry, Ma. I thought it was better."

She squinted at him. "You're paler than I remember."

"Damn that Templeton," he barked, making Grammy start. "I thought so, too. This must be it for me. Knew I shouldn't have agreed to settle this today."

Grammy smiled indulgently, musing whether her son's idea of settling things was even in the ball-park.

"Now, don't go getting that look, Ma. I know what you're thinking, but you know, when a man's got lotsa time on his hands, things start to sink in. You were good to me, Ma. Too good, taking in my family instead of taking a whip to my sorry hide."

Grammy's face fell, and she had to lean on the sofa for support. "I knew it. It *was* my fault. All of it. The racing, the cars—"

"No, I didn't mean that," he said in a rushed breath. "I only meant— Look, there was nothing you could've done to stop me from racing."

"I let you tear around the house in your walker for hours at a time if you wanted. You were so good about not bumping into the furniture."

"Not so good at staying off the walls, I bet."

Now that he was here, nothing was stopping Grammy from saying what she had to say. From laying out all her cards and getting an answer, one way or the other. If it turned out she was to blame, well, she'd just have to deal with it. She was still going to pack up his trophies and move on.

"I bought you that pedal car when you were just a toddler. Lord, sometimes the only way I could stop you from crying was to put you in it."

"See there? I was headstrong."

"Still."

"Ma." Lawrence sighed and stepped closer, bringing a chill with him.

"If I hadn't done that, you might never have taken to cars. Might never have raced." Grammy sucked in a breath and persisted, fresh tears popping out as she said, "Might never have hit that wall."

"Ma, that wasn't your fault. If I hadn't run around in a walker or that ol' pedal car, I would've eventually turned my tricycle into a hot rod."

"I don't know . . ." she said, thinking he was being nice, giving her an easy out. Probably couldn't stand to see her cry. Didn't mean this was the truth.

"And before you start feeling guilty for giving me a trike, too, just remember you couldn't stop me from growing up. I got a two-wheeler, like all boys do, and even if it'd been my first set of wheels, I would've ridden that like I was possessed." He grinned then, and stroked his chin thoughtfully. "Oh wait, I did ride that like I was possessed."

Grammy smiled at his humor, then winced when she remembered how she'd scrubbed gravel out of his knees and had his arm stitched twice.

"See?" he said.

Lawrence stepped closer, closing the gap between them. Grammy could tell he wanted to hug her, watched as he reached out to her, but there was no substance there. Nothing to feel. His arms dropped to his sides, defeat registered not only on his pale face, but in the uncharacteristic slump of his shoulders.

"Nothing coulda stopped me," he said. Suddenly, he straightened up again. "Look at it this way, Ma. Thanks to you, I was getting experience from the first time you set me in my walker and my feet touched the floor. Lessons that were better learned before I ever rolled onto a track, that helped me avoid a lotta mistakes later, when it wasn't so safe. You couldn't stop me from racing. You helped me be good."

Grammy wanted to believe him. Needed to believe him.

"I mean it, Ma," he said, fading even more.

"Lawrence—"

"Bye, Ma. Tell the girls I love them."

"Lawrence!"

But he was gone.

It didn't hurt, not really. How could it?—he'd died a long, long time ago. No, it was more . . . relief. She'd spent a lot of years feeling guilty, and when she wasn't feeling guilty, she felt just as bad for forgetting it for just a little while.

She was ready to move on. The girls were both busy. What's-his-name was answering Maggie's phone. Ruby had packed a small bag and taken off on a road trip with Jeremy. Finally, an empty nest.

The cordless was still in her hand. Grammy dialed, and when Milton answered, she said, "Hi. Are you busy for dinner tonight? It's just us; Ruby's out, and Maggie's in Chicago."

 *Chapter 20*

Maggie soared out of the plushest elevator she'd ever ridden in and glided across the massive three-story marble and polished granite lobby. There were some nice lobbies in St. Louis, but wow, these Chicago builders took *grand* to a whole new level.

She should have been calmer now that her interview was over, but who could be calm at a moment like this? Were other people calm after making decisions that changed the course of their lives?

She gazed around the lobby once more. *What would it be like to pass through here every morning? How impressed were clients when they walked through these massive front doors?*

Her phone beeped receipt of another message, reminding her that she had calls to make, news to share. This phone was new, though, a different model, and it took two tries before she managed to access her old voice mail. Ruby and Grammy both wanted to talk to her; she'd call them back. Ike's message took more time and thought.

"Maggie, it's Ike. Great news. I don't know if your father got some good advice somewhere, robbed a private museum, or just got lucky, but we found some really valuable items in the old barn. Let's see . . . there was a Lalique box, signed; Tiffany lamps—one of those went for three grand alone; so did the pate-de-verre and wrought-iron lamp. The gem, though, was the Mitsuhiro statue. Twenty grand."

"In the *barn*?" Maggie just about dropped the phone.

"There was quite a collection of fans, too," the message continued, "all put away real nice. Ladies' folding fans, you know what I mean. One of those brought over five thousand. And so on and so on. All buried under crapola, of course. No way you could have known. Good thing it didn't get struck by lightning and burn down all these years. Anyway, just wanted you to know you made a helluva profit on both auctions. I don't have the final numbers yet, but let's just say on this go-round alone?—Ruby could buy a Hummer to go with her combat boots. And, oh, that reminds me, I held out half a dozen ladies' Rolexes; you and Ruby may want them. If not, they can go in the auction next week."

Sorry, Pop, for every unkind word I ever thought about your collectibles. Except how insane *do you have to be to bury Lalique and Rolex and Mitsuhiro in a barn?*

"Say, Maggie, one more thing. You know, with a windfall like this, you could afford to retire from that high-stress job and come back to auctioneering. I'm getting old; I could use a partner. Think about it. Give me a call when you can."

Wow, two job offers in one day.

In spite of the interview team making her meeting last-minute—a test to see how serious she was, no doubt—it quickly became obvious during the meeting that they wanted her really bad. They'd kept her busy for two hours. They gave her a tour. Showed her the new office; told her to furnish it the way she wanted. Invited her to dinner.

She'd thanked them for their confidence in her and politely declined dinner. She had to get back to Kevin's.

First, though, she wanted to call Scott. He'd be racing; she'd leave a message.

Scott was doling out bills to the taxi driver when he happened to look across the street and saw Maggie sail out of the high-rise office building.

God, she was a sight for sore eyes. If his duffel wasn't already in his hand, he would've forgotten it in the single-minded joy of seeing her again. Maggie in a slim black skirt and jacket, with a sky-blue top underneath, was nothing less than the sexiest woman he'd ever seen. Lord, those legs alone should require a permit.

"Hey, man, you're Scotty Templeton, aren'tcha? Can I have your autograph?" the driver asked.

"Keep the change," Scott said gruffly, thrusting more bills through the window before dodging traffic to cross the street. Easier said than done when he couldn't take his eyes off Maggie, who practically floated on air down the five granite steps. Blond hair flowing. A smile so wide, she was nearly laughing.

Bad. Very bad.

So. She got the job. What came next? Flying to Vegas to tie the knot? Moving to Chicago to be with Killjoy?

Shit, just shoot me now.

Scott dodged a van and stepped onto the curb. His heart suddenly felt like a heavy lump in his chest, not strong enough to beat without Maggie in his life. When he'd met her that first day, charging between the patrol cars in a very sexy rage directed at him, she was rushing to get to an interview. Well, obviously she'd finally had it, and just as obviously, she was overjoyed with the result. And why not? She was brilliant. Focused, attentive, obsessed. Smart. Intelligent.

They'd be fools not to hire her. She'd be with Killjoy every day. Every night.

Am I too late?

And here Scott was, dodging cars, charging after her. His pace slowed once he was on the sidewalk. There were enough pedestrians around that Maggie hadn't seen him yet. He should save face, turn away, not intrude further on her life. But then that'd make him a fool, too. They'd had something special. *Still* had something special, if he hadn't misjudged the tone of their phone conversations these past two weeks. Hell, if he could be that wrong about anything, he shouldn't be *allowed* behind the wheel of a race car again. Ever.

He had, perhaps, made one tiny miscalculation. He'd held back when it came to their future, determined to let Maggie make up her own mind, to find her own path, make her own decisions. But did he have to shelve a future with her because some jerk she'd been dating didn't respect the line?

Hell, no.

There had to be a mid-ground.

His cell phone *vroom*ed, but it was a number he didn't recognize, so he didn't pick up. He couldn't if he'd wanted to, because just then Maggie slipped off her jacket.

Good Lord, she went to an interview wearing *that*? A beaded blue bustier? That put her breasts right out there, like melons on a plate? That emphasized the smallness of her waist? No way they didn't hire her, even if she'd left her jacket on the whole time.

His fantasy—and Killjoy was about to reap the rewards?

No friggin' way!

Maggie reached a hand up, adjusting her earpiece. Snippets of information barraged Scott: an unknown number ringing on his mobile, right now; Killjoy in possession of Maggie's phone last night, maybe still; Maggie right out of a meeting, most likely making a call. Hope against hope, he snatched his phone off his belt before the call went to voice mail.

He must have said hello, because Maggie sounded surprised when she responded. Across the plaza, Scott watched her lips move as she said, "I was going to leave you a message. What happened?"

"What?"

She glanced at his Rolex, still on her wrist; *minus one for the home team.* "You wrecked the car already? Tell me you're not in the hospital."

Oh. The race. "I don't crash regularly, you know."

She snickered. "As opposed to crashing irregularly?"

"God, I missed your sassy mouth."

Her nose crinkled impishly, and he wanted to run up to her and kiss it.

"As long as you walk away," she said. "That's all I care about."

"You sure about that?"

After a beat of silence, Maggie said, "What do you mean?"

"How was your interview?"

"Oh, that. Great," she said enthusiastically. "Red carpet treatment. More money, bonuses, vacation condo on a Caribbean island. Wait a minute—what do you mean, am I sure? And how did you know I had an interview today? I wasn't going to tell you until it was over."

She turned and looked straight at him then. A breeze teased and lifted her hair. Beckoning him.

"Hi," he said simply, holding her gaze from the distance.

Without hesitation, Maggie rushed across the wide expanse of concrete, the brilliance of her smile allowing Scott a smidgen of hope. She was happy to see him. Rushing toward him. So she'd gotten the job of her dreams—so what? She'd been calling *him*, not Killjoy.

She ran in a tippy-toe jog, the way women do in high heels. And as beautiful as she was, as sexy and enticing, this wasn't all about the physical. His feelings weren't about that. This was about who he knew she was inside and how much he loved her. How he wanted the best for her.

Maggie stopped in front of him and said, "I can't believe you're here."

The fact that she didn't throw her arms around him said everything he was afraid to hear. Happy to see him, yes. Going to kiss him and tell him she'd waited for him, no.

Was she playing him?

Getting ready to deliver the let's-still-be-friends speech?

He couldn't wring her pretty neck, so if she started that speech, he'd just have to kiss her senseless.

At the same time, they both realized they were burning up minutes and laughed self-consciously.

"Guess we can hang up now," Maggie said with a shrug and a cute smile.

"You have a new number," Scott said as he, too, disconnected.

"You're all right. Nothing's broken."

"I'm fine. I called you last night. Woke up Killjoy."

She shook her head, perplexed. "Was there an earthquake I don't know about? A tsunami washed the track away? Why are you here *now*?"

"Because my plane landed an hour ago? There, see, I can be sassy, too," he teased, because he didn't want to say what he'd come to say on a public sidewalk. "Look, is there someplace we can go for a drink or something?"

"Sure. Oh, here, before I forget." Maggie slipped off his pride and joy and held it out between them.

Not a good sign.

Scott didn't reach for it. "It's yours. I gave it to you."

"It was a loan. Besides, Ike found some in the barn, ladies' models, so if I keep this one, you'd be forcing me to start a collection."

"Heaven forbid."

She waggled the watch between them, encouraging Scott to reach for it, but he wasn't persuaded, because once he reached out, once his fingers touched hers again, it'd be too hard to let go.

Let her make up her own mind. Show her he was best. He had to figure out how to cover both ends of the spectrum with Maggie looking up at him like that? His gaze never left her eyes, which sparkled back at him, playful and proud at the same time.

"You have to take it," she said.

"Would it be so bad?" he asked, stalling, hoping that if she stopped to think about this, she'd think through everything more carefully. "Having more than one of anything? How about kids?"

Maggie's hand stilled in the space between them. "Kids?"

"Yeah. You want more than one, don't you?"

For once Maggie was speechless, baffled, nothing coming out of her mouth. Scott seized the opportunity; he leaned in and took that kiss he'd been missing.

Her lips were warm, inviting, and he felt them spread into a slow smile beneath his own, but not for long, because he teased her lips, coaxing them into a deeper kiss that had one passerby applauding and another advising them to get a room.

"I'm sorry," he said.

"For kissing me?" She sounded appalled, as if she'd clobber him if he said yes.

"No. Never for kissing you." Careful to avoid his watch, Scott took Maggie's free hand in his and led her along the sidewalk. "This the right direction?"

"For, uh, what?"

"That drink we talked about." Because he couldn't take her to a hotel room until they had this sorted out.

"Wait—did you fly here?" she asked, tilting backward, trying to stop, but in heels she was no match for him, and Scott drew her patiently along. "What happened to 'Flying's for birds'?"

"Yeah. Well. I was dumb as a bird not to tell you I love you before I left. This place any good?"

Maggie stared at the door to a restaurant, then as Scott tried to steer her through the entrance, she spun him around on the sidewalk and said, "Wait, I get it. You're here because somehow you heard I came to Chicago. You're afraid I came to see Kevin."

"I flew here"—he wanted to be sure he said this just right—"because whatever decision you make is yours to make. But a very wise man pointed out to me that if I let you make that decision without having all the information you need, then I was a dumber ass than he took me for."

Maggie laughed. "Pop?"

"Please, don't tell him I said that he was wise." Scott glanced over his shoulder, afraid he'd see Coop, steeling himself for that annoying cackle, but all was blessedly silent. "I'd never live it down. I'm only sorry I didn't tell you sooner. So if you came here to see Killjoy because you don't know how much I love you, then let me make this very clear—"

"You're growling."

"I'm wondering where you spent the night," he said, throwing his arms up in the air rather than grabbing her and shaking the information loose. "There, I said it. I can't help it. I thought I was better than that, but it turns out I'm only human."

Maggie bowed her head and said nothing.

"Oh please, put me out of my misery."

She tossed her head, a haughty gesture meant to put him in his place. "I'm not sure you deserve it," she said.

"Why the hell not?"

"For making me wait."

Scott leaned against the building, not knowing what to say, what to think. He had no right to be angry. No right to feel he'd lost something he'd never taken the pains to ensure he had. He'd been so concerned with what was good for Maggie, with what she needed, that he hadn't let her know what he needed.

He reached out and touched her arm. Would he grovel?

Damn straight. He was comfortable enough in his own skin to know that sometimes a man's gotta do what a man's gotta do.

The narrow-eyed squint she gave him would've scared off a lesser man, but Scott was undaunted because just as he'd known since the day they'd met, Maggie in a snit was better than no Maggie at all. He caressed her arm, and really, he deserved some sort of award for keeping his gaze steady on her face when it was dying to wander south.

"I couldn't pressure you," he said. "He's controlled your life so much, and I told myself I had to let you choose. Had to hope you'd come to realize on your own that he's a slug, but when I went to his place today, I didn't know if I was going to be able to leave there without punching him out."

"I broke up with him."

"Oh, thank God," he said, sagging with relief. His heart thumped in his chest, as though allowed to beat again.

"I tried to do it before, but I made it official yesterday as soon as I got here. My cell phone was on his plan, so I returned it, got a hotel room, and bought a new one this morning. Feeling better yet?"

"You have no idea." Recognizing the teasing light in her eyes, Scott leaned into her, lowering his voice intimately. "Can I attack you now?"

She punched his arm.

"Yeah, didn't think so." Okay, he'd play the game. "Glad to hear your interview went well."

Maggie's grin spread into the same ebullient smile she'd been wearing when she'd exited the building. "You wouldn't believe the money they offered me! Let's walk."

Scott obediently kept pace beside her. Hell, now that

Maggie'd seen the light and made her own choice without any pressure from him, he'd jump through any number of hoops for her today. As long as they got a hotel room in the next block.

"Will it be a problem for you, working with him?"

"Worried?"

"Nope," he said honestly.

"Good. I didn't take the job."

"But— I thought you were going to injure me for delaying your interview, and you turned it down?"

Maggie shrugged dismissively, though she figured Scott deserved some kind of explanation because, after all, he'd been one of the motivating factors in the reexamination of her life. In finding her life, really, because she'd been on the path to living someone else's.

"The job was Kevin's idea," she said. "The move was Kevin's idea. I figured out before you left town that I just got caught up in his excitement. It never was what *I* wanted."

Unlike Ike's offer, which she definitely did want.

Their steps slowed as they came to an intersection. There were other pedestrians around, so Scott pulled Maggie into a cozy nook just outside a store's threshold where they'd have a modicum of privacy. "You never said anything."

"I had to work it out for myself. I had to work out a lot of things for myself." She owed it to him to be totally honest. "See, I was pretty sure you loved me, but I didn't know if *you* knew it, and if you didn't, how could I even hope you'd be around forever? So, that aside, I realized the only way to be truly happy was not to settle."

She'd cleared the negative out of her life. Set a new course. Made her own decisions.

"I didn't know if the famous Scotty Templeton was in for the long haul. I didn't know if you'd be able to—or even *want* to, after a while—find time for me and our children."

Scott leaned in close, and Maggie thought he was going to kiss her again, but he said, "And what conclusion did you come to?"

"That I'm crazy in love with you."

"Hm." He narrowed his eyes at her. "Define *crazy*."

She took a moment. It was important to get this right. "Me standing here. You right there, not kissing me, just touching my arm—when God knows, I want you to kiss me so bad it hurts. And I'm thinking, *Sure, he's a race car driver and annoying as hell, but who knows? We might have a future.*"

Scott's grin was slow, and sexy as hell. "I'm never going to be able to one-up you, am I?"

"We could take it a day at a time and see."

"We could."

"Except—" They'd never discussed the future. Tipping her head to the side and studying him intently didn't tell her squat, so, trying not to cringe, she came right out and asked, "Do you have a five-year plan?"

"Sure."

Oh. Great.

"Doesn't everyone?"

She muttered, "Not *every*one."

Scott didn't seem to notice. "I'd like to win a championship each year. And then—what do you think of Team Templeton?"

"Sounds pretentious. But I didn't mean business. I want to know if you have your personal life mapped out."

"You mean, wife and kids? House? Dog? That sort of thing? Are you kidding? I'm having trouble figuring out if you'll still be talking to me in five minutes, much less five years."

The light changed. Pedestrians moved on. They stayed in the nook, though, each heartbeat drawing them closer. Maggie eased into Scott's space, feeling his power, his love. Wanting to reassure him that she'd rather be doing something more than talking in five minutes. And for a lot longer than five years.

Scott's lips hovered inches from hers as he leaned into her, radiating a vitality that she could drink on forever. Wanted to drink on forever.

"So, you want talk?" she said saucily, feeling relieved and mischievous now that she had the answer she'd wanted. "Did I tell you about this great guy who comes to town?"

"Better be me."

"Moves into the house."

Maggie shivered in delight as Scott's hands grazed her arms, sliding upward to her bare shoulders and the nape of her neck. Not one to let a good deed go unrewarded, she brushed her mouth across his cheek, the hard plane of his jaw, his earlobe, hoping she was arousing him as much as he was her.

She picked up where she'd left off. "Shows me what love's all about— Stop beaming, I'm not finished."

Wisely, Scott wiped the stupid grin off his face and looked as if he were listening really hard. But she doubted it, because his hands never stopped their sensuous assault on her skin.

"I can't think when you do that," she whispered, leaning into him until the breasts he'd had his eyes locked on were mashed against his chest, measuring every erratic beat of his heart.

"You think too much," he rasped.

"I love you."

"Then again, I love the way you think." Scott's kiss was slow and hungry at the same time, setting Maggie's insides on fire so hot, she wasn't surprised when he growled against her mouth. "You wouldn't happen to have a hotel room around here, would you?"

"In the next block."

"Dang, what're we waiting for!"

"We've got the light."

In one smooth motion, he had her pointed toward the intersection and on her way across the street. Fortunately going the right direction.

She'd been on her way back to Kevin's to pick up a few things she'd left behind. What the heck; she had better things to do. He could keep Slightly Wilted Elvis, which, according to the Chicago expert she'd consulted, was worth next to nothing. He could mail her anything he thought was important. What was really, truly important to her was right here, right now.

As they stepped on the far sidewalk, she indicated which way to go.

"Team Templeton, huh?"

"Grows on you, doesn't it?"

"But, Scott." How to say this without bursting his bubble. "You walked out on a race. A really big race. You think someone's going to sponsor a team with you on it?"

"Yeah, there is that. I thought I was screwed, too, until I spent hours on the plane with nothing to do but puke or think."

"Poor baby."

"The thing is, racing was so important in my life because, without you, I had no life."

Maggie thought that was probably the sweetest thing anyone'd ever said to her, but before she could let Scott know it, he was barreling full speed ahead.

"Now that we're on the same page," he said, "I'm going to liquidate all my cars. Clean out the garage; parts, engines. The basement. My brother's garage. His basement. My best friend's—"

"Enough!" It was worse than she thought; she clapped her hands over her ears. But not for long, because Scott grabbed one again and held it.

He grinned. "I can call in some favors. And grovel. Did I mention groveling?"

"Hey, I'd hire you."

He raised her hand to his lips and kissed it. "I know

you would, babe. But you love me. It's different."

"Did I mention that I have some extra disposable income from the auctions? Maybe I could invest in Team Templeton?"

"Think there's enough left of your father to roll over in his grave?"

When they rushed through the ostentatiously wide front doors of the hotel Maggie'd stayed at last night, she said, "Here it is," and Scott growled, "About time."

"What?" She turned and grinned over her shoulder at him. "You don't move so fast in your condition?"

"A little louder, please. Not everyone in the lobby heard you."

Maggie's laugh wavered and died as she heard "Scotty Templeton" float on lips around the lobby.

Drat. Recognized.

She knew what came next; didn't mean she was happy about it.

"Scotty." A woman was first to move, rooting through her purse as she rushed toward him, two teenage boys flanking her with smirks as big as Texas. Pen in hand at last, she approached Scott in spite of the murderous look Maggie tossed her way. Though Maggie was pleased to note that the teenage boys had difficulty deciding which of the two of them was more interesting, Scott with his reputation for speed and danger, or her in a bustier and short skirt.

But *still*.

"Sorry, ma'am. Maybe later," Scott said, no dimple in sight. He wrapped his arm around Maggie's shoulders and headed toward the elevators like a Porsche off the pole. "In case you didn't hear, I have the hots for this lady."

Scott was all over Maggie in the elevator, coming up for air only once before they reached her floor.

"In case you don't know it," he said, his voice thick with heat and desire. "I'm gonna have the hots for you for the rest of my life. You think you're crazy in love now? Wait a few years."

Next month, don't miss these exciting new love stories only from Avon Books

Two Weeks With a Stranger by Debra Mullins

An Avon Romantic Treasure

Lucy, Lady Devingham, has been content to let her husband gallivant about London while she enjoys the pleasures of country life. But when she receives word that Simon's mysterious activities now involve another woman, Lucy throws caution to the wind to prove once and for all that she is a force to be reckoned with—and a woman to be loved.

Beware of Doug by Elaine Fox

An Avon Contemporary Romance

Meet Doug, the match-mauling canine. No matter what kind of man Lily Tyler brings home, casual friend or romantic contender, Doug is there with a nasty surprise. It'll take one very determined man to woo Lily . . . and sexy pilot Brady Cole thinks he's just the man for the job.

Night of the Huntress by Kathryn Smith

An Avon Romance

Bishop has spent centuries trying to heal the wounds between humans and vampires. All is put to the test when he is captured by a mysterious woman, the vampire slayer known as The Reaper. Bishop knows this is his last chance to prove to this woman that all is not as it seems.

Good Groom Hunting by Shana Galen

An Avon Romance

Josephine Hale is every bit the granddaughter of a pirate, and she is determined to track down her grandfather's lost treasure, no matter where the trail might take her. But when her search lands her in a partnership with the Earl of Westman, Josie finds herself suddenly in the middle of the adventure of a lifetime.

DISCOVER CONTEMPORARY ROMANCES *at their*
SIZZLING HOT BEST FROM AVON BOOKS

Avon Romantic Treasures

Unforgettable, enthralling love stories, sparkling with passion and adventure from Romance's bestselling authors

SCANDAL OF THE BLACK ROSE *by Debra Mullins*
0-06-079923-4/$6.99 US/$9.99 Can

PORTRAIT OF A LOVER *by Julianne MacLean*
0-06-081935-9/$6.99 US/$9.99 Can

PROMISE ME FOREVER *by Lorraine Heath*
0-06-074982-2/$6.99 US/$9.99 Can

DUKE OF SCANDAL *by Adele Ashworth*
0-06-052841-9/$6.99 US/$9.99 Can

SHE'S NO PRINCESS *by Laura Lee Guhrke*
0-06-077474-6/$6.99 US/$9.99 Can

THE DUKE IN DISGUISE *by Gayle Callen*
0-06-078412-1/$6.99 US/$9.99 Can

TEMPTING THE WOLF *by Lois Greiman*
0-06-078398-2/$6.99 US/$9.99 Can

HIS MISTRESS BY MORNING *by Elizabeth Boyle*
0-06-078402-4/$6.99 US/$9.99 Can

HOW TO SEDUCE A DUKE *by Kathryn Caskie*
0-06-112456-7/$6.99 US/$9.99 Can

A DUKE OF HER OWN *by Lorraine Heath*
0-06-112963-1/$6.99 US/$9.99 Can

A̶

978-0-06-089022-3
$13.95 ($17.50 Can.)

0-06-081588-4
$12.95 ($16.95 Can.)

0-06-087340-X
$12.95 ($16.95 Can.)

0-06-113388-4
$12.95 ($16.95 Can.)

0-06-083691-1
$12.95 ($16.95 Can.)